Paul Finch is an ex-cop and journalist turned best-selling author. He first cut his literary teeth penning episodes of *The Bill*, and has written extensively in horror and fantasy, including for *Dr Who*. He is also known for his crime/thriller novels, of which there are twelve to date, including the Heckenburg and Clayburn series. Paul lives in Lancashire with his wife and business-partner, Cathy.

Also by P. W. Finch

The Wulfbury Chronicles

Usurper
Battle Lord

Battle Lord

P. W. Finch

CANELO

First published in the United Kingdom in 2024 by

Canelo
Unit 9, 5th Floor
Cargo Works, 1-2 Hatfields
London SE1 9PG
United Kingdom

Copyright © P. W. Finch 2024

The moral right of P. W. Finch to be identified as the creator of this work has been asserted in accordance with the Copyright, Designs and Patents Act, 1988.

All rights reserved. No part of this publication may be reproduced or transmitted in any form or by any means, electronic or mechanical, including photocopy, recording, or any information storage and retrieval system, without permission in writing from the publisher.

A CIP catalogue record for this book is available from the British Library.

Print ISBN 978 1 80436 218 1
Ebook ISBN 978 1 80436 219 8

This book is a work of fiction. Names, characters, businesses, organizations, places and events are either the product of the author's imagination or are used fictitiously. Any resemblance to actual persons, living or dead, events or locales is entirely coincidental.

Cover design by kid-ethic

Cover images © Shutterstock

Look for more great books at www.canelo.co

Printed and bound in Great Britain by Clays Ltd, Elcograf S.p.A.

For my parents, Brian and Margaret, both of whom instilled in me an abiding fascination for the past.

PROLOGUE

The Vikings came downhill.

It was a bitter February day. The bracken growing in the fields where crops had once stood was brown, thick with frost. Snow still covered the unburied bones of villagers. But, inch by wretched inch, winter was loosening its grip. Birdsong sounded; the river flowed free, cakes of ice trailing on its surface.

The Norman vanguard waited on the river's south bank, their horses skittish. The Vikings approached from the other side, halting when they came to the water's edge. There were twelve of them, their jarl's *drengr*: the tallest and brawniest. They wore hauberks of ring-mail or banded leather studded with nuggets of steel. Each carried his circular linden wood shield on his back, and by his side his weapon of choice. For all this show of martial strength, they also flew a banner bearing the crossed staffs of the *Vaergenga* – a peace sign.

The sixteen Norman knights lowered their metal-tipped lances to the ground. They, too, were in full battle-harness. A single pennon fluttered above their heads: the White Leopard of Tancarville rearing on a black weave.

The groups eyed each other warily. The Vikings, on foot, were concerned about the Normans' battle-steeds. The Normans kept one eye on the hill to the Vikings' rear, and the sturdy palisade at its crown bristling with bows and blades. A flag bearing the image of a great black raven billowed over the battlements.

One of the Vikings ventured forward until the ice-cold waters sloshed around his bearskin boots.

In faltering Frankish, he said: 'My name is Sigfurth. They also call me "Blood-Hair".' And indeed, his dense beard and luxurious locks were so red they were almost crimson. 'Wulfgar Ragnarsson offers parley. He lays rightful claim to these lands, the earldom of Ripon, by right of battle and right of ancestry. The English thief and whoremaster, Sigobert, who by guile and cowardice seized these lands from Jarl Wulfgar's forefathers, is long perished, and all his seed scattered in the mud and carrion of Senlac Hill. With whom do I speak?'

The Normans' clean-shaved faces remained inscrutable behind the nose-guards of their conical helms. One of them urged his horse forward and pointed with his lance at a crow-picked skeleton slumped by a mooring pillar. Only threads of flesh and sinew remained on it, but its wrists had been fixed above its head with iron nails and its ribcage split by a hammer and chisel to allow the rending out of heart and lungs.

Blood-Hair shrugged. 'A ragged folk came to live here. A nameless rabble who thought they had earned their place in the world. Jarl Wulfgar taught them truth. As you yourselves now teach truth to many English in this land.'

'Pagan,' the Norman knight said simply, which surprised the redheaded Viking, not least because it was spoken in English.

'Jarl Wulfgar pays all honours to his family's gods. But the Allfather has many names. Jarl Wulfgar has no dispute with followers of the White Christ.'

'You mean if that's what is required to hang on to your ill-gotten gains?' Again, it was English. Spoken like a native.

The Viking frowned, switching also to the local tongue. 'Who are you?'

'You may well ask.'

'I offer parley, yet you say nothing.'

'You offer parley?' The knight's tone was contemptuous. '*You?*'

'Jarl Wulfgar knows your laws. He will swear all oaths of allegiance required by your king in honour of his conquest. He will make a strong ally.'

'There can be no parley here,' the knight replied. 'Your allegiance is not required, nor your oaths. Especially not your oaths... for Jarl Wulfgar won't survive to make good on them.'

'A third time, I ask your name,' Blood-Hair said.

With deliberate slowness, the Norman lifted his helmet.

No Viking ever showed fear or even surprise in the face of a foe. That was part of their creed. But even Sigfurth Blood-Hair, a time-served slayer of men, sucked in a startled breath. The stunned silence lingered, before he hawked and spat, a rotten, black gap showing where his upper front teeth should be.

'Any further questions?' the Norman, who was remarkably young, asked them.

The *drengr* turned and headed back up the steep track towards the palisade. Only Blood-Hair remained behind.

'You and all your people will die here,' he warned.

'You said that once before,' the young knight replied. 'The difference is, on that occasion you believed it.'

PART ONE

SOWN WITH FIRE

CHAPTER 1

Five days after the battle on Senlac Ridge, in that region called Haestinga, Cerdic Aelfricsson, sole surviving heir to Earl Rothgar of Ripon, found himself trudging eastward along the Roman road that followed England's south coast. Stripped to rags, filthy, wet and weary, he and a few other ragged English survivors, roped like animals to the rear of carts in the Norman cavalcade, plodded tiredly along.

Much of the route was closed in by that great, semi-mythical woodland known as the Weald. This was the southern outskirt of the forest, and a key region of that vast and wealthy earldom, Wessex. A northerner by birth and breeding, Cerdic had never been here before, but he'd heard much about it. It should have been a wonder for him merely to be present in this place. But his feet by now were lumps of sores and blisters, and he had bruises and open wounds all over his thinly clad body. His wrists chafed under stout ropes that were bound so tightly his fingers tingled. He was a captive, a prisoner of war, now the property of the Norman conquerors, who would occasionally make time in their journey to kick him, or whip him, or spit on him.

A loathing curdled inside him, so intense that it burned in his mind, firing his imagination to a vast range of unnameable atrocities, all of which he yearned to wreak on his captors.

Mainly though, he reserved this for the Viking war band that had broken away from the invading army of Harald 'the Hardraada' Sigurdsson and captured, ransacked and finally occupied Cerdic's Northumbrian home, Wulfbury burh, slaughtering in the process his mentor and tutor, Aethelric, Letwold, his dearest friend, and Eadora, the flower of Swaledale, among countless others.

'Are you unwell today?' Yvette asked, interrupting his thoughts. 'You seem distracted.'

She had lifted the cloth at the back of the wagon in which she was travelling, the one to which Cerdic was fastened. She, too, was a prisoner, and the experience of captivity was taking its toll on her. At roughly seventeen years old, she was a natural beauty, with long brown hair, dark doe eyes and fine cheekbones, but increasingly she looked drawn and pale. The interior of the awning-covered wagon that had become her home was crude and basic, and though it rendered her situation vastly more comfortable than Cerdic's, as the former ward of a titled lady, it was like nothing she'd ever been used to. She already looked thinner than when Cerdic had first seen her, only a few days previously. Her white kirtle and white linen veil, an ensemble that had rendered her an ethereal vision on that first night in the grey mist covering the battlefield, now looked worn and drab.

Before he could reply, a sound to the left caught his attention, drawing his eyes to the wall of yellow undergrowth hemming the road from the north. It was late October, so there were great gaps in it, and for half a second Cerdic thought he spied furtive movement in the rank, dripping depths beyond.

'Would you rather not work today?' Yvette asked in her French-accented but nevertheless perfect English.

'Work?' He glanced round at her, fleetingly puzzled. 'No… no, we can work.'

She nodded, huddling into her cloak. 'You're coming on very well. Quicker than I expected.'

He shrugged as he trudged. 'I speak Latin, as you know. That seems to be half the battle.'

He glanced into the woods again, and as he did, he tripped, toppling forward, landing hard on his knees. The road might have been Roman in origin, but what remained of its paving was buried under layers of soil and trodden leaf-mulch, and thanks to the on-off autumn rain and the passage of at least ten thousand men, it had been churned into a black, stinking slurry. Wrists burning as the rope bit deep, Cerdic fell forward fully and was dragged through it on his front, thrashing about in his efforts to get up. Yvette tried to help by leaning out of the cart and tugging on the rope, but it proved difficult. Calling to the wagon-master beyond her awning would have made no difference. When Duke William the Bastard's army was on the move, it neither stopped nor slowed unless by the Bastard's own command. To the rear of them, meanwhile, perhaps twenty yards behind, a phalanx of Norman infantry, primarily men-at-arms, several of them wounded, most dirtied and bedraggled, marched disconsolately, paying him no heed. It didn't matter to them that he could die this way. So many of the duke's English prisoners already had. Only after much scrambling and struggling, and a huge effort on his own part, as well as Yvette's, did Cerdic, newly filthied down the front of his body, regain his feet.

The girl watched him, visibly saddened by his tattered state, by his painful limp, by the livid gash still visible on his scalp thanks to the moist air that had plastered down his fair Saxon locks.

There was no official relationship between them. Cerdic was the son of an English earl, captured after he was knocked unconscious during the butchery on Senlac Ridge. Yvette, meanwhile, was the daughter, and only child in fact, of a Norman count so at odds with his duke that he now lived in exile in Anjou, and had refused to participate in the Norman invasion of England. Years ago, when her father had first drawn steel against his overlord, she had been smuggled across the Channel to live in the care of an old family friend, Edith Swan-Neck, the Lady of Walsingham and the common-law wife of the late King of England, Harold Godwinson. However, now she had been recognised by one of Duke William's great lords and taken as a captive herself. No doubt she'd be useful leverage when the duke finally returned to Normandy and sought terms with her father. Hence, she received better treatment than common prisoners-of-war like

Cerdic, though the war was far from over yet, and her future remained uncertain.

Cerdic and Yvette had formed an unofficial kind of alliance, a connection that had strengthened as, at Cerdic's request, Yvette taught him the language of her people. Daily now, as he stumbled at the back of her cart, she gave him lessons, but thanks to the damp and the cold, and the poor, meagre food he received, he was weakening all the time. Up until now, at least, it had seemed to her that Cerdic's dauntless defiance – a product of youthful naivety, she suspected, rather than adult reason – would be adequate to see him through, but just at this moment he seemed wearier and more tired than at any stage of the journey so far.

'You've spent no time grieving for your lost ones,' she said, seeking to distract him from his fatigue. 'You cannot contain that within yourself.'

Cerdic fought down thoughts of his father's grave far away in the north, on that desolate road outside York, and of the corpse of his brother, Unferth, which still lay on Senlac Ridge and was now most likely clustered with scavenger birds.

'In times of war, grief is for the weak,' he muttered.

She rolled her lovely eyes. 'That's a foolish thing to say.'

'Your father wouldn't say that?'

Yvette's father, Rodric of Hiemois, was a famous commander of men, but the girl remained unimpressed. 'My father *would* say that, yes, but it would still be foolish. Besides, did we not agree that your war is over now that you're a hostage?'

'We agreed nothing of the sort.'

'I told you I would teach you our language so there'd be better understanding between you and my people, so that you could find common ground with them.'

'And I told you I would learn it so they wouldn't have mastery over me.'

She sighed.

'Yvette... you expect me to surrender without striking a blow?'

'From what I understand, you struck many blows on Senlac Ridge.'

Cerdic was grim-faced. His memory of that fateful battle was a whirlwind of blood and blades, much of it vague thanks to his head wound. It was true that he'd sundered skulls and severed limbs, had driven sword and seax through the flesh and ribs of more opponents than he could count. But in the chaos and frenzy and that foul, crimson fug of close-quarter killing, he didn't see what else he could have done. He had been driven purely by the animal instinct to survive, rather than courage.

'I mean blows in retaliation,' he said, 'not blows in self-defence.'

Her eyes still hinted at reproach. 'Hatred only begets more hatred, Cerdic.'

'The hatred ends when the war is over. And one battle does not make a war. Look at your duke's army.'

She became cross. 'I told you, he is not *my* duke.'

'They are tired, too, and hungry. And their numbers are depleted.'

It was true. The footmen behind them weren't the only ones marching in poor order. Many others in the Norman host, knights included, were dishevelled and mud-spattered, a significant number groaning from dirtily bandaged wounds. Several carts were crammed with men too maimed either to walk or ride, blood still dripping through the planking underneath them. Frequently, Cerdic and Yvette passed small burial parties interring the newly deceased in roadside clay. After Senlac Ridge, Duke William boasted that he'd slain many more than he'd lost. But Cerdic had been there too, and he doubted that. The Normans might have had the day, but it had cost them dear...

A crackle in the foliage again drew his attention to the woods.

'But none of that is good news for us,' he mumbled to himself.

'Do you wish to learn today, or not?' she asked.

He nodded distractedly, still listening, though any further sounds from the forest were lost in the creaking of cartwheels, thudding of hooves and tramping of feet.

They proceeded with their lessons, Yvette imparting her knowledge to Cerdic as the memories of her own lessons in English dictated. From the beginning, she'd said that she felt the best way to teach him was to converse with him in French, and use little of his own language, forcing him to concentrate on the meaning of words and sentences and committing them to memory. As she'd already remarked, he'd proved an able student.

Around mid-morning, a Norman knight called Roland Casterborus, who had now bypassed the duo several times as he rode back and forth along the column on his master's business, finally noticed what they were doing and slowed his horse to a walk alongside them.

Cerdic and Yvette's official captor was Count Cynric FitzOslac, the Leopard of Tancarville, one of the Bastard's closest deputies, and it was his personal household that held them in custody. The knight Roland was Cynric's seneschal and standard-bearer, which said much about him as a warrior, though in appearance he was a sombre fellow, short-haired as all the Normans were, but wearing a trim beard and moustache. An old horizontal scar marked the left side of his face, hinting at the many battles he'd fought before ever coming to England. He regarded Cerdic curiously and spoke to Yvette in French.

Cerdic was surprised to find that he'd already, in only a few short days, picked up enough of the language to at least partly comprehend their conversation, the knight-seneschal asking the female hostage what she was doing, the hostage replying that she was teaching Cerdic their language. Roland gave the boy another look, this one more interested than hostile.

'*Pourquoi pensez-vous que cela vous aidera?*'

Cerdic didn't completely understand the question, but got the gist of it, replying that he would feel less like an animal if he could converse with those who had taken him prisoner.

Roland nodded soberly, before riding on. Like Turold de Bardouville, Count Cynric's champion, the knight-seneschal was one of the few among Cerdic's captors who had not seemed inclined to vindictiveness. He was undoubtedly one of the leaders here, an elite warrior and commanding figure, who issued orders curtly and, if not contemptuous of the defeated English, was mostly indifferent to their beaten, bedraggled state. But he was not in the business of being cruel for the sake of it.

'He isn't like the others,' Cerdic commented.

'They say he follows the code of *chevalerie*,' Yvette said. 'Or seeks to.'

'Chivalry?' Cerdic had never heard the term.

'As I understand, it's a new way to behave… for knights, I mean. I heard mention of it at my father's court. It first spread through Francia in ballads and written tales of love and heroism, though many feel it should guide the conduct of real knights. It espouses courage and loyalty in battle but calls for Christian restraint, even kindness to one's foes.'

'Kindness?' Cerdic almost laughed. 'I hate to tell you this, Yvette, but I think there's quite a gulf between your people's dreams and their true selves.'

'I know,' she replied. 'So be wary of him. Be wary of de Bardouville, too. He is more civil to you than the rest, but he is Count Cynric's personal warrior. This means he has slain many in single combat.'

'You were just saying I should make peace.'

'Make peace, but remain watchful. *Tous les hommes ont le bien et le mal en eux*. You understand this?'

He mused. 'I think you said that men can be good or bad.'

'*Non*. All men are both good and evil. But be careful around those to whom evil comes easily.'

Cerdic thought on that as he trudged along. 'Frankly, I'm amused you still harbour such simple ideas as good and evil.' His eyes roved to the trees on their left.

'What do you mean?' she said, following his gaze.

'I fear there are men out here who are past such notions. Think about that. Men who'll be crazed, deranged by what they've seen and done, by what's been done to them.'

The damp autumnal spaces they could see were bare of life, but there were shadows in there, too, and deeper recesses thick with mist.

'Out *here*?' She sounded surprised. 'In *this* forest?'

'Where else?'

'You think they'll attack us?'

He scanned the treeline. 'If they *are* here and I'm not imagining it, I don't think they're here to – how did you put it – find common ground.'

'But we are a full-sized army, and they were defeated.'

'Men who've lost everything tend not to understand such terms.'

She gazed into the trees again. 'I thought you'd welcome an ambush?'

'Not if I'm caught up in it.' He held up his tightly bound wrists. 'It's not like I can run away.'

Only now did their predicament really seem to dawn on Yvette, her surprise turning to visible concern. 'We are halfway along the column,' she said. 'Surely that's the safest place?'

'There'll be no safe place.' But seeing her deepening concern, he added: 'There's unlikely to be a massed assault. The southern earls are all dead, and we're on the outer rim of the Weald. There'd be greater danger in its depths. But listen to me, if there is an attack, the best thing you can do is lie low in your cart.' He looked uncertain how to phrase his next snippet of advice. 'And if they capture you, you must impress on them forcefully that you're a ward of the Lady of Walsingham. And I mean *forcefully*. You have a Frankish accent, Yvette, and if they think you're with the Normans...'

If she'd been concerned before, that thought struck her with something like terror. Without a word, she shrank back into her private compartment.

The Norman host rested that day about two hours after darkness had fallen, which in late October was all-consuming. Unable to find dry or level ground on which to build a fortified camp, they were forced to bivouac along the road for nearly a mile. It was during these dark, silent hours that a number of Norman sentries were felled by axe-blows, the assailants always melting back into the night, though not without freeing some of the prisoners and setting fire to a couple of supply wagons first.

Cerdic was not one of those released, but the next day he was even warier as he plodded behind Yvette, his wrists burning as he twisted at his ropes, his eyes spearing the walls of decayed foliage. So narrow was the route now that his captors hadn't been able to post flanking guards, and several times he thought he glimpsed indistinct figures moving parallel to the column. The deep chop-wounds on the previous night's victims suggested their assailants were housecarls, almost certainly survivors from Senlac Ridge, so they'd be in no mood to be merciful. Theoretically, Cerdic would be spared, but as he'd said to Yvette, once the affray was on, anything could happen.

It started shortly before noon, arrows suddenly whipping back and forth, striking Norman horsemen or punching through the awnings of vehicles.

'Yvette, get down!' Cerdic shouted. 'Lie flat.'

There was a half-foot of wooden rim around the bed of the cart in which she was travelling. It provided a minor bulwark but not much more. Meanwhile, there was chaos all along the column, shields hefted outward, harsh orders shouted, which Cerdic gauged were for the march to proceed.

They pressed on as though fearless, though in truth they had no option. They straggled over a considerable distance. Anyone who halted risked being cut off from the rest. Even small numbers of ambushers could then engage hand-to-hand.

More missiles flew, Cerdic ducking as best he could while stumbling along. Just ahead of Yvette's wagon, on the left, one of Count Cynric's knights fell from his saddle. An arrow had pierced the left side of his neck, though it wasn't an ordinary arrow, Cerdic realised as the body approached. It was a crossbow bolt. He'd never seen or even heard of English soldiers using this weapon, so clearly these had been pillaged from the dead Normans on Senlac Ridge. That explained why they weren't using fire-arrows, though these high-speed darts were no less deadly.

As the knight's body passed, Cerdic swooped on it.

He was attached to the back of Yvette's wagon by five or six feet of rope, which, once it had been knotted around his wrists and a steel ring on the vehicle's tailgate, gave him about four feet of clearance. It was all he needed to grapple quickly with the slain knight's harness, ripping out a dagger and then a larger, heavier seax, which had once presumably belonged to an English carl. He scrambled forward, pushing both under the hanging cloth.

'Yvette, hide these.'

The girl had been lying flat, as instructed, and it was a second or two before she took them off him and secreted them somewhere. A bolt then struck one of the iron hoops over which the awning was drawn, splintering with the force, a shard of it almost blinding the lad.

'Christ's sake, don't you know English prisoners when you see them!' he bellowed.

The missile storm ceased about a minute later, but several hundred yards further on it recommenced with greater intensity. This time, javelins were flung as well, and heavy spears. The column pressed on grimly, no one breaking ranks, though Cerdic was increasingly aware that he wore neither mail nor helmet.

They passed more corpses. One with a throwing-axe buried in the side of his skull. One with a crossbow shaft sunk in his eye. *A greeting from King Harold*, Cerdic thought, though he drew no satisfaction as stray bolts continually glanced by, some within inches. At length, he had no option but to openly defy his captors. There were only companies of footmen to the rear, and they'd be more concerned about themselves than watching him. So, he dashed forward, vaulting up and over the tailgate of Yvette's cart, crashing in through the opening.

The girl knelt up, shocked. 'What are you doing?' she hissed.

Daylight speared in where a couple of missiles had already punctured the awning.

He lugged her down again. 'What do you think? I want to live too.'

They lay nose-to-nose. 'But what if they see you?'

'I think they're a bit busy just now... Sorry I haven't a prettier face to show you. It's been pummelled of late.'

She nodded her understanding, eyes moist with fear. Then, making a visible effort to pull herself together, she reached up with her left hand, tilting his head forward to examine the scalp wound left by Turold de Bardouville's longsword.

'It's healing,' she said, 'but it should have been stitched. I used to stitch my father's wounds. But I have no such materials with me now.'

He glanced up at her, fascinated. 'You stitched your father's wounds? You can only have been a child.'

'With a father like mine, you grew up quickly.'

'I can't say the same for mine.' He cocked an ear to the events outside. They heard shouts of anger and pain, gasps, yelps, a horse squealing as its flesh was pierced. 'But I've grown up too these last few weeks.'

With a shuddersome *bang*, a crossbow bolt flew clean through the canvas. Yvette clutched his arm with fright.

'Is it true?' she whispered. 'If your people catch me, they'll kill me?'

'I won't let them,' he said. A pounding of fast-approaching hooves sounded outside. Cerdic levered himself up, risking a glance over the tailgate, and saw a line of Tancarville cavalry, again notable by the rearing white leopards on their black surcoats, advancing up the column on the right-hand side. At their front rode Joubert FitzOslac. Even with his helmet on, his shield up and a studded leather neck-guard tucked into place, his thickset form and fierce eyes gave him away.

Of all his Norman captors, Joubert was the one Cerdic reviled the most. It was an open question whether the count's son saw repeated acts of savagery as the only way to impress his father, or whether he was simply doing what came natural to him. Cerdic had already seen the young Norman lord, who was only two or three years his senior, murder and brutalise a number of defenceless prisoners. Joubert seemed to despise the English simply because they weren't Norman. Even to a crushed and broken enemy, there wasn't an inch of compassion in his whole battle-hardened body. Alongside him rode a squat, black-bearded brute whom Cerdic had seen several times before. A bodyguard or deputy of some sort.

Ten yards short of the cart, they veered into the trees, thirty mounted men-at-arms behind them. They'd had enough. It was a skirmish party aiming to flush out the enemy. Cerdic kept low, only his eyes peeking over the woodwork, hoping he'd see something that would please him, such as Joubert's party returning in defeat. Preferably without their captain. He'd love to know that Joubert had died in there, or better still, been crippled and left to the mercy of men whose homes and families he'd aimed to despoil.

After twenty minutes, occasional horsemen rejoined the column. Several lacked helmets and were bloodied, their shields bristling with arrows. When Joubert returned, he and his bearded sidekick were in a similar state, but both still very much alive.

Cerdic tried to count the others. About twenty remained in total. Out of thirty, that wasn't a grievous loss, though it still might reflect badly on their leader. He hoped so, at least.

'What am I to do with these weapons?' Yvette asked, producing the two blades.

'One is for you,' he replied. 'To protect yourself.'

'You mean in case you *can't* talk your people out of carrying me away?'

Cerdic shook his head. The woods seemed to be quiet now. 'It isn't my people you need to fear. If this is the best they can do, launch a few missiles and run for cover, then an army like this can easily withstand them. And in another day or so, we'll be out of the Weald properly – I'd imagine that's why we came by this route – and then even this minor resistance will end.'

She didn't answer straight away, evaluating his mood.

'You shouldn't be too disheartened by that,' she said.

'I'm not,' he shrugged. And in a strange way that was true.

He'd partly hoped to be released by whoever these desperadoes were, but would they really welcome him? He was Northumbrian, almost as much an alien to these southerners as the Normans were. He knew no one down here. He'd hold no rank among them, would likely be seen as nothing more than an extra mouth to feed. In any case, he'd already seen enough to persuade himself that the ambushers were little more than hunted men themselves, a straggle of remnants from King Harold's vanquished host, doing as much damage as possible before they too succumbed to wounds or hunger or Norman steel.

Yvette offered him the seax. 'Why don't you cut yourself free? Escape?'

He took it, but pushed it out of sight under a blanket, along with the dagger. 'There'll be better opportunities than this.' She looked bewildered. 'Yvette... Duke Bastard lost men today. He'll retaliate for that. Better for me if I stay hidden in the back of your cart, a flyspeck beneath his notice, rather than get caught wandering some woodland path as a freeborn Englishman.'

'So, what will you do?'

'A plan will suggest itself. I'm sure of it.'

CHAPTER 2

Duke William of Normandy had a formidable record when it came to war.

To begin with, the fiery Norman suzerain fought his battles differently from most others. The cream of his warriors were mounted knights rather than axe-wielding infantry like the housecarls, and yet they weren't some elite hardcore always located at the heart of his army. They were immense in number and were spread across it extensively. In return for land or a privileged place in the household, they offered martial service to their overlord and basically that was *all* they did. When they weren't fighting for real, they were training or engaging each other in mock-battles called tournaments or jousts, so their expertise was high. Their armaments were superior to many of their opponents'. They wore chain-mail rather than ring-mail, which was lighter but more impenetrable, while their shields were rectangular or kite-shaped, instead of circular, which left less of their body exposed. They were adept with all kinds of weapons, but the Norman longsword was their preference; though it took time and skill to master, there was surely no more effective a weapon from horseback. Cerdic had seen that for himself. And felt it. Six days since Senlac Ridge, his scalp still throbbed.

Before they'd even come to England, this highly mobile and motivated force had proved itself during several battles in Normandy, always against numerically superior opponents, and in each case the duke had led his men personally. He'd shown the same fearlessness on Senlac Ridge, where on more than one occasion, the Normans had only rallied against the English because the duke himself had charged King Harold's shieldwall on his own. And yet, to look at him, this Duke of Normandy, whom they called 'the Bastard', seemed an average specimen. It was no myth that he was a great commander, but where inside him that power resided Cerdic couldn't imagine.

Aged somewhere in his late thirties, the Bastard clearly retained youth and vigour, but in terms of stature, he was shortish and tubby. His dark hair was hacked down to a thicket of flat-topped bristles, which seemed to be the fashion of his countrymen, but his face was pale, almost unnaturally so, and unusually round, his jaw heavy, his eyes large and protuberant, almost froglike. There was nothing obvious of the warrior about him. For all this, even from the little Cerdic had really seen of the duke since Senlac Ridge, a mounted, scarlet-liveried figure moving back and forth at the front of his great army, or standing alone by a campfire, brooding, the lad had deduced that this was one of those ever-suspicious and unsmiling lords, who brooked no resistance to their will. Even the remotest hint of opposition would provoke a ferocious response.

Earl Tostig had been one such, Harald 'the Hardraada' Sigurdsson another.

But the true depth of the Norman Bastard's fury would only become plain to the lad nine days after Senlac Ridge, when the Norman host left the Weald road and deployed in wide formation, facing towards the coast, an infantry line to the fore, cavalry companies behind.

It was a dry day, the sun having finally emerged through the ceiling of autumn cloud. It wasn't giving off much heat, but the air was clear, the level landscape, cut by the odd drainage channel, lying russet and gold all the way to the sea, which was just visible as a dim blue line. The army commenced a slow advance, weak sunlight glimmering from their heavy chain-mail coats, the tips of spears, the edges of drawn longswords.

The baggage train drew up, one vehicle behind the next, at the rear. Cerdic was glad of the unexpected rest, and had good vantage across much of the plain, though what Duke William was actually advancing against he initially wasn't sure. However, this didn't worry him as much as the size of the Norman host which, now that it was laid out, he could see in its entirety. There were more of them left than he'd expected. For all their losses, at least twelve thousand remained under arms. And it was still a trained, disciplined force.

His heart sank as he struggled to picture any English army left that could challenge it on the open field. There was sufficient manpower, that much was certain, but were there sufficient professional soldiers? Those scattered in the Weald had clearly felt their numbers inadequate to meet the invaders face-to-face. But did any of England's remaining commanders have the mental wherewithal to fight the invaders through insurgency?

Somehow, Cerdic couldn't see the brothers Edwin and Morcar, the earls of Mercia and Northumbria respectively, taking up that mantle. Though their forces had been badly mauled by Harald Hardraada at the battle of Fulford, they still commanded significant numbers, and yet had failed to arrive at Senlac Ridge. Cerdic had set eyes on them once only, post-Fulford, and had been unimpressed by their reluctance to answer a royal summons. They'd done their part of the fighting, it had seemed to imply; the rest of it was someone else's responsibility.

For that reason alone, he doubted that whoever was offering resistance here on a bleak section of the south coast would have any connection to those northern lords.

'It's a town called Romney,' Yvette said, appearing at the back of her wagon. 'I overheard the driver speaking to one of the guards.'

'Romney?' he said. The name wasn't familiar to him.

'One of the Five Ports. Apparently, they are special harbours along England's south coast. I don't really understand why.'

Cerdic said nothing. From conversations with his father and Aethelric, he understood that the Five Ports were recognised entryways into England but in addition held duties to provide ships for the royal fleet.

Yvette looked at him, pale-faced. 'They're going to destroy it.'

'But that makes no sense,' Cerdic replied, thinking how much use they could make of a town like this. 'Surely, they'll just capture it?'

'All I know is what I heard,' Yvette said.

Cerdic had just enough spare rope to allow him to climb up on the side of Yvette's wagon, and from there he could see over the heads of the advancing cohorts. Habitations were just about visible: straw-roofed cottages leading along a narrow lane, which the Norman force entirely straddled, towards a clutter of similar, small buildings and beyond those a palisade, on the other side of which there were higher, sturdier rooftops.

A small group, unarmoured by the looks of it, had come out from the main gate and were approaching. Many carried boxes or bulging sacks, or simply walked with their arms outspread. A deputation, no doubt, offering silver in return for clemency.

Before Cerdic could see more, he was grabbed by his belt and yanked from his perch.

He landed with gut-thumping force in the hummocky grass. When he looked up, winded, Joubert glowered down from his saddle. He made some typically belligerent statement, which was too guttural and quickly uttered for Cerdic even to partially translate, before turning his animal away.

'He says that condemned men can have no interest in the affairs of the living,' Yvette said.

Cerdic got back to his feet and watched as his pig-like tormentor returned to another group of mounted knights waiting close by. Most likely, the count's son was angry because it was House Tancarville that had been left behind to guard the baggage train. Cerdic wondered if this was in punishment for Joubert's decision to lead a mounted troop into the cover during the forest ambush and throw away half a company of men.

It was noticeable that Count Cynric himself, astride his own horse, sat apart from them by several dozen yards. He was a naturally gaunt man, lean of body, long of limb, with a white beard and moustache and unruly white hair. At present, only part of his sallow features were visible above the heavy cloak wrapping his slumped, crooked form. Cerdic knew that the count had been wounded on Senlac Ridge, but now he seemed to be ailing from it. By the nobleman's haggard expression, he wasn't seeing very much. The knights Roland Casterborus and Turold de Bardouville were mounted up a few paces behind him, watching in silence as the great army converged on the citizens sent out to greet it.

A baying of horns split the mid-morning air, followed by a thunder of pommels on shields and then a roaring of men seized by bloodlust.

'Time for another lesson?' Cerdic suggested, taking Yvette by the shoulders, pushing her gently back under the awning, and climbing in after her.

She tried her best to tutor him as they sat face-to-face, fighting to blot out the dirge of horrified shrieks from across the coastal plain and, as the autumn day grew dull and grey, the rising orange glare and thickening stench of smoke. Her eyes welled with tears, her mouth trembling as she sought to converse with him. However, in the end, struggling simply to breathe, she pushed past him and leapt out of the wagon.

Cerdic swore, lurching to the tailgate, gazing after her.

Yvette held her skirts up as she fled away on foot. The nearest groups of Count Cynric's men, who still sat on their horses or leaned on spears, chattering, unmoved by the inferno on the horizon, didn't notice at first.

It was a moment of sheer peril, which tore Cerdic two ways at once.

But there was only one solution.

He fumbled under the blanket, locating the seax and, turning it in his hands, pressed it crosswise against the top of the tailgate, then ran his bonds up and down its edge. A weapon honed for war, the ropes were no match for it.

He cast them loose but hesitated before scrambling out of the cart.

Roland and Turold still sat alongside each other. Of the two, Turold, as Count Cynric's champion, was the most obviously fearsome. Though he was the one who'd finally struck Cerdic down on Senlac Ridge, he'd been inclined to show warmth to the lad ever since. He spoke English for one thing, one of the few Normans who could, which helped them converse. But physically, he was a giant, inches taller than Cerdic's father had been, and vastly broader across the chest and shoulders, an immense stature often enhanced by the bearskin cloak he wore. It would be no joke to enrage such a fellow. At present of course, both Turold and Roland were deep in discussion, their attention elsewhere.

Cerdic took his chance, scrambling out of the cart and running after Yvette, tucking the blade into the back of his belt as he did.

She was no longer in sight, but he saw a clutch of autumnal trees just ahead, with a path leading through them. He followed it, and now heard angry shouts at his rear. The route wound on. There was still no sign of her, and for half a moment he wondered if he'd come the wrong way, only to emerge on the edge of a wheatfield that, during the harvest, had been stripped to stubble. He stumbled to a halt, watching helplessly as a band of raucous mercenaries, Bretons by the looks and sounds of them, rode back and forth with nets and ropes, chasing down the screaming female captives they'd rounded up in one of the villages earlier, and who now had been released just for sport. Clearly, the Bretons had been ordered to stand aside while Romney was sacked, the finer plunder reserved for the Norman lords themselves, and thus had found other entertainment.

Cerdic's mouth dried, his heart thumping in his chest.

Movement on his periphery drew his gaze southward, and he spied Yvette. She watched goggle-eyed as the Bretons played their sickening game, but at the same time backed slowly into a bank of ferns that were still deep and lush, though reddening as October drew on. She turned with an air of panic as well as horror, and plunged away through them.

Cerdic hastened over, tearing into the vegetation himself, though almost immediately the loamy ground crumbled beneath his feet. He'd reached the edge of a deep gulley, at the bottom of which a creek meandered seaward. Some thirty yards along it, Yvette had dropped to her knees at the waterside, the hem of her kirtle torn and dirty. Her head hung low, her back heaving as she wept. Cerdic stumbled down over loose stones, slipping at the bottom and finishing up ankle-deep in water. He blundered along it, finally taking her in his arms.

At first she resisted, struggling like a cat, only to realise that it was Cerdic. She sagged in his grasp. 'Why are they doing these things?' she sobbed. 'Why?'

'Because they were attacked,' he replied. 'Duke William is teaching his enemies a lesson.'

She pulled back from him. 'You're making excuses for them?'

Cerdic shook his head wearily. 'I'm explaining what's happening. This is war.'

'But those people out there are not warriors.'

'The duke can't find the warriors...' Despite all, Cerdic was surprised by how simply the explanation came to him. 'So, he punishes their loved ones instead.'

She shook her head, too appalled to try and rationalise it.

'All that matters is you and I survive,' he said. 'And *you* won't if you make it plain to them that you'll run at every opportunity.'

Sensing a presence, he glanced up. Turold had appeared at the top of the slope. He'd removed his helmet, but his lance lay across the front of his saddle. He watched them sternly.

'We're coming back!' Cerdic shouted, helping Yvette to her feet. 'I found her. She was... the slaughter, it was too much.'

The knight said nothing as, arm in arm, they ascended.

'Yvette's not a combatant, Turold,' Cerdic said when they reached the top. 'She shouldn't be treated like one.'

'How is it you're free of your bonds?' the Norman asked.

Cerdic reached around his back, pulled the seax into view and offered it hilt-first. 'I took this from one of your fatalities back in the Weald.'

The knight accepted it, sliding it in among his saddlebags. However, he didn't look satisfied. 'You got loose, and didn't seek to rejoin your compatriots?'

Cerdic unhanded Yvette, who pushed irritably past the knight's horse and fought her way through the ferns towards the wheatfield.

Cerdic watched her. 'Maybe I have other interests now.'

He made to walk back, too, but Turold's lance fell across his path.

'You think me a fool?' the knight said. 'I know a freedom fighter when I see one. Why didn't you go to your people?'

'They're not my people. I'm a northerner, remember?'

'You stood with them on Senlac Ridge.'

'The situation's changed. You have the south. I can't roll back time. But my interests lie north. Things may be different there.'

The knight regarded him long and hard. His scarred, stony visage was the last word in intimidation.

'I'm being honest with you, Turold,' Cerdic said. 'I could be halfway back to the Weald by now, but to what? Homelessness? Beggary? And with winter coming?'

Several taut moments passed before the lance was lifted.

'Put her in her wagon,' Turold said, as they pushed back through the ferns. 'I'll tell Roland it was a misunderstanding.'

'Will he believe that?'

'He'll believe it because he'll want to believe it.'

Cerdic was interested by that. He remembered that Roland Casterborus was, or sought to be, an adherent to this new form of thinking among the Frankish military elite. Cerdic knew nothing about it other than Yvette's brief explanation. Though if it was supposed to limit the brutality shown by men under arms, and made demands upon them to defend the weak, how Count Cynric's seneschal could reconcile that with the events beyond the small wood, both the screams and wails, and the stench of burning that now filled the coastal air, was beyond his imagination.

Back on the wheatfield, they saw that Yvette, who was still a dozen yards ahead, had come to the attention of the Bretons, two of whom stalked towards her in their mismatched mail, laughing leerily, offering her wine from a slopping gourd.

Turold barked out a thunderous command, and kicked his horse forward, the sellswords immediately falling back, eyeing his spear-tip. For her part, Yvette spared the champion a single sullen glare, then stalked into the trees, head held proudly.

Cerdic made to follow, only for the lance to drop across his path a second time.

He glanced up. Turold's expression had softened, but his eyes were bleak.

'This can't happen again, you understand?' he said. 'As far as I'm concerned, you're an English soldier and an enemy. Yvette of Hiemois meanwhile is the daughter of a rebel and a traitor. That means she, too, is an enemy. Don't force me to prove whose side I'm on.'

CHAPTER 3

Cerdic was nudged into wakefulness by a leather-booted foot. He looked groggily up from where he lay curled against the rear wheel of Yvette's wagon.

Dawn appeared to be breaking, because though a dank mist hung over everything, he could sense movement in the camp and muted conversations. Two figures towered over him. One was Roland Casterborus, the other Turold. Both were fully mailed and wearing their black surcoats emblazoned with the White Leopard of Tancarville. Neither smiled.

'*Votre nom est-il Cerdic?*' Roland asked.

Cerdic struggled into a sitting position. 'Yes, my name's Cerdic.'

'*Apprends-tu notre langue?*'

Cerdic replied in broken French, attempting to explain that yes, he was learning their tongue, but that he didn't understand it very well. Not yet. Roland glanced at Turold, who merely shrugged. The knight-seneschal strode away. Turold hunkered down.

'In that case, I'm to come with you,' he said.

'Come with me where?'

'Don't ask questions.' The knight produced a blade, took his wrists and sawed through his bonds. 'Do as you are told and all will be well.'

He walked away, beckoning as he did. Cerdic stumbled after him, still stiff with cold. The column had left the road the previous day and was now bivouacked on a broad stretch of upward-sloping heathland. This meant that the ground was mostly dry, but also that Cerdic's Norman captors had been able to spread out, their tents, pavilions and breakfast fires now ranging off in many directions.

'What is this?' he asked. They continued uphill, which meant they were headed towards the next object of Duke William's anger, the old Roman fortress overlooking the seaport called Dover.

'You can be useful,' the knight replied. 'And that's a good thing. For you, I mean.'

'What will I need to do?'

'For the moment, be quiet. Speak only when you're spoken to.'

Soon they were on significantly higher ground, where the mist had cleared. The fortress in front of them was perched on an elevated shoulder of rock, occupying a strong position. From this vantage, the port was no more than a clutter of shops, houses and boatyards, with innumerable masts of fishing boats and transport cogs lined up alongside its piers and jetties. No people were visible, the majority no doubt hiding in their homes.

The fort's original Roman walls were much eroded by time, though a massive timber breastwork had been added along the top by Saxon lords of more recent vintage. In total, the ramparts stood twenty-five feet tall, which wasn't even close to the height of the curtain walls encircling London, and probably wasn't even as high as those at York, but its position on that high, natural platform meant that it could only be assaulted from one direction, the northwest. There was a road and an entrance gate on that side, the shallow slope leading right up to it, but this was deceptive even to Cerdic's untrained eye, because though the main gate was traditionally the weakest section of any fortification, an army approaching this one would suffer protracted missile attack before it could even get close.

It was little wonder the Norman encampment ended several hundred yards short of it and was protected by a hastily dug ditch and several rows of sharpened stakes.

They halted here. A dozen yards off, Count Cynric sat astride his horse. Again, only his white face was visible above the heavy cloak wrapping his slumped outline. Roland was close by him, on foot but clutching the reins to two other steeds.

'Your count appears to be sickening,' Cerdic said.

'It's the injury he suffered on the Ridge,' Turold replied. 'Something inside him broke. He'll recover though. At least, you'd better hope he does. Else Joubert will command. In the meantime, you have other things to concern you…'

Cerdic looked again towards the edifice of the fortress. Now, as pale sunlight crept across the land, he could make out the motionless forms of several fallen men on the open ground in front of it, which hardly boded well. Meanwhile, behind him, other figures emerged from between the canvas structures of the camp. They too were armoured and, in most cases, attended by grooms and camp-boys, who busily handed them weapons or adjusted their cloaks and war-harness.

Cerdic had only been a prisoner of the Normans for eleven days, but already he recognised several of their highest-ranking men, or 'barons' as Yvette referred to them.

The duke's half-brother, Robert of Mortain, was there, as well as Count Eustace of Boulogne, Ralph de Tosney, William de Warenne, William FitzOsbern. Loyal warriors in their master's cause, all of whom partook in the bitter fighting on Senlac Ridge, but who, from what Yvette had said, were also a pack of rapacious jackals, each with his own private army, which he could and might mobilise swiftly should he feel he'd been inadequately rewarded for his services.

Other lesser men who'd also appeared on the camp's outskirts, knights and men-at-arms, dropped hurriedly to one knee. Turold did so too, dragging Cerdic down with him.

Directly behind them, another horseman had emerged from the maze of tents.

It was the Bastard himself, distinctive as ever in his polished chain-mail and brilliant blood-red livery with its Golden Lions insignia. Several moments passed as the duke simply sat there, his helmet tucked under his left arm. He looked at none of those around him, but instead was focused on the ominous shape of the stronghold. He gave some low-voiced command, which Cerdic barely heard, though it was sufficient for his followers to relax, all rising warily to their feet. When the duke spoke a second time, it was to Turold, though his gaze remained distant.

From what Cerdic could make out, the duke had asked: 'This is him?'

With much bowing and scraping, Turold replied in the affirmative.

The duke spoke again, and this time Cerdic's hair prickled. These words were for *him*.

Turold translated: 'Tell the garrison in Castle Dover, that William of Normandy is their lord and master... by reason of the pact he agreed with and the oath that was sworn by the late and dishonoured usurper, Harold Godwinson. And by the law of battle, by which means he overcame Godwinson in a fair contest in that place the English call Haestinga. There is no cause to continue this resistance on behalf of a cursed rogue who now lies slain. Tell these men that they were loyal servants indeed. That much is plain. They fought hard under Godwinson's banner. No man will condemn them for performing this duty. No lord will deny their courage and zeal. But that cause is lost. Therefore, we instruct them, for the sake of their wives and children, to end this war. If they abandon the castle and lay down their arms, they will be treated leniently. These are the terms we offer: a full amnesty for those Norman knights they have laid in their graves, and our unconditional pardon for their resistance to our rightful claim. It is our vow, our word as duke and future king, that they may live their lives as before, unchained, unmolested. But there is more yet. Those who are inclined might even enter our service as warriors, knights, in pursuit of which career there are great rewards... all they need do is bend their knee and offer homage and fealty.'

Without another word, without even waiting to ensure that he'd been understood, the duke turned his horse around and rode slowly back into the camp. For all his loathing of the invaders, it was only when the intimidating presence was removed that Cerdic felt able to vent his feelings.

'Why must *I* deliver this message?' he hissed. 'Count Cynric has other prisoners.'

'Some escaped during the forest ambush,' Turold replied.

'Some, not all.'

'The rest died.'

'Died?' Cerdic was shocked. 'All of them?'

Turold shrugged. 'Many were wounded already. The others lacked the guile you showed.'

By that, Cerdic assumed that the other captives either didn't think to or weren't able to ride in the wagons to which they'd been tethered during the worst of the last two weeks' weather.

'Some would call that murder,' he said.

'If you don't want there to be further murders, I advise you to carry out the duke's orders.'

'*You* speak English... you could do it.'

'You think they'd trust *me*?' Turold replied.

'I'm not sure they'd trust me either.'

'They'll *listen* to you at least... you ought to be able to get close to the walls without their bowmen sewing you to the ground.'

Cerdic glanced back towards the fortress. In particular, he eyed the twisted shapes littering the slope to its fore.

'*Que se passe-t-il?*' Roland asked, leading the two horses forward.

Turold explained to him in French, the knight-seneschal snapping back in words too quick for Cerdic to catch, before handing the two sets of reins to Turold and walking away again.

'Roland says you must *make* them trust you,' Turold said. 'If not, the consequence will be dire. I should explain... last night, not long after our arrival here, Duke William sent an embassy to the castle gate to seek parley. As you can see, they were shot down. In response, the duke planned to bring townsfolk up and execute them in front of the walls. Ten for every hour that passes while the garrison holds out.'

If anyone else had announced a scheme as outrageously harsh as that, Cerdic might have doubted their word, but in response to that minor ambush in the Weald, the town of Romney had been sacked and burned, the townsmen slain to a man and the women and girls handed to the army's lower orders. What he and Yvette had witnessed in the wheatfield outside the town had only been the start of it. There was no question that when Duke Bastard, the Church's current favourite, threatened heathen barbarity, he was fully capable of it.

'What changed his mind?' the lad asked.

'Count Cynric.'

Cerdic was surprised, and glanced again at the nobleman still seated on horseback some distance from the rest, seemingly indifferent to events, apparently wilting by the hour.

'Well... in truth, it was Roland.' Turold rubbed his chin, clearly unsure how much of this information to divulge. 'He persuaded the count that you, as captured English nobility, might speak to them, talk them into a peaceful surrender. The count took this message to the duke.'

Cerdic pondered the several other occasions during his captivity when his captor-in-chief might have avoided violence and how he'd chosen not to. 'Was that because Count Cynric is ill, and fearful of punishment in the afterlife?'

Turold gave a wry smile. 'I doubt it, but there were other advantages to be had. Understand this, Cerdic... with Duke William, one must continue to win his favour, or others will get ahead of you. The barons of Normandy seek always to find new plans and ideas to put to him, but most involve battle and slaughter. On this occasion, he saw the value of negotiation.'

Cerdic was intrigued. The night before Senlac Ridge, King Harold had offered parley and the Bastard had refused. Perhaps because his army was then at full strength? Did this mean he was less certain about his fighting capability now? If the garrison in the fortress refused to be cowed by the executions of townsfolk, maybe even were so infuriated that it would galvanise them to resist all the harder, the duke would have no option but to storm the mighty redoubt... and was he concerned that it might prove impregnable to his weakened force?

Roland now reappeared, mounted on his own battle-steed. In one hand he carried a long pole, from the end of which a white flag hung unfurled.

'*Montez sur vos chevaux*,' he said.

Turold handed the reins of one of the two horses to Cerdic. 'You can ride, I assume?'

Cerdic nodded and clambered lithely into the saddle.

The three of them rode out from the camp together, weaving through the defences and heading up the gently sloping grassland towards the fortress, the upper sections of which were now bathed in morning sunlight. As they did, Roland issued more instructions.

'Roland reminds you,' Turold translated, 'that I speak...'

'That you speak English like a native,' Cerdic cut in. 'So, if I try any trickery, you will know?'

The knight nodded. 'I'm impressed you've picked up so much of our language.'

'I don't understand everything said to me, but each day I learn more.'

'In such a short time, that is admirable.'

'It's not as if I've had much else to occupy my mind...'

'The fact you've done this while suffering is even more to your credit.'

Cerdic wondered if this was true. Had he not focused as hard as he had on Yvette's lessons simply to blot out his pain, to numb himself to the horror of this new existence? There were other reasons too, of course.

'My old teacher said I have a gift for...'

'*Que dit le garçon?*' Roland interrupted, evidently tiring of this conversation in which he could not participate.

Turold replied, presumably explaining that Cerdic was learning their language with unfeasible speed. Roland was slow to respond, but when he did, his expression was grave.

'Roland advises you be wary,' Turold said. 'He says there are some here who will deem superior intelligence a threat.'

'Roland would care?'

'Roland is a chivalrous knight. You understand what that means?'

'That even amid all this blood, he seeks to follow Christ's teachings?'

'That is a good way to put it. Though for many, it remains an ideal, not a reality...'

Roland, who'd blushed a little, almost as if he knew they'd been discussing him, reined up sharply. He pulled on his helmet and handed the flagpole to Cerdic.

'You go from here alone,' Turold said, also fitting his helmet in place.

Cerdic, who wasn't even mailed, let alone helmeted, surveyed the ground ahead, seeing the first of the corpses some forty paces to his front. From their garb, they were Norman men-at-arms, but so thick with arrows they were more like hedgehogs. A huge, ugly raven hopped about between them, strands of meat dangling from its curved, black beak.

He swallowed a gobbet of saliva. 'You realise you're sending me to my death?'

'Not if you're who you say you are,' Turold replied.

Slow and cautious, the lad urged his horse forward, holding the flag of truce high.

'English!' he shouted. 'I am English!'

At first, back in the camp, he'd been outraged by the mere suggestion he do this, that *he* should be the one to tell his countrymen – and most likely they'd be housecarls, warriors to their marrow – to lay down their weapons. Now he was simply afraid.

'Don't shoot!' he called again. 'I am English.'

He passed the slain men-at-arms, the dark blot of the raven flapping lazily away. A number of figures on the wall watched him silently, but still no missiles had come his way.

'I'm English!' he shouted again.

Another ten yards after that, and several goose-shafts whistled down, one of them biting the earth just to the left. His mount whinnied, shying to the right.

'That's far enough!' came a harsh northern voice.

To Cerdic's surprise, and to his relief, it was a voice he thought he recognised. He raised one hand to shield his eyes.

'Gerlac?' he shouted. 'Thegn Gerlac?'

After a brief, astonished silence, the voice came back again. 'Who is that?'

'I'm Cerdic. You know me... we've spoken many times.'

'Lord Cerdic?' The thegn sounded incredulous. 'Lord Cerdic... is that you?'

CHAPTER 4

'*Qu'est-ce qui se passe?*' Roland asked, to which Turold replied that Cerdic was clearly acquainted with one of the men holding the rampart.

Cerdic, forty yards in front, and well within range of the defenders, all of whom would now be holding bowstrings taut, just waiting to launch missiles, couldn't help but remind himself that this wasn't entirely true. Gerlac had been Thegn of Easingwold, only one of numerous tenancies on his father's vast estate. The duo knew each other well enough to nod in passing, but no more than that. Though of course the Normans didn't need to know this. On reflection, there was much they shouldn't know.

'I pray you don't mention my father's name or the location of our home,' he called up.

There was no initial response to that. No doubt, the men on the rampart were trying to work out whether this was a friend or a foe. That in itself agonised the lad, to have his loyalty called into question by former comrades. Requesting their silence on matters of his lineage would only confuse them more, but there was no time now to explain.

'You're with the Bastard now?' Gerlac called down, sounding confused.

'Unwillingly. I'm a hostage.'

Another silence. Did they consider that unmanly of him? Unlordly? Would it have been more appropriate to his rank if he'd died alongside his brother?

Maybe, but then maybe not. These men hadn't died in the battle either.

Cerdic wondered how many they numbered. He estimated there were fifty or so on the breastwork. There were glints from iron caps and shirts of tarnished rings, but thanks to the sun, which had now cleared the battlements, he could see that more than a few of the defenders were visibly decked in ragged, bloody bandaging.

'Let me guess…' Gerlac's new tone was subtly different, almost scornful. 'They've instructed you to order our surrender?'

Rather to the lad's surprise, he realised that this had not in fact been his task. Most likely because his captors doubted he'd have the authority to do any such thing.

'They *request* it,' he responded. 'To prevent more of us dying.'

'Prevent us dying?' The voice betrayed open mockery. 'Is that some kind of jest?'

'I'm only the messenger. But I think they are sincere. The Normans have lost men too. They know you hold a strong position. The terms are that if your garrison surrenders, all will be spared. There is an additional offer. Those seeking employment may find it as men-at-arms with Duke William.'

Hoots of derision sounded all along the breastwork.

'We'd rather have our eyes plucked out,' Gerlac growled.

'I understand that,' Cerdic replied. 'Maybe the duke will too. But if that doesn't suit you, walk away. You can do that if you put down your swords.'

There was no immediate response, though he could hear further discussion, several more figures having now appeared on the breastwork.

'Gerlac, how many are you?' Cerdic called, only to immediately realise what a tomfool question that was. 'Forget I asked that. But consider this. There can't be enough of you to hold out for long, and Duke William is not a man to be trifled with. I fear that if you force him to break in, which he will, for I've seen siege weapons packed into his baggage train, his wrath will fall heavy on you.' The lad paused, wondering if such a threat made him sound like one of the enemy. 'Forgive me for bringing this news.

I feel like a traitor, but there are some in Duke William's camp who genuinely wish this slaughter to end.'

He wondered if this was even true. Some distance behind him sat Roland Casterborus, who, thanks to this strange concept of chivalry, seemed sincere in his desire to save the lives of beaten enemies, and yet even his solemn, priest-like features were bisected on their left side by a scar inflicted in battle; he was no stranger to killing. Likewise Turold, who of them all had been most inclined to be Cerdic's friend, seemed indifferent to the fate of most of those around him. Count Cynric had only sought a peaceful solution here because it would enhance his standing with the duke.

'They wish this slaughter to end?' Gerlac said derisively. 'Lord Cerdic, the slaughter has only just begun. Do they understand how much of England remains? Do they understand how many Englishmen wait north of here, how many will raise arms in resistance?'

Cerdic didn't like being the butt of scorn, but the defiant tone stirred his blood.

But then Turold's voice carried from behind. 'Tell him that with every seaport we capture, further shiploads of the duke's followers will arrive. They will bolster his forces until the army is immense. All his losses on Senlac Ridge will be accounted for and even then, it will swell further. To fight on is futile.'

'They're aware the war isn't over, Gerlac,' Cerdic called up. 'But they are geared for it.'

'Tell him that Duke William is not cruel,' Turold added. 'Tell him he will make similar offers to those English lords located north of here. Peace and prosperity in return for fealty. Their old master is dead anyway. Where can the harm lie?'

Cerdic repeated this, adding variations of his own. 'Regardless of what happens in the north, and we all know there are many strongholds remaining, your deaths here will serve no purpose,' he shouted. 'You will not hinder Duke William for long. I pray you, Gerlac, walk away from here with your lives.'

'Are you a master of tactics, Lord Cerdic?' Gerlac jeered. 'The Romans constructed this fort to control the most important harbour in Britain and our most prosperous sea lane. How can we just gift it to our enemies?'

'Tell them we will have their fort anyway,' Turold said.

'He knows that!' Cerdic spat back. 'But he's a warrior, like you. He won't just roll over.'

'For his sake, he needs to.'

Cerdic urged his mount forward another few yards. 'Gerlac, don't you think you've done enough? Why die when you can live? I pray you, my friend. Think of your families. Don't throw your lives away when you don't need to.'

There was more discussion along the breastwork.

Cerdic turned in his saddle. 'What other inducements can I offer?'

The two knights regarded him blankly.

'Consider it,' he said. 'All their comrades are food for worms. It's likely there are lords in there who now are lords of nothing. And you ask them just to accept that? What else can I offer to sweeten the pill?'

'*Argent*,' Roland said simply.

Which Cerdic was surprised by, because he knew enough Frankish now to know that it meant silver. Even Turold seemed puzzled. This hadn't been mentioned by anyone before.

The lad shook his head. 'They won't believe that. You know why? Because I don't believe it either.'

The knights conferred.

Turold turned back. 'If Count Cynric can convince the duke to spare these bandits, he can likely convince him to pay them. Even if it's a token sum.'

Cerdic glanced from one to the other. 'You give your word on that?'

The knights spoke together again.

'Roland gives you his word that he'll try,' Turold said. 'It would make sense after all. Whatever happens, these men must surrender their arms and armour. And if they walk away with nothing, they might die anyway. To persuade them to take that chance, it would only be sensible to put silver in their purses.'

Cerdic supposed this was true. The likes of Gerlac would have an especially long distance to travel, on foot and with winter imminent. Even those who weren't wounded, and that seemed to be precious few, would have little chance of survival.

'Gerlac!' he called. 'They will pay you to surrender.'

The silence this time was more prolonged.

'You must think us fools, Lord,' Gerlac eventually replied.

'The Normans would think you fools to accept any other terms.'

Another silence, then more discussion. By the sounds of it, heated.

Eventually Gerlac called back. 'How much?'

'A purse of silver each,' Turold said from behind.

Cerdic relayed the message, adding: 'Gerlac, I implore you… there is no army anywhere close who can help you. There may be further fighting north of here. No one thinks otherwise. And yes, the tables may still turn. But that won't happen *here*. Surrender is your only hope.'

Even Cerdic was surprised by how hard he was pleading to them. On one hand, he wanted the resistance to go on. He wanted more Normans slain, but it was his younger, headstrong self who demanded that. On the other, a wiser voice told him that last stands were nearly always futile, and that bravery was wasted when nothing was gained by it.

'End this thing,' he begged. 'There are gifts on the table. All you need do is accept.'

Long minutes then passed, during which conversation spread again along the parapet.

Cerdic rode back to the two knights and reined up.

'I hate myself for what I've just done,' he said.

'You hate yourself for saving former comrades' lives?' Turold replied.

'I've betrayed everything I stand for.'

The household champion looked amused. 'I wonder if you really believe that?'

'It makes sense to end the killing,' the lad agreed. 'But I've asked them to admit defeat.'

'Someone has to lose. But that doesn't mean they have to die.' Turold eyed Cerdic craftily. 'Especially not when, as you yourself have just suggested, it might mean living to fight another day.'

Cerdic shook his head. 'I didn't say that.'

'You implied it, *non*?'

The lad glanced at Roland, whose gaze was locked on the fortress. 'Not purposely...'

'Have no fear,' Turold said. 'No one else understood you, except me. And that's what I'd have said too. It's a gamble one takes when sparing foes. But often, if one holds the upper hand, gambles can be worth the risk...'

A hefty timber *clunk* drew their attention to the fort, and they saw that the front gate had opened. Already, it seemed, a group of dingy and ragged individuals were straggling out from it. Roland straightened in his saddle. Turold's hand moved instinctively to the hilt of his longsword, but he kept the steel in its scabbard.

Cerdic glanced to the parapet again, seeing that it was now bare of life.

'Wonders never cease,' Turold sounded genuinely surprised. 'You've accomplished your task. Go on, go forth. Greet your countrymen.'

Still unsure that he'd done the right thing, but glad at least that no more blood would be shed, Cerdic advanced up the slope to meet what was clearly a sorry and pitiful band.

He'd wondered briefly if there'd been an official garrison posted here, though by the looks of these men they'd nearly all come from Senlac Ridge. Thegn Gerlac, who led them out, certainly had. Most likely, the others hailed from various shattered companies who'd been scattered through the Weald, finally coming on this place as a last resort.

All were now out, but they were no more than a hundred. Many, as he'd already seen, were bound and bandaged, but those bindings were thick with blood, ordure and other filth. Some limped or leaned on each other. Others used improvised crutches. There was minimal ring-mail on view. Doubtless, they'd thrown off the bulk of their armour, in most cases even their leather hauberks, in order to escape more speedily. All were en route to emaciation. A week and a half without any food at all could easily do that to a man.

Gerlac of Easingwold appeared to be the least grizzled. He was tall and strong-boned, with a shock of golden hair and a ruddy complexion. He still wore his ring-mail and carried an unsheathed broadsword over his left shoulder. Perhaps he'd assumed the leadership role here because he was the one most fit to fight, or maybe the only man left with any seniority.

Cerdic reined his horse up.

'You must disarm yourselves, Gerlac,' he said as they approached. 'All of you. Those are the terms. Please do it now, before you come any closer.'

Gerlac stopped, the rest of his party stumbling to a halt. Up close, their thin, grey faces were pinched with pain, gaunt with misery. They stank of sweat and sickness. Many of their rag-wrapped wounds were likely rotting. For the first time, Cerdic was pleased that his own features carried cuts and bruises. His fellow English wouldn't now think that he'd gone into captivity without a struggle.

Grim-faced, the thegn threw down his sword and commenced unbuckling his mail. One by one, the rest did the same, weapons and other fragments of war-gear piling up where they discarded them. It was noticeable though that, several times, both Gerlac and the others stared past Cerdic towards the Norman camp, increasingly fearful. Cerdic understood that. To voluntarily disarm in the face of an adversary must seem like madness. Thankfully, Gerlac possessed a broader vision. Clanks and clatters sounded as axes, flails and spears were deposited. Cerdic wheeled his horse around.

And was startled to see a wall of Norman cavalry, all mounted, all fully girt in chain-mail and helmets, and bearing shields and lances. They'd come up from the camp without him realising, and were now spread out across the entire breadth of the heath.

Suddenly, he understood why Gerlac and his troop had seemed so concerned.

Of Turold and Roland, there was no sign. Except that Cerdic thought he heard Roland's voice as he argued with someone. '*J'ai fait une promesse,*' the seneschal protested.

I made a promise...

'Christ,' the lad whispered as the Normans advanced, spear-points lowered. Even then, he'd have hoped it a mere show of strength, had he not spotted Joubert riding among them, grinning eagerly.

Frantic, he spurred his horse away across the rugged turf, and only just in time, for with a wild shout, the mounted horde surged forward. Furiously, chaotically.

'Lord Cerdic!' he heard Gerlac cry, but he didn't look round as he kicked his horse again and again, madly, cruelly, to escape the deluge of sharpened steel.

'*Cerdiiic...*' Gerlac's frantic cry became a shriek of rage and terror and then was lost under the thunderous pounding of hooves.

Cerdic only just made it clear, reining his mount up in the shelter of a copse of silver birch, before wheeling around and looking back. The garrison were mostly hidden, the Norman horsemen flying pell-mell among them, those whose spears and lances had already transfixed their initial targets now laying on all sides with longswords or chain-maces.

Cerdic forced his mount out from the trees and reined up on the very edge of the grass, eyes darting back and forth. At one point, he glimpsed Gerlac, a tallish figure who'd somehow retrieved his broadsword, but now blundered blindly and helplessly from one blow to another, his head and upper body drenched crimson. Another Englishman, no one Cerdic recognised, broke free from the slaughter and lumbered towards the copse, only for two knights to pursue him with lances levelled. It was difficult to see which of them speared him down first, but when they turned about and headed back to the fray, both shafts stood side by side, quivering to his twitching death throes.

Cerdic jolted with fright when another rider emerged from the trees directly alongside him. But then he saw that it was Turold, who was pale-cheeked as he sat hunched over the pommel of his saddle, eyes roving the carnage.

It ended almost as quickly as it had started, the horsemen still careering around, threading in and out of each other, seeking fresh victims, but in most cases finding none, their beasts' iron-shod hooves ploughing a gory carpet of broken corpses. Their blood-rage now abated, their anger turned to mirth. Dripping blades were lowered or sheathed, shields slung down among saddlebags or thrown over onto backs. They returned to their camp in small groups, talking together, guffawing. Only one or two, lesser individuals, men-at-arms rather than knights, had dismounted and now rummaged in the heap of abandoned arms. One who made his way back alone came particularly close, whistling as he ran a dirty rag the length of his blade. When he removed his helmet, it was the brutish black-beard Cerdic had so often seen in company with Joubert.

Turold addressed the fellow in his own tongue as he passed. When Blackbeard saw that it was Turold, his goblin features split into a huge grin. He replied with brash self-confidence, but Turold's second comment landed less agreeably. Blackbeard snorted to himself as if it was all too amusing, and rode on.

'Yvo de Taillebois,' Turold told Cerdic. 'I said to him: "An excellent day's sport, Slayer? Spearing the innocent is your game, is it not?"'

'I didn't ask what you said to him!' Cerdic replied quietly.

'And he said to me...'

'I didn't ask what *he* said, either!'

Turold persisted. 'He said: "You have a strange understanding of innocence, Bardouville. Those filthied curs defied our lord."

And I replied: "In my experience, it takes one cur to know another."'

Cerdic snorted. 'I'm sure your disapproval cut him to the bone.'

Turold said nothing else, just kicked his mount forward, coming out properly from the trees and heading back towards the camp. A second thought then occurred to him. He halted and looked back. 'When you fight that one, Cerdic... I mean Taillebois...'

Cerdic stared at him. 'You're so sure that will happen?'

'I *know* it will. But when that day comes, don't concern yourself with the rules of fair play. Because Yvo de Taillebois surely won't.'

CHAPTER 5

As Cerdic returned to the camp, Bishop Odo cantered by in his bulging hauberk, a posse of toadying sidekicks behind him, all armoured but all monks by their tonsured heads, one of them carrying the papal banner.

Cerdic marvelled as they passed him, assuming they were set to deploy across the bloody field to pray for those left lying out there. But as he watched, the bishop's party proceeded onward up the sloping heath towards the fort, not sparing a glance for the slain. And then he remembered why. Ever since he'd been captured, he'd heard rumours that Bishop Odo had persuaded his brother, Duke William, to grant him the earldom of Kent. And what better way to ensure that than to take possession of its main stronghold? From here, he could also control the earldom's busiest port, which also meant that he'd control its trade. No doubt the corpulent but ever-hungry prelate already pictured the situation once England was pacified, the treasure pouring in through his open front gate.

He looked again, glassy-eyed, over the butchered remnants of the garrison. The likes of this he'd never seen in his life prior to the commencement of this darkest autumn of all, and yet now it was such a common sight that he didn't even flinch. He even tried to rationalise it. Like it or loathe it, Duke William was the dominant lord in this corner of England. And as Yvo de Taillebois had said, these men had defied him. Not only that, they'd slain his emissaries. As the new *seigneur* of this region, was this not his right? To punish transgressors?

None of it rang true, of course.

Duke William was the intruder here, the invader, the criminal. Not only that, he'd killed these men by the vilest deception, and Cerdic, through utter folly, had colluded with that.

Desolate, he dismounted and led his horse back on foot. Only when he'd passed through the outer defences and then was weaving among the tents and cooking fires did it seem strange to him that he was no longer bound and in fact had possession of a steed.

How easily he could ride away. And yet he didn't.

For the same reasons as before.

Where would he ride to? Who would he find for allies?

He glanced around, assuming that one of Count Cynric's guards would leap upon him, probably beat him again, and then re-tether him to the back of Yvette's cart, like the beast of burden he was. But the camp was half-empty.

He didn't understand this, until he heard the distant dirge of screams.

The populace of Dover had been spared the sword when it suited the duke to find non-violent means by which to subdue the fortress that had guarded them. But now the fortress had fallen, the people were fair game.

—

An hour later, with the wails and cries from the town still loud on the smoky air, Turold came up to Cerdic and Yvette, who sat staring into the meagre fire beside their wagon. Food bowls lay beside them, but in both cases the pottage with cabbage leaves crushed into it was largely uneaten. As usual, Yvette had shared her extra rations with the lad, giving him a hunk of loaf and a rasher of bacon, but they too were untouched.

Neither looked round as the knight sat himself down, his mail and leather creaking. He too carried a bowl, but was eating only half-heartedly.

'One day after fleeing my father's homestead,' Cerdic said, still gazing unseeing at the flames, 'I found myself asleep in the open countryside. When I woke, a lone wolf had come up to me. It could have attacked while I lay there. Could have torn out my throat before I'd even known I was in danger. But it didn't. It sniffed at me... it was curious. Then it went back into the trees and was gone. There was no need, you see. The wolf was neither hungry nor frightened. It saw no reason to draw blood.'

'What's your point?' Turold mumbled through a mouthful of stale bread.

'That wolf had more honour than your duke.'

'I warned you it was a gamble,' the knight said sullenly. 'A gamble for your people, too. A gamble they lost.'

'So... you condone what happened?'

'I condone nothing of the sort.' Turold lurched to his feet. Briefly, his handsome, scarred features were twisted with anger. 'That garrison surrendered to us in good faith. But war is war. Men should know what they're getting into.'

'Quite right,' Cerdic said. 'It's their own fault for assuming the enemy would be as honourable as them.'

'You've seen how things are. We must constantly raid to keep our supplies adequate. Even then, we're forced to eat filth like this.' The knight slung the contents of his bowl into the fire. 'We can hardly feed a wagon train of prisoners, too.'

I wonder whose fault that is? Cerdic thought. *Perhaps the man who through sheer hubris expected a lightning victory in a foreign land, over a people he didn't understand, against leaders he didn't know? And all that with the winter coming.*

Tiring of the conversation, Turold wandered away.

'I don't think it was his fault, Cerdic,' Yvette said. 'He didn't know that massacre was going to happen.'

'Neither did Roland Casterborus. But it happened nevertheless.'

There was a long, painful silence, the lad refusing to look at her as he glowered.

'Your people keep thralls...' She shook her head. 'Slaves. My people don't.'

A second passed before he realised what she'd said. He gave her a puzzled frown. 'So, what are you saying? My people are bad, so they deserve what's happening to them?'

'No...' She looked close to tears. 'I'm saying... I'm saying that all men do evil things.'

'And that exonerates these murderers?'

'No, I...' She shook her head. 'Forgive me, I don't know what I'm saying.'

Sniffling aloud, she got to her feet, walked doggedly to the wagon and climbed inside.

Cerdic got up as well, the smoke from the flames, thick and pungent thanks to the dampness of the wood, swirling around him, cloying, stinging his eyes. He'd stand here anyway, he told himself. Listening to the hellish racket from the town, and he'd soak it up, and let it fuel the flame inside him. Not just the flame of hatred, the flame of determination too... determination that he would act on this, that it could never be his destiny to sit here a slave or hostage, a mere spectator while his people were mutilated to death...

'You wouldn't be so free with your hostile pronouncements,' an English voice said, 'if you knew how many here understood your tongue.'

Cerdic swung around, startled.

A man he hadn't seen before had approached the fire. He wore his pale copper hair shaved at the sides and tied on his scalp in a complex Celtic-style topknot. His red beard was trimmed to a peach-like fuzz, revealing hard, angular features, while his eyes were scheming slits of emerald. Whoever he was, he was clearly a native of the British Isles. However, he was no prisoner. He wore a hauberk of thick, banded felt embedded with nuggets of steel, and over the top of that, an orange, travel-stained tabard emblazoned with a black ram's head. His leggings, which, like Cerdic, he wore cross-strapped over his breeches to thigh-height, were of mud-spattered fleece, while his cloak, which was heavy, shapeless and trailed behind him, looked to have been stitched together from numerous other sheepskins. More bewildering though, was his accent. Speaking perfect English was one thing – Turold was possessed of that skill – but to do it in a native Northumbrian accent was something again. As was the broadsword buckled at his waist, its pommel worked in gold and silver, not to mention the two-bladed battle-axe suspended over his back.

'What I'm saying is… there are more English speakers here than you realise,' the man said, toeing at the embers of the fire.

'Who are you?' Cerdic asked.

'No one of consequence, yet.' The newcomer chuckled to himself; it was an ugly, guttural sound. 'But you… you, I hear, *are*.'

'I can't harm anyone,' Cerdic said guardedly. 'If that concerns you.'

Another short, guttural laugh. 'I sincerely doubt the truth of that.' The stranger glanced round at him. 'They tell me you're heir to a great estate somewhere in the north?'

'I won't tell you where.' Cerdic was unapologetically blunt; English or not, he didn't know this fellow, and already he didn't like him. 'I won't tell anyone.'

'Very wise of you. I wouldn't either. And I have higher-placed friends here than you.'

'I ask again, who are you?'

'There's no need for me to be secretive.' The stranger squatted down to warm his coarse warrior's hands. 'Your countrymen know me as Copsi. In title, I am Thegn of Holburn.'

Cerdic tried not to show how shaken this left him.

He'd only heard talk of it in his father's hall, but the Copsi he knew about had been a man of extraordinary wickedness. One of Earl Tostig's closest confederates, one of his deadliest warriors and a persistent thorn in the side of his official master, the loyal and noble Gospatric, Lord of Bamburgh, whom in due course he had treacherously murdered.

'I see you've heard that name?' Copsi said.

Cerdic hesitated to respond. He must mind his words from this point on if he didn't want this reputedly very dangerous man to work out exactly who he was. The mere fact that Cerdic's name was 'Cerdic' might already have given the fellow a clue.

The thegn's green eyes narrowed imperceptibly. 'You don't like it either, do you?'

Cerdic shrugged. 'It means nothing to me. But if you come and go as you please here, if you're a true Northumbrian and yet are entitled to bear arms in the camp of the Normans, I can only assume the friends you boast of are *genuine* friends. Which makes you a traitor.'

Copsi snorted, amused again. He rose. At full height, he was a good head taller than Cerdic. 'Such a traitor that I'd lure my own countrymen to their deaths without a blow struck in their defence?'

'I...' Cerdic struggled. 'I was misled.'

'We all of us have explanations like that to offer. What it boils down to, lad, is you'll do what you must to survive. And in that, you are no different from me.'

He didn't bother waiting for a reply. The conversation clearly over, at least as far as Thegn Copsi was concerned, he turned and ambled away.

Cerdic watched his broad, fleece-covered back recede into the camp.

In truth, it was probably no surprise that old foes of the English state would finish up here. After Tostig and the Hardraada were slain on the River Derwent, it must have been a Godsend to all embittered rebels like Copsi when Duke William invaded. What Copsi had been able to bring to the duke's table was less certain, of course. And what he might be offered in return for it even less so. But the presence of such individuals made it more dangerous for Cerdic to bide his time; men like that would forever be spying, prying, looking for any gains they could make, particularly at the expense of Englishmen who'd stayed loyal. But the lad still couldn't be rushed or panicked into making a mistake. As yet, he was in no position to do anything. He trudged to the wagon, where he pre-empted his captors by binding his own wrists and hitching himself back to the vehicle's tailgate.

Somehow, he *had* to find himself a position of power, or at least influence.

And then he'd strike. And the likes of traitors like Copsi would pay, as well as these Norman hounds. He clenched his fists, screwing his eyes shut in a semblance of angry prayer. On his own life, he swore this would be so.

CHAPTER 6

In the final week of October, the weather broke properly. Leaves spun on rain-filled wind; grey mist drifted. The hours of daylight shortened, and it was much colder now.

The army headed northeast towards Canterbury, but sluggishly, recrossing the earldom of Kent in zigzag fashion, repeatedly stopping to sack towns and villages, though this time the plunder they acquired was for provision rather than to enrich themselves. Churches were left unharmed, there was no wanton destruction. The grain, fodder and animals they couldn't take they left for the ceorls, who in most cases were still hiding. Even those halls they encountered, so long as they were undefended, their gates left open, were spared the firebrand, though all were searched for money boxes, jewellery and weapons.

Cerdic couldn't help wondering if the reason for all this again lay in Bishop Odo's designs on the earldom. Doubtless, he had no desire to inherit a wasteland.

Restraint wasn't always shown. On the second day, when a fieldworker threw a stone and ran, Norman knights rode after him and chopped him down, then scoured the nearby coppice, flushing out a number of others, all of whom were herded into captivity. A convenient branch was then chosen, from which they soon dangled side by side. Only Father Jerome, Count Cynric's personal chaplain, seemed perturbed by this, his distinctive figure in his hooded maroon cassock sitting alongside the grisly exhibit for a long time afterward, presumably praying, though also wearing a glazed, unseeing expression.

Cerdic meanwhile sought to ride more often in Yvette's cart. That wasn't just so that he could focus on his lessons, but because if they were bound for London once they were finished at Canterbury, he'd by then have walked a very considerable distance, at ponderous pace but along routes that were little more than rutted, rocky tracks, and now were so sodden by autumn rain that they were degenerating even past the stage of being quagmires. It made exhaustive trudging, and the rope burns on his wrists became raw and purulent.

A day or so short of the holy city, the rain eased off, and though a biting wind moaned across the desolated land, he opted to walk again. Mainly, this was because Roland Casterborus was riding close to the rear of their wagon, and though he seemed preoccupied with his own thoughts, for their prisoner to claim himself a ride directly under his nose might be too much of an impertinence for him to ignore.

For her part, Yvette was glad. Partly for that same reason, but also because there was very little space under the awning, and Cerdic, a cold companion since the incident at Dover, had become sullen and withdrawn, interested only in learning the Frankish tongue. He dedicated himself to their lessons with intense concentration, and pestered her non-stop.

And yet, they were midway through one such session when the lad's attention broke of its own accord, and he turned from her, addressing the knight-seneschal in his own tongue.

'What is this strange thing... this thing, chivalry?'

At first, Roland didn't realise he was being spoken to. They hadn't seen much of him since the Dover massacre, and when they had, he'd seemed morose and distracted.

'What is this thing?' Cerdic asked again, in French.

Roland gave him a quizzical stare. 'You've learned our tongue quickly.'

'Your mad duke drive me to it,' Cerdic said, aware that his pronunciation of the new language was crude and doubtless heavily accented, but determined to show these dogs there was nothing they could do that he couldn't.

'A week and a half ago, you still needed Turold to interpret for you.'

'I am closer than thought you.'

Roland smiled, though there was little mirth in it. He eyed Yvette, still sitting in the back of her wagon. 'You're quite a teacher, *mademoiselle*. Or young Cerdic here is quite a pupil.'

'He concentrates very hard, my lord,' she said. 'When there are things he must blot out.'

Roland considered that, glancing past her. Dull brown fields, recently stripped of their crops but not yet tilled, stretched away indefinitely. The odd cluster of trees stood bare, only shreds of red leafage remaining. The sky was slate-grey in every direction.

'This chivalry thing?' Cerdic asked again. 'What is it… Lord?'

The knight didn't look at him. 'Why do you ask?'

'It push you to spare life of garrison men at Dover?' The lad glanced at his tutor. 'This is correct?' he asked her in English.

'Mostly,' she said, also in English. 'The little you get wrong we can easily fix. Conversing in our tongue is the best way to do this.'

He nodded, turning back to the knight, switching to French again. 'This chivalry thing… you cling to it, I hear. Turold tell me this. But no one else in Norman camp believe same.'

Roland sniffed. 'The laws of chivalry are many and complex. Few ordinary men, I fear, can adhere to them for long.'

'Too difficult?' Cerdic asked.

Roland gazed at him again, perhaps wondering why he was even exchanging words with this tattered, filthy scarecrow who was tethered like a dog and plodding ankle-deep through liquid filth, this brutish enemy of his people who doubtless would murder them all in their beds if he got the chance. And yet, Roland Casterborus, probably the one knight in Duke William's entire host who *did* believe in the tenets of chivalry, or who tried to, felt compelled to answer, and to answer truthfully.

'Many in our equestrian order think the chivalrous ideal a good thing.' He spoke loudly and slowly so that the prisoner's attempt to converse with him in his own tongue would not be foiled. 'But it isn't some fad.'

The lad glanced at Yvette. 'Fad?'

'A short-lived thing,' she replied in French. 'Something you only do once or twice.'

'It's no fad,' Roland said again. 'But a meaning all of its own. A way of life.'

Cerdic pondered this. 'Where it start?'

The knight frowned. 'Do you mean that as it sounds? When did it begin? Or do you mean where does it come from?'

Cerdic shrugged, interested in both.

Roland considered. 'As to where it came from, I can't really say. But there are many old songs, poems, tales of heroes... they date to the reign of Charlemagne...'

'King of Franks,' Cerdic interrupted.

Roland stared at him again, fascinated that one so ragged and dirty could possess knowledge of this sort.

'A king of... paladin?' Cerdic asked.

'You know about his twelve paladins?' Roland was now seriously impressed. As Turold had said, the boy *was* intelligent. Even educated.

Cerdic made a vague gesture. It wouldn't serve to pretend that he knew more than he did, though Aethelric's vivid and colourful history lessons had ranged far beyond the shores of Britain and the writings of Bede.

'Charlemagne had twelve companions,' Roland said. 'Paladins, great knights all. They led his wars against the Saracen...'

'As written about in *The Song of Roland*,' Yvette put in. 'Your namesake perhaps?'

The knight tinged red, seemed awkward. 'If I were to admit that I was always interested to know who my father named me after, it wouldn't be a lie. Whether that influenced my views, who can say. But to answer your question properly, boy, the twelve paladins of Charlemagne were great and honourable men...'

'Roman *palatinus*?' Cerdic said. Again, it was half a question and half a statement.

'Indeed,' Roland replied. 'So-named because they were the emperor's most trusted swords. But also because they conducted themselves with discipline and *probity*. You understand this word?'

Cerdic shook his head.

'Honour, Cerdic,' Yvette said. 'They had virtue. They were morally correct.'

'This is the origin of chivalry,' Roland added. 'There are many rules, which someday I'll be pleased to discuss with you in detail. But you also asked where does it start. The answer to that is *here*.' He struck his own chest. 'In the heart of every man who takes knightly vows.' He'd spoken with increased enthusiasm, the hood of his cloak falling backward. But now his face fell again. 'Or that is where it *should* start.'

'Why do men fail?' Cerdic asked him.

'Another good question. I see now why Turold has taken you under his wing.'

'Why?' the boy persisted.

The knight looked saddened. 'Because it cannot be.'

Cerdic frowned, confused.

The knight shrugged. 'Because its main purpose is to tame the warlike spirit. Don't look surprised. What other role can it play? All across Christendom there are great lords, their households filled with knights. Men like your housecarls.'

'I know knights,' the lad said.

Roland didn't dispute that. From what Turold had told him, this strange, tormented youngster had killed more than a few of them. 'Men who are trained to fight,' he explained. 'Who live to fight. Who do nothing else but fight... for that is their purpose. But when there is no war, what then?'

The lad snorted. 'Your duke will bring it.'

'Alas, boy, if only it were that simple. It's not every day that a kingdom as wealthy as England is available to be conquered.'

'You conquer nothing yet.'

'You need only give the duke time on that, trust me. My point is that sometimes there is peace. It may last days, weeks, months, years even. And what do these fighting men do then?'

He posed this as a genuine question, but Cerdic shrugged. 'You tell me. You are knight.'

'Yes, I'm a knight, and I *can* tell you. We carouse, we brawl, we whore. My apologies *mademoiselle*, but the truth is the truth.'

He didn't really expect Yvette to flinch at the immodest reference, which was a good thing, as she didn't even blush. The things she had seen in recent days made certain of that.

'Peace becomes anarchy,' he added, 'when the forces of the lawmakers become lawless themselves. I tell you, Cerdic... I've known tournaments set whole towns afire. I've seen tavern disorder turn into feuds that lasted for generations.'

Again, the lad frowned, puzzled. 'Knights make this havoc? Happen often?'

'Not often, but enough for it to be a scourge on Christian society. A time may come when the pope and his minions will feel a need to drive all these dogs of war from out of Christendom. To unleash them in far-off lands perhaps, on pagans. How they will do that, Heaven only knows, but in the meantime, we have the chivalrous code... which has one function only, to rein in the violence and cruelty that lurks in the souls of those men who live only for war.' His shoulders seemed to sag as he pondered the complexity of such a thing. 'As I've already explained to you, it's something of a contradiction.'

Again, Cerdic glanced at Yvette. 'Contra...?'

'When one thing needs another to survive,' she explained, 'and yet they cannot coexist.'

He contemplated this, not understanding entirely, but trying.

'Only special men can make this impossible thing real, Cerdic,' Roland said. 'And they are few and far between.'

'You are special man?' the lad asked, quite sincerely.

The knight stared into the distance. 'I try to be, but I fear I don't try hard enough.'

'You fight and you love?'

'That's an amusing way to put it.'

Cerdic's frown became a scowl. 'I can never fight and love. All love has left me.'

Roland thought on this. 'Fortunately, boy, you will never need worry about it.'

Clearly feeling that he'd said enough, he spurred his horse onward, cantering away along the column. The moment he'd left them, Cerdic scrambled forward and clambered onto and over the tailgate, settling himself under the awning again.

'How did I do?' he asked in English.

'I've already told you.' Yvette made space for him. He was rank with sweat and dirt, though she hadn't bathed in a while herself and was wearing the same clothes she'd been taken hostage in. 'You are an excellent pupil. I am proud of you.'

'That's good to know.' He pulled off his mud-encrusted boots, rubbing at his swollen feet.

Yvette tugged the cloth down over the opening. 'If Lord Joubert catches you in here, he'll break your legs.'

'Lord Joubert now rides as close to the front of this happy parade as he dares. Turold told me that. Daily, he offers impertinent advice to the duke.'

'Is it working?' she asked. 'Is the duke getting to know him?'

'Probably the way a beast of the field gets to know a gnat it's too lazy to swat.'

'And what of Lord Joubert's father?'

'I hear tell he rides near the back, in a cart that may shortly become his bier.'

'I only hope he has the good grace to live until we get to Canterbury.'

'Why Canterbury?' Cerdic asked.

'If Archbishop Stigand crowns Duke William, the new king will be forced to settle with his lieutenants. There'll be much debate, much disagreement, but it may be that our futures are finally decided.'

Cerdic shook his head. 'Archbishop Stigand refused to offer the crown only a couple of weeks ago.'

'Will he refuse with a Norman sword at his throat?'

'All I know about Archbishop Stigand is his trickster reputation. They'll need to find that throat first.'

On the final day of their approach to Canterbury, they were met on the road by representatives from many habitations in its hinterland, townsmen, merchants, clerics, all offering gifts and subservience.

For the first time since Dover, Duke William was inclined to accept these gestures as acts of good faith, sending small detachments under trusted men to garrison the towns in question rather than ransack them.

'He thinks he's close to realising his ambition,' Cerdic told Yvette. 'No man rules by terror alone. He'll still take everything that's ours, but if he can make it seem like he's a gracious lord, England's religious capital will be the place to do it.'

And indeed, the following morning, it looked as though the occupants of Canterbury would reciprocate. It wasn't as ominous an obstacle as York, and it didn't come close to the indomitable appearance of London, but the River Stour, a large waterway, ran close to its ramparts on both the north and west sides. The stone walls atop its original earthwork were battlemented. However, no helmet or ring-mail gleamed from their parapets. No martial banners flew. The only flag the Normans saw when they deployed on the huge meadow to the south of the city billowed from the spire of the white stone basilica's square central tower, which was the highest point of any building inside. The banner was emblazoned with a white cross on blue, with some black configuration in the centre. Cerdic didn't know what such arms denoted, but suspected they held religious significance. It certainly wasn't the Fighting Man of House Godwinson, the White Dragon of England or even the White Horse of Kent.

Most curious of all, the city gate stood open. No deputation waited there, which might have been deemed an insult, but Cerdic suspected, and he imagined Duke William would think the same, that most of the city dignitaries might still be anticipating violence and therefore had hidden themselves. That would certainly apply to Archbishop Stigand. Even if the old fox had changed his mind about crowning the new monarch-in-waiting, which appeared to be the case from the city's undefended state, he would still be expecting some form of displeasure.

Cerdic saw all this from a position on high ground to the rear of the army, where once again the baggage train had been left under a small guard, though this time it wasn't House Tancarville, Joubert's efforts to curry favour having paid some dividends. For late October, it was a fine day, cool but dry, fragments of fleecy cloud scudding across a pebble-blue sky. The meadows in front of the city, though cropped by sheep, were emerald green. Cerdic climbed onto the side of the wagon, to see properly. Yvette watched from the opening.

'What's happening?' she asked. 'I can't see anything.'

'Nothing yet,' he replied.

Down at the front of the army, he spied the duke himself, his scarlet cloak whipping in the wind, as he sat astride his black destrier. Some distance ahead of him, another horseman, corpulent but draped in episcopal purple, rode forth at the front of a small troop of mounted monks. Yet again, they carried the papal gonfalon.

Cerdic snorted.

Bishop Odo remembered he was a churchman when the situation warranted it.

The bishop's party slowed as they approached the open gateway. A single figure had appeared there. A monk in a black habit. He was clearly of great age, for he leaned on a staff that was almost as crooked as he was. His bald head shone in the autumn sun; his white beard was a low-hanging bush. And yet, his near-casual appearance in the gateway, from which he clearly had no intention to move, seemed strangely ominous. All conversation ceased.

Bishop Odo's party came to a halt some thirty yards short of the entrance. They waited, inviting the ancient figure to come to them. But as before, he remained where he stood. At length, the purple-clad shape of the bishop urged his mount forward, reining it up alongside the monk. Words were exchanged, and even from this distance, Cerdic could see the bishop's posture change. He no longer sat proud in his saddle, but hunched a little, head drooping as he listened to whatever the monk had to say.

Finally, with an audible curse, which they heard even from so far away, he turned his steed and cantered back to his waiting party, whom he briefly conversed with, before one of them galloped back to the duke.

Cerdic was bewildered but felt strange tingles of excitement.

The monk halted beside the duke and passed on the message.

The duke received it much as his brother had: slumped in his saddle, head low. Slowly, he raised his left leg and slid to the ground. Before dropping to his knees, and then onto all fours. For an astonishing moment, Cerdic thought he was going to be physically sick.

A low but rapidly rising ululation wavered across the meadow, a slow-building shriek of rage. The whole army was now astir, mumbles passing man-to-man. Horses turned skittish.

Yvette climbed from the back of her wagon, gazing down at the distant scarlet-clad figure, who abruptly ceased his caterwaul and now sat on the grass in childlike fashion, digging into it with repeated, savage blows of his dagger.

His brother, the bishop, returned towards him, but slowly, the rest of his monks tagging nervously behind. Only after what seemed an age did the duke's senior lieutenants, men like Eustace of Boulogne, Robert of Mortain, Roger de Montgomery, converge upon him. As they did, he leapt back to his feet, gesticulating, issuing harsh but incoherent words. He lurched back into his saddle, wheeled his animal around and galloped across the face of his troops, shouting that they had more yet to do.

Word of what had happened spread through the ranks like a swift fire.

No one told Cerdic. Turold might have, or even Roland, but they were down in the foremost rank of the army, along with the bulk of House Tancarville. Instead, he overheard conversations between men-at-arms, which he now more or less understood.

The monk in the gateway was Brother Edwy, Dean of the Cathedral Chapter. He had said that Canterbury was open to the Normans. None of the basilica doors were locked, and no one would stop them entering or helping themselves to as much gold or silver as they desired, to reliquaries and precious vessels, to the rich vestments and jewelled crucifixes. They could hoard it all. But His Grace, Archbishop Stigand, was not home. He was on official duty in London, for the Witan, which included the northern earls, who had now come south with all their powers, and which had elected a new king. It was Stigand's next task to supervise the coronation.

'Edgar, the one they call "the Aetheling",' Cerdic told Yvette. 'He's only a lad, younger than me by several years, but I remember Aethelric telling me all about him. He was living abroad until recently, but now he's returned. And he's lawfully in line for the throne as he's descended from the house of Edmund Ironside.'

'We have a new king?' Yvette said, scarcely able to believe it.

'We do. And it isn't William of Normandy.'

CHAPTER 7

Cerdic was startled to see that the bridge of boats was still in place, the timber footway lying clear across the Thames, directly linking the southern shore to the city.

King Harold had constructed it virtually overnight, to expedite his army's march to the south coast. It had never been the sturdiest structure, raw planking nailed over a range of bobbing, tilting vessels, but it had sufficed in the role for which it was intended. But there was no earthly reason the lad could think of why it was still here now. Even though Duke William had led his host westward towards London in the closest thing Cerdic had so far experienced to a battle-march, it had still taken them the best part of three days. The duke had been determined to reach the capital in time to prevent the coronation of this latest usurper, but that still should have given the defenders of London ample time to dismantle the structure. Even if they'd left it intact for long enough to permit the survivors of Senlac Ridge to cross over, it ought to have been long gone by this time.

Thanks to the duke urging speed rather than caution, Cerdic had now been instructed to ride rather than walk, which had been a relief to his blistered feet and aching legs even if the vehicle had jerked and jolted incessantly, and had allowed him to continue his French lessons with new intensity. But it might also have been the reason why the Norman army attempted to cross the bridge almost at the moment of its arrival on All Souls' Eve.

Even more startling to Cerdic was the *way* they were attempting to cross it.

They weren't going over on horseback. Duke William was not that stupid. But it was a mark of his reckless desperation to storm his enemy's capital that he'd dismounted what looked like an entire battalion of knights and men-at-arms and ordered them across on foot.

Again on high ground to the rear, Cerdic and Yvette had an unobstructed view.

On the opposite side of the river, just to the right of their position, stood London's southeastern wall, sheer and impenetrable, lighted torches all along its high parapets, the steel of multiple helmets glinting in its many embrasures. The troops crossing the water, meanwhile, resembled one of the old Roman legions that Cerdic had heard Aethelric describe. Not marching carefully, two at a time with significant gaps between pairs, but crammed together in a lengthy phalanx, four or five abreast, heavily mailed and helmeted, advancing behind their shields. The boats rolled and tilted under the weight, their gunwales clunking, their timber under-structures creaking aloud.

'Will it hold?' Yvette said, shouting to be heard over the hubbub of voices.

'It had better,' Cerdic replied. 'Duke Bastard is used to getting what he wants, or hell and fury rains down. Look how many are waiting to go over after them.'

Down on the river's southern bank, a turmoil of men and horses milled about, much shouting and arguing among their captains as further groups were commanded to make ready.

'Though he doesn't take the chance himself, I notice.' Cerdic nodded towards even higher ground on their right, where a distinctive barrel-shaped figure sat astride his horse, silhouetted on the torchlight glowing along the parapets of Southwark burh. The portlier figure seated alongside him was clearly his brother.

There was more creaking and grinding of timbers.

'That's a faster current than when we crossed on the way down here,' Cerdic said. 'When we went over, it was after weeks of sun and dust-dry fields. But it's rained since then. A lot.'

And indeed, even by the flickering light of torches, the Thames wasn't so much gliding now as rushing. The ships twisted in formation, striking each other hard, chains clanking.

'It only takes one anchor to snap loose,' the lad said, 'and that bridge will fall apart like straw.'

But it never came to that.

The Norman vanguard was only fifty yards from the north shore when a bombardment commenced from unseen levies westward of London's outer ramparts. First it was arrows and spears, rattling like hail on the upturned shields. But then heftier payloads: bulging sackcloth bags, which opened in mid-air, releasing showers of heavy stones. These larger objects inflicted immediate and horrendous damage on the infantry at the front, smashing down through the roof of shields, and the boards of the bridge underneath, and the boats beneath those. Shrieks split the air as pulverised men went down through the woodwork with them, or flopped broken over the sides, vanishing into the smooth-flowing waters. With the shield formation shattered, the English arrows found their mark too. The crossing parties behind stumbled to a halt, bottled up all the way to the south bank. From somewhere on this side meanwhile, again concealed in the abyssal dark between Duke William's position and Southwark's outer wall, the next phase of the English attack was launched. This time it was only arrows, but they were arrows lit on fire, seven or eight slim but blazing missiles arcing over the heads of the Norman troops massed on the southern shore, striking the bridge close to the muddy embankment amid its rigging and bundled sailcloth.

In almost no time, fires raged up from under the planking on which men were hopelessly crammed, burning with unnatural force and ferocity, springing from one vessel to the next.

Only then did Cerdic realise why the bridge had not been dismantled.

Having served the purpose of allowing that swathe of Englishmen who'd survived Senlac Ridge to find refuge behind London's walls, now it had been used to store skins filled with some kind of flammable material. Again, he remembered Aethelric's history lessons, in which he'd learned about the Greeks and the Persians, and how they'd used incendiary weapons to reduce enemy fortifications. Missiles from the north bank also cut fiery streaks through the dark. More fire-arrows. This time hitting the other end of the bridge. Again, igniting whatever was packed under the planking.

With further deafening *whumps*, clouds of fire mushroomed skyward, each one engulfing its own ship, the black figures of men twisting and melting in the heart of it like human candles.

Foul smoke billowed across the water. The stench of cooking flesh was abhorrent.

The screams were a discord from Hell. As the fire spread with beastlike speed from both sides of the river, many of those trapped chose death by drowning, jumping over the side or simply falling, their heavy mail dragging them down into the river's muddy bowels. Some waited until the last second and plunged in as living torches. In no time, it seemed, the entire bridge was blazing with an intensity that was almost white.

Cerdic stood rigid, the sweat blown dry on his body by the heat, his hair like stiff grass.

The skeletal wreckage of vessels still immersed in flame now broke loose and drifted downriver. Others tilted under, the Thames hissing and bubbling.

He risked a glance at Yvette, who stood aghast.

'There must've been a thousand men on there,' she stuttered.

Cerdic hated the Normans searingly. The only passion in his heart was for their total destruction. It ran so deep that, had he heard about this event rather than witnessed it, he'd have laughed, cheered, pumped the air with his fist, celebrated joyously. But to be standing here now, the sweat running down his back as the hot, foul smoke still wreathed him, having actually *seen* it, *smelled* it, to have heard the cacophonous screams – prolonged, inhuman wails implying agony and anguish beyond imagining – that was something very different.

His stomach lurched, his skin prickling as though crawling with ants.

Down below on the darkened lower shore, there were howls of rage and consternation. Norman soldiers, both mounted and on foot, bolted back and forth, colliding with each other, slipping and falling in the riverside mud, roaring their outrage. It was chaos, a frenzy. Men called hoarsely upon God, demanding vengeance, clattering blades on shields, enmeshed together as they fought to find a route, any route, that would lead across the river to the stronghold of their enemies.

As Cerdic stood locked in place, a new horror struck him.

'*Turold!*' he stammered. 'My God… Turold.'

At which moment a horseman thundered up, weaving wildly as he sought to avoid footmen blinded by rage. It was the man himself, his longsword drawn, his bearskin cloak swirling.

'Turold!' Cerdic shouted. 'I thought you might've…'

'Been out there?' The knight didn't even look at the river. 'It's no thanks to Joubert I wasn't. He pressed for us to lead the vanguard.'

'Roland? Is he…'

'Where he should be, guarding Count Cynric. Now, you two!' He pointed his sword at them. 'Get into that wagon, you hear? And stay there! You hear me, Cerdic? You hide there and keep quiet. If you value your lives, remind no one of your presence here.'

Without waiting for an answer, he galloped on.

Yvette climbed under the awning, and sat wrapped in her shawl, shuddering. Cerdic clambered after her, pulling the cloth over the opening.

They regarded each other with haunted eyes. They'd both been so transfixed by the bridge incident that neither had initially considered how it might turn out for them. But now they cowered, only thin sailcloth between themselves and a baying horde of men literally screaming for blood.

'I need to cut your hair,' Yvette whispered, producing the dagger. 'Those long Saxon locks are very telling.'

'Yes, yes,' he nodded. 'As short as possible, I beg you.'

She set to work, sawing off his mane in great, unruly hanks. And all the while, the pandemonium raged outside. From out of it, several particular voices became clear. They were strident and authoritative, and bitterly opposed to each other.

'Damn you, Mortain... that was half my men!' one of them bellowed with a rage he clearly felt in his gut.

'I lost men out there, too,' another retorted, equally furious.

Cerdic, who was mostly now able to comprehend their words, couldn't help pulling away from Yvette and pushing the hanging cloth an inch to one side. Close to the wagon, two of the Norman nobles, whom he recognised as Robert of Mortain and Roger de Montgomery, squared up to each other from the backs of their horses. Neither wore helmets, though Montgomery's hand fingered the hilt of his longsword.

'It was *your* idea,' he shouted, 'you brown tongue whoreson!'

'Devil take you, Montgomery!' Mortain spat back. 'I didn't hear *you* arguing against it.'

A third baron reined up alongside them. While the first two were solid, stocky men, with the close-cropped hair and hard-bitten features of typical Norman knights, this newcomer was of heavy, portlier build, and though he wore mail, his flowing blue livery was excessive and patterned with religious symbols done in gold thread: crosses, fishes, even the *Chi-Ro*, the letter symbol for Jesus Christ. Bishop Odo was the religious leader of Duke William's host, but this was his second-in-command, Bishop Geoffrey of Coutance. Not that this prevented Montgomery rounding on him too.

'And you, your grace! You said your spies told you the English were finished!'

The bishop shook his head. 'I said they were finished in the open field. I didn't recommend we attack across a narrow causeway, against a rampart Julius Caesar would have balked it.'

Montgomery was spitting with anger. 'So, no one's taking responsibility? What a surprise!'

A fourth party rode up. From his hulking build and ugly, pock-marked face it could only be Count Eustace of Boulogne, a fellow that Cerdic had come to learn was one of the most fearsome, ruthless and most vauntingly ambitious of all the Norman commanders. 'The duke requires our presence!' he said sternly. 'All of us. Now.'

Mortain and Coutance hastened away, but Montgomery hung on.

'I see you held *your* company back from the bridge, Boulogne!'

Boulogne smirked. 'Maybe I have a brain.'

'I know you. You're up to something, you dog.'

'Only a fool would have chanced that bridge in the dark. You saw it with your own eyes, did you not? If the flames hadn't taken those men, the river would.'

'You could have made that point to the duke.'

'He was already decided.'

'It was that idiot, Mortain, who persuaded him. *You* could have persuaded him otherwise, had you even tried.'

Boulogne's smirk became a scowl. 'You mind your tongue, Montgomery. Need I remind you that half your host is killed?'

'That's what you want, isn't it? You bastard. To see the rest of us weakened, while you remain strong.'

'I warn you, Montgomery. You're in no position to stir the shit pot.' Boulogne smiled again. Grinned, even. 'Not anymore.'

He wheeled his horse around and rode away, brutally forcing it through the throng.

'*Bandit!*' Montgomery howled, spurring his own mount into pursuit.

Cerdic let the drape drop. 'These barons of yours are quite the nest of snakes.'

'I told you,' Yvette said quietly. 'They hate Duke William, but they fear him more. So instead, they plot against each other.'

'And these are the people who now control England.' Another waft of foul smoke engulfed them. Cerdic pictured charred, contorted shapes washing up in the riverside slime. 'Those who aren't now the scrapings of a giant's kitchen.'

They were quiet for a moment, then Yvette said: 'Surely you didn't *enjoy* that spectacle, Cerdic?'

The question shocked him. 'Do I look as if I did?'

'Weren't they your enemy? Those you plan to kill?'

Their gazes locked hard.

'What was it Turold said?' he replied. '"War is war. Men should know what they are getting into."'

She glanced away. 'Turold at least was spared. And Roland.'

'Yes.' It surprised him, but he couldn't deny that he'd felt relief at that.

'It seems you've found some Normans you like.'

Outside, the noise and fury was still so intense that it threatened to envelope them, wagon and all. 'At times like these,' he said, 'one takes all the friends one can get.'

CHAPTER 8

Southwark burh, which of course was significantly smaller than London, and fortified with timber rather than stone, was in the unfortunate position of occupying the river's south bank. And so all that night, the Norman army assailed it. Impatient to slake his anger, Duke William had the many shops and houses on the river's south shore torn apart, and scaling ladders constructed out of them. He then sent companies of knights and men-at-arms forward in *testudo* formation, under roofs made from interlocked shields, but rocks, spears and other missiles rained down almost continuously from the ramparts. The formations broke in many places before they could get sufficiently close to loft their ladders.

Several times this was attempted, with much loss of soldiery, before the duke called in disciplined ranks of archers. One volley of arrows after another slanted upward at the parapets, thinning out the defenders noticeably. But when the escalade companies trundled forth again, this time propping their ladders against the battlements, burning oil deluged down, immersing those detailed to ascend first.

Inside their wagon, Yvette covered her ears against the screams. Cerdic peeked out again, watching agog as figures ablaze from head to foot, man-shaped whirlwinds of fire, stumbled around at the foot of the burning structures. It was the same flammable material, he supposed, that had been used to ignite the death-trap bridge. The bowmen let loose again, flight after flight feathering the upper parapets, but to no avail. The next wave of assault companies were also repulsed by fire and stone. However, the attacking army had now unpacked and assembled its heavy weapons, and by the early hours of the morning, the duke's engineers brought forward catapults and throwing machines of every sort: trebuchets, mangonel and ballistae, with which they bombarded the upper reaches of Southwark's walls with boulders and the trunks of trees sawn into hefty blocks.

Soon, whole segments of shattered timber were crashing down, broken bodies falling with them. After several hours of this, close to dawn, the Norman scaling ladders were raised again and this time there was almost no opposition.

Cerdic was in no position to see what happened inside, though later, again overhearing talk, he learned that almost no fighting men had been found in Southwark. The majority left alive had been simple townsfolk – boatmen and dock workers, day labourers and thralls, stall holders and craftsmen – and on the whole, there'd been more women than men. On the Norman army's arrival, they'd been too terrified to open their gates for fear they'd be blamed for the bridge of death.

Which of course they were.

—

As All Saints' Day dawned, it was dank and misty on the riverside, and the victory seemed like a minor one, if it was any kind of victory at all, for it had gained them nothing.

No trace of the boat-bridge remained, nor of the men who had died on it. The river ran even deeper and faster than it had the evening before, and the remaining Norman host, having afforded itself no time the previous night to build a proper camp, was tired, hungry and cold, not to mention wet, for it was dispersed widely along the river's southern shore, much of which was marshland.

Duke William, still determined to make a show of strength, mainly for the benefit of the defenders of London, who doubtless would be watching, ordered the erection of fifty waterline gibbets, all of them high so there could be no mistaking what they were. The hundred or so English who remained from the garrison of Southwark, men and women both, were unceremoniously strung up. Their dirty, ragged forms were ordered to be left there until the crows picked them to pieces.

By this time, it seemed as though Cerdic and Yvette had sat in frightened silence for hours. At one point, when angry voices had sounded directly outside, a Breton voice telling comrades that if he'd had his way, the captives would have been flayed, not hanged, they clung to each other, convinced they were about to be discovered. A short time after that, when the cloth at the rear of the wagon was suddenly ripped aside, Yvette couldn't conceal a yelp and Cerdic's hand went for the dagger under the blanket.

A youngish Norman knight, who they hadn't seen before, gazed in on them.

Torturous seconds passed as he assessed them.

'A boy and a girl, you say?' he finally told someone they couldn't see.

Another Frankish voice replied.

The young knight nodded. 'They are both here.'

Cerdic swallowed phlegm. His grip tightened on the dagger's hilt. He was adamant that he wouldn't die without taking more of these bastards with him.

But when the knight stepped aside, and his companion appeared, it was Turold.

The champion looked in on them, and had to look twice at Cerdic, his face now clean-shaved, and his flaxen hair cut very close and flattened across the top in the Norman style. He nodded his approval at that, then handed them a flask of wine and a small sack containing a loaf and a block of cheese.

'Keep hiding,' he told Cerdic in English. 'Most of those who'd do you harm appear to have forgotten about your existence... at least for the moment. I'll ensure you continue to be fed.'

Cerdic nodded gratefully but eyed the younger knight warily.

'This is Will Malet,' Turold said. 'He was my squire. He won't reveal your presence.'

Malet regarded them sternly but seemed content with this new responsibility.

Yvette pointed towards the front of the wagon. 'What about our driver?' she whispered.

'An uninterested oaf,' Turold replied. 'He likely doesn't even know who you are, just that he must lug you along. In any case, from now on, Malet will ride close to you. He'll make sure that no one gets curious...'

'What if it's Lord Joubert?'

'Lord Joubert is busy elsewhere. He's the last one you need worry about at present.'

'You say Joubert wished you first across the river last night?' Cerdic asked.

Turold frowned, as if this was a problem he increasingly needed to grapple with. 'He's overly keen to promote House Tancarville. While his father ails, he fears we are losing ground with the duke. Last night, he lobbied hard for permission to take point. If he'd had his way, we'd have died to a man.'

'Why didn't it happen?' Yvette asked.

'Because Roland and I persuaded Count Cynric against it.'

Cerdic was intrigued by that. He'd last seen Count Cynric two days previously, in a roadside camp, where his limp, grey-faced form had needed to be lifted from his bier by others and his breeches let down for him simply so that he could defecate.

'How ill is the count?' he wondered.

'He hasn't lost his mind just yet. We told him the boat-bridge was an invitation for us to cross, and so had to be a trap. Despite his son's protests, he agreed.'

'Why didn't you warn Duke William?'

'The duke is not currently receptive to any idea that might lengthen this campaign.'

'Even at the cost of throwing friends away?'

Turold smiled grimly. 'He has no friends. Every man here is expendable.'

He pulled the cloth down, and they sat back in the dimness.

'God help us,' Yvette said.

'God help those English the duke encounters now,' Cerdic replied.

She hung her head. 'Is there any end to this...'

'It won't be soon. He wants the crown, Yvette.'

'Of course...'

Cerdic shrugged. 'Well, it isn't just men who are denying him now. This is the Thames, our greatest river. The further east you go, it widens into an estuary and then the sea. Go west and it narrows, but not for days, weeks even. It'll be swamp and forest for miles before he finds a crossing point. You understand what I'm saying? It's anyone's guess how long it will be before he can attack London from the landward side. And if by then King Edgar has more than a toehold on power, he could prove quite an obstacle even for Duke Bastard.'

'You mentioned this Edgar before. The Aetheling?'

Cerdic nodded. 'Officially, that title means he's a royal prince. Unofficially, it means he's a green boy. He can't do what needs to be done on his own. He has the northern earls, of course, Edwin and Morcar. But they don't inspire much confidence in me.'

'Cerdic... what are you saying? Your people may surrender?'

The more Cerdic dwelled on the earls Edwin and Morcar, both so famous for putting self-interest first, the more it struck him how distinct a possibility this was. It was heartbreaking to think that England might lose this war after fighting only one major battle, though he and Yvette's prime consideration at present had to be preserving their own lives.

'If they do,' he said, 'as I've just mentioned, it won't be soon. Geography is no one's friend now.'

—

The journey west from the smouldering ruins of Southwark and the line of swinging corpses, which was all that remained of its population, was a stop-start affair, for the riverside track was narrow and rutted, designed mainly for cattle. Whenever Cerdic risked a glance outside, Will Malet rode close by, as Turold had promised, but he also saw that they were embedded in the midst of the duke's army. Those other Normans he saw looked haggard with hardship and loss, but they were also sour-faced with anger.

However, the next few days would soon test even their hardy resolve.

Chill rain swept them, turning roads from swamps to actual streams. Marshes flooded, reaching far inland, causing extensive diversions through thick and trackless forest. In such conditions, the wheels of wagons jammed, axels broke, horses were lamed. Not that this prevented them sacking every village they came to and burning everything they didn't steal, including houses and hovels. Hamlets that had stood for hundreds of years, their occupants surviving by fishing the Thames and fowling in the riverside marshes, were gone in a day. The few whose lives they spared might have wished otherwise, shrieking in horror as they were dragged to the chopping block, the women to lose their hands, the men their genitals, and sometimes, for good measure, their eyes.

When a party of sellswords from Maine and Aquitaine, knights by name but landless rogues in truth, bent on pillage, joined up with them, one of innumerable such bands who'd apparently landed safely in the various ports Duke William had captured and now were fanning out across lower England, they were herding a gaggle of forty prisoners: yet more villagers from the Thames region, men, women and children who'd hidden in the woods and been discovered by accident. Once presented to Duke William, the adults among them were bound to trees and used for target practice by his crossbowmen, while the children were sent back into the wilderness to be hunted by dogs. Another such group of 'outlaws' was rounded up the next day, and hanged in a variety of ways, not just by the neck, but by the feet, the hands, even the hair. On this occasion, Father Jerome made a bizarre, demented figure as he cavorted about underneath them, gibbering in his efforts to offer absolution.

Cerdic wanted to call out to him, to ask if he was enjoying his missionary work in England, but knew that he couldn't risk it. Instead, he sat silent under the awning and brooded, and remembered with a numbing sense of horror the nightmare that old King Edward had confided in his father, in which his sickbed was visited by two long-dead monks who prophesied to him that a dark veil was about to draw over England, and that before the end of this year, a host of devils would sow pain and fire across the kingdom.

After five straight days of this terror, a new succession of intense November downpours put paid to nearly all punitive actions, the army trudging in abject misery, hooded heads bowed under the relentless rain, hooves and feet plunging inches deep into sucking mud. Wagons proceeded at a snail's pace, jolting and creaking like ships on stormy waters. And then, one day, very abruptly, all forward motion halted, and they heard loud shouting directly outside. Cerdic risked lifting the cloth.

They were in a dreary woodland, the overhead canopy so bare of leaves that rain hammered through it unimpeded, but they'd halted at a junction, a woodland track veering left. It was ploughed into equally impassable quagmires to this one, but an extensive cohort of men, mostly Norman knights and mounted men-at-arms, had detached from the main force and was marching away along it.

At their rear, a count with a completely shaven head, whom Cerdic now knew as Duke William's seneschal, William FitzOsbern, swapped commands with several of his deputies. On receipt of their orders, they hastened off towards the front of the column, while he spurred his horse along the side track, hitting a gallop to get ahead of the splinter force. Cerdic watched as it dwindled into the autumn gloom. That was a sizeable portion of the army, he estimated. Eight hundred men at least. As the main column jerked back into motion, he glanced around and, as usual, saw Will Malet close by. The young knight was helmeted and wore his Leopard of Tancarville cloak, but he was still saturated, water trickling from his nosepiece.

'Will?' Cerdic hissed, confident enough to converse in French. 'What's happening?'

Malet indicated that he should lower the drape. As Cerdic did so, the knight urged his horse over until he was close to the back of the cart.

'This morning,' he replied quietly, 'we received a delegation from Queen Ealdgyth.'

Cerdic frowned as he listened. He knew Queen Ealdgyth as the late King Harold's younger sister and the widow of the even later King Edward.

'She wishes to cede her city of Winchester to us,' Malet added.

At first, Cerdic was so stumped by this that he couldn't reply. According to Aethelric's teaching, the city of Winchester had once been the capital of the old kingdom of Wessex. The southern English still considered it the beating heart of England. More troubling, if Queen Ealdgyth was really prepared to surrender it, was that it housed the kingdom's gold reserve. Surely, this couldn't be true? Unless the woman had lost her mind. This year alone, four of her brothers had been slain, and only last January her husband, the one true love of her life, died raving about the dark veil sweeping over his kingdom.

'The terms she offers are favourable,' Malet added. 'And the duke is pleased for once. But it's fifty miles south. He can't send the whole army.'

Cerdic swallowed, tortured. Another easy victory handed to the enemy on a plate. Did the rest of England have the first clue how weary and strung out through woods and mires these invaders currently were? They'd surely be vulnerable now to some kind of attack. And yet there was no one to do that, it seemed.

And now they'd acquired England's royal treasury without even a fight.

'There is more,' Malet added. 'Every day now, the Thames narrows. And so the duke sends horsemen to its southern shore, to launch arrows at buildings on the other side. Arrows carrying parchments.'

'What parchments?' Cerdic asked.

'Threats. To this boy who wishes to be king, and his supporters. If they do not surrender London peacefully, they will all of them dangle from its highest towers.'

'I think they know that already.'

'But also promises.'

'What promises?'

'If they *do* surrender, they may keep their titles and honours. From today, those messages will refer to Queen Ealdgyth, who ceded Winchester with no bloodshed and now will be treated with great reverence.'

Message delivered, Malet edged his horse away again.

'What was that about?' Yvette asked. 'I didn't hear properly.'

Cerdic pondered Archbishop Stigand, whom he'd never met but whose reputation for being a sly one, a survivor of numerous political and religious intrigues, had travelled far and wide, and then the earls Edwin and Morcar, the most powerful magnates of the north, who'd liked Harold Godwinson well enough to see him put on the throne, but who, once their own earldoms had been saved by the king's swift action at Stamford Bridge, decided they didn't like him enough to come and help during his own hour of need.

'What that was about,' he replied disconsolately, 'was the doom of England.'

CHAPTER 9

The first one to approach Duke William's camp was Stigand himself.

It was at a place called Wallingford in the first week of December, the open woodland through which the Thames meandered now a grotto of ice. The loamy vapours of autumn had fled in the face of glistening frost. But the duke rode out all the same into the river, at this point only thirty yards across and so shallow that one could easily see the stones along its bottom. It was part-frozen of course, the waters moving sluggishly, but from the far side a lone horseman advanced to meet him. He wore a white cloak and boots and was about fifty years old, clean-shaved and with a flowing mane of white hair.

It was Yvette who recognised the archbishop, having seem him at the coronation of Harold Godwinson. Though Cerdic was unsurprised, he was confused that the prelate was alone. At the very least, he'd have expected an episcopal entourage.

'Perhaps they're too fearful of Duke William?' Yvette said, as they leaned from the back of the wagon to watch.

'Or perhaps old Stigand didn't tell anyone he was coming?' Cerdic replied.

This would have been much in keeping with what Cerdic knew about the notorious archbishop. But it still felt as though he'd taken a significant risk, coming here unprotected.

Something's happened that has changed the pieces on the board, the lad told himself. *It's persuaded him that his future lies with the Normans.*

What had happened was made plain a short time later.

At the end of their discussion, both Duke William and Archbishop Stigand returned to the southern bank of the river together. The other Norman barons crowded forward on foot, their suzerain remaining on horseback while he addressed them in a voice loud enough for Cerdic and Yvette to hear.

'The walled city of London remains under arms,' the duke began. 'To assault it would cost us gravely. But behind those walls there is weakness, for the earls, Edwin and Morcar, unnerved by our seizure of the English Treasury, have withdrawn their armies.'

An amazed silence greeted this, and then subdued cheers.

'I should have wagered on it,' Cerdic said glumly.

'Fighting men aplenty remain in London,' the duke added. 'Mainly, they are survivors from Senlac Ridge. They're a hardy, defiant breed, I'll give them that. But his grace, Archbishop Stigand, informs us that many are wounded, many tired, and most of them hollow-ribbed with hunger, for this city was not provisioned to withstand a siege. The archbishop also informs us that the English claimant to the throne, this Edgar the Aetheling, this boy who has scarce seen fourteen winters, is not yet crowned.'

Cerdic pondered that. According to Aethelric's teaching, this didn't mean anything. If the Witan had already pronounced him king...

Duke William's strident voice interrupted his thoughts.

'To the English, this is deemed irrelevant. He has already issued writs and even charters under the name "King Edgar II". But we know, with our deeper understanding of Christian law and our truer devotion to the right and proper way of doing things, that this amounts to a pile of horse manure.'

There were loud growls of agreement.

'A crown makes a king, not a throne,' the duke said. 'Archbishop Stigand understands this, and so does the other great primate of this realm, Ealdred of York. The latter, we are told, is firm of the belief that England should be ruled by an Englishman. But he also understands that without the support of Edwin and Morcar, this Edgar wields power in name only, and has no control over the veterans of Senlac Ridge who man London's walls. These men, Archbishop Ealdred fears, will fight to the last.'

'So, he's planning to throw his lot in with a man who's already been killing the innocent for fun,' Cerdic mumbled.

'Probably *because* they kill the innocent for fun,' Yvette replied.

That seemed plausible. Likely, the news of Duke William's fury had travelled widely.

'These prelates are all the same if it's their own hides at risk.' The lad's thoughts lingered on Pope Alexander, so quick to throw a Christian kingdom to the wolves. 'We've come a long way since the first bishop of Rome was willingly nailed upside down on a cross.'

'Without Edwin and Morcar, what can they do?' she asked.

'Edwin and Morcar!' he spat.

He'd seen the Aelfgarsons once: Edwin, the older brother, a leonine brawler, Morcar leaner, less obviously aggressive, perhaps more affable, and yet somehow they'd been unimpressive as leaders of men. Of course, out of necessity they'd have rebuilt their forces since Fulford, and their new warriors would be fresh, not like the poor famished wretches holding out in London. They'd be a mighty loss to the garrison there.

'Because of this,' Duke William added, 'Archbishop Stigand considers that Archbishop Ealdred will also come over to us and might persuade this Edgar.'

Cerdic sighed. Again, he ought to have guessed this would happen.

'In return, we have pledged that there'll be no more harrying of the people…'

Agitation rumbled through the ranks, particularly among those sellsword companies, those *routiers* who'd now been arriving daily at Dover, Romney and Pevensey, swelling the army to enormous size, but not without first ranging across the country doing as much rapine and destruction as they liked, and hopeful of doing more.

The duke raised a hand. The dissent fell quiet.

'This is our command,' he said sternly.

—

Duke William led his host across the river, heading northeast. Most habitations they passed were empty of people and the army still felt it necessary to purloin livestock, but there was less violence and burning, and as word of this spread, ceorls reappeared in the fields, watching, some even cheering, which Duke William acknowledged with a raised hand.

'You shouldn't consider these people traitors,' Yvette said.

'No?' Cerdic replied sourly.

'They want to live. Maybe their previous lords were unjust to them. A change of leadership may not bring benefits, but it may not bring evil either. At least, that's how they're probably thinking.'

'But we've already seen the evil these men are capable of.'

'I told you before, Cerdic... we're all of us capable of evil.'

—

At Berkhamsted, Archbishop Ealdred surrendered.

It was snowing that day, a glimmering white blanket hugging the denuded landscape. Even so, on a meadow outside the small town, an English deputation awaited, glowing braziers set up alongside tents and banners. In an open central pavilion, done in brilliant red with multiple crosses embroidered in silver thread, Cerdic saw a carpet, cushions, and a table laden with food and drink. A bent and aged figure stood outside it, leaning on a jewel-encrusted crozier and wearing Advent vestments of purple and gold.

Another person stepped into view behind him. Tall, with a pale face and a shock of fair hair, but thin, wearing a long light-blue tunic with embroidery around the collar and cuffs. Even from this distance, spots were visible on the boy's chin.

He's brought the Aetheling, Cerdic told himself. *They submit together.*

During the course of that afternoon, Duke William's meeting with the archbishop became a celebratory feast. Word passed through the camp that all had been agreed. Edgar the Aetheling would step down as temporary leader of the English, and Duke William would be crowned in his stead, that duty to be performed by Archbishop Ealdred. Surprisingly, the least enthusiastic signatory to the deal was the duke himself. He had wanted to wait so that he could bring his wife, Matilda, to England, and have her crowned alongside him. But this wasn't to be. The deputation from London was loath to admit it, but they did not, in fact, speak for that great city. Or at least not for the housecarls who held it. London would not surrender, and there were many other English who felt the same. The coronation should therefore be soon, even if that meant it was sparsely attended, as from that point on it would be more difficult for those English not innately hostile to withhold their respect.

On 14 December, Cerdic heard from Turold that several embassies had been sent to London, but as all had been rebuffed at the city's westernmost entrance, having come under showers of stones and faeces, the duke had now sent a mercenary force under a seasoned captain called Brion de Chalot.

'It's five hundred strong,' Turold said, gnawing on a mutton bone as they sat by the fire. 'But it's under orders to make no assault. Instead, it should camp within sight of the city walls. A show of strength. The duke hopes this will sway the people of London against those who only want to fight.'

Cerdic sat dejected across the flames from him. Given that the truly bitter weather had arrived, and because the lad had shown no inclination to flee thus far, Roland had issued orders that though his hands must remain bound, he no longer should be tethered to Yvette's wagon and in fact could ride alongside her full-time, though Cerdic had also been given strict instructions to keep his pego in his breeches.

'Our aim is to return Yvette to her father unspoiled,' the knight-seneschal had said. 'Anything else would be unacceptable.'

At present, Cerdic was too preoccupied with the fate of his country.

London *would* fall. There was no point pretending otherwise. The only questions were when and how protracted and brutal an affair would it be.

The following morning, in the very early hours, the remnants of the mercenary force returned. At first, they came in ones and twos, then in larger groups, but all were bloodied.

The survivors told how they'd been close to London when a vast English army fell on them. How they'd only cut their way to freedom when two hundred of their number had fallen. More and more returnees told similar tales. *Similar*, but not *identical*. And when Bishop Odo advised them that lies would be repaid with rope and gibbet, because the safety of the rest of the army now depended on it, a more convincing explanation emerged.

Brion de Chalot had bidden his followers clear a space amid the shops and shanty houses making up the city's west suburb but within shouting distance of the wall, and there make a camp, where they would roister all night. This they did, having searched the empty properties and procured all the victuals and bottles of drink they could find. However, that night, as they drunkenly slumbered, fire-arrows flew into the camp. As the small army came back to wakefulness, many of its members stumbling about so fuddled they weren't even aware they were on fire, an English force attacked them.

It wasn't numerically immense, the *routiers* sheepishly admitted, but those comprising it came out of the darkness like devils. Mainly, they fought with axes, but also with longswords and crossbows, which they'd clearly stolen from Norman corpses. Chalot himself died when a bolt struck him in the forehead.

According to one lesser mercenary captain, many, unsure what they were facing—

'Or too cowardly to face it,' Joubert interrupted.

The shamefaced officer persevered: 'They managed to break out of the encirclement, and fight their way to the paddock, only to find many of their horses stolen. Those able to acquire one got free. Those who weren't were slain.'

Duke William exploded, swearing and blaspheming. He roared that he'd promised to be a gracious lord to London's inhabitants, pledging safe passage for those survivors of Senlac Ridge. And *this* was the response!

Terrified, the English bishops begged him to resist taking vengeance on ordinary citizens. The duke raged at them that England's citizens were treacherous dogs, that they were forcing him to take these terrible measures.

'I see he attaches no blame to himself,' Yvette said later, when they'd rekindled their fire.

'He offered the city peace,' Turold replied. 'Winchester was ours without a fight. And its population was spared.'

'It sounds to me,' Cerdic said, 'that the men sent to London brought this disaster on themselves.'

'If Brion de Chalot wasn't dead already, I'd have had him hanged,' Turold said.

They relapsed into fretful silence. None could return to sleep now, but half an hour later, Turold, having scouted around the camp for more rumours, reappeared.

'The duke will proceed with the coronation,' he said. 'But instead of using the Saxon minster at Winchester, we head to the basilica on... a place called *Thorney Island*?'

He queried that last part with Cerdic.

The lad nodded. 'The West Minster.'

'Apparently, it's only four miles from the place called Ludgate. Which is where Chalot's sellswords were cut to pieces.'

'That would be a fearless gesture,' Yvette replied.

'And a trap,' Roland Casterborus said, emerging from the icy darkness.

They glanced up at him, though briefly he was lost in thought.

Both Turold and Roland had now become companionable with the two captives, though for different reasons: Turold de Bardouville because, initially at least, he'd been the only one who could converse with Cerdic, though he remained a cynical, hard-bitten character, jocular when the mood was on him, stern and unyielding at other times. By contrast, Roland was a different animal. A stiffer, more upright figure, he held higher rank than the household champion, but he'd been a sad, brooding presence since the betrayal at Dover, and Cerdic felt sure this owed to his pursuit of the ideal.

Again, the lad was intrigued by this concept of chivalry.

To wage war, and yet do it in merciful fashion?

Spoken out loud, it sounded fantastical. And Roland was clearly the proof of how challenging it was. Cerdic couldn't help wondering how the knight-seneschal had managed until now, for he'd clearly fought many campaigns, though perhaps few of those prior to this one had been so laced with cruelty and deceit.

Sensing that all eyes were upon him, Roland deigned to explain himself.

'Despite the papal decree, there are many crowned heads in Europe who consider Duke William's assault on England to be criminal. They particularly disapprove of a mere duke throwing down an anointed king. In addition, His Holiness will be unnerved by the duke's methods. But this new ploy, I suspect, is a way to even that score. If the English can themselves be lured into attacking a lawful coronation, sympathy for their cause might ebb. And even if they don't attack, they might learn a lesson from it… namely, that their new king is here to stay and that he doesn't fear them.'

'When will it happen?' Cerdic asked.

'Christmas Day,' Turold replied.

'That would sanctify the event,' Yvette said. 'One of our holiest days… the commencement of the reign of the One True King commemorated by the commencement of a new reign in England.'

Roland squatted by the fire, pulling off his gauntlets and warming his hands. 'There's more to it than that, I fear. The duke is setting himself out as bait. He's issued orders that, on the great day itself, the bulk of the army is to camp several miles west, with a relatively small force, a handpicked three hundred or so on the island itself. They'll provide a ring of steel around the church, though to the untrained eye it will seem a paltry few. In addition, squadrons of our cavalry will be ready to detach from the main camp at a moment's notice should the need arise.'

'It's a ploy to lure the housecarls out of London?' Yvette asked.

Roland shrugged. 'Maybe. He will also invite London's great and good as guests of course. The genuine hand of peace... or fakery, a bare-faced attempt to make things *look* respectable? I don't know. Either way, the honour of guarding the West Minster itself falls to us. House Tancarville.'

A pensive silence greeted this.

'Lord Joubert has been lobbying the duke again,' he added. 'Pointing out our heroics on Senlac Ridge. Arguing how it was we who captured the Fighting Man banner. It's also the case that few of the other great lords petitioned for it. They'd sooner be inside the church, where they can praise the new king to his face.'

'And where there'll be sturdy stone walls between themselves and the as-yet unknown forces of England,' Turold said.

Roland merely grunted at that.

Cerdic, for his part, contributed nothing to the discussion. It would be another famous day, whatever its outcome. And yet again, he'd be right there to witness it.

CHAPTER 10

In the early afternoon of Christmas Eve, Duke William made camp a couple of miles west of Thorney Island, not exactly on the same meadow where King Harold had bivouacked before crossing the Thames on his fateful journey down to the south coast, though close to there. Where previously the road and the clutters of pens and ramshackle buildings along its edges had thronged with people and their animals, now it was deserted. When they arrived, thin flakes were spiralling down through the blue December dusk, adding to an unbroken carpet of snow.

While a general encampment was made, House Tancarville was martialled into battle formation, a forward march commencing along the London road, goods and wagons at the centre, infantry at the rear, knights and mounted men-at-arms on either side. Cerdic couldn't see who rode at the front, though no doubt it was Joubert, escorted by Roland but revelling in his leadership role. It wasn't Count Cynric himself, for he rode in the vehicle next to them. A couple of times, Cerdic spotted the nobleman lifting the awning. He never saw the count's face, just a limp white hand.

As the abbey church loomed through the Yuletide dusk, its stained-glass windows glittered multi-coloured from the candle-light inside, for it seemed that Archbishop Ealdred had sent word ahead for the full cathedral chapter to be on duty when the king-in-waiting arrived. The outer palisade that encircled the whole of the West Minster precinct was lit by torches but unmanned, the gates wide open. Turold commenced riding back and forth, instructing the captains of the household, sending those infantrymen equipped with crossbows up onto the outer gantry. While this was in progress, the remainder of the company passed inside, following a narrow entry-lane between tall, impressive townhouses, and deploying in orderly fashion in a central paved square in front of the steps leading up to the basilica's front door.

Only a hundred yards to the east, behind a curtain wall made from stone and battlemented along the top, stood the Palace of the West Minster. King Edward had constructed it on the site of the earlier dragon hall erected by the Viking, Canute, and made it his permanent residence. This too was firelit, though all they could see of it in the gathering winter gloom was this outer wall, and a secondary stone structure behind, something the Normans called a *donjon*, which was equally solid and immense to the church, though not as tall, with further battlements along its high parapet. A nervous gaggle of civilians, most likely thralls and other domestic staff, waited by its open front gate.

Cerdic's understanding was that Duke William would take possession of the palace from the moment he arrived here, at dawn, though it would be Count Cynric's duty the night before to inspect it and ensure that all was in readiness. Given the count's condition, this duty now passed to Roland as Cynric's official deputy. Joubert meanwhile was already organising defensive positions.

It was a scene of chaos, with much shouting and rushing about carrying torches. Though the cold deepened with the darkness, both Cerdic and Yvette looked out continually. The impressive houses they'd seen on entering reminded Cerdic that he'd heard how many of London's dignitaries, the leading churchmen and wealthiest merchants, had properties here. According to Turold, one of these properties, one of the best in fact, had been reserved for occupation by Count Cynric and his *seigneurs*. Like all the others, it had been vacated quickly on the news that the Norman host was approaching. Even though its owner was Bishop William of London, a Norman who'd lived in England for years, he'd fled too, fearful that he might be blamed for failing to quell the resistance in the city. Apparently, it boasted several luxurious chambers, though none of these were at anyone's disposal, save for the count himself, who clearly needed rest.

Needless to say, the prisoners would not be ensconced indoors.

Turold brought this news to them late in the evening. The wagon, which was left in a small entry to the front right side of the bishop's residence, looking out onto the square, would be their shelter for the night. The knight also brought them additional blankets and fleeces. He apologised that there was no whale-oil lamp to spare, though it wouldn't have given off much heat in any case.

'Do you think the English will attack tomorrow?' Yvette wondered.

Turold shrugged. 'I'd like to say the English are not fools. But I wish they'd accept their new overlord. I understand that he's been harsh so far, but all rulers are harsh. Godwinson could be harsh, could he not?'

Yvette didn't know in truth, but she imagined it was possible.

'What do *you* think?' she asked Cerdic, after Turold had crunched away across the snowy square.

'Some will always prefer death to slavery,' he said.

'But not you?' She seemed keen to know his answer.

'I believe in surviving so that one can fight another day.'

Visibly disheartened, she handed him several of the new sheep-skins.

But Duke Bastard will never be any king of mine, he wanted to add. He didn't though, because it would have been foolishness. No man got to choose the monarch that reigned over him.

A coronation would put things into a slightly different perspective, of course. Would make William the Bastard even more unassailable than he'd been before. But there were other ways yet to hit back. Cerdic was certain. *Adapt to your new wyrd... but be clever.*

This was among the last but most important instructions his brother had given him.

Well, he'd been clever enough to evade execution when first he'd been captured. He'd been clever enough to survive the hellish march from Senlac Ridge to West Minster, when all other captives had died. So long as he played this thing carefully, he was certain he could be clever enough to gain advantage of some sort for himself and his people.

And increasingly, he felt he knew how.

—

It was like no Christmas Day the lad had ever known. He woke in the dull cold, haunted by memories of happier occasions: candle-fire and prayer in the incense-laden chapel, then raucous feasts in his father's hall. Heavy evergreens suspended overhead, hearths piled with holly logs, songs sung, toasts offered, poems recited. Roaring laughter, the wassail bowl slopping as they filled it with ale or mead. Venison joints simmering in gravy, boar's head, roast duckling, game pie.

In contrast, the precinct of the West Minster was silent and eerie.

It had snowed throughout the night. The white carpet lay inches deep, feather-sized flakes continuing to cascade. Warm light spilled from the church itself, and the palace next door, but the absence of ordinary people going about festive business was oppressive.

There was also a tension in the air.

In addition to the crossbows on the outer palisade, Joubert had placed bowmen on the roofs encircling the central square. Crossing the square itself stood a double line of dismounted knights with shields ready and swords drawn, while men-at-arms were located around the perimeter, one every few paces. Whether these troops had been here all night or were replacements now that morning had come was unclear, but all were struggling to withstand the cold. They wore heavy mail, but surcoats as well, and over the top of those, furs or sheepskins. They stamped their feet and leaned together, faces visibly pinched.

They numbered eighty in total, but there was no sign of Joubert himself.

Cerdic wondered if, once he'd made his deployments, the young lord had secured for himself one of those luxury bedrooms that were closed off to everyone else. As he watched from the back of the cart, Roland, equally well-wrapped to the others, came down the steps from the church's open front door. He pulled his helmet over his coif and buckled it under his chin. Hefting his shield, he issued some quiet command, and the double line of soldiers came to attention. Turold, similarly clad, appeared from the passage to the front gate on horseback. He dismounted, handed his reins to a groom and threaded through the line of men.

'The road's clear a mile in either direction,' Cerdic heard him say. 'If anyone had been creeping around, we'd have seen signs in the snow. But we didn't.'

Roland nodded.

Voices then shouted, and a horn blew.

Soldiers came alert. Turold and Roland went for the hilts of their swords. But then Duke William cantered into view from the entry-lane, forty or so mounted attendants behind him, the bulk of them made up of his leading barons, Bishop Odo and Robert of Mortain at the front. All wore fine robes as befitted the occasion. Duke William himself was resplendent in a lavish flowing tunic of red and gold, though in all cases, chain-mail glinted underneath.

Each one of them, rather than bringing his entire household, had one bodyguard in attendance. In Duke William's case it was his personal champion, Roger Perceval, a tall, spare-framed knight but infamously deadly. Cerdic couldn't be sure, but he fancied Perceval had been the one who, on Senlac Ridge, had slain Aelfrith Eagle-Eye, the fiercest of King Harold's hearth-men.

Last of all came the churchmen who'd officiate, Archbishop Stigand on horseback and, more heavily cloaked against the cold than anyone else there, the older and frailer Archbishop Ealdred, who rode in a tapestried chaise. As the primate of York was helped out by a handful of fussing, black-robed monks, he was already clad in his Christmas vestments of white and silver, with a mitre on his shrivelled, nodding head. Riding alongside him, Cerdic saw the fellow who probably boasted the shortest reign as king in the entire history of the British Isles. Edgar the Aetheling also descended from the chaise, looking pale-faced and dishevelled. He wore the same clothes as before and now seemed lost and bereft, most likely because he'd slowly come to suspect that a future of captivity awaited him.

Duke William and his two brothers repaired immediately to the palace, where they were greeted by toadying domestic staff. The duke's own chamberlains had ridden ahead earlier that morning to ensure all was prepared, and to enforce the much-higher standards that they were certain the staff here were unused to.

The Norman counts and the clerics meanwhile went into the church, Archbishop Ealdred needing to be assisted up the steps.

'I've never seen a coronation before,' Cerdic said.

'You won't see this one,' Yvette mumbled, still hidden under her blankets. 'Unless you can see through stone.'

He watched as the two ranks of knights, having opened to admit the ducal party, now formed up again. Their numbers had noticeably increased. Not only had the bodyguards brought by the duke and his men joined them, Roger Perceval prowling the front as though itching to be the first into any fray, other men-at-arms had also appeared, creating additional ranks behind. With them had come Joubert, yawning and unhelmeted, his red hair sticking up like bits of straw.

'What's happening now?' Yvette asked.

'The count's son's risen from his beauty sleep. As usual, it's done him no good. I swear, there are more soldiers here than guests. Also, it's a confined space.' Cerdic glanced at the surrounding rooftops and the shadowy shapes of bowmen. 'If anyone *did* try to fight their way in here, it'd be a killing ground.'

On this basis, it seemed far less likely to him now that any group of renegades, no matter how much they burned for vengeance, would attempt an assault. He'd wondered on first arriving if the close-packed timber houses, with their multi-levelled thatched roofs, might be vulnerable to fire-arrows. The English defending Ludgate had already used that tactic. But now those roofs were heavy with snow, every parapet an overhanging shelf of white. Flame would pose no risk.

'I suspect it'll be a quiet day,' he said. 'And hopefully a quick one.'

He glanced at the royal residence. It had to be three times the size of his father's hall at Wulfbury. With its stone outer wall and sturdy battlements, it looked like something the Normans would build. He reminded himself that King Edward had constructed it on the site of a Viking long-hall. So, first a Danish king made his mark in this place, then an English king, and now it would be a Norman. It was enough to make him wonder if there ever was any point in a single person trying to influence these tides of history.

Adapt to your new wyrd.

Cerdic shook his head. Not when it involved theft and murder on a scale like this. Englishmen beyond counting had died resisting the Vikings. They'd died resisting the Normans too. He might not be able to reverse this ghastly ruination of all their lives. But there were certain things that he could and would fight for.

All he needed...

Above all, be clever.

...was the chance.

And the chain of events that would give him that chance was set in motion shortly after midday, when, several hours into a monotonous series of Latin intonations sung by choristers, those outside the church heard a voice of concern from high overhead.

'My lord... my Lord Joubert, there's a crowd approaching along the road from London.'

This brought both Cerdic and Yvette to the back of their cart.

The falling snow had eased off, but the air was crisp and still. The alarm had been raised by an archer on one of the surrounding roofs.

Joubert spun his horse to address the captain of his men-at-arms. 'Send a galloper to camp. Tell him to use the postern gate by the river, so he won't be interfered with. He's to tell them the English are here!'

CHAPTER 11

'Wait, my lord!' Roland rode across the Minster square, snow flying from his hooves. 'Wait!'

'*Close the main gate!*' Joubert bellowed.

'My lord!' Roland interrupted. 'The duke himself issued invitations to the people of London as a peace offering. It may be that they've accepted.'

Joubert glared at him, but now seemed undecided.

'Is the crowd armed?' Roland called up.

'I can't tell, my lord,' the archer replied.

Joubert rounded on the knight-seneschal. 'Go and see for yourself.'

Roland urged his horse through the ranks of infantry. 'Don't send that message to the camp, Lord, I beg you. They'll come here with full power.'

Joubert still looked torn with indecision.

'My lord?' the infantry captain enquired.

'Let me think, damn your bollocks! The rest of you be ready. Prepare for battle.'

Inside the wagon, Yvette shrank backward, almost into Cerdic's arms.

'What do we do?' she whispered. He shook his head, genuinely uncertain. She rifled through the blankets, producing the dagger. 'Cut your bonds. You can't defend either of us tied up.'

That made sense to him, but he hesitated to do this, again glancing outside.

Joubert had vanished from view. Cerdic guessed that he too had gone to the gate. At the far side of the square, Turold had taken command. As he drew his longsword, he called up to the rooftops. 'What's happening?'

'My lord, it looks like civilians,' the archer shouted back. 'There are men *and* women. Even children. But there's a considerable number. They're maybe a hundred yards from the gate. Lord Joubert and Lord Roland are on the palisade.'

Turold stepped out in front of the defensive line. 'Everyone stay calm.'

Roger Perceval picked a footman at random. 'Into the church. Bar the doors.'

'There's no need,' Turold argued. 'If these are civilians, they've been invited here.'

Perceval snorted. 'Not by *me*.'

Cerdic watched the stand-off with fascination. House Tancarville's champion against the Duke of Normandy's? Technically, the Tancarville man possessed seniority of command as they had official guard-duty for the coronation, but how willing would any Norman knight be to defy one of the duke's own high-ranking retainers?

Perceval glanced at the footman again. 'Do as I tell you.'

The fellow scampered away. Turold looked as though he still might object. He was taller and broader than the duke's man, but Perceval had a ferocious reputation.

With a skitter of hooves in snow, Roland reappeared from the entry-lane. 'They're claiming to be representatives of the city,' he said. 'There are some fine robes among them, but mostly they look like peasants.'

'Weapons?' Turold asked.

'I didn't see any.'

'How many?'

'Four... maybe five hundred.'

'Devils in Hell.' Even Turold looked shaken by that. Roger Perceval too.

'Go and address them in their own tongue,' Roland said. 'Joubert's on the palisade, but all he's doing is throwing abuse. Not that they understand a word.'

Turold nodded, sheathed his sword and hurried away on foot.

Roland switched his attention to the rooftops. 'Are you men ready?'

'We're ready, my lord!'

He turned to the others. 'The rest of you... no one make a move they don't need to. These people say they are guests.'

'You're not thinking of letting them into the church?' Perceval said.

Roland didn't answer. To refuse them admission would be to flout Duke William's own invitation. But how serious had that invitation been? The rest of the men looked equally uneasy, even though more men-at-arms had now appeared at the rear, mounted, and were forming up in loose phalanxes.

'They're genuinely readying for battle,' Cerdic said, watching, increasingly tense. He took Yvette's dagger, laid it edge-up on the rim of the cart and commenced sawing. 'We stay in here though. The best we can hope for if the English triumph is that they think we're hostages.'

Yvette nodded distractedly. Outside, there were more sounds of dispute.

'The duke issued written invitations,' Roland said. 'They're waving those papers right now.'

'He issued invitations to a few,' Perceval retorted. 'To their bishops and aldermen. Not to some ill-bred rabble.'

'These are the people he needs to win over. These are the ones who'll bar their homes to us, who'll fight us in the streets of London if the war continues.'

'In which case why won't they fight us here too? We should keep them all out.'

Joubert emerged from the entry-lane at full gallop, his steed slithering a dozen yards as he pulled it to a halt, all but colliding with the first line of knights.

'I'm allowing two hundred in,' he said, 'and no more. The rest stay outside. They've no choice. We've closed the gate on them, and it stays closed.'

'Are we searching the ones coming in for weapons?' Perceval asked.

The count's son grimaced as he realised that he'd forgotten to issue this order.

'Too late now,' Roland said. 'Who's controlling the gate?'

'Turold. I've also sent a rider to the main camp.'

'My lord, *why*?'

'Because I'm taking no chances, Casterborus! There are another five hundred of them out there, at least! I said we'd guard the duke, and by God's fiery blood, we will!'

'If our cavalry comes along that road…'

'I've told them there's no emergency, but that we need additional men.'

Cerdic's mouth dried as he overheard all this, while Roland's grim expression offered no encouragement. Either he didn't trust the messenger to deliver the correct wording, or he didn't trust Joubert to exert control when these additional men arrived.

—

The first civilians who ventured into the square looked at least as nervous as the soldiers facing them. They clumped together tightly as they advanced, but they weren't an obvious threat. Most wore commoner garb, while there were women there as well as men, whitebeards alongside pimply-faced youngsters. The immense frames and tough, stony expressions of housecarls were noticeably absent. Even the few younger men Cerdic saw, as he stood on the tailgate of the cart, were pot-bellied and bandy-legged. A couple leaned on crutches. One older fellow, evidently blind, was being led by a hefty woman who was probably his daughter.

Yet the double line of Norman knights, bolstered from behind now by men-at-arms mounted on skittish steeds, stiffened as the small crowd approached. Cerdic glanced to the rooftops, where innumerable men seemed to be perched on snowy edges, taking careful aim with bows and crossbows.

'A lion's den if ever I've seen one,' he muttered. 'These people have got courage even if there isn't a warrior among them.'

The new arrivals had no visible leadership, which was maybe a concern. There were one or two older men, perhaps better dressed than the others, but Cerdic saw no dominant figure in church garb whom he could identify as head of this flock.

'There's no danger from these people at all,' he said.

'What's that?' Yvette was less able to see from her lower position, while his words were drowned out by the rising hubbub in the square.

The mumbling of the people grew in confidence, reaching a gradual clamour as they called for their new king. Frankish oaths grew noisier in return, the Normans ordering them back.

'They're ordinary townsfolk,' Cerdic said. 'A poor few who, for whatever reason, have made a decision that to keep resisting is pointless.'

But he too felt a sense of alarm as ever more civilians spilled into the square. The soldiers reddened and sweated as the English at the front, shunted from behind, crowded ever closer to their wall of shields.

'Keep them back!' Joubert shouted from the rear. 'Drive them back!'

The knights advanced a couple of steps, pushing with spear hafts. Horses snorted and whickered. A cry of pain sounded as the pommel of a sword struck a face, and then from inside the church there came a wild – nay, *ecstatic* – cheering, and the bells began to ring with what should have been joyous celebration. The English reciprocated, thinking this the moment when they'd see their new ruler. Fists and crutches thrust wildly upward; a great belly-roar sounded. In response to which horses neighed in panic. A punch was thrown by a Norman, and then another, before a spear was rammed home. A voice gargled in agony; another cried in outrage. An arrow slanted down, striking an Englishwoman's neck. Angered and horrified, her friends tried to clear space around her. One kicked hard at the Norman shields. Another arrow whistled down.

'*Wipe them out!*' Joubert screamed, his lips speckled with froth. '*Wipe the dogs out!*'

Swords rose and fell. More arrows and darts flickered down.

The cries of acclamation became shrieks of terror and pain.

Cerdic leapt from the cart, blade in hand. But he couldn't do anything, and stood there rigid. Over his shoulder, Yvette watched agog as the Norman war-machine rolled forward, horsemen now forcing their way through the infantry, thrusting with lances, wielding their swords like cleavers.

As the bells overhead tolled and tolled on this new dawn for England, the Norman line advanced, blades flashing, a carpet of flesh and blood behind it. Those English still on their feet were funnelled back down the entry-lane, harried from above by archers and crossbowmen. Cerdic would later learn that, on hearing the frenzy of horrified screams, the much larger crowd of English locked out on the road attempted to force the palisade gate, which led Turold to order the crossbowmen on the gantry to loose. That second crowd fled in all directions. One or two retaliated by throwing stones but were swiftly shot down. By now of course, the cavalry from the main Norman camp was encroaching, and on seeing the violence, spurred their steeds into a gallop. Lances levelled, the charging horde swept all before them, clearing the road to London for a mile at least, littering its sidings with corpses.

Only as Turold stood on the gantry, squadron after squadron of knights thundering past, did he become aware of the discord at his rear. He turned and saw Joubert mounted, lurching back and forth among the surviving scatter of English from the square, striking them down with great blows of his sword. Others of the Tancarville retinue had also arrived, hacking, chopping. Yvo de Taillebois personally felled the blind man and his daughter with savage strokes to their skulls.

Back on the square itself, Cerdic stared hollow-eyed across the twitching human wreckage, the sudden unearthly quiet broken only by gasps and whimpers, and the single croak of a hefty raven, as it fluttered down to take first pick of the gory delicacies on offer. On the far side, Roland slumped in his saddle. He dropped his helmet into the snow, then yanked back his coif and ran a mailed hand through sweat-sodden hair.

'I take back what I said,' Yvette breathed. 'Some of us are indeed more capable of evil than others.'

With a hefty *clunk*, a bar was withdrawn, and the church door swung open. Warm candlelight flooded the steps, and the single male figure that stood at the top of them was silhouetted, though his squat, square-shouldered outline was very distinctive.

As were his purple robes of royalty. And the golden circlet he carried by his side rather than wore on his head.

'And yet, one man's evil,' Cerdic said, 'can be another man's opportunity.'

CHAPTER 12

That evening, Cerdic found Roland on the ground floor of the Bishop of London's house. The knight-seneschal sat alone in what might have been a stone storeroom, though all it contained now was an iron bucket filled with hot coals and a crude table with several stone bottles on it. Most had been uncorked. The air reeked of wine.

Roland, who still wore the loose tunic, leather breeches and boots that he'd worn under his hauberk earlier, was in the process of filling a large goblet from the one bottle still full. From his flushed expression, he'd been here for some time. He glanced at the young Englishman and said nothing. He didn't even seem surprised that he was out of his bonds.

'Why did Count Cynric come to England?' Cerdic asked. 'Back home, is he a count in name only?'

The knight looked puzzled. 'He has splendid estates. Castles, vassals...'

'So... why?'

Roland swilled more wine. Meanwhile, angry exchanges sounded from the floor overhead.

'Because...' he slurred, 'there are some men who always want more. There are some who if you tell them they can't have something, will become ever more determined to make it theirs... whatever the consequence.'

'Can anything be worth all this?' Cerdic asked. 'You've surely all traded your souls by now. In purely earthly terms, you've lost many men already, and more will follow when you storm London.'

'Ah-ha... no.' The knight wagged a drunken finger. 'Apparently, London has opened her gates. That is the latest intelligence. When the city fathers decided to attend the coronation, those housecarls who'd been manning London's walls took the chance to leave.' He sniffed and pondered this. 'I'm under no illusion, though. I imagine they'll make a stand further north, perhaps amid folk they feel they can better trust. But the ones left in the city now... they've no belly for it. After what happened today, they're begging for mercy. Which the duke will show. When he enters the city tomorrow.'

Cerdic was incredulous. Outside, some seven hours later, the abbey chapter were still clearing the corpses and blood, and they hadn't even started on the massacre site along the London road. 'You're telling me this is a victory?'

Roland made a vague gesture. 'Does it feel like one?'

Cerdic listened to the arguments raging overhead, and then thought about the riotous sounds from the palace, wherein the coronation feast had gone ahead as planned.

'I hear that House Tancarville has been banished from the royal banquet,' he said.

Roland nodded solemnly. 'Many could learn from that. Over these years, Duke William – who's now King William, I suppose – has employed men to do grubby deeds on his behalf. But he rarely thanks them. He's the pope's man, you see.' He snorted a bitter laugh. 'God's breath, man. *His* hands must be clean.'

'People won't be fooled by that.'

'On the contrary, my young friend, they are *always* fooled. You know why? Because greed always trumps common sense.'

Throw yourself on their greed. Yet more advice from Unferth, issued to his younger brother on the last night of his life. *Use it against them.*

'Even now,' Roland said, 'though rivers of wine and ale are flowing, there is great debate in the palace about the division of spoils. A debate that House Tancarville is also banned from, incidentally. Much to Count Cynric's chagrin. But few of those men over there will get what they expect. Oh, the great lords will prosper. The king will have no choice but to reward *them*. But the rest…?' He gave an indifferent smile. 'In Duke William's eyes, vermin will always be vermin. Which is why, soon in the new year, once he's commenced building his great London castle, he will return to Normandy without having dispensed any real largesse… save to those he can't ignore.'

Cerdic considered this. And it pleased him. In truth, the timing could not be better.

'Is Count Cynric fit enough to grant me an audience?' he asked.

'Go up. See for yourself. But…' Roland snapped his fingers, 'I'll take the knife first.'

Cerdic showed empty palms. 'Knife?'

'You didn't chew through your leash with those pearly white teeth.'

Realising that he didn't need the dagger anyway, the lad slid it from under his tunic, and handed it over. Roland jammed it point-down into the table, and resumed gulping wine.

Cerdic left the room, followed another passage between storerooms, then ascended a wooden step-ladder into the part of the building meant for occupancy. Here, a timber corridor lit by candles burning in iron wall-brackets moulded to look like gauntleted fists led him to a vast chamber, a hall not unlike that of his father, lacking in the ornamentation perhaps, but larger overall. It was lit by a multitude of candles, but also by a huge fire blazing in a rock-built hearth at its far end, the smoke from which ascended a single rock chimney. Religious tapestries clad the walls, while swags of evergreen adorned the hammerbeams of the roof, indicating that Christmas had been on the lord-bishop's mind before he'd fled. There were countless tables and benches in here, and while some were occupied, many had been pushed aside by the huge number of knights crowded in.

With the exception of Roland, it was the entirety of Count Cynric's equestrian household, some still mailed, some even spattered with dried blood, most of them drinking from flagons of ale or wine. All looked vexed and tired, their clean-shaved faces gleaming with sweat. So huge a congregation, plus the heat from the fire, created a rank, muggy atmosphere.

Count Cynric, looking surprisingly stronger than Cerdic had expected, occupied the high seat close to the flames. He wore ill-fitting clothes, which again hung on him loosely, a clear indication that he'd been unwell, though some of his colour seemed to have returned and his left arm was no longer strapped.

Angry viewpoints were still being exchanged. Not exactly harsh words. There were no insults flying. But the company was unhappy. It only occurred to Cerdic now that they were hardly likely to feel well-disposed towards the English, but he ventured forward anyway, not to the very centre of the hall, where space had been cleared so that different groups could harangue each other from beyond striking distance, but far enough for them all to see him.

Even then he had to shout at the top of his voice.

'My lords... *my noble lords!*'

One by one, they fell quiet, blinking at him in confusion.

'My noble lords,' he said again, in French of course. 'I fear that House Tancarville might have overreached itself in coming to England.'

The silence greeting this was one of disbelief.

It took several seconds for Joubert, still mailed and seated on a stool to the left, to leap to his feet. 'Is that English wastrel still alive?' He seemed astounded.

Cerdic strove on. 'My lords... as well as the many you've lost in battle, you now stand admonished by His Highness, the new King William of England.'

'He speaks our language?' Joubert simmered with both bewilderment and rage. 'How does he speak our language? Shut him up, someone!'

'House Tancarville is one of the great houses of Normandy,' Cerdic persevered.

'*Shut him up!*' Joubert roared. '*Shut the wretch up!*'

'But its fortunes have wilted...'

Joubert lurched to a rack of throwing spears.

'If you hear me out, my lords,' Cerdic said hurriedly, 'I can change this.'

Joubert selected a javelin. 'Let's do with this mongrel dog, once and for all.'

He drew the missile back to hurl it, only to have it snatched by the shaft and lugged out of his grasp from behind. He spun, and even when he saw Turold there, turned crimson with outrage. The rest of the room watched, shocked. The count's own eyes narrowed, but he said nothing.

'You dare interfere?' Joubert hissed.

Turold shrugged. 'If the boy says he can help, why don't we listen... my lord?'

Joubert's eyes shrank to steely points. He gave a grunting, pig-like chuckle. 'Yes, Turold. From the outset, for reasons no one can understand, you've shown friendship to this young and pretty-faced creature.'

'And also for reasons no one understands,' Turold retorted, 'you've shown him hatred.' He turned to his master. 'Lord Count, can it hurt to hear what the boy says? He lives here, he's a native, he's descended from a noble family...'

'We only have his word for that,' Joubert spat.

'He's become acquainted with our tongue in two months. Is that the work of some peasant?'

'Intelligence doesn't grant him noble blood,' someone else said.

'It marks him as different, at least.' Turold stepped forward into the space. 'He says he can change our fortunes, so I ask again... can it hurt to listen?'

All heads turned to their overlord.

Count Cynric leaned forward. When he spoke, his voice was croaky but audible. 'Speak, boy. But make it impressive. I've no room in my house now for idle mouths.'

'My lord, I fear that you and your people have made mistakes.' Cerdic knew that speaking so boldly was a risk, but he needed them to hear everything he said. 'I also fear this owes to a deep conviction you Normans have that right is always on your side.'

Mumbles of disquiet greeted this.

'This certainty you possess that all the time you spend in England, you have no moral obligations.'

'God's bowels, Turold!' someone growled.

'Let him speak!' Turold replied. 'If he fails to satisfy, I'll kill him myself.'

The champion locked gazes with the lad, and Cerdic knew that he wasn't joking. Turold's own reputation now was riding on the spiel he'd prepared himself to give them.

'This led you to make reckless uphill charges against King Harold's shieldwall,' Cerdic said. 'Because you thought the forces opposing you were churlish rogues who'd flee in the face of genuine might. Your duke will boast of his victory that day, but you men of Tancarville know the truth. You saw the piles of Norman dead. Many were your friends and colleagues. Several weeks ago, Lord Joubert requested first place on the boat-bridge because he thought the English subhumans were broken.'

Joubert scowled in response, but there were equal scowls directed at him. If he'd had his way that night, their burnt, drowned husks would all be at the bottom of the Thames.

'It led you to your attack on the citizens of London this afternoon,' Cerdic said. 'Because even though they clearly weren't warriors, to your eyes they were non-people. Rodents, who could be disposed of without a second thought. And now you have besmirched your new king's coronation with the blood of those he hopes to rule. He will never raise you up for as long as he reigns.'

Shouts and curses echoed.

'And *you* can reverse this situation?' It was Roland. He'd come into the room behind Cerdic, and stood with goblet in hand. '*You?* A half-starved wretch?'

'It's true, my lord,' Cerdic said, still addressing Count Cynric, who remained steadfastly blank of expression. 'I *am* half-starved. Only the generosity of a fellow captive, sharing her food with me, has kept me alive this long. But I can forgive all that if you can help me now.'

'Weren't you supposed to be helping us?' Will Malet wondered.

'We can help each other. Lord Cynric... I told you two days after Senlac Ridge, the same day you spared my life, that I am heir to a great estate. I proved it with the ring of my fathers.' He referred here to the signet ring bearing his family's Boar's Head crest, which he'd worn during the battle and which his captors had purloined afterwards, but with which he'd persuaded them that he was of noble blood. 'I stand to inherit an entire earldom in the north of England. It has farm fields and orchards, hunting chases straddling forest and moor, a river that leaps with salmon, trout and pike. There are dozens of prosperous villages attached to it, and many minor holdings... manors, as you Normans would call them. If you'd rather seize portable wealth, there is also silver beyond counting. All of this can be yours.'

'Silver beyond counting?' someone said sceptically.

'Buried on the estate,' he replied. 'And as sole survivor of my family, only I know where it is. So, even if the king demands you stand aside for him, you can carry that wealth away and bury it somewhere of your own choosing first.'

He paused, awaiting a response.

His audience waited also, firelight gleaming on their sweat-soaked faces.

Turold glanced around at everyone. 'You've certainly created interest. But wherever this magical place is, how can it be ours if our new-made king refuses to grant it to us?'

'There's talk that the king returns to Normandy next month,' Cerdic said. 'No doubt he needs rest. But all that time the debates will rage about who is owed what. Already, I hear, certain sellsword captains have slunk away with their companions to seize what they can while the seizing is good.'

There were grumbles of discontent. Clearly, many of those here were concerned about the same thing. It was bad enough that they'd been discredited through Joubert's actions, but even if they hadn't been, the oath-sworn elements of the Norman army were now expected to wait patiently for rewards that might never come while the lawless camp-followers were dividing the spoils.

'My lords!' Cerdic shouted. 'If the king is heading to Normandy, when will he return here? A year from now? Two years? Even then, how soon will he travel north? It could be half a decade, maybe longer...'

Roland settled himself on a bench. 'If you're saying we should just head north because we can have what we like there and no one will interfere, the king has taken measures against that by striking a bargain with the earls Edwin and Morcar.'

Cerdic faltered. This was something he hadn't heard about.

'It's true, Cerdic,' Turold said. 'Aren't they your leading men in the north? Both have agreed to disband their armies and submit to the king at a place east of London called Barking Abbey.'

Cerdic's thoughts raced, but the simplest answer was always to tell the truth.

'Firstly, and I feel treasonous just saying this, my lords, but I wouldn't trust Edwin and Morcar. They could have brought forces to join Harold Godwinson on Senlac Ridge, but they didn't. They could have turned London into a bastion, but they withdrew, left the Aetheling no option but to hand himself over.'

'One might call this sensible,' another said, 'given how much we now hold.'

Cerdic gave him a pitying look. 'You hold nothing of this realm. Your duke calls himself king, but all your soldiers are here, in its southeast corner.'

'We captured Winchester too, you whelp,' Joubert spat.

'One city... the capital of a kingdom that no longer exists. A place of symbolic value because old King Edward's widow resides there.'

'And the home of England's royal treasury,' Roland reminded him.

'All the money in the world means nothing to you here if King William ships it back to Normandy,' Cerdic said. 'My point is that from your perspective, northern England goes on and on. And whatever the earls Edwin and Morcar say, you'll have to fight for every inch of it. Its landscape is mountain and forest the like of which you Normans can't imagine. Even before my people came, a race of Britons lived there. The Brigantes. So fierce even the Romans failed to quell them. You think they are gone?' He shook his head. 'They make up the bulk of the population, though now their numbers are bolstered by Viking settlers from Ireland who only accepted Saxon rule after decades of resistance. And you expect them simply to accept yours?'

Only the spit and crackle of logs filled the cavernous silence. For many there gathered, the fight on Senlac Ridge had been the hardest of their careers. Few had lost so many friends in a single day. The thought of going through all that again, maybe more than once, put a genuine chill in their bones.

'My lords,' Cerdic said, 'your new king may go proudly home to Normandy, so those who were too cowardly to come here can cheer him in the streets. But I assure you, he's king of nothing until he conquers these other lands.'

He paused again, praying that he hadn't overstepped the mark.

'You're quite a speaker,' Count Cynric finally said. 'And a tad cocksure.' He shifted position. Though ravaged by pain and weakness, he remained stolidly cold. Whatever his real thoughts were, the count's key strength was clearly that he never gave anything away. 'You've explained how impossible a task this looks to be. I presume you're now going to tell us why it isn't?'

'My lord, you won't capture anything in the north without a colossal army,' Cerdic replied. 'And without the king, you won't have that. Even *with* the king, it would be a fruitless endeavour on *your* part. After today, you'll gain neither a fishpond nor a beanfield. You know that. It's why you called this meeting. *I*, on the other hand... am more generous.'

For the first time in Cerdic's experience, Count Cynric's mouth hitched itself into a half-smile. 'And just what do you plan to be generous with? This mysterious, silver-rich earldom you won't even name?'

'My lord, withholding the name of my home, retaining this final piece of information, is my last line of protection.'

Joubert snorted. 'This lying Saxon runt has *nothing* to trade. Don't any of you realise that? He has no proof this place is real. And we're listening?'

'Once we get there, there are documents,' Cerdic said. 'Deeds, titles. All the proof you will need.'

'You won't even tell us where it is, you little bastard!'

'Why would I?' Cerdic said. 'You think any Englishman would trust *you*? Your cutthroats have killed and raped…'

'Enough of the insults!' someone shouted.

'These insults are facts!' Cerdic shouted back. He swung to face Cynric again. 'They're also the reason I'm only telling you what I trust you to know. There's a vacant seat in the north, an earldom. I can lead you to it, and I can share it with you.'

'The northern earls are Edwin of Mercia and Morcar of Northumbria,' Cynric replied. 'They will shortly surrender to the king. We know of no others.'

'Well, my lord…' Roland stood up, 'that's not strictly true.'

The room switched its attention to him.

The knight-seneschal was still a little drunk, and struggled to get his thoughts in order. But all here present knew that he possessed extensive knowledge of England and her customs. He'd made it his business to acquire such when the invasion plans had first been mooted.

'When it comes to fiefs and tenancy, the English have a strange system,' he said. 'As well as the earldoms, they have what they call "holds". Minor earldoms, semi-independent of their overlords. Over the years, several have been raised to full earldom status in response to brave deeds or useful service. This lesser magnate, who apparently will surrender with Edwin and Morcar… Waltheof, I believe he is called…'

'That's correct,' Cerdic said, remembering the name from conversations he'd overheard at Wulfbury.

'He is Earl of Huntingdon,' Roland added. 'A place we've never heard of.'

'My father benefitted from a similar promotion,' Cerdic said.

'Who was your father?' the count asked.

'I won't tell you who he was, my lord. Or where he ruled. But as I say, I *can* show you.'

'So, not only will you lead us north,' a knight called Milo de Hauteville said, trying not to scoff too obviously. 'You will also protect us from your fellow English?'

'That's my plan,' Cerdic replied.

'And will they even know you? Will they recognise your authority?'

'Some will, not all. But some is better than none, no?'

'Won't they be more inclined to listen to Edwin and Morcar?' Cynric wondered.

'Again, some will, not all. And from what I know of Edwin and Morcar, they won't care who the new lord is so long as he proves strong and loyal.'

Another profound silence followed as the count pondered.

It was Roland who broke it. 'And if we get there, won't there be a battle to fight?'

Cerdic nodded. 'Yes. Against a certain Wulfgar Ragnarsson. As I told you before. I've hidden nothing from you.'

Roland shook his head. 'I don't like this, my lord. There are many uncertainties.'

'The only certainty if we stay here is that we'll be denied the reward we were promised,' Turold replied.

Another long silence.

'How far is it?' Roland asked. 'You can tell us that much, at least.'

'I can't be exact,' Cerdic said. 'Maybe two hundred miles as the crow flies.'

The silence tautened, every man present thinking the same thing.

Two hundred miles in enemy territory...

'But we can't go as the crow flies,' Cerdic added. 'The roads will be dangerous.'

Joubert laughed. 'Even with *you* to persuade your English rats that we are virtuous men?'

'We'll be in defiance of the king,' Cerdic explained. 'And if your progress north is reported to his regents, they may send someone in pursuit.'

Fresh debates broke out. Clearly, no one was sure whether this was likely or not. The new king had been furious about the ruin of his coronation, but whether his anger would extend to prohibiting those deemed responsible from exploring possibilities in other parts was uncertain.

Now Turold spoke. 'If anyone is sent north in pursuit, they can take their pick of prey. Lord Cynric, do we seriously think we'll be the only group doing this? It isn't just the sellswords who are carving up the spoils. Bishop Odo already has the earldom of Kent, while the Count of Mortain is proclaimed Earl of Cornwall. The regents this boy talks about include William FitzOsbern and Odo himself. Can you imagine two worse hellhounds to put in charge of your enemy's corpse? There won't be a scrap of meat left for the rest of us.'

The count thought on this.

Cerdic watched him carefully. No doubt he shared his champion's concerns, but maybe wondered if there were closer demesnes he could lay his hands on when the scramble for land commenced. Not that this would help when the new king returned from Normandy, as anyone within reach who'd defied his orders would be smitten easily. It was just conceivable that someone he disliked might be tolerated if their acquisition was so far away that it would take a huge effort simply to reach them.

'The way I see it,' Turold said, 'we may miss out on a great deal more in England than we ever anticipated.'

'And we may die chasing a faerie tale,' Joubert objected.

'You weren't chasing a faerie tale when you came here,' Cerdic countered. 'The pot of gold was yours. It's no one's fault but your own that it's been withdrawn.'

The count's son's face creased with anger. He slid his longsword from its scabbard. 'I've had just about enough of you...'

'Put that steel away!' his father said sternly.

Joubert blinked at him in surprise.

'Do as I command!' the count insisted, immediately cringing and gasping, though Joubert, chastened, did as he was told.

Roland approached the high seat, but the count signalled that all was well. Gradually, he recovered himself. 'Roland... we will discuss this further. But not in the presence of this boy.' He directed a narrow glance at Cerdic. 'I don't trust you, sirrah. You're English, you hate us. But we must weigh that...' the glance he gave his son was brief but disdainful, 'against other matters.'

Joubert stood rigid, humiliated as well as enraged, but holding his peace.

'Leave us.' The count waved Cerdic away. 'We'll talk on this more.'

Roland marched the lad to the door, one hand clamping his shoulder.

'You're certainly brave,' he said quietly. 'To promise so much.'

'There'll be blood too, I fear. A lot.'

'There always is.'

CHAPTER 13

'What are you doing?' Yvette said. 'You're going to give them your earldom?'

Cerdic ought to have known she'd have followed him into the bishop's house, even though he'd advised against it. She was waiting outside the main hall, clearly having heard every word.

He walked away. 'You must be aware I've been teasing them with that all along.'

'Only to save your life.'

'And that worked... but I can't back down from the promise now, can I?'

'And the silver beyond counting?' She sounded astonished that he'd made such an offer.

Cerdic wasn't so much astonished as uneasy, because that part of it had been the biggest gamble. Wulfgar Ragnarsson found only eight chests of silver in Wulfbury. He'd told Cerdic that himself, but Cerdic knew that his father had buried many more. Highly likely, the first eight had been left somewhere they'd be found, meaning that any miscreant who discovered them wouldn't think to look for any others. At least, he hoped that was the case. Aethelric himself had made some reference to his father having made provision for a *geld* payment. Cerdic didn't dwell on the possibility the Nordic whoresons might have found the rest since then.

'Cerdic... the silver?'

He shrugged. 'I had to tempt them irresistibly. Their biggest fear is that any estates they seize will later be confiscated by the king. But treasure can remain undeclared. It can be moved and hidden.'

'And you're really going to give it to them? Your entire inheritance?'

'That's the carrot I dangled.' He descended the step-ladder to the ground floor.

Yvette lifted her skirts as she scrambled down after him. 'And what is your real plan?'

Cerdic walked to the storeroom where he'd seen Roland drinking wine. 'You mean at what point do I lure them all to their deaths?'

'Of course. Not that I'd approve of such.'

'At no point. At least, none of my choosing.'

As he'd hoped, there were a couple of kegs still intact. He picked one up, punched its lid loose and cast around for a cup. Two goblets sat on a shelf. He blew the dust off them, handed one to Yvette and poured them both a generous measure. He was no connoisseur when it came to wine, but it seemed a certainty the Bishop of London would only stock his home with the finest vintages. Either way, Cerdic quaffed thirstily.

'Why this change of heart?' Yvette asked, sipping at her own. 'All along, you've threatened to have vengeance, to kill them all.'

She didn't seem angry, but neither was she obviously happy. If anything, she seemed confused. And clearly was still suspicious.

He sighed. 'It's not so much a change of heart. More a change of circumstance.'

'I don't understand.'

'Duke Bastard is now King Bastard. And it's lawful. England's only contender for the throne is in the same Bastard's grasp. And he won't be released again, whatever they told him.'

'So, what are you saying? This is no feint on your part? You don't plan to lead an uprising?'

Cerdic snorted wine. 'An uprising?'

'That's what I've feared all along.'

'How could I do that with Edwin and Morcar compliant?'

'When you regain your earldom.'

'An uprising.' He shook his head. 'Forgive me, Yvette, but regaining my earldom feels like challenge enough.'

She thought on that. 'This Viking... this Wulfgar...?'

'Yes, he's currently in the way.'

'But if Count Cynric kills him, as you intend, you'll then have House Tancarville in your way.'

'What remains of them.' He poured himself another foaming cup. 'Wulfgar won't be easy to dislodge. In addition to that, I undersold the dangers House Tancarville may face on the road north. I anticipate that whenever this thing is over, they, or the Northmen, or whoever is left, will be considerably weaker than they are now.'

'And what then?'

'Give me a chance, Yvette. I'm doing this on the hoof.'

'You're still playing a dangerous game.'

'You heard Count Cynric.' He gulped away the last of his second cup. 'I've no future as a hostage.'

She watched him as he refilled for a third time. 'And now you plan to get drunk?'

'It's Christmas Day, remember.'

'I can think of a better way to spend it.'

Suddenly, he was intrigued. 'You... you can?'

She took the cup off him and snatched his hand. 'Come.'

'Where?'

'This is something you'll enjoy. I found it earlier, while looking for you.'

More than curious, he allowed her to lead him down a flight of stone steps into a chilly undercroft, where they passed beneath a stone arch into an open paved area, in the middle of whose floor there was a deep recess. It was rectangular in shape, perhaps six feet by ten, and about three feet deep. Its interior was lined with colourful mosaics, images along its sides and bottom depicting fishes of various sizes. Similar decoration adorned the room's neatly plastered walls: frescoes portraying brown-skinned folk in togas, standing in fruit gardens or dancing in gay parade.

'A bathhouse,' she said.

'A bathhouse?' He'd heard of such things, but never thought he'd see one.

'A luxury the Roman people enjoyed. Lady Edith had one installed at her home in Walsingham. It seems that Bishop William enjoyed his comforts too.'

'How does it work?'

She approached a stone dais to one side of the recess, on top of which sat a fire-blackened stone box with a hinged door on the front, clearly a stove, and a hefty steel tank on top. She opened the door, exposing a pile of ash, though dull orange light glimmered at its heart.

'You see these coals?' she said. 'They're still warm. One takes these.' She lifted a pair of bellows from a hook on the wall, pumping air into the stone box. Immediately, small flames flickered to life. She grabbed a handful of kindling from a basket on the floor, fed it into the flames, to raise them higher, then shovelled in some coal from an iron scuttle. She closed the door again and tapped the steel tank. 'This is called the cistern. At Walsingham we filled it via a natural spring. Here, we open this, I think...' She lifted a slat blocking a copper pipe slanting down to the cistern from the wall, 'and water sluices in from the river.'

Cerdic listened as water pattered into the steel interior.

'And the hot coals heat the water?' he said.

'And when it's piping hot, we open this gate.' She indicated another slat, blocking the end to a second pipe, which dropped from the cistern to a narrow gutter cut into the paved floor. 'This in its turn leads to the bath.'

Cerdic looked askance at the cistern, which was already shooting steam from two different vents. 'And we climb into it?'

'Of course.' She threw off her shawl.

'Won't it scald us?'

'You have to be wary of the temperature.' She crossed back to the cistern, opening another small hatch and peeking in. More steam pumped out. 'But your body can adjust. This will soon be ready.'

She opened the second gate, and hot water gurgled down the pipe, running freely along the gutter and pouring into the bath. Pleased, she removed her cloak and unlaced the front of her kirtle.

He eyed her nervously. 'What are you doing?'

'You northerners don't bathe with your clothes on, surely?'

'We usually just go in a quiet part of the river.'

'This will be more pleasant.'

He watched, captivated, as she lifted off one garment after another.

Eventually, wearing only a thin, thigh-length shift, she crossed the room to where a bundle of towels hung alongside the cistern. She glanced at him again, arching an eyebrow at the fact he was still fully dressed.

'Surely you're not embarrassed after everything that's happened between us?' She took off her shift. 'The other night we had to put our feet in each other's crotches just to prevent our toes freezing.'

He nodded vaguely.

The bath was now several inches full. The water, though brackish from the river, swirled and steamed enticingly. He said nothing. He was simply too distracted by the sight of Yvette nude, displaying a body a goddess would have been proud of, as she lowered herself into it.

'Look, there's even some soap.' She pried a bar of tallow-coloured material from the tiles on the bath-side. 'Get in. Try it.'

'Soap?' he said warily.

'Your English soaps stink foully.' She was already working the bar across her hands and slender arms, leaving creamy suds in its wake. 'They're pure animal fat. This one is a recipe from the Romans. It has olive oil in it too, and perfume. Lady Edith had this imported for her own bathhouse. It's much softer and it smells better. Get in while the water's hot.'

Slowly, helplessly self-conscious, Cerdic stripped his ragged clothes off, and climbed gingerly down alongside her. It was hotter than he'd ever experienced before, but not unbearable, and he soon found himself relaxing. The gashes and bruises covering his wasted form were immediately soothed, the stiffness eased from his joints. The soap suds filling the water only helped with that. He found himself lying flat, even submerged. The slow dissipation of the dirt encrusting his hair and flesh was rapture. When he broke the surface again, he sucked in lungfuls of air. It was warm and wet, but invigorating too.

Yvette though, despite having encouraged him to strip, had flinched at the sight of the scars criss-crossing his limbs and body.

He saw her face. 'What's the matter?'

'You must be strong to survive what they've done to you.' She blinked away a tear. 'I'd never have thought my people could be so cruel.'

'Even after everything you've seen them do?'

She bit her lip, unresponsive to that.

Fleetingly, he was puzzled, though he supposed that you could witness atrocious deeds and block the horror out if the victims were people you didn't know. Maybe he, Cerdic, was the first person of genuine acquaintance whom she'd seen brutalised. It gave him a strange feeling in his stomach. On one hand, it was nice to be liked so much that your pain made others sad. On the other, he didn't want her to think him a victim. He didn't feel like one. All wheels turned. This one would too, and when it did, he'd be ready.

'I'm sorry you've been mistreated,' she said again.

'Well... I did kill a number of your duke's men.'

She slid forward until she was directly alongside him, motioning for him to dip his head. He complied. 'At least the wound on your scalp has healed,' she muttered.

He felt at it, touching the jagged line of tissue. It had stung for days, but there was no sensation there now. Yvette sat back, her eyes moist.

'Such cruelty. All those people today. They died, doing nothing wrong. And we're sitting in a bath.'

'If we stayed dirty, would that bring them back?'

'So many people, Cerdic...'

'They tend to blend into one after a time.'

She shook her head. 'We shouldn't let them.'

'We can try, but we can also be clean.'

He took the soap off her and rubbed it between his hands, creating a rich lather. She was right; the only soaps he'd known prior to this had felt like stone and reeked of rotten flesh.

She watched him. 'How do you keep your spirits?'

He shrugged. 'Hatred gives you a reason to live.'

'Some would say the wrong reason.'

'Right, wrong... I fear things aren't that simple anymore.'

'You see.' She placed a hand on his shoulder. 'You said "fear". That means you know it for a bad thing.' Her fingertips traced a delicate path across his chest. Suddenly, she was sitting so close that it was impossible to ignore the curves of her body just below the water. 'Life should be about love, Cerdic. Not hate.'

'We...' He could barely speak. 'We don't create hatred, Yvette. It's imposed on us.'

'So can love be.' She leaned forward, brushing his lips with her own.

They kissed. Lightly at first, then properly, their lips fusing together, tongues probing the insides of each other's mouths, only for Cerdic to break away again.

'Yvette, we can't do this.'

'We can't?' She arched an eyebrow. 'I don't understand... you have some incapacity?' Her hand slipped down to his groin. 'Everything seems to be working.'

'We *mustn't* then.' He slid away. 'You heard what Roland said. If you go home to your father spoiled...'

'Ah yes, because then I'd be much less of a prize...'

'I'm more concerned that his anger would fall on you.'

She shook her head. 'How old are you, Cerdic?'

'I've passed my eighteenth birthday,' he said defensively. 'Four weeks ago.'

She looked surprised. 'You never mentioned that.'

'We were hanging villagers at the time. It didn't seem appropriate.'

'Well… I turned eighteen one month to the day before I met you. If I was at home, and none of these terrible things had happened, I'd be married. Most likely to a man I'd never even seen before we attended the altar, who was probably much older than me. I'd likely be working on my second or third child by now. That would be my sole duty in the world. To produce heirs for another Norman lord with more use during daytime for his longsword than his spouse…'

'What're you saying… that we're no longer children and should determine our own fate?'

'Isn't that what *you* are doing? Setting one band of foes on another, hoping you'll be the last man standing?'

'But for you it's different.'

'Why? Because of my father? Where is he now… when I need his protection most?'

'Yvette, you're more precious than I am.'

Being honest, he never felt he'd spoken truer words. She was still alongside him, and to be in such proximity to loveliness like this was tantalising. The heat and sweat of the bathhouse enhanced it. Added glow to Yvette's skin, lustre to her dark eyes, to her glistening wet tresses. The fact she was suddenly angry was provocative all on its own.

'This moment is precious,' she said. 'Or it *should* be.'

He swallowed, looking away, though his loins were on fire.

'You don't want me?' she asked.

'Of course I want you, but why would you want *me*? You've heard my scheme. You must know my chances of survival are slim.'

'That doesn't affect us *now*. Cerdic… you're the only person who's been kind to me since I was kidnapped. And you did this despite suffering terribly yourself.'

'We were two souls in torment together.'

'And now we're not. Not for this moment, at least…'

She leaned forward, but still he drew back.

'There's... something else,' he said. His pink hue owed to more than the sultry heat of the bathhouse. This was a difficult admission. 'I'm... *new* to this.'

Yvette seemed genuinely surprised. 'And you the son of an earl?'

He shrugged. 'I didn't want to mention it... didn't want to look weak.'

'You've never even lain with a village girl?'

'My father disapproved of such things.'

'I like your father the more I hear about him.'

'Many would agree. And much good it did him.'

'Well, there's no coercion here. Not now, when we're both so in need of solace.' She took his hand and put it on her left breast. He didn't grip tightly, didn't dare, but the thrill it sent through him was immeasurable; how soft and pliant the flesh, how hard the nipple. 'You like that?' she asked, the tip of her tongue running teasingly along her upper lip.

'Of course.'

'You'll like this more...'

She leaned forward a second time, and they kissed again, mouths agape, arms slithering around each other, the lad drawing the lass's supple body hard into his own.

'Well, well!' came an amused voice.

They sprang apart. A tall indistinct figure stood over them in the steam.

'And all this time in that covered cart, Cerdic,' – it was Turold – 'I thought you were studying the Frankish tongue.' He guffawed. 'I didn't realise you were studying *a* Frankish tongue.'

'We weren't doing that,' Cerdic hastened to explain.

'I don't blame you, by the way.' Turold eyed Yvette so lustily that she covered herself with her arms even though she was mostly under the soapy water. 'But you two are fortunate it's me who came in here and not someone else.'

'It's a private thing,' Yvette said flatly. 'No one else needs to know about it.'

Turold laughed again. 'There are no private acts here. Not at present.'

'We're not children, sir knight.'

'So I can see.'

'You could look away, at least.'

'Why should I? I've long been an admirer of beauty.'

Yvette scowled. 'You certainly can't be referring to Cerdic. You see the hurts your friends have inflicted on him?'

Turold became serious. 'Not my friends. But trust me, those marks would be nothing if Joubert had found you in here.'

'I agree,' Cerdic groaned. 'This would be all the excuse he'd need.'

'Why does Joubert hate Cerdic so?' Yvette demanded.

Turold mused on that. 'Because he was put aside once before, and now he senses it again.'

'He has an older brother?' Cerdic asked.

'The count has two other children,' the knight replied. 'Aliza, his daughter, is the youngest. But Dagobert, his other son, is the eldest. He wields power in Tancarville currently, in lieu of his father's return, and will inherit all on Cynric's death. But he's only one year older than Joubert, and something of a dunderhead. Joubert has long believed himself a better option. Other observers would make it even money who'd be the worst, though Joubert, I think, has sharper instincts. And right now, his instinct tells him there's more to Cerdic than meets the eye. And that troubles him.'

'It doesn't trouble you?' Yvette asked.

Turold chuckled. 'Cerdic is clearly more of a wolf than even I thought, my lady. But no, it doesn't trouble me. Nothing troubles me. I've never met a problem yet I couldn't cut down with my longsword. And that goes for Cerdic too. As he well knows.'

Cerdic nodded grudgingly.

'Lord Joubert would have you hobbled for this,' the knight said. 'He's sworn as much. He'd have your ankles broken. He'd have you crawl to your northern stronghold on all fours. Just to ensure you know your place.'

'Wouldn't his father overrule him?' Yvette asked.

'Maybe. Now that he needs him to show us the way.'

Cerdic sat bolt upright. 'You're saying we're going north?'

'We are. And this time you ride your own horse. Count Cynric says we can't be weighed down by a baggage train.'

'Yvette can ride too,' the lad said hurriedly.

Turold glanced from one to the other, amused. 'Yvette comes with us?'

'Isn't she Count Cynric's hostage?'

'The count is holding her for the king.'

'Has the king demanded she be turned over?' Cerdic asked.

Turold mused on that. 'Not as I'm aware. But he will.'

'When? When he's learned that the Leopard of Tancarville is already defying him by seeking his fortune elsewhere?'

Turold smiled at that. 'In truth, I don't think the Leopard even remembers that we have Yvette in our charge.'

'Is it your duty to remind him?' the girl asked.

'It would make more sense if you didn't,' Cerdic said quickly. 'At some point the king will demand to know why one of his barons has seized an earldom. There'll be a debate, maybe a dispute, maybe worse. Yvette will be an effective bargaining chip.'

'Plus, if you handed me over now,' Yvette added, 'the king might wonder why. It might be forewarning him that Count Cynric has other plans.'

The knight glanced from one to the other, noncommittal either way.

'I understand that you're loyal to your overlord,' Cerdic said. 'But things could be much worse for Yvette than they are with us. Count Eustace already has half an eye on her.'

'Would you even be showing disloyalty if you let me stay?' Yvette asked. 'You've received no orders to hand me over. When you proceed north just take me along. You are only doing as you were told.'

Turold snorted with laughter. 'You two could convince a man the sky is green and grass blue.'

'You're a good friend to us, Turold…'

The knight raised a hand. 'I'll need to consult Roland first. But he likes you both. And that's in your favour.'

'When do we leave?'

'Tomorrow, cockcrow.' He retreated through the steam. 'So, whatever you're doing here, don't drag it out.'

Cerdic swung to face her. 'We're going north. I can't believe it. Yvette, I'm going home. Oh, did I do the right thing asking for you to be brought with us?'

She sighed. 'Should I say it again? You're the only person who's been kind to me since I was abducted. Why would I want to go anywhere else?'

'You don't seem happy.'

'Our moment has passed, I fear.'

Cerdic had to admit that his own ardour had cooled a little. 'It's probably for the best.'

'Of course.' She climbed from the bath. 'Now you can get on with your war.'

'I've told you, there won't be a war.'

'The war in your head, Cerdic.'

Grabbing a bunch of towels, she rubbed herself down. His desire stirred again as she stood on the bathside, shamelessly naked, rolling wads of fluffy material up and down her shapely legs, across her belly and breasts. But she'd stung him too.

'You talk as if I've no right to feel angry,' he said.

'What does my opinion matter? I'm a mere chattel, a bargaining chip.'

'I only said that to make Turold see sense.'

'I know it's not your fault.' She pulled her clothes over her head. 'Even if every word of it is true.' She left the bathhouse without a backward glance.

Cerdic sat confused. He wasn't quite sure how he'd vexed her, but he wondered if that momentary spark between them – which had definitely been there, of that there'd been no doubt – was something she now regretted, and maybe she wasn't content to blame herself for it, but him too. Women were a foreign land in so many ways.

More understandable was her reluctance to condone his scheme for their arrival in the north. However he dressed it up with his grandiose plans to unleash one foe on another, he'd still be making war. She'd been right about that. But where she was wrong was in her assumption that the war started in England by Harald the Hardraada and William the Bastard was otherwise over. The new maleficent King of England might now be crowned and enthroned, and already drunk on his own triumph, while Cerdic's fanciful ambition to destroy him – which he'd once boasted about to Yvette's face – might now have been tamed into something more manageable, but this war was not over at all.

'Not yet.' He settled back into the water's soapy caress. 'Not by half.'

PART TWO

VARGRKIND

CHAPTER 14

The village fields had been stripped of their crops. There'd been time enough for that. But they hadn't been cleared of stubble and no one had re-tilled them, hacked brown tussocks still poking through the uneven blanket of snow. Quite close to the edge of one, just beyond the ditch separating it from the trampled lane, the cross-like timber structure where once a ragged, straw-stuffed mannequin had hung, now bore a different burden, though its purpose was still to serve as a warning.

It was anyone's guess what age the fellow had been when they'd put him there, or whether he'd still been alive or was already dead when they roped him in place, his arms extended and looped over the back of the crossbeam, but the few tatters he wore were stiff with frost, his ribs and limbs withered to greyish sticks. More snow sat unbroken on his head and shoulders, while icicles hung from the blackened remnant of his face.

Cerdic reined his horse up in shock. Roland, riding beside him at the head of the troop, also slowed to a halt. A single raven perched on the dead man's shoulder regarded the newcomers with a near contemptuous lack of fear or even interest.

'So, now crucifixion returns to England,' the lad said, to which the knight made no reply. 'Well, if nothing else, my lord, your ancestors would be proud.'

Ahead, the muddy, icy road opened out into what might once have been the village centre, though it was mostly still covered with unbroken snow, while the houses and shops encircling it were blackened ruins.

'What's this?' a Frankish voice called. 'The arms of Cynric of Tancarville, no less!'

The entire company was girt for war. Even Cerdic wore a thick woollen jerkin with a coif attached, and over that a chain-mail hauberk and a heavy Norman cloak. Roland wore his mail coif and a helmet, while atop the pole slotted into the leather pannier on his horse's flank, Count Cynric's Leopard banner billowed in the winter breeze.

Another Norman walked across the snow towards them, leading a sleek beige mare and carrying his own helmet. He was of brawny build, his heavy brutish features riven by aged scars. He smiled as though amused, exposing brown spades for teeth. 'So, you haven't been sent back to Normandy to wallow in your disgrace?'

Roland didn't smile back. 'Who are you?'

'Hugh d'Ivry.' The knight offered a curt bow. 'I fought on the duke's right flank at Senlac Ridge.'

Roland didn't bow in return. 'What's happened here?'

'This is my claim,' Hugh d'Ivry replied.

On raised ground to the right stood a five-sided stone tower, doubtless Roman in origin. Firelight shone within and smoke hung overhead. Men appeared to be working on its roof, replacing many of the old and broken tiles with new timber slats. Down below, villagers in tatters, many caked in blood and dirt, passed logs uphill in a human chain, while others near the top fought to erect them into a crude palisade. Mounted figures in mail shouted curses at them.

'They call it Harlow,' D'Ivry said. 'Or so I'm told. It matters not. I'll shortly be renaming it. Comprises ten manors at a rough estimate. Runs from here to a river called the Stour, and even beyond that.' He climbed proudly into his saddle. 'As of this moment, I'm lord of all you can see.'

'All I can see is fire-damage,' Roland replied.

D'Ivry shrugged. 'There are five villages in this vicinity alone. I thought we could live without one if it taught the others their place in the world.'

'What about the people who lived here?' Cerdic asked.

D'Ivry glanced at him curiously, presumably wondering about his English accent.

'They have no complaints,' he said. 'Most are over there.' He nodded to a distant ditch, the jumbled contents of which were half-concealed by snow.

'Burying the evidence?' Roland asked.

D'Ivry gave another brown-toothed smile, but his eyes were colder now. On the hill, Cerdic saw that several additional mailed figures had emerged from the tower.

'What did they do to deserve that?'

'Defied me,' D'Ivry replied.

'Defied *you*?' Roland feigned outrage. 'How dare they?'

The knight glared at him, which Cerdic could not have imagined happening back in Normandy. Roland Casterborus was of visibly higher status than this fellow. A banneret in the service of nobility, a count's seneschal. But here in England where many were only present because they'd been told they could glut themselves on English wine and women, and pocket all the riches they could seize, things were different.

'Hugh d'Ivry!' another voice said in greeting.

Turold approached, his longsword slung over the back of his bearskin cloak, a chain-mace coiled at his waist. He removed his helmet as he drew closer.

D'Ivry laughed aloud. 'Turold de Bardouville. You scoundrel. So, you found your rightful place... in a legion of the damned.'

'My mother said I'd never come to anything good,' Turold replied.

D'Ivry laughed again. 'You could learn much from this fellow, banneret. He lets his sword do the talking.'

'You need a lesson in manners,' Roland replied.

Again, D'Ivry looked amused. His followers, such as they were, and all had the looks of rogues, had now ridden down the tower track to join him, but hung back uncertainly as more and more retainers of House Tancarville poured into the village.

For his own part, Hugh d'Ivry was not intimidated.

'Don't pretend you people have the right to teach us,' he said. 'I know what you're about. After that debacle at the West Minster, our new king won't give you a share in anything. You might serve a mighty name, but here you're in the shithouse with the rest of us. You'll get nothing unless you take it yourself.' He glanced past them, spotting someone else approaching. 'My noble lords!' He leapt from his horse, affecting a humble bow. 'What a fine winter's day. Might I welcome you to Harlow?'

'You've had trouble here?' Joubert asked, noting the pit filled with corpses.

Count Cynric sat mounted alongside him but said nothing. He was cocooned in furs, but he watched their host through slitted eyes.

'Nothing we couldn't resolve very quickly,' D'Ivry said.

Joubert nodded. 'These English need a firm hand. I don't think they've quite realised that yet. But in time they'll get used to it.'

'My thoughts too. My lords, why don't we repair to my tower? I can offer a warm fire and refreshments of a sort.'

Joubert glanced at Count Cynric, who, after brief uncertainty, gave an imperceptible nod. Like his seneschal, he appeared to have taken an instant dislike to this new fellow, but they'd been in the saddle for several hours, and a rest was called for. While the noblemen proceeded towards the tower track, D'Ivry hurrying alongside them, ingratiating himself, Roland turned to Turold. 'Who is he?'

'Nobody,' Turold replied. 'A penniless vagabond who I wouldn't trust to look after my worst enemy's pet hounds.'

'He's obviously captain of this band of jackanapes.'

'If so, it's a position he'll have appointed himself to.'

'Is this the way of it now?' Cerdic asked. 'Any low-born beast can claim a lordship?'

'You yourself said it,' Roland replied. 'Even William of Normandy can't capture every part of this land on his own.'

'But if it's dog eat dog, won't that attract the worst of the worst?'

'Whatever works,' Turold said. 'Just remember, the most dangerous dog of them all is still our new king.'

—

After Harlow, they headed northwest to avoid the fen country. All the way, mile upon mile, every habitation lay in Norman hands. Often, there was an air that these forced occupations had been long in the planning. The standards of high-ranking barons fluttered from elevated points of land, and normal business, such as was possible on a snowy day in January, proceeded, only now with Frankish spearmen astride horses watching villagers and townsfolk with quiet menace. In larger homesteads, hearth-smoke rose from the long-hall chimneys, servants hurrying about their duties, but it was Norman men-at-arms who manned the stockades.

At a place called Luton, an enormous earthwork was under construction. A range of men, women and children, all dirtied and frostbitten, struggled against the hard-frozen earth with picks and shovels, while men-at-arms bearing the colours of Ralph de Tosney stalked back and forth.

'The king's standard-bearer is building his own damn castle,' Roland said. 'The cat hasn't even returned to Normandy and already the mice are playing.'

Cerdic was fascinated but appalled too, though every day now he understood better the nature of the Norman baronage. Though William the Bastard's army had proceeded in good order from Senlac Ridge, laying waste to English holdings regularly and purposely but never once breaking into anything resembling a chaotic horde, many parts of it had splintered away to stake their own claims while their commander-in-chief was preoccupied with advancing on London, and not just those mercenary scum who'd been known as robbers from the outset.

'None of these seats are officially vacant,' he said. 'The title holders might just be in hiding.'

Turold shrugged. 'Any English who fought on Senlac Ridge will be disinherited as punishment. I hear tell the Abbot of Saint Edmund's has been invited to prove his loyalty by surrendering all those estates once belonging to thegns of his slain in the battle. As for the living, there's no point them even returning to these properties. And most likely, they've realised that.'

'And if they died, and left heirs?'

'Those heirs might be able to redeem their family lands... for crippling ransoms.'

'What if they died at Fulford or Stamford Bridge, fighting the Hardraada?' the lad wondered. 'He was a mutual enemy of ours?'

Turold chuckled as he kicked his horse ahead of them. 'That, I feel, is a question for our honoured seneschal.'

Roland gave it only brief thought. 'If and when the king sees fit to hold hearings to establish who possesses what in this new kingdom of his, they'll be invited to make a case.'

'You mean they would if it was *you*?' Cerdic said.

Roland didn't reply but gazed directly ahead.

Cerdic persisted. 'I wonder, Roland, how all this rests with your chivalrous ideals?'

'A key aspect of the code is the obedience one shows to his overlord.'

'No matter how foul the orders he issues?'

'Knighthood is about service, Cerdic. And loyalty.'

Cerdic thought on this. 'I discussed it with Turold the other day. He is less impressed by the code than you.'

'You tell me this as if I'd be surprised.'

'He tells me that other aspects of chivalry involve the defence of Holy Mother Church, the defence of the weak and vulnerable, and particularly the defence of women and children.'

'All this is true.'

'It's laudable. But what about Hugh d'Ivry? He boasted that he'd filled an entire trench with villagers' corpses, women and children included.'

'We weren't there to prevent it,' Roland said quietly.

'But we could have taken appropriate action afterwards, could we not? Instead of supping with those responsible, we could have killed them.'

'That would have been revenge, not justice.'

'Sometimes I confuse the two.'

'*Don't!*' Roland turned in his saddle. For half a moment, he was uncharacteristically angry, his scarred but solemn face flustered, as though he was engaged in some deep struggle underneath. With an effort, he got control of himself, turning frontward again. 'There's something you need to understand, Cerdic, which you plainly don't as yet. The best way to protect the inhabitants of this realm is to restore order.'

'Ah... *that's* what we're doing?'

'*We?*'

'I'm one of you now, whether I like it or not.' Cerdic was openly vexed by the mere thought of this. 'At least, what remains of my people think I am.'

'They don't understand either. All that's happened here is that one dynastic power has replaced another. The people themselves needn't suffer.'

'Perhaps you can tell them that. Those who once had land, homes and families.'

Roland gazed stubbornly forward. 'Once resistance ceases, the reprisals will end.'

'These aren't reprisals, Roland. These are cruel, verminous men doing cruel, verminous things. And to people who have no one left to fight for them.'

'Restore order, and law will follow. And it will be a good law.'

'It won't be the law of chivalry. Do right on every side. Is that not another of its key commandments? Always be generous? Give largesse to all?'

'In due course, Cerdic, the law will prevail.'

And that was all the knight-seneschal would say on the matter, though the further north they ventured, the more the Norman occupation thinned out, and the more that rule of law appeared to diminish.

Crossroads gibbets and leafless winter trees dangled with frozen, creaking forms. More and more, they encountered small refugee camps tucked away from the road amid copses or thickets, huddles of frightened country folk scampering off into even deeper, darker places. Many of those they caught bore the marks of whipping or branding. Others had had limbs lopped or broken, but all wore the haggard expressions of the terrorised and traumatised. They couldn't look their Norman captors in the eye, but chose to crawl on their bellies, gibbering, rather than stand up and answer questions. When the company came to farms or villages now, they found the defences torn down, the buildings and granaries gutted by fire. Animals lay slaughtered in fields or fishponds, fouling the latter with blood and offal. Orchards and vegetable gardens were reduced to charcoal.

'Why do this?' Yvette protested. 'Stealing is one thing, but why desolate the land?'

'More likely these people did it themselves,' Turold replied. 'What say you, Cerdic?'

Cerdic couldn't deny the possibility that some of the English landowners who'd survived the Senlac apocalypse might have come home with only one course in mind: deny the invader everything. And when they came to properties that remained intact, it was easy to see why, for these companies on the extreme edge of the enemy's advance were the true flotsam of Normandy. Masterless men who were less than sellswords. Cutthroats and ruffians from the gutters of Nantes and Rouen, who announced themselves with drunken, ribald shouts from the interiors of halls, whose savage hounds roamed freely, nuzzling at corpses, who'd fitted locks to outbuildings so they could fill them with captives, for the most part these handsome, golden-haired women of a type they'd never seen before, but who now they used as sexual playthings, and when they were done, turned them into skivvies and scullions.

One such group of human dregs had even posted a guard. This was at a place called Woburn. The lone guard leaned half-asleep on his spear beside a fire-blackened gateway. When he saw the new arrivals, he dashed into the hall, shouting. A crowd of men came out, most only half-dressed, brandishing a variety of mismatched weapons.

If Cerdic had been armed, he'd have ridden into them at full pelt.

And for once, he wasn't alone.

'Inbred, gap-toothed swine!' Joubert roared. 'Whom do you serve?'

'You, my lord... if you'll have us,' one replied with an idiot grin. Clearly he was their leader. He was obese and wore a leather corselet which came halfway down his bowlegs and was stained by wine and food.

'Whoreson dog,' Joubert snarled. 'Get your egg-sucking rabble out of that building. Because *we* want to use it. And make sure they take their shit with them. Have them do this in the next half-hour, and maybe – *maybe* – I won't mount your heads on every gatepost from here back to London.'

The rabble bustled wildly in their efforts to comply.

'Finally see something in Lord Joubert that pleases you?' Turold said quietly.

Cerdic stiffened. 'You expect me to admire a man because he steals from other thieves?'

'Why not? That's what you aim to have us do.'

Turold and Roland joined the rest of the count's men, dismounting in the long-hall yard.

'I know you hoped the north would be free of this,' Yvette told Cerdic. 'It *will* be. We're surely into the Danelaw now. A little further, and uncouth vermin like these won't dare show their faces.'

'It isn't just the uncouth ones,' he said tightly.

Nearby, an outbuilding had been opened to reveal a band of cowering figures. Whether they were thralls or servants or even members of the former household, it was impossible to tell. Even now they were shouted at and kicked, ordered to take care of the horses and baggage. One tall, older man, who might once have had an air of dignity, an ex-steward perhaps, was cuffed so hard by Yvo de Taillebois that he fell face-down, the knight pressing the back of his head with a boot sole until a nose bone audibly cracked. Father Jerome jerked around to look away. Cerdic thought the priest was going to vomit.

'Your flock are molested again, Father,' the lad said. 'What would the Good Shepherd say?'

The priest gave him a haunted look, the eyes wide and bright as coins in his skeletal face.

'Cerdic, don't lose control,' Yvette pleaded.

'I appreciate it's in my interest not to,' he replied. 'But it gets harder.'

'Which is why we haven't given you a sword, sirrah,' came a thin, nasal voice.

Cerdic spun around, shocked to see Count Cynric dismounting close behind him. A couple of his men assisted him, but he now seemed to have regained much of his health. There was clearly nothing wrong with his ears, because he'd evidently overheard their conversation. Fleetingly, Cerdic's blood was so hot that he didn't much care.

'We *could* have armed you,' the count added, not looking at the lad as he straightened himself. 'It might have been for the best...' He sucked in a painful breath. '*You* leading *us*... and maybe the first into any battle.' He nodded gratefully as an attendant helped him with his cloak, lacing its folds over his narrow chest. He still didn't look at the lad. 'But Turold tells us you were quite the butcher... on Senlac Ridge.' He coughed. 'So... arming *you* is not a risk we care to take. Not till the prize is in sight.'

'And as prizes go, it had better be damn well worth it,' Joubert said, also riding up, swinging down from his saddle and flinging his reins at one of the bedraggled servants. 'If it were down to me, I'd dispense with you now. Throw you to those rancid curs over there...' He indicated the mercenary band that had formerly occupied the hall, now standing on the far side of the yard, their weapons and loot heaped at their feet as they waited, somewhat hopefully, for employment. 'I'd tell them you're a princeling worth a small fortune. It wouldn't matter whether it was true or not, but I'd enjoy watching what happened when they found out you weren't.'

He strode off, pushing Yvette out of his way.

'My son harbours a deep antipathy to your people,' Count Cynric said. 'Part and parcel of being the second son. The one who must *take* things if he wishes to possess them.'

If nothing else, Cerdic understood that frustration.

'The world is his enemy, but particularly *you*, it seems.' The count smiled thinly. 'You, he fears by instinct. And after what I just overheard, maybe his instinct is correct.'

'Forgive me, Lord.' Cerdic bowed, hating himself for grovelling, but knowing when it was necessary. 'I spoke out of anger.'

'Anger is a useful thing to a warrior, young Cerdic. But pray, don't misdirect it.'

Cerdic was startled. Not just because it was the first time Cynric of Tancarville had called him by his name, but because it was near enough the first time the nobleman had spoken to him at all.

'There could be better things in the future…' Cynric coughed again, 'than you imagine.'

He hobbled off towards the long-hall, an attendant at either arm.

'What did he mean by that?' Yvette asked.

'I don't know.' But Cerdic felt uneasy. 'Better things' to a Norman could be very different from those to a Saxon.

CHAPTER 15

Concerned that too many of their countrymen were taking this unconquered part of England lightly, Count Cynric's host, which was just five hundred strong in total, now advanced north in disciplined fashion. Not that they had much choice. In normal times, Cerdic learned, it would be their strategy to leave defensible posts behind them – small, stockaded camps located every few miles in case an urgent retreat was necessary – but very soon the distance was too great for that. It would have meant leaving more and more men behind, progressively weakening their main thrust.

Thus, on open land they marched in arrowhead formation, Roland, Turold and the other leading knights at the tip, alongside Cerdic, of course, to direct. The count and those pack-animals they needed to transport vital supplies were placed in the middle where they could best be protected. The rest of the knights occupied the left and right flanks, under the command of Joubert and Yvo de Taillebois respectively, the infantry at the rear, and behind those, tagging along in sullen, disorderly fashion, the mercenaries they'd encountered, whom the count had finally employed at a staggeringly low rate (on the tacit understanding with his son and knight-seneschal that they'd be used as front-line fodder in every situation that arose).

In closer countryside, in dense woodland or traversing narrow valleys, they fell into a more regular column, but always posted flanking guards and, whenever they camped, extensive numbers of picquets.

North of Tamworth, they detected no further Norman presence, and now found homesteads occupied by their owners and closed firmly against them, farms and village huts shuttered and locked, palisades fully manned, mostly by fyrdsmen it seemed, but all of them armed. At certain times, parties of helmeted horsemen rode parallel at a distance or on high ground, and on the first couple of occasions, Joubert issued quick, curt orders, and he and his companions charged them, and always they scattered, much to he and his knights' amusement. But all this told Cerdic was that the occupants of these midland shires were alert to their presence, that they weren't looking for a fight unless pressed, but that this was their land, and the new king was king here in name only.

As the numbers of these observers grew, others in the company became nervous. Joubert and his men stopped finding it funny. No one had attacked or impeded them, but it occurred to them that the majority of the estates they now crossed were held by vassals of Earl Edwin of Mercia, and that maybe it was only the peace Edwin had made with the new monarch that prevented such a thing. So, their fate relied on the good will of an English earl they'd never met, but one whom rumour had it was notoriously fickle and who, if it suited him, could change his allegiance at a whim.

It also depended on Cerdic, who claimed to be the scion of a noble house and only had a simple carved ring to prove it. And increasingly, Cerdic heard Joubert arguing with his father about the wisdom of this.

'The English whelp is leading us to destruction!' the count's son said.

'And why would he go to all this trouble to do that?' the count replied.

'Because we slew his household on Senlac Ridge?'

'So, you admit he had a household?'

'The point is, Father...'

'The point is, Joubert, you ruined our chances of advancement with the king. And by "you", I mean *you personally*. You slaughtered innocents on the day they were supposed to become his lawful subjects, on a day that should have been glorious for him.'

'And so we head blindly into the barbarous north? Literally, into the unknown.'

'It's for *your* sake that we do this. You need land, you need a title…'

'And what will I be, Father, the Earl of Far Away?'

'We could stake your claim here, or further south. But when the king returns from Normandy, which he will, he'll snatch it off you again. How long, for instance, do you expect Earl Hugh of Harlow to last?'

Joubert never won these exchanges. Mainly because he was the one who'd muddied the waters for them. He could argue the English had tried to storm the West Minster on Christmas Day, that he'd only been defending the new king, but most of these men had been with him, and they'd know it for a lie. In response to this, Joubert said that they needed to be more aggressive in their northward march. If that meant sacking towns and villages, maybe burning a long-hall or two, so be it. To Cerdic, this was a plan that verged on the ludicrous. Here they were, driving deeper and deeper into hostile territory, continually watched by those who might turn on them, and the count's son wanted to start killing people?

Thankfully, the count overruled him on this as well.

To compensate, Joubert demanded more speed. Wherever they were going, they had to get there soon. If for no other reason, he said by the campfire one night, having guzzled more wine than was good for him, than to prove as soon as possible to 'dear old Papa' that the English wolf-cub, Cerdic, was leading them into a trap.

The following day, it was bitter again, their breath misting, fresh snow blanketing the ground, but as before, Joubert demanded speed. The sight of Yvette riding side-saddle because she hadn't been able to procure any riding clothes infuriated him. He reined his beast up, leapt down, grabbed her hand and pulled her from her mount.

Cerdic also reined up, tingling with concern.

There'd always been the potential for this to happen. Yvette was comely, and none of these men had had the company of whores for days now. When Joubert pulled a dagger and grabbed a handful of Yvette's skirt, Cerdic made to jump from the saddle himself, only for Turold to clamp his shoulder. Joubert meanwhile slid the point of his blade into the bunched material. 'Ride like a man, or you don't ride at all,' he said.

Hot saliva fizzled between his bared teeth; there was lust there as well as hate. He ripped the steel downward, slicing the garment from its waistband to its hem.

'What's happening here?' Count Cynric asked, approaching from behind.

'Speed is all, Father.' Joubert unhanded the girl and put his dagger away. 'If we wish to survive this campaign, we need to be quicker on our feet.'

Later, Cerdic dropped back until he was alongside Yvette, who now rode humiliated, her left leg exposed all the way down to her boot.

'Are you all right?' he asked, aware of the knights and men-at-arms casting lewd glances.

'If you want the truth,' she said, 'I'm not so much embarrassed as cold.'

'Of course.'

Later, they separated from the main company so that Cerdic could take off the wolfskin leggings he wore over his trousers. Yvette put them on gratefully, cross-strapping them into place, but even they only came to mid-thigh, and when she rode, a glimpse of her upper leg was still visible, and brutish men continued to steal furtive glances.

'You need to be careful of Joubert,' Roland said when Cerdic returned to the point.

'I'm well aware he hates me.'

'Are you also aware that he has many friends in this company?'

'I've been warned that Yvo de Taillebois is one I should watch.'

Roland nodded. 'He's a sword-master almost on a par with Turold. At Varaville, he killed so many French knights in nose-to-nose combat that he earned himself the soubriquet "Slayer". He carries that name still.'

Cerdic thought hard on the pugnacious black-beard. 'How is it that he rides with Joubert?'

'Joubert was squired to him when he was ten years old. They've formed a natural bond. But there are others like Taillebois in Joubert's personal *mesnie*. That's a small group within our larger group, who have sworn their fealty to him foremost. They're maybe not so deadly as Taillebois or Joubert, but they're equally pitiless.'

Cerdic pondered that. 'I don't wish to insult you, Roland, but in my eyes at least, *all* of your people are pitiless.'

'Be assured, there are some who are worse than others. And a man like Joubert will attract them all to his banner. Especially in a place like this, where men were told they could have whatever they took.' The knight paused, perhaps wondering just how much he should confide in someone who was still, basically, a prisoner. 'Count Cynric is the Leopard of Tancarville, one of Normandy's greatest nobles. And you won't need me to tell you that he didn't win that position through his generous nature. But he is a thinker as well as a fighter. And for that reason, he knows he must have limits, because without limits there will be consequences. In contrast, Joubert knows only…'

'That he'll never have power unless he seizes it for himself,' Cerdic cut in, reiterating the words of the count himself.

Roland nodded, by now getting used to the youngster's ability to read people. 'That's correct. But the men who follow him feel the same. They know they can wreak blood and havoc, because in Joubert's minor household there are no laws against it.'

'I suppose I should be glad the count has recovered.'

'We all should. But hear me out, Cerdic…' Roland's tone became deadly serious. 'The majority of Count Cynric's men are household knights. Loyal, well-trained warriors who are nevertheless desperate to be awarded lands and titles of their own. In due course, a few of their kind will earn themselves tenancies, but most know that someday, somewhere, they will die on a battlefield, never having fulfilled their dreams. That's why this group have risked everything coming to England. It was nothing to do with the pope, or the greater glory of Duke William. That's why they'll risk everything following you on this final leg of the journey. But woe betide you, Cerdic, if, when you come into this kingdom of yours, there's nothing to be had. In that case, Joubert's doubts about this mission will be seen as justified. And then there'll be nothing either I or Turold can do to protect you.'

'I appreciate the warning,' Cerdic said. 'But I've made no secret that, if there's nothing to be had, we'll all of us die there together.'

'Good.' The knight nodded again. 'Just remember... there are different ways to die. And Joubert knows them all.'

—

It was mid-afternoon, when on open pasture to the left, they saw a sheepfold under a straw-thatched roof. Ten fleecy bodies were crammed inside. On Joubert's orders, his men dragged as many out as they could, cut the animals' throats and commenced butchering them. Moments later, an outraged farm-lad came running over the meadow, wielding a crook. His eyes were crossed, his features dull-witted, but village idiot or not, he was brave when it came to his sheep.

Joubert strode towards him, sword drawn. 'What's that you say? You threatening me? In your guttural, mongrel tongue?'

The farm-lad waved the crook, protesting again. It was incoherent even to Cerdic, because the young shepherd clearly had speech impediments.

'Another unfitted to live,' Joubert replied, driving in with a single thrust.

The boy collapsed, gurgling on his own blood. Joubert yanked his sword free, then squatted down to check a shiny cross tied on a neck-thong.

'Iron,' he spat with disgust, leaving it be.

No one else in the column had participated or even openly condoned the act, though a couple muttered about the folly of having threatened Joubert with a stick, but neither did they display obvious disgust. The count himself was simply grateful to dismount, take his seat by one of the new-built fires, and anticipate his mutton dinner.

Later that evening, once the meal was complete and even though both Cerdic and Yvette had eaten their share, because though the meat was stolen, they knew they must restore themselves to strength, Cerdic requested permission to bury the shepherd boy. It was granted without a second thought, and he left the camp with a pick, a spade and an oil lamp. To his surprise, Father Jerome fell into step alongside him.

'Why are you here?' Cerdic asked.

The priest seemed surprised he should ask. 'To say the rites.'

'Aren't you tired of that? Offering prayers for the murdered, but never once condemning the murderers?'

The priest's mouth trembled, but he gazed dead ahead.

'You wouldn't be thinking of checking to see if that cross the boy wore was actually silver?' Cerdic asked. 'And that maybe Lord Joubert made an error?'

'When it comes to enriching himself, Lord Joubert seldom makes errors.'

But when they arrived at the scene, they found only a spattered gory trail leading away across the snow amid a frenzy of pawmarks.

'Wolves.' Cerdic edged backward. 'I wouldn't pray here too long, Father. They'll now have a taste for dead flesh. Even the sort that's walking around wearing priest garb.'

—

Wolves were a sure sign they were into the northern half of England. And indeed, later that night, they heard distant howls. To Cerdic, it seemed more than a little ominous.

'What if someone comes after us, seeking *wergeld*?' he asked Turold.

'*Wergeld?*' the knight replied, gnawing shreds of flesh from a sheep bone.

'The blood price. For the shepherd boy.'

Yvette watched from across the flames, visibly unsure that this was a sensible line of questioning. But the knight seemed to understand.

'You mean the murder fine?'

'That's probably a better way to refer to it, yes. But my question stands. If someone comes, will Lord Joubert kill them too?'

'What do you think?'

'Aren't we deep in enemy territory? Won't that just be inviting an attack?'

'Doubtless the lack of enemy action has made him bold,' Turold said.

Cerdic wondered about this too. Initially on embarking north, he'd been concerned that they'd be confronted by war-bands of vengeful hearth-men. That they might face battle after battle, during which he had no idea on whose side he'd be fighting, but because of which they'd lose so many that they'd be forced to retreat south. He'd purposely not sought the north–south road that King Harold had used to march from York, because it had seemed a near-certainty that ambushes would await them there. But now, it seemed, the opposite was true. No one at all had opposed them. Not yet.

Where were the housecarls who'd escaped from London? There had to be several hundred to have manned the walls of the capital alone. Had they gone to the far north, to regroup with those survivors of Fulford and Stamford Bridge? Or were they still here somewhere, refraining from attack because Edwin and Morcar had stood them down?

It was strangely disappointing to see no resistance, even though he hadn't wanted full-scale carnage. But he couldn't help wondering if the killing of the farm boy might change things. In the blackness of the Mercian night meanwhile, the wolves howled on.

'You can only prod fate with a stick so many times,' he said. 'I can smell it.'

'What's that?' Turold grunted.

'Violence.'

And before morning, violence came.

But not from the place they expected.

CHAPTER 16

The attack came while he lay huddled under a pile of fleeces in his one-man tent.

The first Cerdic knew of it, hard, sweaty hands had slammed down across his mouth and eyes. Then heavy, mail-clad bodies were on top of him, the small canvas structure crammed to bursting with bulky forms. Purely for comfort's sake, Cerdic had ceased wearing his hauberk when sleeping, but now fists rammed down into his body, driving the wind from his lungs. He had no weapon to reach for, but even if he had, it would have been no use; strong hands had pinioned his arms and wrists. He uttered muffled roars as a wad of dirty material was crammed into his mouth, then a foul-smelling sackcloth hood was pulled over his head and tightened at the neck with a tug-cord.

Bound at the wrists and ankles, he was lifted bodily outside. He heard grunting voices, feet crunching in snow. The blackness beyond the sackcloth indicated that it was still night, or at least the early hours. Then he heard muffled yelps, which sounded female.

Yvette! Her tent had been set alongside his…

He writhed in his bonds as he sensed rather than saw her being carried alongside him, but for no gain. Their assailants were too many and too strong.

The brittle cold intensified as they travelled, which meant they were moving away from the camp and the embers of the fires. Cerdic roared and struggled again, still to no avail, except that it earned him another punch in the belly, which twisted him in agony.

As their abductors put distance between themselves and the camp, they whispered less, and spoke more. To Cerdic's surprise, he heard Frankish voices. He'd expected the English, goaded by the slaying of the shepherd. As they descended a steep hill, someone slipped and fell, cursing. Cerdic dropped downward from the waist, his shoulders and the back of his head striking thick, icy snow, which slithered into his jerkin. More blows landed, as if somehow the accident had been his fault.

'God's breath!' someone swore. 'Stop arsing around! Get him down here!'

Cerdic heard that voice clearly. And recognised Joubert.

Yvette did too, because despite her gag and hood, she commenced a desperate wailing.

'Shut that bitch up!' Joubert spat.

A resounding impact sounded, a hefty hand against the side of a head, and the wailing ceased. Cerdic roared again, struggling as hard as he could.

They were carried another couple of dozen yards and dropped again, this time deliberately. He fought to get up, but a foot landed on his chest, pushing him back down.

'Don't worry, Cerdic of House Unknown. You'll get to see everything.'

Yvette's muffled wailing recommenced, briefly becoming shrill and clear. She screamed loudly, only for what sounded like another hand to slap her. Then she was muffled again, as if a fresh gag had been inserted. At the same time, Cerdic heard the distinctive *skrik-skrik-skrik* of a flint being struck, and somewhere on his right an orange glow blossomed. It reproduced itself rapidly until there were blobs of light on all sides.

'Up with him,' Joubert said.

Cerdic was lugged to his feet, only for his shins to be kicked from under him. He dropped to his knees. A hand fiddled with his neck-cord, and the hood was ripped away. He knelt blinking in the glare of several torches, unable to make out at first what was happening, though it rapidly fell into place. They were on some kind of narrow path, which ran between an upward slope on the right and a downward slope on the left. Trees grew above and below them, the snow hanging heavy on their branches and plastered up several of their trunks.

Cerdic gazed at his captors. Joubert stood on his right, grinning gleefully, his breath smoking in the orange light. Of the others, and there was a significant number, maybe twelve, he recognised all as members of Joubert's *mesnie*. He knew none of their names apart from Yvo de Taillebois, who now stood directly facing him, about ten feet away, clinging to the lower end of a rope, which led tautly upward to where it had been thrown over a bough some eight feet overhead, and then down again, to where it had been fastened around Yvette's neck.

Cerdic's damp hair prickled. Rage boiled inside him. He made to leap to his feet, only for a drawn sword to touch his throat.

'Look again,' Joubert said. 'More carefully perhaps.'

Cerdic did as instructed, eyes bugging with horror.

Yvette, who had ceased her wailing abruptly, stood stiffly on the path. Her hood had been removed, though the new gag they'd used had been tied clean around her head. Her hair hung in an untidy mess and she regarded him with sheer terror. Just to her left, he saw why. She stood on the very edge of the path, on a point of ground where the lower slope simply fell away. And even as she stood there, though she was doing everything in her power not to move, that edge, which was mostly snow rather than soil, was crumbling under her feet.

Cerdic leaned over and looked down. Twenty feet below, firelight glimmered on the glazed surface of a pond. Reeds stood up from it, sheathed thick with frost. But falling even that distance onto ice, which almost certainly would break, was hardly the problem. The problem was the noose, and Yvo the Slayer at the other end of the rope, also grinning like a demon through his dense black whiskers, and clearly strong enough to let her plummet to midway and then jerk her to an abrupt and final halt.

'For Christ's sake, Joubert!' Cerdic stuttered. The blade at his throat pressed harder. It cut the skin, blood welling out. 'This is madness! In God's name... your father holds Yvette for the king, as a means of ensuring the compliance of Count Rodric.'

'Which is why neither the king nor my father know anything about this.' Joubert walked to a point on the path halfway between the two prisoners. 'Even now my father sleeps the sleep of the dead, which I fancy may soon be a real state for him. But until that happy time, the rest of us must hide our true purposes under bushels.'

'Don't do this, I beg you.'

Joubert shrugged. 'I don't wish to. But you've forced my hand.'

'This is lunacy.'

'No. Heading north on your say-so alone, that's lunacy. You see, I know treachery when I see it.'

Because you're a master of it yourself? Cerdic thought to ask, but now was not the time.

'As such, we've reached the unhappy situation,' Joubert said, 'where this female of yours needs to hang. My father will never know, of course. He'll be told she ran away during the night. And he'll believe it, because there'll be no trace of her body.'

'We can lay her to rest down there, my lord.' Yvo the Slayer pointed at the sheet of ice. 'It'll have frozen over again by morning.'

'Perfect,' Joubert replied. 'So, it's your choice, English ratling. Tell us the truth about everything, and the girl lives. Refuse or lie… again… and she hangs.'

Cerdic met Yvette's gaze, her eyes wide and rabbit-like.

He had no doubt that Joubert meant what he said, and that he'd cover everything up as promised. It didn't matter whether Turold and Roland believed him, so long as Count Cynric did, and Count Cynric would because they were the same flesh and blood. But if he admitted now that their destination was the minor earldom of Ripon, in the greater earldom of Northumbria, of which Wulfbury, in the heart of Swaledale, was the capital, neither of their lives would be worth a penny. Joubert could dispense with both and as soon as tomorrow grab any peasant and have him show them the way.

It didn't even matter about the legal documentation Cerdic had promised. Because without Cerdic there'd be no one to be disinherited. The earldom would be vacant. All they'd need to do was take it by force of arms, and hold it until King William finally came north, at which point he'd probably grant them ownership anyway. Despite the error made at the West Minster, he'd need strong, loyal men in a region like Northumbria.

It was an impossible decision.

'You...' Cerdic's voice was querulous. 'Even if you find out where my earldom is, you won't be able to walk through the burh gate. The Vikings will slaughter you. But there's a secret way I can show you... and only *I*. So, if nothing else you need *me* alive. And that means you can't kill either of us. Because if anything happens to Yvette, I'll tell the count exactly what you did.'

It was weak. It shouldn't have made any difference. But to his surprise, Joubert seemed to take it seriously. He stood with arms folded.

'An unwise threat, English,' he said. 'I believe you would. And yet, though it might indeed be important for me to keep you alive, it would be less so for you to keep a tongue in your head.' He shrugged sadly, as though imparting a distasteful truth. 'Because, as you say, you'd still be able to *show* us.'

'And what would your father say if he wakes up tomorrow morning and finds...'

'You overestimate my father's concern for you!' Joubert lurched forward, kicking him in the ribs. 'You haven't realised that yet? You think Count Cynric's never maimed a malefactor? Never lopped a peasant's hand off for being caught with a hunting bird? Never put his eyes out for gazing on my sister? I'll tell him your constant, God-damned insolence had become too much for me. And he will accept it.'

Cringing with pain, Cerdic glanced again at Yvette. She stood with head down, her long, tangled tresses glistening with firelight. She'd accepted her fate, he realised, shocked. Was even resigned to it. She knew that he couldn't possibly tell them. For half a horrible moment, he wondered if she was going to leap over the precipice herself, to pre-empt her own murder.

'Are you actually listening to me?' Joubert wondered.

'I *am* listening, my lord,' Cerdic said. 'I just... I can't...' Suddenly, he shouted. '*Help! Someone! Turold, Roland... help us, please!*'

Joubert and his men laughed. Loudly, uproariously.

'You've really no idea how far we've brought you?' Joubert said. 'Most of them are coifed and hooded anyway. Hoods, you know... those things that cover your ears.' His men laughed louder. 'On top of that, on a night like this they're under cloaks, pelts. They won't hear a sound. And the picquets, well...' he threw another amused glance at his retainers, 'they *like* me.'

They roared their mirth again.

Apart from the one on Joubert's right.

Whose mouth was wide open, but who suddenly was gagging and choking.

He flailed about as he dropped his torch. It was only when Cerdic saw the feathered end of a crossbow bolt that he realised what it was.

A second bolt flickered through the torchlight, striking another knight in the throat.

Only then did the panic ensue.

As the first two victims toppled over, Joubert and the rest drew their swords, spinning where they stood. A third knight shrieked, pierced through the left cheek, dashing his firebrand into the face of a colleague. Another dropped his torch, clamping hands to his belly.

'Torches down!' Joubert bellowed. 'They're picking off the flame-bearers!'

The remaining lights were cast onto the path, but they still gave off sufficient glow for the marksmen to choose targets and hit them cleanly. Yvo the Slayer released the rope and scrambled forward, grabbing Joubert's arm, hustling him up the slope into the relative cover of the snow-laden trees.

The others followed, but not all quick enough, more bolts striking backs and arses.

All Cerdic could do was kneel and stare, firstly at Yvette, who still stood rigid with terror, no longer in danger of the noose, but easily vulnerable to the criss-crossing missiles, then at the several corpses already adorning the path. As he got to his feet, he sensed a Norman standing on his left. The fellow had doubled over in his efforts to extract a bolt from his thigh. He'd stood his longsword in the ground as he did, enabling Cerdic to buffet him from behind, sending him somersaulting down the slope, shattering the pond-ice and vanishing, his chain-mail carrying him straight down. Hurriedly, Cerdic slid his ropes along the upright sword's edge, shearing through, then working his ankle-blonds loose with his fingers.

Arrows still flew, but Yvette remained frozen with shock, and even as Cerdic watched, tilted slowly, the loose, snowy edge giving way. Jolted into action, she scrambled sideways, wrenching her noose off as she crossed the path and threw herself into the snow at the foot of the slope. Grabbing the longsword, Cerdic joined her. They lay together panting, more bolts flitting by overhead.

'Can you run uphill?' he asked, cutting her bonds.

She nodded, wide-eyed.

'On my count...'

'Let's just go!' She tore her gag off and jumped to her feet.

The upward slope was torturously steep, but pure fear drove them, Yvette as swift as Cerdic thanks to the slit in her skirt. They passed bloodstained snow where others of Joubert's men had been wounded, but soon were on the flat again, weaving through the trees towards Count Cynric's camp, which was easy to locate because they could hear wild shouts.

'This is a full-scale attack.' Cerdic slithered to a halt, the sweat streaming off him.

Nearby, another member of Joubert's *mesnie* lay slumped amid a tangle of roots, bolts protruding at various angles. Behind meanwhile, they sensed movement. They glanced back and saw shadowy forms prowling forward through the trees. Most carried crossbows, while others were armed with axes and spears. Thinking quickly, Yvette dropped to the ground, dragging Cerdic after her, ensuring that both of them lay on the broad bloodstain that had spilled from the dead man amid the roots. This was likely the sole reason the warriors encroaching on the camp, dozens and dozens soon stealing past this position alone, ignored them, trampled on them even.

When the horde had passed, the duo glanced up.

'Congratulations,' Cerdic breathed. 'A good ploy.'

'Except that I'm now covered in blood,' she complained.

'So long as it's not your own.'

Stumbling on through the wood, the hubbub from the camp grew louder.

They came in sight of it long before the trees ended.

Whoever the night's assailants were, they might have gone silently in among the tents and the glowing relics of the campfires, thrusting their blades into men as they slept, but by the looks of it, Joubert and his handful of survivors had got there ahead of them, alerted the picquets and now were dashing back and forth, shouting, grabbing up shields to go with their swords. The attackers thus abandoned stealth, coming out from the trees in a ragged line, their crossbowmen, who appeared to be dead-shots, at the front. As Cerdic watched, they took an immediate heavy toll, the bulk of them dropping to one knee when they loosed, each quill hitting its target squarely. Only when Count Cynric's own crossbowmen assembled along that eastern edge of his camp, still fuddled by sleep but finally returning missiles, did the enemy draw hand-weapons and charge.

Cerdic pulled Yvette down. He'd heard more voices behind them, slower units looking to rejoin their main company. Their shadows passed swiftly, hurrying out into open space. They too were carrying crossbows. Most likely, they'd been the ones who'd taken pot-shots at Joubert's men across the pond. Yvette tried to move again, but Cerdic held her tight, rising only to a half-crouch himself.

'What are we doing?' she asked.

'Waiting. I'm not getting into a fight with my own countrymen.'

'You can't fight the Normans either,' she said.

'I know...'

'Not if you need their help!'

'*I know!*' He was torn by indecision.

But then they heard the attackers shouting to each other as more of them flooded out onto the snowy meadow. And it was not in English.

To Cerdic's disbelief, it almost sounded Frankish.

He glanced at Yvette. 'What tongue is that?'

'Flemish,' she said. 'I think. I recall Lady Edith saying that Duke William brought many nationalities to feast on England's corpse.'

Cerdic wondered fleetingly if the king had caught up with them. But on reflection, it could not be that. If they'd come from the king, they'd have sought a parley first.

'Freebooters, by damn!' He jumped up, hefting the longsword. 'Good. That means there are no rules.'

CHAPTER 17

In the camp of the Normans, it was total chaos.

Many still barely aware what was happening had already been hit by missiles. Most, when they realised they were under arrow attack, took shelter behind tents and shields. Turold, who'd reacted quicker than most, still carried no shield nor wore a helmet, and was struck twice by crossbow bolts. But the iron mesh of his mail turned the first point, while the second projectile glanced away.

He ran through the camp, longsword in hand, shouting commands, detailing two strong fighters in particular, Alain le Roux and Ivan d'Avranches, to protect the count. Roland, meanwhile, issued orders for the count's own crossbows to form a defensive line and return volleys, then moved on to the paddock, recruiting more men as he went, instructing them to mount up and counterattack on horseback.

At which point, the enemy, whose total number was not far short of the count's own, five hundred, maybe more, charged in.

Turold halted, puzzled. They mostly wore heavy leather brigandines studded with steel and fitted with immense shoulder-guards. It was almost a uniform, which suggested they were an organised company. Their helmets looked Danish in that they were rounded at the crest, their nose and cheek-guards ornamented, but they weren't Vikings. Vikings didn't use crossbows, yet these fellows made excellent use of them. Even as they ran forward, they reloaded and loosed, reloaded and loosed, every bolt claiming its mark.

Another dart hurtled towards him. He evaded it, falling and rolling, and then springing back to his feet, to find himself facing several axemen who'd already hacked their way through the Norman foot. He swung in with his longsword, striking a neck with such force that his opponent went down truncated, but with his blade lodged in the exposed vertebrae. Unable to yank it free in time, Turold loosened the chain-mace from his waist and twirled it ferociously, smashing one opponent's helmet, crushing the bone beneath, and catching another across the temple, the blood and brains flying. A spear was flung. He knocked it down, but then an axe slashed the front of his hauberk, shearing it open, and as he pulled the rent links together with his free hand, someone caught the chain of his mace and tore it from his grasp. Encouraged by this, more and more of them closed in around him. Turold roared and cursed at them, but curses meant nothing when a man had no weapon.

It was the first time Cerdic had wielded a longsword in real combat, and immediately he sensed advantage in the extra half-foot of perfectly balanced steel. Back home, he'd preferred the broadsword to the battle-axe. The battle-axe had great strike-power, but was ungainly, difficult to manage at protracted close quarters. The longsword, however, had all that extra strike but was dexterous in the hand as well.

The first three he encountered, he despatched with relative ease, though they'd only been half-aware he was there, spinning to face him but too late. The fourth and fifth gave him more of a fight, but again his extended steel found their vital organs.

He raced on into the camp, where the melee was in full spate, every man for himself as a wild, disorganised battle raged between the tents. Another Fleming ran towards him, hurriedly reloading his crossbow, which, this close, Cerdic saw was of a lighter sort than that used by the Normans. The bowman glanced up at the last moment, taking desperate aim, but Cerdic's steel pierced him to the heart. Then he spied Turold, his mail hanging open, armed only with a broken spear as a whole pack of them circled him. Cerdic lurched forward, grabbing up a discarded longsword.

'Turold!' he shouted.

The knight turned, reached out and caught the thrown weapon by its hilt.

They weighed in both at the same time, slicing bone, cleaving helms and skulls. When they came together in the middle, the knight threw one arm around the lad's shoulders, clamping them together in a half-bearhug, before they went their separate ways.

Now that they were wide awake, the Normans' superior armour and weapons were telling. While overhead, the sun rose in a silver disc amid tumbles of ice-grey cloud, its bleak light spilling over the carnage, the attackers backed out of the camp towards the line of trees. Only for Roland to reappear at the head of the mounted troop he'd put together, some sixty knights behind him as they galloped through the snow on the east side of the encampment.

Many of the Flemings were so entangled with the Norman foot that they didn't see the lowered lances until they were spitted on them. Others were ridden down from the side or behind, heads smashed like turnips, bodies torn by clashing hooves.

Dozens fled into the woods, but many more found themselves corralled inside the camp, footmen blocking their front, horsemen their rear. The Normans pressed in from all sides, swords rising and falling in a bloody rain. Shields thundered as they splintered apart, blades dashed sparks from bucklers and brigandines.

Cerdic now saw that there was a handful of Vikings with the Flemings, men of infinitely larger stature, men who were hairier and more brutish, men who wore ring-mail under fur and elaborate faceplates, and who fought with the dreaded Dane-axe. This small group alone, even though they were scattered sparsely, had already accounted for many adversaries. Even the Norman cavalry suffered losses, riders yanked to the ground and smitten by seax, mattock, cudgel. Roland was unhorsed himself when a spear caught him in the armpit. It failed to penetrate his hauberk, but he fell heavily, his nose gouting blood as he scrambled back to his feet and fought with his animal's reins.

'Kill them!' Joubert howled. 'Kill them all!' He galloped into their midst like a battering ram, hacking to left and right, striking any Flemish head within reach. The Slayer was close behind, though swaying in the saddle, the result of a gruesome gash to his face.

Cerdic meanwhile battled his way through to Roland, who'd got control of his animal and now was smearing blood across his cheek and along his mail sleeve.

'Roland!' Cerdic grabbed him. 'We mustn't kill them all!'

'And what do we do, take them prisoner? They're as many as we are!'

'We need to speak to them. Find out who they are... what they've come for.'

The knight-seneschal looked bewildered. 'Who they are is Flemings with a smattering of Danes. Sellsword rubbish if ever I saw any. What they came for is our food and drink, our horses and pack-animals, our weapons, our armour!'

'Roland, we're a large target to have fallen foul of routine banditry.'

'These are hardly bandits.'

'That's my point.'

Roland shoved him away, clambering back into his saddle. Cerdic looked around. Fifty yards from the midst of the violence, Count Cynric sat mounted under his Leopard standard, a shield over his body, a circle of knights around him. However, it didn't escape Cerdic's notice that a couple of bolts had embedded in Cynric's shield – these Flemings were lethal shots, even in the filth and chaos of battle – and then, a blink of an eye later, a small group of them, led by a colossal Viking with an axe in one hand and a broadsword in the other, threshed their way out through the hedge of men and blades, most likely to make a run for it, but by sheer misfortune choosing the direction of the count.

Numerous knights broke from the main fight to intercept them. Both Alain le Roux and Ivan d'Avranches spurred their beasts forward, lances lowered, skewering a man each. Even Cerdic found himself running at them, chopping one at the ankles, and meeting another face-on, parrying his counterstroke and severing his jugular.

None of them got close to the count, the giant himself wrestled down under a mass of mail-clad bodies. Cerdic spun and saw Roland, eyes bulging at the disaster that had nearly just befallen them. Cerdic snatched his bridle. 'We're losing too many men.'

'*We* again? So, are you really one of us now?'

'I've told you why I need you. Norman corpses are no use to me. If it's different for you and your master, there's nothing I can do, but this slaughterhouse is serving no one. For every twenty of theirs, we lose ten of ours. How many will remain?'

This at least seemed to make sense to the knight-seneschal. He yanked his reins back and wheeled his horse around to view the battle, which was progressing much as Cerdic had said. The Normans, led by Turold, were carving inroads into that final phalanx of Flemings, but more and more dropped or stumbled away with wounds of their own.

He kicked his animal forward, riding hard for the Leopard banner. Cerdic watched as Roland and the count exchanged words, then spotted a red-bearded Fleming leaping to his feet. He'd been faking death so the Norman encirclement could pass over him, and now, with crossbow already loaded, he levelled it at his shoulder and aimed at the count.

Cerdic charged, longsword raised.

The redbeard spun around, swinging his weapon and loosing its quill.

Only by pure luck did Cerdic's blade strike the missile. Redbeard drew a seax and threw himself forward, ducking inside the reach of the longsword, but Cerdic kicked at his groin, and as he doubled over, slammed its pommel onto the back of his helmet, dropping him into a stunned squat, before kicking him over onto his back. Quickly, the lad stepped astride the fallen foe, jabbing the longsword's tip at his Adam's apple.

At which point, a deafening horn blew several rapid blasts.

The Normans in the thick of the fight looked around, recognising the horn as their own but bewildered, before slowly backing away, creating a gap between themselves and the enemy. Shields remained in place; blades were levelled. But suddenly the clangour of battle was ear-pummelling in its absence. Instead, the air was riven by a frantic rasping of breath.

The remaining Flemings, sodden with sweat, wreathed in blood, clung together in confusion. They were still encircled and so still offered weapons.

Cerdic peered down into the eyes of the fellow at his feet. They peered back with defiance.

'In case you hadn't realised it,' Cerdic told him in French, 'you and your *routier* brigands are beaten. If they don't wish to be hanged and burned and maybe worse, they should throw down their weapons.'

Redbeard's mouth remained clamped.

Cerdic leaned on his longsword, drawing more blood. The sellsword gasped.

'I've seen good people die by the cartload these last few months,' the lad said. 'It will only balance the scales to send some Godless, heathen pigs in their wake.'

'We're no heathens,' the sellsword hissed.

'Then you know that only hellfire awaits you here! *Tell them!*'

With no choice, Redbeard called out a set of semi-incoherent instructions to his beleaguered colleagues. At first there was no response, the Flemings, still panting hard, but with eyes and faces strained, threatening more blood if the battle continued. Then a gruff, bass voice sounded amid their ranks, and after another breathless moment, one by one, their weapons clattered to the snow.

CHAPTER 18

The Flemings still clumped together tightly, but now they sat, a huddled, weary, bloodstained rabble, unarmed and with bulwarks of shields and levelled spears hemming them in from all sides save the front, where Count Cynric and his lead knights sat astride their destriers.

Roland kicked his horse forward a couple of paces. 'If your senior man remains,' he shouted, 'stand up. Identify yourself.'

There was some brief muttering among the surrendered troops. Then, one of them rose stiffly to his feet. To Cerdic's surprise, it was not the gigantic Viking who'd fought with a weapon in each hand, and now sat sullenly in the front rank, but the more diminutive fellow with the red beard who'd made a desperate ploy to shoot the count down from close range, and whom Cerdic himself had overcome.

'Take your helmet off,' Roland instructed.

The Fleming did so, revealing matted red hair and a great axe-head of a nose in a face no more than thirty years old. He didn't look especially frightened, more grudging, which was either a testimony to his courage or suggested he had no idea who he'd fallen foul of.

'What are you called?' Roland asked.

'Arne,' the redhead replied in Flemish French. 'Of Brabant.'

'You command this company?'

'I am their captain. For what it's worth.'

Joubert urged his horse forward, his face written with contempt. 'You don't look like much, Arne of Brabant.'

'We are chosen by election,' Arne replied. 'Not from right of birth. Wisdom and intellect are deemed to be crucial.'

Joubert bared his teeth. 'We should hang this impudent turd.'

'I mean no disrespect, Lord,' Arne added, addressing Count Cynric himself. 'But we are promoted on the basis of leadership ability. We must prove our quality first.'

'And you've proven yours?' Joubert scoffed. 'Is that what you're telling us?'

Arne sighed. 'I thought so… until today.'

'Indeed,' Roland replied. 'It wasn't particularly wise to attack *our* encampment.'

The Fleming shrugged. 'The winter's been hard, and we need supplies. We're as much strangers in this land as you. No one will give us shelter or food.'

'Have you tried offering payment for it?' Cerdic called out.

Arne glanced at him, recognising the hard-fighting lad who'd bested him. A lad who spoke French, but with an English accent. Clearly, this puzzled him.

'A new idea to the likes of you, I'd guess,' Cerdic added.

Arne glanced again at Cynric. 'We were promised loot when we came to England. Instead, we're lucky to have our lives. Our battalion was a thousand strong when we arrived last September. We've been foraging off the land ever since.'

Cerdic stepped closer. 'You came with Earl Tostig? And the Hardraada?'

For half a second, his thoughts were alive with sudden possibilities. Perhaps it had been a lucky stroke that Roland had gone along with his desire to spare these wretches.

Joubert read the revelation differently.

'You sided with pagans against fellow Christians?' he sneered.

Arne shrugged. 'The King of Norway was a Christian. Tyrkil here…' he pointed at the giant Viking, 'sole survivor of the Hardraada's personal *drengr*, is not.' That much was obvious from the sign of the hammer, which the Northman wore at his throat. 'But all his life he served Christians. So, it would be truer to say that we sided against Christians with other Christians. Which is much as you have done, is it not?'

Joubert ruddied in the cheek.

'What have you been doing since?' Turold asked. He stood closest to them, leaning two-handed on a longsword they had all of them seen slice men into ribbons. 'Raiding?'

'On occasion,' Arne admitted. 'But it hasn't been easy. Many communities here have come together for fear of you Normans. Young lads have been trained in weapon use to support their fathers and uncles.' He caught a few knights exchanging grins. 'You may smirk. But when they stand behind rock walls now fully rebuilt, or on palisades restored, and they've stockpiled all the supplies they need and have fletched thousands of new arrows, it's a difficult prospect.'

'And why would they do this?' Joubert demanded. 'The northern earls have given fealty to Duke William. He is now their king.'

Arne smiled at that. 'The people of the north hear only what has happened to the people of the south. The whole of Wessex and Kent, they say, is ravaged. Villages and granaries burned. Those villagers not killed outright condemned to the lingering death of starvation.'

No one challenged this. They'd all partaken in Duke William's vengeful march across the land he'd claimed he wanted to rule benevolently. As such, they too had found every door barred to them since they'd entered Mercia.

'Let me understand this,' Turold said. 'You won't attack villages with new fences, but you would attack *us*?'

Arne shrugged again. 'Desperation makes men bold.'

There seemed to be less confidence in him now. Suddenly, his gaze was averted.

'You think we're fools?' Cerdic said. Arne glanced at him distractedly, again wondering who this unusual youth might be. 'Someone paid you to attack this column, didn't they?'

There was a protracted silence. All eyes now fixed on Arne.

'Talk to us,' Roland said. 'We have power of life and death over you.'

Arne glanced at his comrades, who seemed equally uneasy.

'Whoever it was, he must have paid a lot to buy such loyalty,' Cerdic said. 'I imagine he told you we are heading north to claim a vast but vacant earldom?'

None of the captives replied, but they watched him closely.

'But I'd be surprised if it was that solely?' Cerdic said. 'None of Count Cynric's rivals know where this northern estate lies. They can't be sure they'll derive any wealth from it until they set eyes upon it. And that clearly isn't going to happen for years, not with King William bound for Normandy. In that case...' he walked forward until he stood alongside Turold, 'was this attack of yours connected to events down *there*... across the narrow sea?'

Again, the Flemings said nothing but remained tense.

'Talk to us, you fools,' Roland urged them. 'Whatever contract you signed, it's broken now. You've no reason not to speak.'

'Especially as we'll kill you if you don't,' Turold said.

'And maybe pay you if you do,' Cerdic added.

'Enough!' Joubert interjected. He spurred his horse round to face his father. 'This English whelp has no damn authority here. He can't negotiate on our behalf.' He pulled out a riding crop as though to beat the object of his anger again. 'You dare promise these bandits pay? And from *our* war-chest!'

'From my own!' Cerdic retorted. He turned to the count. 'My lord, when I come into my inheritance, there'll be more than enough to go around. And I don't see skulking murderers here. I see trained soldiers. Their bowmen in particular have exceptional skills.'

Joubert spluttered, only for his father to gesture for quiet. And then to speak. As usual, his delivery was slow, cool and deliberate. 'All you Flemings who are masters of the crossbow, stand.'

The prisoners watched the encircling shields and spears with increasing alarm.

'Stand,' the count said again, though his tone now was surprisingly conciliatory. 'This is merely a headcount.'

Slowly, warily, the Flemings rose to their feet. Not all, but most.

'I count seventy-five,' Cerdic eventually said. 'Perhaps forty others. At a guess, we've just lost a hundred men. Don't we have tried-and-tested replacements right here?'

'We can't trust these dogs!' Joubert protested. 'They'll want paying upfront and we can't do that.'

'When their only alternative is death?' Cerdic replied.

'Or hunger?' Turold said. 'Wandering these northern snows, this time without weapons. Or clothes.'

Cerdic addressed the Flemish captain himself. 'Arne of Brabant, my father lost many thegns and carls at Fulford and Stamford Bridge… maybe they were fighting your men. The rest, or most of them, died on Senlac Ridge. So, there are manors aplenty where I come from, all of them awaiting new occupants. We have silver too, if that's more to your liking.'

'Have you heard this?' Joubert hissed at his father. 'This *prisoner* is being generous with *your* demesnes.' He paused, baffled. 'Father, why are you looking at him like that?'

Count Cynric barely seemed to hear. 'The boy negotiates well. And he can fight.'

'You're not thinking of agreeing to this?' Joubert was incredulous.

Roland steered his horse over to them. 'We could use the extra men, my lord.'

'Count Cynric!' Arne called over, having conferred with his confederates. 'I understand you have a female with you? Yvette of Hiemois, daughter and heiress to Count Rodric?'

The silence of the thunderstruck greeted this.

It broke only when Yvette pushed her way through the mailed ranks, regarding the Flemings with more than a degree of disdain. They eyed her back, perhaps unsure what to make of her. She was beautiful of course, in her delicate, elfin way, yet was dressed now mostly in clothes that were dingy and torn, her hair tied in a scarf that more befitted a peasant than a lady of repute. Despite all, she stood among the Norman horde with the air of an equal.

'You were after this girl?' Roland demanded.

Again, the Flemings spoke among themselves.

'The king sent you?' Turold asked.

Still, Arne resisted answering.

Cerdic's thoughts ran riot. King William had already learned about their mission to the north, and considered it treachery? And unable to pursue them himself, had sent a small but professional force to waylay them? Except that King William knew better than to make enemies when he didn't need to. By express understanding, the Count of Tancarville was holding Yvette of Hiemois on his behalf. In the first instance, he would send a messenger to request the girl be sent south again. If that failed, he would order it. Only then, if that failed too, would he despatch soldiers, and they'd be trusted knights, not mercenary scum.

'Let me guess,' Roland said with a thin smile. 'Count Eustace sent you?'

The mercenaries' mouths stayed shut.

'I see you don't deny it.' The knight-seneschal turned to his master. 'Only two weeks after the coronation, my lord, and Eustace of Boulogne is plotting again.'

Cerdic listened with interest. He could put a face to Count Eustace, and knew that he was a powerful Norman magnate, but there his knowledge ran out. Clearly though, from Roland's tone, Eustace exemplified the Norman political wolf-pit.

'Probably thinks he's been inadequately rewarded,' Milo de Hauteville suggested.

'Like us,' Joubert replied.

'Except that we're adventuring in pursuit of our goal,' Roland countered. 'But Boulogne's solution, as usual, is rebellion.' He turned back to Cynric. 'If Boulogne joins forces with Count Rodric, Yvette's father, that makes the rebel alliance very strong. And taking the girl to her father would be a sign of his good faith.'

'Perhaps we should throw our lot in with Boulogne and Hiemois,' Joubert said. 'Abandon this insane march north. Go south again, join the faction.'

'While the king is in Normandy?' Turold said. 'Tancarville itself would be vulnerable. My lord, your son, Dagobert, won't be able to hold it on his own. Not against William himself.'

'If it came to a war, at least in the south we'd have allies,' Joubert retorted. 'Who will we have where we're headed now?'

Even though it had become common knowledge that they were journeying north to provide Joubert with a powerbase of his own, the count's son's disgruntlement seemed to grow with each day. Clearly, he thought their destination, if it even existed, too far from anywhere, too scant for his needs. No doubt he'd want it when he saw it, Cerdic thought, and maybe he suspected this deep down, hence his ever-increasing hatred for their prisoner, who of course might rival him for that title.

Count Cynric meanwhile heard out the arguments with impassive consideration.

'Whatever you decide, my lord,' Cerdic said, 'it's still better if we head north and take Yvette with us. For safekeeping if nothing else. In due course, you can donate her to whichever side you see fit, but there's no need to rush a decision.'

'This is dangerous counsel,' Roland said, 'but it makes sense. As far as the king is aware, we're looking to capture land far from his sphere. We're treading on no one's toes save these renegade Northmen the boy talks about.'

At this, Cerdic noticed the Viking prisoner, Tyrkil, perk up, as though he'd finally heard something that interested him.

'He's unlikely to be offended,' Roland added. 'And if we're holding the child who is key to preventing a potential full-scale revolt in Normandy, he'll be actively pleased. Of course, on the other hand, as Cerdic says, if the revolt goes in favour of the rebels... well, the choice will be yours.'

Cynric thought long and hard before straightening in his saddle. 'We continue north.'

Joubert snorted with dissatisfaction.

'You!' the count said. 'Arne of Brabant!'

'My liege?' the Flemish captain replied.

'You and your remaining men will serve?'

Arne looked wary, though there were hopeful expressions on his men's faces. Clearly, they'd still been expecting death. These were Normans who held them, after all.

'Until?' Arne asked.

The count looked amused. 'Until such time as we make a settlement.'

Arne made an awkward gesture. 'We have a basic rate…'

'There'll be no basic rates,' the count replied.

'Your pay is we don't slaughter you,' Joubert said.

'Until we are able to redistribute the land and goods we capture,' the count added.

'Just don't expect lordships.' Joubert glanced irritably at Cerdic. 'I strongly doubt there'll be many of those to toss around.'

'We at least get an equal share in rations?' Arne asked.

'Rations we can spare,' the count replied. 'Now that you've cut our numbers down.'

'And don't make the mistake of thinking *that* will happen again,' Joubert scowled. 'Try it, and the word "punishment" will have new meanings for you.'

Arne nodded. Roland trotted his horse towards them. 'As Count Cynric's knight-seneschal and banneret, you'll be under my command. Is that understood?'

'Of course.' Though there was more than a hint of grudge in Arne's voice.

'Then fall your men in for breakfast. Any too wounded to continue should be placed with ours. Our next task is to find a religious house where they can be cared for.'

Roland signalled the troops hemming the prisoners in, and they broke apart, lowering their shields and spears. The prisoners visibly relaxed, those still seated now climbing to their feet, brushing the snow from their backsides. Yvette, meanwhile, approached Cerdic.

She arched an eyebrow. 'The count may *donate* me?'

'You've suddenly become a very important person,' he replied.

'And you're holding me for *safekeeping*?'

'You surely agree with that, at least?'

She remained unimpressed. Tingeing pink, he spied Arne standing alone and pensive now that his men had been led away to be fed, and moved over towards him.

'My name is Cerdic,' the lad said.

Arne eyed him with interest, taking in his blood-spattered woollen jerkin, the great cross-hilt of the longsword, which Cerdic now wore over his back the way Turold did.

'An Englishman?' he said. 'Among Normans?'

Cerdic shrugged. 'I've had to adapt to a new world. Whether I've managed it, I'm unsure.'

'You speak well for a youngster.'

Cerdic reflected on that. Oratory and rhetoric were skills he'd been tutored in by Aethelric, though until now he'd never had cause to put them to use.

'And this is the young woman we were sent to rescue?' Arne said.

'Do I look as if I need to be rescued?' Yvette asked tetchily.

Arne smiled. 'I wouldn't know, my lady. I'm confused by this whole situation.'

'Speaking of confusion,' Cerdic said, 'how is the north?'

'Tense.'

'Are there many under arms?'

'As I said, we've encountered...'

'I don't mean farmhands defending villages. I mean housecarls. Are there armies in the field?'

'You're aware the earls Edwin and Morcar have submitted?'

Cerdic shrugged. 'I know about that. But Edwin and Morcar are not the only leaders north of the River Thames.'

'There are other groups like ours. English groups. Warriors who have not surrendered, but they mostly live scattered, like outlaws. The housecarls who held London have left England altogether, to serve in distant lands. I hear that a certain Eadric is building resistance in the west, but at present is hiding in the

Welsh hills. It would take a mighty man indeed to pull all these forces together.'

One of his underlings now called to him, offering an iron bowl and spoon. Arne nodded to Cerdic, bowed to Yvette, and limped away.

'Please don't tell me you want to be that mighty man?' Yvette said.

'All I want, Yvette, is to be lord of the land to which I was born. But at present…'

Before Cerdic could finish, a rider reined up beside him, so close, kicking up so much snow with his hooves, that he was forced to step back.

'It isn't over between us!' Joubert gazed down at him with raw hatred, though for once he was pale rather than ruddy. There was a repressed but desperate anger there, as if somewhere inside he'd finally realised that things were spiralling out of his control. 'You may have fooled my father with that glib tongue of yours, but I take a different view.'

'It's a good thing you were foiled last night,' Cerdic retorted. 'Otherwise, you'd have denied your father a considerable advantage today.'

'Oh, it's clear we now need your little traitorous bitch. But I'm far from convinced we need *you*.'

Joubert reined his horse around and hit an immediate gallop, others having to jump out of his way. It was several seconds before Cerdic realised that Turold had come over.

'I'll need to take charge of *this*,' he said, patting the longsword on Cerdic's back. Grudgingly, the lad unslung it and handed it over. 'But every chance we get from now on…' Turold also gazed long and hard after the count's son, 'I'm going to give you tuition in its use. Because you need it.'

Cerdic was surprised by that. 'Didn't I do well last night?'

'You did very well. But you can do better. And with me to teach you, you will.'

CHAPTER 19

Even though Cerdic was still prohibited from bearing arms, Turold, clearly envisaging some future time when this wouldn't be the case, was determined to teach him the full range of skills associated with the Norman longsword, and to do it quickly. Their very first lesson came the following morning, before the rest of the camp had even stirred, the champion marking out a frozen square of woodland with burning torches, the lad still yawning as the two of them confronted each other. As per Turold's instruction, Cerdic had donned his chain-mail and brought his helmet, while the knight had given him a shield and the blade that he'd confiscated after the battle with the Flemings.

'We need to make this as much like a real fight as possible,' Turold said. 'It's the only way for a warrior to learn.'

'You know I've trained with weapons before,' Cerdic replied.

Turold said nothing, simply spun his sword front to back and then back to front as they circled each other.

Cerdic stopped in his tracks. 'But I've never learned to do *that*.'

'We call it a flourish.' Turold went through the motion again.

The weapon dropped first to the forward horizontal, the knight turning his palm up and then inward, gripping the hilt solely by forefinger and thumb, the blade hanging down, then, when he thrust with the palm, swinging back over the top, returning to the horizontal. Done swiftly and smoothly, it was a clean, elegant manoeuvre.

'I want to do that,' Cerdic said.

'I'm teaching you to fight, not put on a show.'

'I want to learn both. If I can do that before a fight, I'll be showing my enemy I'm an expert with my weapon. It may weaken his resolve.'

The knight nodded. 'You have the correct instincts, Cerdic, but I've already seen that. I'll show you how to flourish, but first, I'll show you the basics.'

For the next ten minutes, he encouraged the lad to come at him, evading every strike with a variety of cuts, thrusts and parries, many of which seemed obvious to Cerdic and were easy to pick up once he'd been shown how. For the more complex moves, the fight was halted, Turold explaining each one in detail, demonstrating in slow, purposeful fashion.

'Remember not to attack the shield blindly,' he said, handing over a water-skin for their first break. Despite the deep cold and their billows of foggy breath, both of them sweated fiercely. 'I noticed a lot of you English doing that on Senlac Ridge. I suspect it's because the majority of your older warriors learned to fight with the axe rather than the sword. And it can work. A continued bombardment will eventually break even a Norman shield. But the blade can lodge, at which point you'll be vulnerable, particularly to a skilled swordsman.'

'You have exceptional skills,' Cerdic said admiringly.

Turold shrugged. 'Fighting's the only thing I've ever been good at.'

'How do you become a champion of the tournament?'

'By enrolling in as many as you can.'

'Are they like real battles?'

'They can be.'

'Do men die?'

'Yes.' Turold went back into the fighting square. 'Often. If there's dislike between households, it can be more or less the real thing.'

Cerdic went back out and faced him. 'But don't you have this belief... this cult called chivalry? Aren't you supposed to spare lives, forgive indiscretions?'

Turold smiled. 'And how much of that have you seen since we've been here?'

They fought on, working through patterns of familiar moves, as much to train Cerdic in hand-and-eye coordination as anything else. It was, Turold said, about becoming one with the additional length of blade. Knowing instinctively where your steel was even in the midst of chaotic battle, turning it into an extra limb.

'When I was... young,' he grunted, as they swapped blows. 'Normandy was a cauldron of war. If we weren't under invasion, we warred with... each other. That changes people, Cerdic. Makes them harder, crueller. My father was a good example. A household knight in the service of Count Guido of Cherbourg, he fought continuously. Sometimes against men who the previous year he'd been... allied to. Eventually, he received a reward of sorts. *Good!* Good... you didn't overextend that time but pulled back. Remember, your foe won't always be as skilled as you, but if he is, he'll punish every mistake.'

Cerdic mopped fresh sweat from his eyes. He knew that he'd performed well in the battle against the Flemings, but the longsword had still felt like an alien weapon. As on Senlac Ridge, he'd brawled rather than fought. Now though, after only twenty minutes' hard practice, he was thinking and watching rather than simply flying in, addressing each attack on its own merits, responding appropriately, counterattacking, attempting to penetrate his opponent's defences rather than simply hammer them down, and the longsword was the ideal weapon for that.

'Cherbourg gave him a keep by the River Odon,' Turold said. 'A few... acres of land. A village of serfs to work it. But then Cherbourg died, and his sons squabbled. My father had to choose a side. It was a minor war as wars go, but it dragged on for years. He was landed gentry, you might say, but it was always... saddle and sword, at which he excelled. By 1027, the year... the year Duke Robert came to power, he held several fiefs, had become a minor lord in his own... his own right. Good! Yes... *yes!* I like that feint, but don't overuse it. An experienced opponent will read it.'

They halted, panting, still circling, then closed again, blades clashing continuously as they shuffled across the well-trodden snow.

'Father married twice, but his first wife died young. His second was daughter to an... to an English merchant based in Saint-Omer, who'd made good importing wool products. Fine cloaks and such, into Flanders and Normandy...'

They broke again, panting, drinking from the water-skin.

'The Englishman's daughter?' Cerdic said. 'Your mother?'

The champion nodded. 'She gave my father three sons and two daughters. I was the youngest. She was the youngest child too, so when her own father died, his profitable business was divided between his offspring. Already married to a landed knight, it wasn't held that she needed any further money. My father was angry, but he had no claim. Of course, it meant he couldn't expand his own fortune except...'

'By war?' Cerdic said.

Turold returned to the fighting square. He seemed grim, almost sad, as if this was the first time he'd looked back on these details of his early life. They joined again, Cerdic employing everything he'd learned, lunging, feinting, parrying, striking, the knight blocking each move.

'This time... he waged it mostly against his neighbours,' Turold said. 'Or on any campaign Duke Robert, or his son, Duke William, happened to call. At Val-ès-Dunes, Father captured... he captured forty French knights. Ransomed them all. By this time, I was in the saddle too.'

Cerdic paused, gasping, the sharp, cold air stabbing his lungs. 'You must've been young?'

'Your age.' Turold came on the attack. 'But I'd seen combat several times by then. In Normandy... we were... squired as soon as we could ride a horse.'

'You learned *real* fighting at an early age?'

'If it wasn't real fighting, it was the tourney... the next best thing.'

They rested again, having sparred now for a good forty minutes. Sounds of voices cut the frosty air; there was a smell of breakfast fires.

Turold took his gauntlets off and removed his helmet. He became thoughtful. 'It's a warrior culture over there, Cerdic. I wouldn't say you people didn't stand a chance against us. You've fought your share of Vikings, and you've fought them well. I understand that, and you almost won on Senlac Ridge. But Duke William brought twenty thousand men here at the most. And you have… how many million? And yet, where are they? The only English I see now are hanging on gibbets or working with whip-shredded backs under the yoke of new foreign masters.'

Cerdic couldn't deny it. There were still some who'd give the Normans a fight. There had to be. Arne claimed that the housecarls who'd resisted in London had left these shores, maybe never to return. But there had to be others somewhere. Eadric, the warrior now hiding in the Welsh hills? But who knew where he actually was or what extent of power he commanded? It was also true what Turold said about England and the English. Until 1066, the kingdom had been at peace for five decades. Even Cerdic's father's campaigns against Llewelyn and Macbeth were relatively minor affairs conducted by small but professional forces, with few ordinary citizens called into service. The country had sleepwalked into a form of disarmament, become lax in matters of war without even realising.

'I'm the scion of a military family,' the lad said, 'but I'd never killed anyone until Senlac Ridge.'

Turold slid his sword back into its scabbard. 'There's a first time for everything. And you acquitted yourself well enough.'

'Acquitted myself? It's a strange phrase to use for the slaughter of men. But it's also strange how quickly I've become used to it. Slaughter, I mean.'

Turold clapped his shoulder. 'A good thing too. It makes no sense to lose sleep over what may now be your day-to-day existence.'

They trekked back through the snow-laden trees. 'Turold,' Cerdic said, as he handed his sword back, 'don't assume there's no one left here to fight you.'

'I never assume that. None of us do. That's what keeps us in trim.'

'And yet, I think of you in particular as superior to these others.'

The knight laughed. 'Don't be fooled. God granted me size and strength. My mother taught me English. My father's knights taught me skill at arms. But from my father himself... I learned ferocity, ruthlessness. None of those things make me superior. Maybe as a warrior, not as a man.'

The camp lay just ahead, movement visible between the tents. Cerdic halted before they entered. Turold glanced round at him.

'You don't approve of this, do you?' the lad said.

'This?'

'The rape of another country.'

'I have no feelings either way.'

'I don't believe that.'

Turold strode on. 'Believe what you wish.'

Cerdic hurried after him. 'You trained to be a knight from a young age. This idea of chivalry... perhaps it means something to you after all?'

'Don't put it to the test.'

'It means something to Roland.'

'Roland's an idealist. He became one when his wife died.'

Cerdic hadn't known about that, and so refrained from comment.

'She died from the same ague that claimed his infant child,' Turold said. 'That's why he threw himself into the code. He needed something to live for. He wants to believe we're fighting a religious war. But in his heart, he knows we aren't. I don't know, maybe that makes him an even worse sinner. To participate in cruelty when you don't really want to.'

'It has to be better than participating when you do,' Cerdic said.

'Doesn't it make you weak... make a mockery of your principles?'

They were now among the tents, so Cerdic reverted to English. 'Principles, I now believe, are a luxury. I never knew my mother, but my father was a statesman. He'd fought wars, but always preferred diplomacy. All my life, I was schooled by a gentle and intelligent priest. Of course, I learned about war from my brother and the housecarls, but only when I confronted it face-to-face did I realise what it actually was. Maybe my civilised upbringing hadn't prepared me. And yet, I dived in. I slew your people. I'll slay more of them if I get the chance. I may even slay you, Turold.'

The knight arched an eyebrow.

'What does that say about my principles?' Cerdic said. 'What does it say about any of us?'

'It says war is Hell, lad. That's a lesson for life we all learn. But at least for the moment you and I can be friends.'

'Yes,' Cerdic replied. 'Yes, I'm glad of that.'

―

Later that day, it snowed again. More heavily than they'd seen at any stage during the journey thus far. Intense northern winds whipped up blizzard conditions, and by midday it became obvious that to persevere was folly. Even someone who knew for certain which direction was which, and that was not Cerdic, would have struggled to make headway. In the end, Count Cynric instructed that they bivouac early.

This time, after their experience with the Flemings, they were more cautious, finding a low hilltop, which even though it meant they were exposed, also meant that an enemy would struggle to approach them without being seen. Once the camp was built, they encircled it with fresh-cut thorn switches and posted more guards than usual, though it was a hellish experience for the men chosen, the wind sharp as a blade, the snowflakes driving into them like arrows, nothing visible for more than two dozen yards on any side.

Nevertheless, the Normans being the Normans, they opted to make good use of this break in their routine. They'd replenished their dwindling food supplies by slaughtering the flock of sheep the day before yesterday, the remaining meat now crammed into sealed, salt-filled barrels, to be carried on the backs of their pack-beasts, but despite having lost men in the battle with the Flemings, the addition of the mercenaries had resulted in their now having more mouths to feed than before. So, any extra food would be useful. A hunt was thus called.

They'd done well out of England's countryside so far. It was alive with game, particularly deer and boar, while any wetlands they'd encountered, though frozen, were thriving with winter fowl, their rivers and streams crammed with fish. Cynric's company in particular had reaped it, though, conscious they were deep in enemy territory, they'd always been quick and careful. Today's hunt would be no exception. The difference this time was that Roland told Cerdic he could come along. The lad was even trusted with a hunting bow and a bag of arrows. It occurred to him as he rode out with the others that a chance to escape had again been laid on a platter. He didn't even need to kill anyone. He could simply gallop off and lose himself in the snow. But what would even his chances be, alone on this tundra?

So instead, he'd gone hunting, riding mostly in the company of Turold.

Neither of them put arrows into anything that day, though after two hours they came to a clearing in a snow-filled forest, where inside the circle of an ancient, tumbledown wall, smoke rose from a hole in the roof of a large timber structure, a roundhouse of the sort built by the Britons rather than the long-hall more characteristic of the Saxons. The outer wall was fitted with a new pair of wooden gates, complete with an arch over the top, on which was mounted a crudely carved crucifix, but the gates stood open.

They watched from astride their horses as women in shapeless monastic garb, wrapped also in shawls, their long hair tied in scarves, walked into the enclosure and out again, carrying pails of water from a nearby brook, the ice on top of which they had recently broken.

'A nunnery,' Turold said, amused. 'A shame for poor Joubert. I doubt even he could justify attacking this place.'

'But he will, if he learns that it's here,' Cerdic replied.

Turold mused on that. 'It looks like a subsidiary house, to me. A priory. They'll have nothing of value to us. Except maybe those outhouses inside their compound.'

There were indeed several additional but smaller roofs visible behind the wall, and Cerdic remembered Roland's promise that all those severely wounded would be left at the first religious house of convenience.

'This is a good find,' Turold said, walking his horse forward. 'Worth more to the count than any stag or hind we might fetch.'

The nuns were frightened to see two mailed horsemen enter through their gates, darting away in various directions. However, the prioress of Oakthorpe, Mother Agnetha, as they later learned she was called, a thin, elderly woman, though far from frail, confronted them at the roundhouse entrance, barring them access with her own wiry frame. This was a holy place, she said in English, and none could enter while carrying weapons. When Turold explained who they were, she seemed unsurprised. They had heard there was a great war in the south, she replied, and much loss of life. Interestingly, she didn't appear to distinguish between English and Norman, or even English and Viking. Perhaps they were all the same to her, warrior cultures on the rampage, led by rapacious nobles who, whatever their blood, only ever sought power for themselves. Of course, if that was her attitude, it was useful to them. It meant she wouldn't hold any preference for the ethnicity of the sick and dying they were about to deluge her with.

She seemed unhappy when they told her, but they weren't asking.

To soften the blow, Turold said they would make donations of food and drink so the community would not be forced to dig any deeper into its own supplies than necessary. As a woman of God, she could hardly refuse such a generous offer. The sight of the longsword on Turold's back, and the chain-mace coiled at his waist, the handle of which he fingered throughout the conversation, assisted.

Later that day, they returned to the count's camp, and despite the weather, which remained severely inclement, those men too wounded to participate further were wrapped in extra cloaks and blankets, loaded onto horses and led in solemn procession the three miles to their new place of refuge. If a couple fell dead from their mounts on the way, there was nothing to be done. It was less work for the nuns of Oakthorpe. At the end of all this it was late in the day, flakes still swirling but now in mid-January darkness. Cerdic was crusted white when he finally stooped shivering into his tent. So preoccupied was he in shrugging off his snow-caked outer garb that he didn't at first notice Yvette in there, sitting upright, watching him with tear-glazed eyes.

'My lady is no more,' she said. 'Neither body nor soul.'

Her words baffled him. 'What?'

'My Lady of Walsingham.'

Cerdic dropped the rag he'd been using to dry his hair. 'The Swan-Neck?'

'She is destroyed by her own hand.'

He sank to his knees alongside her. 'What do you mean?'

Fresh tears beaded her cheeks. 'I can never go back there, Cerdic.'

'But... how do you know?'

'I heard it from one of the Flemings.'

'A sellsword? What could he know?'

'I heard them discussing it. I asked for more. They told me with shrugs of their shoulders. As if it means nothing to them...'

'What did they say?'

More tears trickled, but she fought to get her thoughts in order. 'Bishop Odo was charged by the king with finding King

Harold's corpse, so they could put it on display... prove once and for all that he is dead. But he has never succeeded. The bishop then heard rumours that Lady Edith had removed it. He despatched a trusted knight of his... Radulf the Staller, a Breton.' She shuddered at the name. 'He was here in England before the Normans, part of Harold's court, but Lady Edith always considered him a spy, which clearly he was... for Radulf, they say, will now be the next Earl of East Anglia.' She shook her head at this news. 'His instructions were to burn my lady's hall, sack her villages, bring my lady back to the bishop so that he might question her personally.'

Cerdic shivered. He knew what this would have meant. He'd seen the thinly veiled lust on the toadlike face of Bishop Odo, that blob in ecclesiastical garb, when Edith Swan-Neck had arrived in Duke William's camp the day after the battle. He'd called her a harlot and a slattern, but he'd yearned to feast on her. That much was obvious. The brutal power he'd exercised simply by denying her possession of her lover's remains had given him pleasure all on its own. Cerdic could only imagine the toad-bishop's enthusiasm when he'd learned that his next duty would involve arresting and interrogating the unfortunate woman.

'My lady got word of it before the Staller and his war-band arrived,' Yvette said. 'She had no household left to fight for her. Even her servants and bondsmen had fled. When the Staller got there, she was all alone. In her bed, lifeless. She'd drunk an elixir made from wine and hemlock.'

Yvette wept again, the anguish etched deep on her face.

Cerdic cursed himself. It had been too easy thinking that, just because Turold and Roland were men of honour, just because even Count Cynric now approved of him, the rest of the Norman hell-horde wasn't riding roughshod in other parts of the country, the population not sobbing with despair.

'Yvette...' He attempted consolation. 'I can't imagine Lady Edith was in her right mind as she awaited those men. Surely, God will understand...'

'She is cast into Hell!' Yvette blurted. 'Or so Father Jerome told me.'

'*Father Jerome!*' Cerdic struggled to say the name aloud without contempt.

'"There is no exception," he said. "Our bodies are temples of the Lord. Whoever sunders one is damned. Even if one does it oneself."'

Cerdic nodded. 'Father Jerome ought to know about Hell.'

'He also said she led a bad life. Without shame or remorse. That she was Harold's whore. I begged him to pray for her, but he said there was no hope.'

'Indeed?'

'To his credit, he wept.'

'He *wept*?'

'He wept for her sins. And for her fate. And for mine.'

'*Yours?*' The anger now gripping Cerdic almost felt physical.

'He said I should make a confession. He said that you and I have been lying together. The sins of the flesh, he says, are the worst.'

'We haven't been. We could have, we nearly did... but we resisted.'

'He didn't believe me when I told him that.'

Cerdic didn't think it was possible to feel colder than he had on returning from the afternoon's hunt, but the chill that pierced him now was deathly.

Throughout his life, he'd encountered priests. Some were unimpeachably wise and good, the likes of Aethelric. Others more workmanlike in their faith, but impressive, like Aethelbald and Osric. Then there'd been Brithnoth, who was strange and eccentric, but harmless. Since the Normans had come, however, he'd met a new breed. They claimed to be devout, zealous even, but in truth they wore their heartlessness like a leprosy. They took their example, it seemed, from Pope Alexander himself, who, to bolster his own power, had approved this holocaust against the Christians of England. Little wonder the likes of Father Jerome, a simpering weakling yet a fellow of high ambition, had quickly dispensed with his own humanity. If he'd ever had any at all.

Father Jerome's problem, of course, was that while those others were out of Cerdic's reach, he wasn't. Yvette wept with head in hand for another moment, and only then noticed that Cerdic had vacated the tent, its open flap fluttering on the bitter wind.

CHAPTER 20

'I seek to be shriven,' Cerdic said.

The priest glanced round, shocked that someone had disturbed his privacy. Even Cerdic, for all his anger, was surprised by the change that had come over Father Jerome. He hadn't seen him up close for several days, and what faced him now was the scrawny relic of a man.

The cleric was literally skeletal. His cassock, stained with filth around its hem and rank with the stench of sweat, hung on his shrunken form like a shroud. His face, thin before, was waxen and shrivelled. The horseshoe of bristles on his bone-white cranium had turned grey. His tent was also a mess, clothing scattered, a prayer book lying torn to shreds, a chest on its side, a thurible, a chalice and other sacred vessels spilling out of it.

He'd been kneeling in front of a suspended crucifix, a whale-oil lamp on one side, a brazier filled with orange embers on the other. His face betrayed no emotion, remained impossibly blank, but he shook his head. 'I'm tired, my son,' he said. 'Perhaps tomorrow.'

'Tomorrow we may be dead,' Cerdic replied. 'Some of us.'

Father Jerome gave no hint that he considered this a threat. Looking closely, Cerdic saw that his cheeks were deeply tear-stained.

He wept for her sins.

For *her* sins. Somehow that enraged the lad almost as much as any atrocity he'd witnessed since Jarl Wulfgar's assault on Wulfbury.

Sighing, the priest reached long, bony fingers into his cassock pocket, taking out a stole and draping it over his shoulders. At the same time, he indicated a cushion.

Cerdic knelt on it, his hands by his sides rather than joined in prayer, each of them clenched into a knot of bone. The priest stood painfully, leaning on the lampstand to keep himself upright. He indicated that Cerdic could start.

'Bless me, Father,' the lad said, 'for I am a terrible sinner.'

The priest nodded, attempting to moisten his lips. 'Look into your heart for...'

'My last confession was long before this war of annihilation was brought on us by the Duke of Normandy, with the full permission of the Norman Church and our Father in Rome.'

Jerome blinked as though only now recognising the person in front of him. 'My son, I...'

'I've killed many men,' Cerdic said. 'Normans, all. And I've enjoyed it. And I will kill yet more, and I will enjoy it then too...'

'One...' the priest stuttered, 'one cannot confess sins one has not yet committed.'

'Who are *you* to say what I can or can't confess?' Cerdic's voice betrayed no anger, only curiosity. 'Who are *you* to say which wretched soul is bound for Heaven and which for Hell?'

'I... I am ordained. I took Holy Orders at...'

'They were rescinded the moment you became chaplain to a pack of murderers.'

The priest's eyes glinted with confusion, but also, for the first time, fear.

'I've seen you, Father Jerome,' Cerdic said. 'Horror-stricken by everything that's happened here. Unable to understand how you've become part of it. I must admit, I don't understand that either. Because you're not like any of the priests I knew and loved.'

Cerdic rose to his feet. He didn't tower over his host. Jerome was taller than he, but stick-thin. 'Father Brithnoth, our village priest, was set on fire and dragged behind a horse rather than submit to a pagan horde. Father Aethelric, my father's chaplain, was rent to the heart by Viking steel. So...' he shrugged, 'when do you make *your* stand against evil?'

'My son, I...' A note of pleading enfeebled the nasal voice even further. 'I understand your confusion, but please, I...'

'*My* confusion?'

'I... I can't... explain to you how... but sanity will prevail.'

'When? When every Englishman is dead, every Englishwoman raped?'

'No, I... *no!*' The priest finally became angry, or tried to. That last question had stung. He waved at the tent's entrance. 'I... won't hear this. You befoul the sacrament of penance...'

'Oh no, Father, I value penance. I'm just wondering what you'll be doing for *yours*. Whether there's distance enough in the world for you to walk it barefoot. Or enough ashes for you to wear in the whole of this ruined kingdom.'

'How dare...' The priest's eyes bugged like veiny pebbles, though somehow Cerdic felt that if there was anger and loathing there, it wasn't aimed at him. 'You dare mock the Church?'

'Not true. I grew up in a *happy* Christian world, where God's word was respected, and men lived in peace and only the guilty were punished. Where churches and abbeys were seats of learning, not broods of vipers...'

This particular passage from Saint Matthew had always caught Cerdic's interest, Jesus calling the corrupt priests in the temple vipers, warning them of God's wrath to come. It persuaded many of them that Jesus was too dangerous to be allowed to live.

It hit its intended mark here as well.

Wordless, Father Jerome lurched forward, grappled with Cerdic physically, then shoved him out of the way, and fled into the blizzard.

—

A few minutes later, Cerdic sat down in the darkness of his tent. Yvette had declined to return to her own, and now lay still, having wormed her way under his furs and blankets.

'All is well?' she asked, her back turned.

'Hardly.'

So sullen was his tone that she chose not to pose further questions.

Cerdic didn't feel better in any measurable way. That so-called Norman priest had been nothing, a pathetic specimen of failed manhood, typical of so many who finished up in the Church simply because they couldn't face the hardships of life. But none of England's ordeal had really been his fault. He'd come along for the ride, probably expecting to preside over a few military funerals, and then enjoy swift promotion to high office.

To rant at him that way had been pointless, an act of crude bullying. But someone from the Church had to pay for Pope Alexander's role in all this.

He reached down and put a hand on the girl's shoulder, but she lay rigid, cold as the winter wind banging and flapping the tent on its flimsy framework. Any ardour she might have felt for him in the Bishop of London's bathhouse had clearly long cooled. Though it couldn't have helped that Edith Swan-Neck, her beloved guardian, a gentle beauty famed across England for her compassionate ways, now writhed in hellfire, or so this new version of the Church claimed, simply because she'd coupled with King Harold outside of wedlock.

Cerdic burrowed down under the covers but lay separate from her.

Sins of the flesh are the worst, the priest had told Yvette.

Cerdic wasn't naïve. Such sins were not to be discounted. He'd seen the troubles they'd caused for Unferth and his concubine, Eadora.

But at present, there were other priorities.

What about sins of the steel? Cerdic wondered.

There'd be many more of those in the days to come.

Jerome de Soussa stumbled through the intensifying blizzard, past the picquets, who stood beside flaring braziers, but were little more than muffled shadows in their cloaks and helmets. One of them called after him, but he made no response, kicking through the thorn-switches and blundering downhill into swirling greyness.

He was completely unprepared, of course. There was mail under his cassock, but he wore no hose, no leggings or trousers, and only unlaced shoes on his feet. He hadn't bothered with a cloak, fur-lined or otherwise, a scarf, or even a pair of gloves. Because punishment was what he sought. And punishment he was already receiving, his mind twisting through torturous loops.

The horror they'd inflicted on this land was of Hadean proportions.

And all of it in God's name. *Dear Lord, in God's holy name!*

Who knew what the penalty might be? Who could imagine what demons the Almighty would unleash?

Jerome was only vaguely aware that he was already among trees. The wind wove the flakes around him in sheets. They plastered one whole side of his body and face, filling his nose and mouth with ice. 'God save me!' he tried to scream. But also: 'God *forgive* me...'

What had they done to this land? This simple, pastoral land, which, before the winter had come, had seemed as serene and beautiful as any he'd ever seen in Francia. A home to people who *did* attend Mass, who *did* say prayers, who *did* venerate holy icons (the shepherd boy, dear God the simpleton shepherd boy, and his crude iron crucifix, so sacred to him that he wore it at his throat!), who lived in settled towns and villages *without* decadence, *without* corruption, *without* the pagan practices and orgiastic revels that Archbishop Marilius had so luridly described that day at Lillebonne.

Even now, in the ongoing blast of wind and snow, he had to stop his ears to blot out the voices of those people, their screams filled with such pain and dismay that they scarcely sounded human.

'Oh God, what have we done, what have we done…?'

And what would *He* do?

The answer to that came in short order, for very soon afterwards, Jerome saw the first of the demons. It rose out of the murk, a shapeless, deformed monstrosity, its arms arcing up and out, its raking claws impossibly long, its eyes and mouth – huge, distorted holes of hunger and misery – set in its belly rather than its face.

Shrieking till he was hoarse, he turned to stumble the other way.

To be stopped dead by a blow in his midriff.

It didn't entirely knock the wind from him, not so much that he couldn't look down and see the shaft of the throwing spear quivering in the gale.

Two lumbering forms approached.

Jerome's first thought was to tear the spear from his body and fend them off with it. He could tell just by feeling that it had barely penetrated the steel mesh under his cassock, but it was fixed there, and he couldn't get it loose.

They came on apace. He turned to run the other way.

And was struck in his face and chest by another blast of wind and snow, and then by the demon, which was no figment of his tormented mind but reared there still, just waiting to embrace him. His shrieks choked off as the spearhead tore deeper, driven through the mail and the wasted muscle beneath, and the innards beneath that. Hot gore sprayed from his lips as he tottered, unbelievable pain transfixing his body, which only worsened when those others came from behind, muffled in cloaks and furs and stinking sheepskins, and taking him one per shoulder, rode him brutally forward along the hard ash shaft.

As Jerome's wails became frantic gurgles, his lungs filling with his own blood, the little light there was dimmed in his eyes, and the last thing he saw was a crude iron cross on what might once have been a neck-thong, as it was dangled in front of him.

Roland reined his horse up. 'What happened?'

'See for yourself,' Joubert replied.

He, Yvo de Taillebois and Milo de Hauteville had returned from scouring the nearby woods. It was a crisp, clear morning, the winter sky a pearlescent blue, but the snow lay a foot deep and mostly unbroken. There hadn't been a trace of Father Jerome's outward journey, his tracks filled in by the blizzard long before it had blown itself out, but the guard who'd seen him depart had still reported it, and they'd commenced searching before breakfast.

Even then, none had expected this.

The priest, frozen solid in a dog-like attitude, his hands clawed and body bent, lay sideways on a spread cloak, which they dragged behind them. A throwing spear had skewered him clean through. His head was turned sideways, the rigid rictus of his face a true mask of agony and despair, his gaping mouth clotted with crimson ice.

'This is one of our spears,' Roland said, shocked.

'We've left spears wherever we've been,' Turold said. 'Most of them sticking in Englishmen.'

'We think he did it to himself,' Joubert remarked.

Roland was even more shocked. 'Suicide? A priest?'

'There was a mark on the tree,' Taillebois said. 'As if he'd braced a spear there and run forward.'

Joubert snickered. 'Ugly damn tree. Holes rotted in it. Like a face.'

Roland shook his head. 'It doesn't make sense. He'd know he'd be damned.'

'You think he didn't fear that already?' Turold replied.

Joubert was particularly dismissive. 'He's been acting like a madman these last few days, anyway.'

No one could argue with that. Their chaplain had behaved strangely of late, gabbling his way through each morning service, his whole body shaking, most likely drinking more than his share of the Eucharistic wine.

'Hardly matters,' Joubert added. 'If we ever find this northern bloody earldom, he'd only have wanted to be its new bishop. Would probably have claimed a lion's share of everything.'

'There's no one now to say Mass for us,' someone complained.

'And that's *our* fault?' Joubert scoffed. 'I'm sure the pope will understand if you miss a few Sundays.'

'A real pope would have excommunicated us all anyway,' Turold said.

—

After breakfast, Cerdic returned to his tent to find Yvette still waiting there.

'Do you know something about this?' she enquired coldly.

'Me?' He didn't need to ask what she meant. 'Why would I?'

'You went to see Father Jerome last night.'

'To remonstrate with him for the way he upset you.'

'Cerdic, look at me. Please... look!' He turned to face her. 'What happened?' Her gaze was intense, her voice hard, penetrating.

He shrugged. 'I told him what I thought of him. Which he didn't like.'

'Is that all?'

'I didn't kill him, Yvette. Of course I didn't.'

'He told me yesterday that you said something to him... that he was "dead flesh walking".'

Cerdic was puzzled, but then remembered the murdered shepherd boy. 'I meant that his soul had perished. Him and the rest of these lying Frankish prelates.'

'Why would you say that to him?'

'Why? Are you serious? Because in giving their blessing to these horrors, they've broken every oath they've taken in their lives.'

She shook her head. 'Our priests haven't *caused* this bloodshed.'

'They haven't? Do you include Bishop Odo in that? And Father Jerome had some curious ideas about it. Have you forgotten his views on Lady Edith?'

Fresh tears sparkled in her eyes. 'All he did was tell me the truth.'

'What truth? That a woman driven to a madness of grief and terror is condemned to Hell? That's not the God I know.'

'Cerdic, it's because of Lady Edith that I believe him innocent of his own death. He was so appalled by the thought of her self-destruction that it moved him to tears.'

'He was moved to tears by the thought of what awaited *him* in the afterlife. But even if he didn't do it himself, Yvette... this land is strewn with the slain. You think their friends and relatives are asleep? You think the danger of vengeance from the bereaved is past?'

'So, we're siding with priest-killers now?'

'You're wrong if you think Jerome was a good man,' Cerdic said. 'He might not have murdered anyone himself, but his presence gave the rest of them licence.'

'But it wasn't his fault...'

'Why didn't he at least condemn them?'

'You know why.'

'Because he'd have been martyred?' He snorted derisively. 'I doubt it, somehow.'

'So... did you opt to martyr him yourself?'

He looked at her long and hard. 'I honestly thought you knew me better.'

'I know you intend to flout God's law. Which whether he was good or evil, Father Jerome represented. I imagine you'd like a land without priests. Is that right, Cerdic? So that when you unleash the mayhem in your soul, there'll be no one to remind you how far you've strayed from the light.'

He absorbed this with an attitude of indifference. 'You know, Yvette, my father taught my brother and I that we should always accept our new *wyrd*.'

That comment bewildered her, so she tried to dismiss it. 'I don't understand...'

'It means that our destinies can change very quickly. Those who rule now may be lying in the gutter tomorrow. Others who are beggars might blink and the next thing they've become kings. This is the way life is, it's the way it's always been. And we should prepare for that possibility because accepting it – making peace with it, if you like – may be the only way to survive.'

'I've already said that your father was very different from mine...'

'But I'm not the only person here whose *wyrd* is unravelling.'

'Cerdic...'

'Lord Joubert is the same. Count Cynric too, even Roland and Turold. Even you, Yvette. No one knows where all this will end, and until we do, we must all of us keep our swords sharp and our senses about us.'

'I still don't understand.'

He made to leave the tent. 'That's a problem I can't fix.'

'Cerdic...' Her tone was suddenly softer. He glanced back. 'You'll think me a fool for saying this...' she blinked away tears, 'but these last few weeks, I've increasingly thought you were someone I could love.'

He said nothing.

'And I've seen the way you look at me when you think I don't notice, and I suspect that you may feel the same.'

'Love? Yvette... I've never even touched you.'

'Maybe such gallantry encouraged me.'

'And now you've decided differently? Is that what you're saying?'

Her tone became a plea. 'It's just that every day you become more like these men you claim to hate.'

'I'm not just going to lie down and die, Yvette.' He opened the tent flap. 'If that's the price of love, then it's too damn high.'

CHAPTER 21

All the way from the south of England, having no map to hand, Cerdic had used a variety of means to direct Count Cynric's retinue north. Sometimes he was steered by the sun, sometimes by the stars, though quite often at this time of year neither of those were visible, and so he also had to speak to the odd peasant, usually someone too bold or dull-witted to run as they approached. As such, the journey overall was a piecemeal affair, the company navigating across Mercia under the control of a guide who occasionally had no idea at all where they were headed.

Of course, he never revealed this ignorance on his part to his captors, because, if he did, they'd quickly realise they were just as able to adopt the same approach and would be minus one more reason to keep him alive.

To maintain the illusion, Cerdic took point at all times with a swagger he never felt. But it wouldn't have been a straightforward journey in any case. Sticking to the byways rather than the highways, they came up against rivers, which, even if they were frozen, were immense obstacles, causing them to divert sometimes for miles before they could find bridges or fords. It added days to their journey, though this suited Cerdic to a degree, because it was almost February now, and though the winter chill lingered, the sun rose for longer, the snow cover gradually thinning. The flurries of flakes that had struck them on and off since their departure from the West Minster now gave way to sleet and bitter rain. It made for miserable travel, but at least it meant the spring was coming.

The constant detours also created more time for him to acquire skill with the longsword. As they'd agreed, Turold tutored Cerdic each morning, for forty minutes or so, before they broke camp, the knight ever more impressed with the lad's ability. On occasion, other knights like Will Malet and Milo de Hauteville joined them, at first only to watch, but then to offer advice of their own, sometimes to engage in tough but friendly combat, Turold spectating from the side, eager to see if his pupil was able to put his new learning into hard practice.

Mostly, he was.

Perhaps the one thing Cerdic took most from these sessions, aside from proficiency with the Norman longsword, was how many different fighting techniques there were.

He'd grown up in the world of the housecarls and had spent most of his time on the hewing block either with axe or broadsword, the purpose of that to build up his body-strength and battle rage, and to hone his precision-strike so that, when the time came, he could stand in the shieldwall with his comrades. As he understood it, the Vikings hadn't waged war in a vastly different way. In ancient times, or so Aethelric once told him, the *berzerkers* fought without ring-mail, relying purely on wolf-like aggression and personal prowess. In due course though, as the Viking raiding parties had enlarged into campaigning armies bent on conquering England, these elite warriors had become more precious to their leaders and were encouraged to fight armoured and in formation.

For all that, both the English and the Norse, while they valued the disciplines demanded of one-on-one combat, had clearly not put them to as much use as these Norman knights, who could fight either on foot or from horseback, and for whom the skills of the individualist were an intrinsic part of the tournament.

But there were other ways to wage war too.

Cerdic had initially perceived the Flemings as light infantry. They wore no encumbering mail and carried only minor side-arms, their primary weapon the crossbow. This too, as he'd already seen, was lighter than the Norman model, and thus more manoeuvrable in the midst of battle. But after they'd agreed terms with Count Cynric, the Flemings had returned to their own camp, about a mile away, to retrieve the rest of their equipment, and their horses. Ordinarily, it seemed, they rode into battle too, and so would be classified as light cavalry rather than infantry. But not only that; they could wield their crossbows just as effectively from the saddle. This explained their weapon's more diminutive design, but also the very high level of marksmanship demanded of the bowmen themselves, as it meant that nothing less would enable them to hit their targets cleanly.

On viewing them mounted and fully equipped, Count Cynric nodded with approval. As Roland said to Cerdic in a quick aside, it was yet another occasion when advice offered by the 'little earl-in-waiting' had proved useful. The count now positioned his new mounted crossbows on the outer flanks of their advancing column, an extra outside guard and a mobile force that was more than capable of meeting any ambushers head-on.

Arne himself, the Flemish captain, was something of a mystery. He mainly rode at the point with Cerdic and Roland, but seldom spoke, save to offer the odd snippet of laconic advice, perhaps if they'd reached some point of the journey where a path unexpectedly divided, or a bridge they'd hoped to find had collapsed.

Two weeks after the Flemings had joined the company, Roland was summoned back along the column to confer with Count Cynric, and Cerdic and Arne rode alone.

'She's quite a prize,' the Flemish captain said.

Cerdic was so surprised to hear him say anything that wasn't a response to a direct question, that at first he assumed he was talking to someone else.

But then the Fleming added: 'The daughter of House Hiemois. Your woman.'

'She's not my woman.' Cerdic tried his damnedest not to show the pain this caused him. 'We were friends, briefly. But we come from different worlds.'

'Worlds that still exist?' Such optimism seemed to amuse the sellsword.

Cerdic shrugged.

'I wonder where you are taking us? Do you even know?'

The lad threw him an irritable glance. 'Has someone been speaking to you? Lord Joubert, perhaps?'

'Lord Joubert is no one's ally, least of all ours.'

'You apparently share his opinion.'

'It's a genuine question, I assure you. Because from what I can see, you don't really know where you're going.'

Cerdic tried not to stiffen in his saddle. 'That's nonsense.'

'We're heading vaguely northward, albeit taking many diversions, and are only making any progress at all because I occasionally correct our course.'

Cerdic clamped his mouth shut, nervous but determined to hide it.

'I take it you're grateful?' Arne asked. 'I mean that I always take pains to disguise this assistance as nothing more than the odd helpful suggestion?' He chuckled. 'Don't fret, Englishman. At the moment we Flemings are being watered and fed at least. That's more than I could have offered my troop for much longer if we hadn't caught up with you. But of course, there's a limit to everything. At some point, if we continue endlessly into these northern wilds, I'll be forced to air my suspicions.'

'And what are your suspicions?'

Arne thought before pronouncing further. 'I think you speak truth about your noble heritage. I've seen the way you fight with the household champion. You've already had training. That much is evident. You fought against us with confidence. You're not some farm-lad trying his hand. But as for this earldom you're looking to share... that I'm less sure about.'

'We'll get there soon enough,' Cerdic responded. 'Then you'll see for yourself.'

'How soon? Do you even know?'

'Listen, *routier*...' Cerdic felt he'd heard enough. 'Just because the geography of England is no strength of mine, that doesn't mean I'm not what I say I am. In truth, until this year... until I was driven out of my home, I'd barely travelled anywhere. Anyway, how do *you* know where we are? You're not even English.'

'Travel is part of my profession. When I first came to this island, we had maps. Harald Sigurdsson's ambition did not end in the north. He wanted to be the new Canute, a king of all England. Once we'd destroyed your northern force, and your king had abdicated...'

'Abdicated?'

'Or been slain, it was all the same to the Hardraada, we'd have headed south. We had all of us memorised the roads, the towns. But as I say, your secret lack of knowledge is safe with me. For the moment.'

Cerdic was almost too embarrassed to ask the next question that occurred to him, but he suspected that Roland would be back with them shortly, and then he wouldn't be able to.

'Where are we headed now?'

'Two days to the west of here stands an old hillfort,' Arne said. 'All that remains of the old kingdom of Elmet. You know this place.'

Cerdic nodded. He had heard of it, though glancing west across the thinly wooded plain, still partly covered in snow, no such high point was in evidence thus far.

'They called it Dore,' Arne added. 'The Danes camped there for a time, but more importantly, you should know it as the entrance from Mercia to your great earldom of Northumbria.'

Cerdic nodded, pleased about that at least.

'We continue this way,' the sellsword said, 'and a week from now, maybe a little longer, we arrive at York. Which is your home, *ja*?'

'How do you know that?' Cerdic said. 'How do you know my earldom lies east of the Pennioroche highlands and not west, in the Ribble lands or Cumbria?'

'You have an accent.'

It was such an obvious explanation that Cerdic couldn't reply.

'The main question in my mind,' Arne said, 'is do we approach this city of York, or not? How safe can it be for us?'

Cerdic shrugged. 'I'm sorry to say it, but I think, if we were going to be ambushed by an army of displaced housecarls, it would have happened by now.'

'I agree. But my concern is not with them, it's with you.'

'With me?'

'If you're who you say you are, what happens if a great force of your supporters is in York? Just waiting to pour out on us?'

'Even if they were, which they aren't, Earl Morcar has forbidden it.'

'Earl Morcar.' Arne considered. 'I never think of him as a great commander.'

'His rank cannot be discounted. There are many awaiting the outcome of he and his brother's talks with King William.'

'They will wait a long time. Morcar and Edwin are going to Normandy.'

Cerdic was shocked. 'With the king?'

'Who else?'

'When was this decided?'

'I imagine as soon as they surrendered.'

'The northern earls are William's prisoners too?'

'Very much so, I'd say. Along with the Aetheling and Archbishop Stigand. The only reason Archbishop Ealdred will be spared this indignity is his age. You know of a thegn called Copsi?'

Cerdic nodded, still struggling with the news that Edwin and Morcar were no more. 'Yes. I even met him once. He's an arch traitor.'

'A dab-hand with a dagger, I'm told?'

Cerdic was still distracted. 'Why do you mention Copsi?' An ugly thought then struck him. '*He's* not been granted one of the northern earldoms?'

'Northumbria,' Arne replied. 'I heard this just before we headed north in pursuit of you.'

Cerdic sat rigid. Copsi the traitor... Copsi the assassin. He would have harboured the deepest grudge imaginable against Earl Rothgar, were Rothgar alive. Whatever happened when they got to Wulfbury, it was impossible to imagine that Cerdic, even if he managed to retake it, would hold it for long if Copsi, with King William's backing, was now Earl of Northumbria. Not that it seemed likely, surely? Copsi was a disinherited thegn, a camp-follower of the Normans. It had to be a temporary measure, if it was any measure at all.

Though who knew in times of turmoil like these?

'You seem troubled?' Arne said.

Cerdic shook himself. 'It's nothing. I'm just saddened that so many good men perished during this war, while so many vile men survived.'

'A good response. And you've answered my question. Wherever your father's earldom lies, you wouldn't be so unnerved by the prospect of Earl Copsi if you had an army of your own lying in wait.'

'Neither would I have recruited a Norman horde to help me retrieve it.'

'You *recruited* them, I see.' Arne smiled all the more. 'I admire the way you think, Cerdic of House Unknown. Something tells me these next few weeks will be interesting for all of us.'

'Arne of Brabant?'

The sellsword had wheeled his horse around, but now he turned it back.

'If you were part of the Hardraada's army,' Cerdic said, 'did you ever encounter a Viking jarl named Wulfgar Ragnarsson?'

The Fleming mused. 'An illustrious name. I should know if I ever had. Would this be the same Northman who stole your father's earldom?'

'I've answered enough of your questions. Can you not answer one of mine?'

'The Northmen in my company are remnants of many Viking crews destroyed at Stamford Bridge. The only thing they have in common is they failed to reach what remained of their fleet before it sailed away. It was the obvious thing for us to join forces. There are few of them left, but I can ask among them.'

Cerdic nodded.

'But bear in mind,' Arne said. 'Wulfgar Ragnarsson is presumably descended from Ragnar Lodbrok? A name to stir a Viking's blood. As things are, I have only narrow control over them. I can't guarantee even that will hold should they learn a Ragnarsson is in the field.'

'How many remain exactly?' Cerdic asked.

'A handful.'

'A handful is neither here nor there.'

'Including Tyrkil?'

'The giant?' Cerdic said. 'I saw him fighting. He's slow. I'm not.'

Arne chuckled again. 'As I say, Englishman… interesting times.'

CHAPTER 22

It was the second week in February, late evening, when they arrived in the vicinity of York, pitching camp a mile west of the city, on wooded ground protected by a loop in the River Ouse. There were strong signs now that winter was receding. The air was milder, though there was no immediate thaw, many patches of snow and ice remaining, but mostly the sky was blue. It would still be more pleasant for the leaders among them to find lodgings in the city itself, or so Joubert argued. However, in the debate following this, Arne of Brabant reminded them all that Morcar had been deprived of his earldom, and that Thegn Copsi now ruled the north. This was a new name to most of them, and though Joubert contended that if this Copsi had been appointed by the king, it meant he'd be friendly to the king's men, Roland replied that they were no longer the king's men. They were seeking to seize lands of their own, which the king might object to.

In addition, he said, Cerdic had insisted that this Copsi was a rapacious bastard unlikely to offer welcome to anyone, English or Norman, if he considered them a threat to his power.

Joubert became wild-eyed with annoyance. 'Are we still heeding the words of this English vagabond? Who won't even tell us where we're bound for.'

'All I can say, my lord,' Cerdic replied, standing up and addressing Count Cynric, whose chair had been set up on the other side of the campfire, 'is that Copsi is unsuited to be earl of anywhere. I met him once, and it was inconsequential. But at home, my seniors spoke nothing but ill of him. He's a self-serving traitor and a proven assassin.'

'He's your countryman, is he not?' the count said.

'Which shows I do not make these accusations lightly. If Copsi is now in York, and you go there, you'll be received. But once he learns you're not on the king's business, you'll all die in your sleep, probably with throats slit. That is how he murdered Lord Gospatric.'

Joubert gazed sullenly at him. Count Cynric remained in thought.

'I'll go to the city anyway,' Joubert said. 'We can't ignore it. It's the centre of everything that happens in this part of the kingdom. It's the second high seat.'

Count Cynric glanced at him. 'You wish to spy?'

'Exactly. We can go incognito.'

'And who, pray, is "we"?'

'Yvo and me,' Joubert said. Then he nodded at Cerdic. 'And the boy. We'll need an interpreter.'

'And if Cerdic goes with you, he won't return,' Roland interjected.

Joubert glowered. 'What do you accuse me of, Casterborus?'

Roland appealed to the count. 'My lord, this is ridiculous. There was an incident only one month ago...'

'Some of my men became impatient,' Joubert retorted. 'They died when the Flemings attacked. Justice has been served.' He glanced at Cerdic, and then at Yvette, daring either of them to counter his claims. 'Someone *must* go to York, Father. We can't keep bypassing these hubs of activity. We need to know what's happening in the kingdom, if nothing else. It would be madness to miss this opportunity.'

'Take Turold,' the count said.

'What's that?'

Turold stepped forward.

'Take Turold,' the count said again. 'You need an interpreter, as you've said. Plus, he'll give you extra fighting prowess if it's needed.'

'Very well.' But Joubert only veiled his frustration thinly.

'On that basis, the plan is good,' Count Cynric said. 'Learn everything you can but keep a low profile. I want no incidents of any sort, if they can be avoided.'

'As you wish. One question, Father.' Joubert pointed at Cerdic. 'You don't believe these scurrilous stories that I intended to murder this... most valuable possession of ours?'

The count sipped wine. 'If I did, I'd be highly displeased. I have my own business with young Cerdic. And that will commence tomorrow, while you are in York.'

Puzzled, Cerdic glanced at Turold, who looked equally surprised, and then at Roland, who simply shrugged.

—

The following morning, before it was even light, Turold, Joubert and Yvo de Taillebois, wearing peasant garb over their mail, their weapons concealed among their saddlebags, rode out, heading for York.

It made sense to do that, Cerdic supposed. The count's small force was so deep in enemy territory now that if they met serious organised opposition, they would struggle. Of course, if they'd asked him, he could have told them, as he'd told Arne of Brabant, that if they hadn't attracted a major English attack by now, it was unlikely to happen at all. He didn't want his own plans capsized of course, but any sign, no matter how small, that England's military forces were not totally scattered, even if it was only up here in the north, might have given him a smidgen of hope for the country's future. But ultimately, it all depended on the political situation. By the sounds of it, both Morcar and Edwin's acquiescence to the invaders had paid them no dividends. Meanwhile, given his history as a ruthless, self-interested rebel, there had to be uncertainty about how Earl Copsi would govern Northumbria, but even if he could actually find any other English thegns and hearth-troops who'd follow him, he was clearly bought and paid for by the Norman king.

But much of this was supposition. Count Cynric wished to know things for certain, and that was the reason behind Joubert's reconnaissance. It all made perfect sense. Except that now there was something else in the wind. Something Cerdic hadn't seen coming, despite his constant attempts to understand his captors better.

'What's this business Count Cynric has with you?' Yvette asked.

Cerdic looked around. He'd been standing alone by the river, watching the waters gush past a section where the sheet ice had broken. She'd approached unheard from the concentric circles of tents around the breakfast fires and now stood wrapped in a heavy pelt.

He straightened. 'I don't know. I've an audience with him in half an hour.'

She pondered that. It was the first time she'd spoken to him since the death of Father Jerome, and disapproval was still written all over her stiff, anxious posture.

'He doesn't seem angry with you,' she said.

'Why would he be angry with me?'

'But then, he often conceals his true feelings.'

'You mean does he plan to torture our destination out of me?'

'Can you think of a better reason for him to want to see you?'

'I doubt he'd have sent Joubert away if that was the intention. Have you eaten?'

'If you can call it that.' She huddled deeper into her fur. 'More salt mutton and tasteless vegetable broth.'

'Yvette?' he asked. 'How is it that you... of all people, can believe I murdered that priest? I'm in the camp of my enemies, and yet none of *them* thinks that.'

She looked sad. 'Maybe I'm just the only one who cares.'

'What does that mean?'

'Cerdic, these Normans...'

'*You* are a Norman.'

'No!' she said forcefully. '*These* Normans... these warriors who've come across the sea with Duke William. Why would they care about one more death? You've seen how many they've already slaughtered. And against all my warnings, you too are becoming part of it.'

Again, he was stung. 'How can you say that when I fought so hard against them?'

'How can you deny it, Cerdic? Every morning now, I see you with Turold.'

'Sparring.'

'Learning different ways to kill.'

'Learning how to fight.'

'You can already fight.'

'But not like them,' he said.

'That's my point. Do you want to become a Norman?'

He shook his head. 'I never said that.'

'I've heard you asking Roland about the code of chivalry. What it means. What it involves. You want to join them, Cerdic. You may not realise that, but that's clearly what it is.' She walked a short distance along the riverbank, boots crunching the snow-crust. 'I don't blame you for being confused. You've nothing left. Your home is gone, your family dead. But I can't pretend it's all right.'

'Perhaps you'd be happier if I was roped to the back of a wagon again?'

She glanced round. 'At least then you'd be the oppressed, not the oppressor.'

'You call *me* the oppressor?'

'Don't pretend you're insulted.' Pinkish dots had appeared on her cheeks. 'I think you're a good man. Or you were. But it just goes on, doesn't it? This fighting, this killing. It goes on until there's no reason for it, until it's become an end in itself.'

For the first time in several days, Cerdic felt angry with her. Not just affronted now, but actually angry. 'You know, Yvette, when Eadora... a girl I once knew...' She watched him carefully; she hadn't heard this name before. 'A girl I imagined might once have been mine... when she was *murdered* by the Vikings...'

Yvette flinched. 'When they severed her spine with a throwing-axe, I swore I wouldn't rest until I drove them out of Wulfbury.'

He let that hang. A second passed before she realised what he'd said.

'Wulfbury?' she asked.

'There, I've told you. That's my home. Or it was.'

She shook her head. 'You shouldn't have told me...'

'I didn't tell the others. *These* Normans who I'm now indistinguishable from.' She turned away. 'Yvette.' He took her by the wrists, not hard, but sufficiently to hold her in place, not that she resisted. 'I know what I am. And I will be that again. I'll not be tossed out like household rubbish. I'll not see my family name vanish from history at the hand of a...'

'At the hand of a pirate,' another voice said, 'and no more than that.'

They spun towards the trees and saw Arne of Brabant approaching.

Cerdic released the girl, but cursed himself, unsure how much the mercenary captain had overheard.

'I asked among my men,' Arne said, 'and while we know no Viking nobleman who calls himself Ragnarsson, you mentioned that he also goes by the name Wulfgar?'

Cerdic nodded.

Arne smiled to himself. 'It seems that among my company once there was a half-Dane and half-English who called himself Wulfgar. I was a ranker myself at the time, but I have memories of him. A good soldier... housecarl standard I'd say. Who once, when drunk, admitted that he'd fled his home in England after killing his father during a quarrel. This Wulfgar did not stay with us long. He left to join Earl Tostig, who was seeking recruits to help him reclaim Northumbria, a land he boasted was filled with golden halls and great hunting estates, all of which would be gifted to his followers should he triumph.'

'It doesn't sound like the same man,' Cerdic said. 'My Wulfgar claimed...'

Arne held up his hand. '*My* Wulfgar also made claims, though only in his cups. He was descended from a line called Ragnarsson, he said. From Ragnar Lodbrok himself. The rest of the company doubted this. He was Danish on his father's side, but they knew him as a common sellsword, a man who only left England for Flanders to evade the price of his father's murder.'

Cerdic shook his head. 'It still doesn't sound like…'

'He had a single mark on his shoulder.'

This time, Cerdic said nothing. Though it seemed a thousand years ago now, he remembered that night in the stable, when Jarl Wulfgar had pronounced death upon him. He'd been stripped to the waist at the time, and he too had borne a mark on his shoulder, a single but very distinctive tattoo.

'Odin's wolf-headed staff,' Arne said. 'Crossed over by Thor's hammer, to make a saltire. All of it in deepest black.'

Cerdic felt a tremor of excitement, which he fought hard to suppress. 'You're saying this man was *not* a Viking lord?'

'Not to the knowledge of my men,' Arne replied. 'Though later, I hear, when he joined with Earl Tostig, he made great play of this lineage he had imagined for himself… most likely to recruit more Northmen to the rebel earl's cause, and later to the cause of the Hardraada.'

'Whom he abandoned in his hour of need,' Cerdic said.

Arne nodded and smiled. 'This was new information to my friend, Tyrkil.'

Cerdic remembered again the giant Viking captured with the Flemings.

'He served in the Hardraada's personal *drengr*,' Arne said, 'where he earned the name "Widow-Maker". I told you he is all that remains of them. So, he too would like to meet this imposter who took his army away before the vital battle was fought.'

'He'll have to stand behind me,' Cerdic said. 'Though I'm glad to hear we have a common cause.'

'I thought you should know this. And now, I understand, the Count of Tancarville is searching the camp for you.'

Cerdic nodded his thanks, turning to Yvette as Arne moved away.

She regarded him uncertainly, worriedly.

'Wulfgar Ragnarsson,' he said. 'A fraud. A pretender. An Englishman. He has no connection to the earldom of Ripon… he's a renegade, like Arne said.' He shook his head. 'He'll still take some beating. But you know, Yvette… I don't care if you disapprove that I must become a Norman to make that happen. I'll not see everything my family ever worked for seized by some everyday bandit.'

She clearly wanted to reply, but from her expression knew that it was pointless.

'*Cerdic!*' he was hailed from the camp. It was Roland. 'You're summoned.'

Cerdic turned back to the girl. 'I'm sorry, Yvette. My new *wyrd* is at last taking shape.'

She looked away, and he left her.

Yvette assumed it was only natural that anyone, even an affable young man, as Cerdic had been when they'd first met, fresh-faced and sunny-haired, not much more than a boy, would degrade into something darker and more vengeful the more pain was forced upon him, and especially so when he finally felt his own power returning.

Partial, near-imaginary power at present, but power all the same.

She didn't understand this Saxon/Viking concept of the *wyrd*, but if it had a human form, which she couldn't help but envisage, the one beckoning Cerdic was a humped and twisted thing indeed.

CHAPTER 23

They circled the camp on its outskirts, Count Cynric and Cerdic riding alongside each other. The nobleman was fully mailed, but wore his cloak wrapped around him. His helmet and weapons hung among his saddlebags. Cerdic, unarmed as usual, sat stiffly in his own saddle, still bemused to have been asked to this meeting. Ten yards back, also mounted, Roland scanned the snowy woods. Behind him, by another twenty yards, six mounted men-at-arms additionally kept watch.

'Doubtless you're wondering what this is about?' the count asked.

He wasn't yet fully restored to health. It was a crisp, cold morning, but not unbearable, yet he shivered under his wrappings. Up close, he seemed thin and frail.

'I think I've an idea, my lord,' the lad replied.

'Ah, you do?'

'You've come a long way on my say-so. You've lost men. But we're now in the north, York less than half a day's ride. You want to know where we're going.'

The count only spoke again after a moment's thought. 'You understand that I'll lose considerable face if, when I finally arrive at this earldom of yours, there is nothing left of it? Assuming there was something there to begin with.'

'My lord, I can only pose the question: what would I gain from having lied to you?'

'It's kept you alive, has it not?'

'But it wouldn't for much longer.'

Cynric pondered. 'I will ask you this, young Cerdic, and on this occasion, I *expect* an answer. How far away are we now?'

'Two or three days, at a fast march. A week at our current pace.'

'In your estimation, do I have the manpower to recapture it?'

'That all depends on whether the Viking horde has strengthened or weakened, my lord. I won't know until I'm able to see for myself. Their force, initially at least, was significant. And unless they've literally destroyed everything, which would make no sense, they'll now be in a highly defensible position. My father's main fortification was notoriously strong. But I know ways we can get to them. I *do* have a plan.'

Cynric gazed ahead. 'And when do you propose to share it?'

'Only when I must.'

The count pondered again. 'My son, Joubert, believes we could draw this information out of you with the branding iron or whip.'

'I dare say I'd crack, my lord. But how would you know it's the correct information? The day you arrive at the destination my tortured person advised you about, and find it's a barren waste?'

'This doesn't demonstrate trust on your part.'

'My lord, trust must be earned. I don't need to remind you what's happened in this country of mine. I'm not the only one here clinging to life by my fingernails.'

The count rode on, still staring directly ahead. It was a disconcerting habit of his, this refusal to make eye contact. It always seemed to imply that there were more important things on his mind than you.

'I can only say what I said before,' Cerdic added. 'I'm heir to an extensive and prosperous earldom. It can be yours, if you'll spare me long enough to show you exactly where it is.'

'And what do you expect in return? An equal share? You must know that's not possible.'

Cerdic shrugged. 'My freedom perhaps. Some means by which to survive and lead a tolerable life.'

'In service to a foreign master?' Cynric sounded sceptical.

'In the end, my lord, we all of us serve someone. You and your men seem less foreign to me now that I've learned your language.

I imagine that will happen across the whole of England in due course.'

'What do you know of my family?'

It was such a change of direction that, briefly, Cerdic was thrown. 'Erm… that they have a long and exalted history. They must have, for Tancarville is a great lordship. I know also that your eldest son, Dagobert, is heir-in-waiting to all your estates. Also, that as well as Joubert, you have another child…'

'My youngest, Aliza.' Cynric seemed thoughtful. 'She is fourteen this year, and eminently marriageable.'

'I see.' Though in truth, Cerdic didn't see at all.

'Do you understand how dynasties grow strong?' the count asked.

'By having enough men and swords to defend them.'

'That is how they survive. A dynasty grows strong by forging alliances with other dynasties. And the easiest way to do this is by marriage. What do you think of this?'

'I'm young,' Cerdic said. 'But even I know marriages that haven't lasted.'

'When there's nothing to be gained, that is sometimes the case. But when there's *everything* to be gained, the sacrament of marriage can forge very strong bonds.'

Cerdic listened on, feeling they were approaching the key point.

'The new King of England has a dilemma,' the count said. 'The men he brought here are baying for their rewards. Some, the lesser ones, will be paid off and seek those honours to which they'll never be entitled in other lands. But in the case of those who are mightier, it must be different. Some, the king will trust implicitly and be glad to invest with lands and titles. It will benefit him too, as they'll help him rule effectively. Others, those who are *truly* mighty, he must reward whether he trusts them or not. That is the price a potentate pays for building an army so vast. Of course, this still leaves many titles open, and here is the crux of it. To fill these remaining vacancies, does he restore those English lords who once held them?'

'It will be difficult,' Cerdic said. 'Many are dead.'

'That is true, while some he can never trust in any circumstance. But all these seats of power must be filled, so at some point even Duke William, now a king, will be forced to compromise.'

'Forgive me, Lord,' Cerdic said, 'what has all this to do with alliances between dynasties? More to the point, what has it to do with me?'

Cynric spoke on as if he hadn't heard. 'The threat of dynastic strife is another problem the new king faces. Overmighty lords will become mightier yet if their new lands are physically adjoined to those they already hold.'

Cerdic understood this much at least. It made no sense to allow mini empires to grow within the boundaries of one's own.

'I, for example,' the count said, 'have extensive estates in Normandy. If I sought new lands adjacent to those, especially now there are questions about my loyalty, the king, or the duke, as he would be there, would refuse by instinct. But if I sought my new acquisitions far from Tancarville, say… here, in the north of England, he might, in that spirit of compromise we have already discussed, consider it a risk worth taking.'

Cerdic remained puzzled. 'Is this not what we're planning already, my lord?'

'That *was* my plan, but plans evolve.' The count looked round at him. 'Do they not?'

'The best ones, yes.'

Cynric nodded and smiled. 'Which is why, when we arrive at this earldom of yours, I intend to install you as the earl.'

Cerdic almost reined his horse up.

'It's this compromise business again,' the count said. 'The king will only sell properties back to those few English he has genuine faith in. You, he doesn't know. Even if my entire retinue dies in the battle with these Northmen, and only you survive, it will count for nothing. However, if you aspired to retrieve your earldom as my son-in-law, the outcome might be more favourable.'

This time, Cerdic was convinced he'd misheard. 'My lord, I... your...?'

'I told you I have a marriageable daughter.'

'I understand, but...' Cerdic's shorn hair prickled. His heart thudded.

'Don't be too quick to dismiss this idea, boy. We've already discussed how when dynasties join, they can be stronger.'

'But, my lord, my... *my* dynasty is...'

'Exhausted? Of course. In truth, you have nothing. So, you're wondering what *I* would gain from this?'

'Well...' Cerdic's thoughts still raced, 'yes.'

'Again, it's a compromise. The king may grant me this mini earldom of yours simply because it's far away and he doesn't wish to be troubled by it. It may also allay my minor rebellion. There is advantage to him, even if he doesn't like me.'

'So, why not give it to Joubert, as you intended?'

Cynric frowned. 'Joubert, I fear, will bring infamy on our name. No doubt you think we're already infamous? For partaking in slaughter?'

Cerdic flushed a little. 'If I don't say it, my lord, others will.'

'That's one of many things I like about you, boy. You speak honestly. So, I must be honest too. Joubert is ill-suited to high office in England. For reasons I can't understand, he hates the English with a passion. And they will hate him back. However, if *you* ruled here, part of our family but also a native Northumbrian, I fancy you'd win the people's hearts and minds.'

Cerdic frowned. This was actually an ugly thought. 'They'd consider me a traitor.'

'Simply for marrying? I fear you misunderstand me, Cerdic. You won't be a puppet. You'll be the *real* earl. You can advise the king, enforce his laws, tax the people, build your own house...'

'But still I'll be answerable to you?'

'I'll be your ally. No more. And a distant one at that. There may be times when I call on your help, but it won't be an exacting relationship, and at least my daughter's future and the future of my grandchildren will be assured.'

'I'll still be part of the Norman hegemony.'

Cynric's thin lips twisted. 'This is something you need to respect, Cerdic. Duke William... now King William, is a single-minded beast, a true devil of his line. No doubt the English will rebel and rebel, and each time he will quell it and each time there'll be blood and horror across the land, and eventually they will accept, because the downtrodden must always eventually accept. But that won't be the case *here*. Because you, Cerdic the Englishman, Cerdic the Northumbrian, will be master.'

'But why would the king accept it?'

'For the reasons I've outlined. You say you have documents proving your right to this inheritance. If so, that will make it easier for him. He can simply let it happen. The people hereabouts can offer no alternative to *you*. In his mind, only one thing will be better than a loyal Norman hand on the tiller, and that is a loyal English hand. There'll be no greater guarantee of stability.'

Cerdic pondered, their slow hoofbeats echoing from the rind of frost coating the ground. It could be made to work, he supposed. But there were serious obstacles.

'Joubert will object,' he said.

'Joubert will do as I tell him,' Cynric replied. 'I have other plans for my second son...' Before he could elaborate, a shout reached them from the camp.

'Count Cynric! Lord Joubert has returned... with important news.'

'Already?' the count muttered. He threw a lingering glance towards the tents. 'You resist telling me your plan, Cerdic. But I have trusted you with mine. Think on it. Few great lords would ever make such concessions.' And he cantered away, snow flying at his heels. The mounted men-at-arms scrambled in pursuit.

Cerdic looked at Roland, who hovered there, his face written with disbelief, though it was Roland of course who'd proclaimed Count Cynric *a thinker as well as a fighter.*

'You heard all that?' Cerdic asked.

'How could I miss it?'

Cerdic shrugged. 'I'm speechless.'
'Don't get too excited.'
'Why?'
'Remember Saint Benedict?'
'Who?'
The knight spurred his horse towards the camp. 'Beware of golden chalices… they often contain poison.'

CHAPTER 24

'The city of York is gearing up for war,' Joubert said, looking amused by the very notion.

He stood beside the campfire, now built up to a warming blaze despite the midday hour. He stripped off his peasant garb item by item, revealing the chain-mail below.

'They know we're here?' someone asked, sounding nervous.

'I doubt it.' Joubert accepted a flagon of wine from a camp-boy and sloshed at least half of it into his mouth. 'They don't seem well organised. We were able to walk into the city through its open front gates without even being asked our names. But a mercenary company has arrived there. Not the quality of your troops, Arne of Brabant. An unwashed rabble of rapists and child-killers masquerading as soldiers.'

Cerdic glanced at Arne, who stood among his men, listening. Almost the entire company ringed the fire. Count Cynric was back in his chair of judgement, Roland next to him. Turold, still dressed as a peasant, albeit the burliest and most menacing that any village in England had ever seen, stood to one side, arms folded. To Cerdic's eye, he seemed subdued.

'Did this rabble cross the sea with the duke?' someone else asked.

'Some may have.' Joubert handed his flagon to the camp-boy, indicating that he wanted it refilled. 'There were Bretons and Franks among them. But some were of Norse stock, others Frisians or Flemings.'

'How many?' Roland asked.

'It's hard to be certain. At present, they're occupied in the taverns and brothels. At a guess, four to five hundred.'

'I myself can't be sure there are so few,' Turold ventured. 'It was difficult to make any kind of headcount.'

'So, if they came this way, they *could* pose a threat?' Roland said.

Joubert sneered. 'I told you they're trash. We'd destroy them in half a day.'

Roland glanced towards Turold. 'Do you concur with that at least?'

Joubert scowled. 'What's the matter, Casterborus? You won't take *my* word for it?'

Roland glanced at the count. 'Turold has seen many battles, my lord.'

The count raised an eyebrow at his champion.

'Mostly, I concur, my lord,' Turold said. 'The ones I saw were low quality, but as I say, I can't confirm their numbers. However many, a substantial force has clearly been sent ahead to prepare the ground for this new fellow, Copsi.'

There was a prolonged thoughtful silence.

'*You* know all about this Copsi, of course,' Joubert suddenly said. 'Do you not... *Cerdic*?'

Cerdic was surprised by Joubert's near-friendly use of his name. Everyone looked at him.

'Thegn Copsi was the subject of much conversation on my father's mead-benches,' he said. 'I believe I mentioned his murder of Lord Gospatric of Bamburgh. At the time, he was notorious as a hired blade. Tostig had several such creatures under pay, but Copsi was said to be the worst, mainly because he and his paymaster had similar ambitions to be much more than they were. Gospatric, in contrast, was known as a good and humble man. His home, Bamburgh, is a hold in the extreme north of Northumbria, on England's frontier with Scotland. Gospatric served as High Reeve of Cumbria. That is also part of Northumbria, but a difficult region to govern. The Britons and Norse-Irish who mostly live there are thinly spread but stubborn and fractious. However, my father always said that Gospatric ruled with diligence and fairness and managed to establish peace. In 1061, though, Malcolm, the King of Scots, invaded that region and captured it. Unhappy that Earl Tostig, his overlord, would take no action against these interlopers, Gospatric travelled to King Edward's court at the West Minster, and there, on the fourth night of Christmas, in the king's own house, was murdered in his bed.'

Cerdic turned specifically to Count Cynric. 'This is the kind of man Thegn Copsi is... I can't bring myself to call him "Earl" because I find it inconceivable that anyone has awarded him such power.'

Joubert drained his second cup of wine and wiped his mouth. 'Well, the good news for you, Cerdic, is that at present his power exists in name only. This place Bamburgh... the lord there now is a certain Oswulf.'

Cerdic nodded. 'Gospatric's nephew, I believe.'

Joubert turned to the others. 'There's talk in York that this Oswulf won't cede an inch of his ancestral land to this new Earl of Northumbria. Apparently, if his uncle's murderer so much as darkens the north with his presence, Oswulf has vowed to kill him.'

'Hence the military advance-guard in York,' Turold added.

'They are not here for *us*, Father,' Joubert explained. 'They don't even know we are here, and probably won't care. For the time at least, we should be unimpeded.' He glanced again at Cerdic. 'That was the good news...'

Again, the tone seemed friendly. Too friendly.

'Are you ready for the bad?' Joubert's smile curved into a grin.

Cerdic said nothing. Turold looked down at his boots.

'We learned all this from a fellow we stumbled on just inside the main gate to the city,' Joubert said, pivoting in a slow circle as he addressed the whole of the company. 'A gibbering fool, we initially thought. A beggar with scattered wits. But then we took a second look at his garb, and we thought it seemed familiar. And so we spoke to him. At first, he was hostile, surly, but his tongue was loosened after we plied him with food and drink.' Joubert glanced at Cerdic again, this time without smiling. 'Yvo!'

Yvo de Taillebois forced his way through, steering someone in front of him, a stumbling wreck in black tatters instead of actual clothes, whose rancid stink entered the open space before he did. When Cerdic saw the fellow, he went numb.

He'd shrunken to a skeletal shadow of his former self, but despite the bone-thin features and straggling, wire-wool beard, there was no mistaking the disgusting strip of ragged, ordure-caked linen binding the gashed holes where the fellow's eyes had once been.

'Turold!' Joubert said aloud. 'You will translate.'

Turold nodded grimly.

'Your name is Haco, is that correct?' Joubert asked.

Turold translated both that and the response: 'He says that's correct.'

Joubert put another question. 'This man, Cerdic, a nobleman's son, who after your brave service in his father's war-band, betrayed you to a life of blind beggary. Is he here?'

Turold translated again. 'He says he is sure he just heard Lord Cerdic speaking.'

'Speak up, Cerdic,' Joubert said. 'Let Haco hear you again.'

'Haco,' Cerdic said hesitantly. 'You don't understand what you've...'

Haco pointed, grinning through his filth and sores. 'That is him!' he shouted in English. 'That is the man. I'd know that hateful voice anywhere.'

Turold translated again.

Joubert looked at Cerdic. 'No love lost, I see.'

There were snickers from his own *mesnie*. Cerdic said nothing.

Joubert turned to Count Cynric, who remained blank and unreadable.

'Father... may I introduce Cerdic Aelfricsson. It may please you to know that, despite his callous betrayal of this formerly loyal hearth-man, most of what he's told us is the truth. Take this, for instance...'

He rummaged among his own rags and drew out a separate bundle of cloth. When he snapped it open and draped it on the ground, they saw what remained of a surcoat with a cloak attached at the shoulders. It was begrimed by blood, mud and other kinds of filth, and slashed and torn many times over. But it had once been white, and the image on the front of it was clearly visible as a blue boar's head.

'See for yourself the crest of the earldom of Ripon,' Joubert said. 'The same crest carved on the ring that our friend, Cerdic, showed us when first we captured him. It's a lesser earldom than Northumbria, but still of significant value. Its capital is the fortress town of Wulfbury, which stands in the heart of a region of green valleys called Swaledale, located some fifty miles north of here. Earl Rothgar, the respected lord of this region, died at the battle called Fulford. His oldest son, Unferth, would have inherited all, but he also died... on Senlac Ridge. Friend Haco, who was wearing this garment when we encountered him, is adamant that one son remained. Name of Cerdic. The same Cerdic who abandoned him after he'd suffered these appalling wounds in defence of his household's banner.'

Joubert fixed Cerdic with a triumphant, derisive smile.

'It... wasn't like that,' Cerdic tried to reply.

'Haco,' Joubert continued, 'does not know for certain whether or not the Norse army occupying Swaledale has enlarged itself since then by attracting additional spears. Stragglers cast adrift after Harald the Hardraada was slain perhaps. Or maybe has shrunk as its chieftains have been allocated their own halls and farms. But blinded though he is, this man, Haco, can lead us there. It was his home too, you see. All he needs in return is food, drink and a warmer bed to sleep in than he's known of late, and he will guide us all the way. We no longer need rely on the word of this snake-in-the-grass.'

He ambled towards Cerdic, one hand clamped on the hilt of his longsword, clearly hoping the lad would give him a reason to draw it.

Count Cynric stood up. 'A splendid day's work. I can't be happier that young Cerdic's credentials are finally proven.'

'Do we execute him now?' Joubert asked. 'For daring to treat us like equals, like fools even, for trying to win back his petty title with the lives of our men?'

Cynric signalled an attendant, who brought him a pelt. Meticulously, he wrapped it around his body. 'We don't execute him at all,' he said. 'Joubert, walk with me.'

He strode from his chair, an alley clearing among the men. When Roland hastened to follow, the count held up a flat hand. 'This conversation will be private.'

Roland glanced at Joubert, who, confused and vaguely truculent, trudged after his father. 'Hold the English villein here!' he said before vanishing through the muttering crowd. 'He doesn't go anywhere!'

Cerdic turned, to find Turold approaching.

'You're truly of noble blood.' The champion seemed happier now, possibly because Joubert's discovery of Cerdic's identity, to which he'd been a party, hadn't immediately resulted in the lad's death. 'I'm impressed.'

Cerdic was perplexed. 'You didn't believe that before? And yet you still became a friend?'

'I take men as I find them. You fight and train well. You show judgement and competence. If you aren't of the lordly caste, you should be.'

'Count Cynric thinks the same,' Roland said quietly. 'He plans to marry him to Aliza.'

Turold looked dumbfounded, though that didn't stop him grabbing Cerdic's hand. 'Congratulations are in order...'

'I'm not so sure,' Roland countered.

A groom handed him the reins to his horse, and he swung up into the saddle. He stared over the heads of the rest of the men after the diminishing figures of the count and his son, already a good hundred yards from the camp, walking westward along the half-frozen river.

'Cynric is a clever man,' Turold said. 'I'd never have considered a ploy like this.'

'Yes, but the cost won't fall on you,' Roland retorted. 'Or on the count. It will fall on Joubert.'

They'd now lost sight of both father and son, the twosome having rounded a bend. A small group of men-at-arms tagged in pursuit, but, having been ordered to keep their distance, were seventy or eighty yards behind.

'How many others know about this?' Turold asked.

Cerdic shrugged. 'None, as far as I'm aware.'

'That's as it should be. The count will want to tell Joubert first.' Turold looked towards Yvette, who stood about twenty yards away. 'Your sweetheart will be disappointed.'

'I don't think so,' Cerdic replied. 'She believes I'm turning into one of you.'

The knight frowned. 'But *she's* one of us.'

'I mean men of violence.'

'She's daughter to the Count of Hiemois. He commands a military power greater than Count Cynric's.'

'She regrets that too,' Cerdic said.

Before they could say more, a cry broke over them.

Prolonged, eerily shrill.

It came from a couple of hundred yards maybe, beyond the nearest clutch of trees. But they heard it clearly, every man coming alert. A second cry followed. This one bespoke horror and agony, and now the direction was clear. Westward, the river.

They turned as one, to see a single figure staggering across the snow.

'Roland!' it cried semi-hysterically. 'Turold!' It was Joubert, his voice cracking with emotion. 'It's Father... he's stepped onto the ice and fallen through. Help us quickly. All of you, in God's name... *help us!*'

As the camp erupted in chaos, Cerdic stood unmoving, locked in place. For the second time in his life, it seemed, the world was suddenly burning around his ears.

Yvette hurried towards him, grabbing his hand, pulling on it. 'We should help,' she said.

Cerdic shook his head, a single thought now lodged there. 'He's already dead.'

'How can you know that…?'

'Because, Yvette,' he took her hand in return, gripping it hard, 'when it comes to killing, Joubert knows too well what he is doing.'

CHAPTER 25

'You know he was *pushed* under that ice, don't you?' Cerdic said.

Turold had returned first from the river. His rugged features were ashen with shock.

'Turold...?' Cerdic said again.

'Of course.' Turold glanced back through the trees, where almost the entirety of the company was crowding its way along the riverbank, shouting and jostling. 'But no one will believe the son murdered his father. The thing now is to stop him murdering *you*.'

Yvette looked horrified and terrified at the same time. 'You think he'll try?'

'Try?' Turold laughed. 'He now has full command. He won't need to *try*.' He swung to one of a pair of camp-boys standing nervously nearby. 'Bring me Lord Roland. Tell him it's urgent.' The boy took off at speed. Turold swung to the other. 'My horse!' The second youngster capered off too. 'Cerdic, I need your full attention. Yvette, we'll need you as well.'

Yvette came forward, while Turold planted his hands firmly on Cerdic's shoulders. 'Do you resolve always to speak the truth, to defend women and children, the weak and helpless, Holy Mother Church?'

'I...' Cerdic didn't know how to respond.

With explosions of earth and flying snow, Roland galloped up. He too was pale. 'We have a catastrophe on our hands!'

'Have they found the body?' Turold asked.

'No. The river's running free under the ice. The current might have carried it for miles by now. They're searching further, though.'

'Then there's nothing more you can do. Stay. Be our witness.'

Roland dismounted. 'To what?'

Turold ignored him. 'Cerdic, kneel.'

Warily, Cerdic dropped to his knees. Roland clung to his steed's reins, looking on in confusion. Yvette joined him, equally bewildered.

'I need your resolution,' Turold said, his steel-blue eyes boring into the young Englishman. 'The question I just asked you…?'

'Yes.' Cerdic's heart thumped, though he didn't know why. 'Yes… of course.'

'Swear it!'

'I swear it.'

'Swear also to defy danger, to always show courage in front of your enemies.'

'I swear it.'

'To be loyal always to lord and master.'

'What is this?' Roland demanded.

'I'm knighting him,' Turold said.

Cerdic was stunned. 'Knighting me?'

Roland stalked forward. 'Have you gone mad?'

'It's the only hope he has,' Turold retorted.

'I've made no preparation,' Cerdic protested.

'It's a "battlefield promotion",' Turold said. 'No one can deny you've earned that.'

'I don't understand.' Cerdic tried to get up, but Turold pushed him down.

'When Joubert returns, he'll seek to kill you. But under chivalrous law, a knight facing sentence of death may claim trial by combat.'

Roland shook his head. 'Turold, you can't do this.'

'Says who? Count Cynric? He'd have *needed* him knighted.'

'The boy's not ready.'

Turold considered that. 'Granted, he didn't keep vigil last night, nor has he bathed recently – but which of us has?'

Roland was visibly torn, his gaze roving between them. The only other person in the camp at present was Haco, the blind man, who'd emerged from the tent they'd loaned to him, but no one having appraised him of events, now sat close to one of the campfires, scavenging what fragments of food lingered in the cooking pots and mess tins. Roland peered through the trees towards the river. A distant furore of voices could still be heard.

'Find me a better objection, Roland,' Turold said, 'and I'll desist.'

'As Knight-Seneschal of House Tancarville, I can *order* you to desist.'

'And will you?' Turold waited grimly. 'Given that the entire structure of House Tancarville is about to change for the infinitely worse?'

Roland's forehead glistened with sweat.

Cerdic understood. Here was a man who for long years had served a noble Norman house embodied by Count Cynric. The count was now gone, shockingly, awfully, but Roland's service to the house went on. Or did it? Normally, yes. But Joubert would not be the next count. That honour would pass to his older brother, Dagobert. Joubert would affect command here in England, but it wouldn't be all-binding. Then there were the circumstances of the count's passing, which were questionable to say the least. The knight-seneschal reached a decision. It clearly hurt him, and still he seemed torn, but he now drew his longsword, standing it upright in front of him, both hands clasped on its pommel.

Turold turned back to Cerdic.

'Surely this is wrong?' the lad said.

'It would have been wrong several weeks ago. But not now. You're a fast learner, Cerdic. Joubert is good, but you can match him. I've seen to that. And don't worry, you can thank me for all that free tuition later. And so, I ask a final time… do you swear to all these things? You're on oath now. Once done, it can't be undone.'

'I swear it,' Cerdic said, his heart hammering even harder, his hair stiffening.

Turold unslung his own sword from his back, slid it from its scabbard, and used its blade to deal him the ritual blow on the left shoulder. 'I dub you a knight.' He resheathed the weapon, then handed it to Cerdic hilt-first across his forearm. 'Rise, Cerdic of Wulfbury.'

Cerdic did so, dazed.

'I'll provide your spurs when I have an extra pair,' Turold added.

Cerdic looked at Yvette, who returned his gaze with a kind of fascinated despondency. He looked back at Turold. 'I don't know what to say...'

'Say nothing. There's no time for celebration.'

A groom arrived, leading Turold's destrier. The knight jumped into his saddle, promptly throwing his spare longsword, the one Cerdic had been training with, over his own back. 'Roland... you've seen what's happened here. You're a witness.'

Roland nodded. 'Where are you going?'

'Half a mile between here and the city, I saw a couple of English priests offering incense and prayers over a mass grave. Probably all that remains of their Fulford dead.' He glanced at Turold and Yvette. 'This time you *do* need to prepare yourselves. Both of you.'

'For what?' Yvette asked.

'Matrimony.'

The girl took a horrified step backward. Cerdic, who hadn't thought he could be any more surprised by the day's events, was equally astounded.

'Put your vanities aside,' Turold said sternly, 'and think this through.'

'Count Cynric!' Cerdic protested. 'He wanted me to marry his daughter.'

'And you think Joubert will, when it will cut him out of your inheritance?'

Roland looked saddened as he regarded the young couple. What remained of his world had finally collapsed, the lad realised.

'Joubert stood to lose everything if you married Aliza,' the knight-seneschal said. 'Can you think of any other reason why he'd push his own father under the ice?'

Meanwhile, Turold had wheeled his horse around and now spurred it to a gallop, hurtling out of the camp in the direction of York.

'How will marrying Yvette help?' Cerdic asked.

'It will make you the son-in-law and heir to Rodric of Hiemois,' Yvette explained wearily. 'A great magnate of Normandy.'

'There you have it,' Roland said. 'Another reason for Joubert to stay his hand. Even *he* would balk at murdering two Norman noblemen on the same day.'

'Roland...' Yvette shook her head. 'There must be another way?'

He glanced at her. 'It will either be Cerdic or Joubert.'

'But that wasn't House Tancarville's plan. I was to be donated back to the king as an act of good faith... so that he could bargain with my father.'

'Yvette. As of this moment, House Tancarville is Joubert.' Roland eyed Cerdic. 'And he's on the verge of a double coup. Seizing both the earldom of Ripon and making himself sole male heir to House Hiemois.'

'If he does that,' Cerdic said, 'won't the king consider it an act of rebellion?'

'The king's already facing rebellion on several fronts. Through Yvette's father and his compatriots in Normandy. Possibly in the south of England through Eustace of Boulogne, and in the north of Northumbria through this Oswulf of Bamburgh, against whom he's already stretched so thin that he's only been able to send a paltry force of sellswords under the first brutish fool who volunteered for the job. Add Lord Joubert to the mix, new Earl of Ripon, scion of House Tancarville, heir-in-waiting to the vast demesnes of Hiemois, and the king is even more likely to sue for peace.'

Cerdic shook his head. 'I'm not sure Yvette's father will be happy.'

'Of course he won't. But what God has put together let no man take apart.'

'I can't pretend I don't yearn for the simpler life we knew before your duke came here,' Cerdic said.

'Plotting is a national pursuit in Normandy,' Roland replied. 'A game they all play. To win, you must keep up with them, or preferably be two steps ahead. Don't look too disheartened, Cerdic... if nothing else, you've got yourself a beautiful bride.'

He turned and crossed the camp towards the river.

'Yvette...' Cerdic felt more awkward than he ever had in his life. 'I didn't ask for this.'

She bit her lip, couldn't even look at him. 'It's not how I imagined my wedding would be.'

He tried to make light of it. 'On the bright side, I could be dead in a few days. Joubert might challenge me anyway, and even if I win, I'll then have Wulfgar Ragnarsson to fight.'

'How wonderful. I'll be a widow at eighteen.'

There wasn't much he could say to that, and so he was relieved, not to mention a little surprised, when Turold reappeared, cantering quickly between the tents, a passenger on the horse behind him, clinging to the knight's waist for dear life.

'You were quick,' Cerdic said.

'I was fortunate,' Turold replied in English. 'This fellow was a short way up the road. Walking and praying at the same time.'

'We call it meditation,' the passenger said, also in English, his tone testy, as Turold lowered him to the ground by the hand.

At first, Cerdic was taken aback to recognise the tall, spare physique under the shabby robe, not to mention the long, thin face. Then he was delighted. 'Aethelbald!'

The young priest recognised him back and was equally pleased. 'Cerdic?'

They came together, clasping hands.

'How do you come to be here?' Aethelbald asked. 'And among Normans?'

'He's not just in our company, Father,' Yvette cut in. 'He's *one of us* now.'

Aethelbald arched a puzzled eyebrow.

'It's a long story,' Cerdic said.

'And we've no time,' Turold interrupted, dismounting. 'You'll do as we ask, Father?'

The priest seemed confused by the whole situation. But on sight of Cerdic, the lad with whom he'd knelt and prayed over the grave of Rothgar after the battle of Fulford, his hostility had abated a little. 'If I must.' He assessed Cerdic and Yvette. 'This is the happy couple?'

Turold glanced over his shoulder at a rising mumble of voices. Figures were reappearing through the trees from the river. One of the foremost was Roland, who signalled to them that time was not on their side.

'Best get things under way,' Turold said. 'As quickly as possible. It may also be that you have a funeral to perform today. Let's hope it's only one.'

CHAPTER 26

'Condolences, Lord,' Cerdic said, standing rigid.

'Gratefully accepted,' Joubert replied, walking across the camp towards him, the entire company at his rear. His face had warped into an odd grimace. It might have reflected the pain of loss – after all, the count's corpse, which they'd finally found tangled in the roots of a riverside tree, was close behind him, wrapped in a cloak and carried at shoulder-height – but it might also have signified angry glee.

'I must admit, however,' Cerdic said, 'I thought you'd spend at least some time mourning your noble father before rushing to send someone after him.'

'My father was a man of action,' Joubert replied. 'He rarely wasted time.' With a steely rasp, he drew his longsword. 'Neither will I.'

Roland stepped forward, not exactly between them, but into the young nobleman's eyeline. 'May I ask what you propose, my lord?'

'What I propose, Casterborus, is to end this charade once and for all. We now know exactly where we're going. And we have a man who can lead us.' He pointed at Haco, standing a short distance away. Despite the grisly tragedy that had befallen him, the blind beggar, who'd finally been told what had happened, gave a leering, near-feral smile, as if there was still enough of a man inside his scarred, emaciated shell to bring pain on those who displeased him. 'More importantly, we know what we need to do when we arrive there, and we won't have time to discuss matters of ownership or division of spoils.'

'So… you intend to kill Cerdic?'

'I do indeed.'

'On what grounds?'

Joubert looked at his knight-seneschal askance. 'On the grounds that I don't like him. I apologise if that offends your chivalrous sensibilities.'

'No need to apologise, my lord. But if Cerdic of Wulfbury is condemned to die, spurious reasons or not, he has the right to a defence.'

'Indeed?'

'And in our trade, my lord,' Turold said, 'we call it trial by battle.'

Joubert glanced at him, baffled.

Turold shrugged. 'As a knight facing a direct threat to his life, whether it's by lawful accusation, or otherwise, it's his entitlement.'

Seconds passed as understanding dawned on Joubert. Only now did he seem to notice that Cerdic wore a longsword on his back. 'You bestowed the honour of knighthood on this Saxon wretch?' His voice cracked with anger.

'It seemed the generous thing to do,' Turold said.

Joubert's red face split into a deranged grin. 'I don't believe you. It's a lie.'

'*I* saw it, my lord,' Roland said. 'I can offer witness.'

Joubert's mouth quivered with rage, white froth blossoming at its corners. 'You have disgraced your station, Turold de Bardouville. And besmirched one of our most sacred institutions.'

'How so, my lord?'

'He's a damn commoner!'

'But we know that not to be true. Thanks to this blinded fellow you've become so enamoured with.'

They all knew Joubert well enough by now, even Cerdic and Yvette. His plans might have been stymied in the lawful sense, but that wouldn't be the end of it. Roland's hand stole to the hilt of his sword; something to do with the entire household now slowly encircling them. They weren't hostile to a man; most just wanted to get a better view of these remarkable proceedings, but Joubert's personal *mesnie* was bulked at the back of him, their eyes narrowed on their leader's enemy.

'How many here,' Joubert asked aloud, 'consider this English ratling a worthy inductee into our ranks?' Only one or two voices mumbled in response. Joubert shrugged at Turold.

'It's already been done, my lord,' the big knight replied. 'It was my gift to him.'

'Gift?'

'My wedding gift.'

The silence in the camp following this was thunderous, ear-splitting. Joubert could only look from one to the other in stupefaction. Then, Yvette went and stood alongside Cerdic, and took him by the hand.

'What's this?' Joubert growled, his face darkening from red to purple.

'What it appears to be,' Turold said.

'And all done correctly... in the eyes of God and law,' Aethelbald said, hustling his way through the crowd, addressing them in stilted but understandable French.

'Who the devil is this streak of windblown piss?' Joubert demanded.

'Aethelbald,' the priest said. 'I am pastor to the Chapter of Saint Peter in York.'

Joubert stared at him with utter disbelief, before rounding on Cerdic and Yvette, and then at the two impudent knights who had engineered all this.

'You've been busy in the forty minutes since my father's accident,' he hissed.

'Count Cynric's demise, my lord, was most untimely,' Roland retorted. 'It threw everything we thought we knew into a melting pot of uncertainty.'

'Meaning what, exactly?'

'Meaning that our future now is unmapped. And that we are in danger enough here without making things worse.'

'*I* would make things worse, Casterborus? Is that what you're saying?'

'We didn't know, Lord,' Turold said boldly. 'We couldn't be sure.'

'We needed to make a decision,' Roland added. 'For all our sakes. If we'd allowed Cerdic of Wulfbury to be slain now, where would we stand legally? We could go on and attack this fortress of Wulfbury, but as nothing more than freebooters. That would make it much easier for the king to evict us when he finally comes north. Whereas, if we had legal documentation, no doubt witnessed by an Archbishop of York still in office…'

'I appreciate the law doesn't trouble you, my lord,' Turold said. 'But the rest of us, in good conscience, as members of *a holy institution*, could hardly join you.'

Joubert's breath came slow and heavy. Even his hair seemed redder, almost like fire. 'You realise I can undo all this with a word?'

'You think so?'

'I am Count of Tancarville! I could have all four of you arrested and then do what I will with you. You think this English whoreson has protection under chivalrous law? There's no law out here. You know how far we are from home?'

'How many agree that Lord Joubert is Count of Tancarville?' Turold called out.

Again, only muted mumbles responded.

Joubert gazed round at them. 'You dare? What's the matter with you all? Are you mad? My father died in an *accident*. I command now.'

'You command while we're in the field, my lord,' Roland said, 'but strictly speaking, your brother Dagobert is Count of Tancarville.'

'Dagobert is five hundred miles away!'

'You've dispensed with the law of *primogeniture* too?' Turold said. 'Who are you, God?'

Joubert pointed savagely. 'You've done this to undermine me. The pair of you.' He turned to the rest. 'You hear that? They've always hated me. They'd side with this Saxon wolf-cub rather than their own lord and master. Well... it won't stand.'

Spitting in rage, he raised his sword on high.

'Careful, my lord!' Roland warned. 'Cerdic may bear arms in his defence.'

'We've done with the law.' Joubert advanced. 'Yvo! The rest of you, kill the traitors!'

The majority of the company hung back, reluctant to draw steel against their seneschal and their champion, not least because most of those present had seen Turold in particular carve men like bread. But Joubert's *mesnie*, at least twenty of whom remained, including Yvo de Taillebois, were right behind him, blades gleaming.

Cerdic pushed Yvette backward, drawing his sword. Turold unsheathed his own. Roland hesitated, but then another party stepped in, Arne of Brabant appearing next to Cerdic, his crossbow loaded and levelled at the shoulder, its bolt trained on Joubert.

'I think not, my lord!' the Flemish captain said.

The rest of his men, who had circled to the rear of the smaller party, also stepped into view, each man training his weapon on a different member of Joubert's retinue. The hostile group came to a stumbling halt, even Joubert regarding these new opponents with livid but frightened eyes. They'd seen the effectiveness of these bowmen for themselves.

The silence tautened slowly, painfully, then Joubert whispered: 'You too?'

'You misunderstand, my lord.' Arne didn't whisper. He spoke loudly, clearly. 'I'm not governed by your rules of nobility. I had a contract with your father. He may be dead, but the contract isn't. And these men, I think... this boy in particular, are more likely to honour it than you.'

'You dare...' Joubert stuttered.

'Think long and hard, Lord Joubert,' Turold interjected. 'You set your dogs on us, and you'll kill us eventually, but you know that Roland and I will take half a dozen each, maybe more. You lose them, and then lose these marksmen too… what are you going to use to assault this stronghold of Wulfbury? Apart from your trusty new friend, the blind man?'

Joubert's face had turned blood-red. He looked as if he was contemplating attacking anyway. But now Cerdic spoke.

'Lord Joubert! I understand that you feel undermined by this, and that you hold me the cause.'

'You are the cause of everything, you English catamite.' Froth literally fizzled from Joubert's mouth. 'I swear I'll kill you.'

'So, the challenge stands,' Cerdic said. 'And I accept. But might I suggest you and I meet when this is finally over, and the earldom of Ripon is in our grasp? It will just be the two of us, knight to knight.'

'Knight to knight!'

'No one else need shed their blood over our personal quarrel.'

The two sides continued to face off, but the tension was leavened a little.

'It's a brave offer, Lord,' Turold said. 'The best one you're likely to get today.'

More seconds passed, before Joubert's hoarse breathing eased and he slowly sheathed his sword. His men, somewhat gratefully, did the same.

'Just don't stray too near any frozen rivers in the meantime,' Turold told Cerdic. 'Not when Lord Joubert is close at hand.'

'And when I've finished with him, I'll deal with *you*,' Joubert spat.

Turold smiled. 'I doubt it. Unless your friend, the Slayer, fancies it. Trust me, Taillebois, I'd like nothing better.'

Yvo the Slayer, for all his reputation, said nothing.

CHAPTER 27

The last time Cerdic had travelled between York and Swaledale, it had been at the end of a hot summer, the road surface baked hard, the meadows bleached yellow, sun-dappled paths lost in shadow as they wound off under the matted leaf-cover of the woods. Now, the scene was a desolate wilderness, the trees naked, the ground lifeless. Where the thin carpet of snow broke, only tufts of brown desiccation peeked through.

The atmosphere inside the company was wintry too.

The shock of Count Cynric's death was still reverberating, of course. The fact they hadn't been able to give him a proper funeral hadn't helped. It might have been possible to have arranged that in York, but it would only have drawn further attention to their presence, which wouldn't have been wise given the expected imminent arrival of the new earl. Instead, they'd lodged the count's body with the monks of York Minster in a temporary casket and paid the chapter to offer regular services for his soul until such time as they returned and were able to transport him home.

However, the real change had come through the emergence of irreconcilable factions. They still rode in rigid, disciplined formation, but the mood now was dramatically different. It was sombre, uncertain. There was no laughter, little idle discourse. An air of suspicion lingered, as if no man really trusted the fellow to his left or his right.

Joubert rode near the back, his face etched with discontent as he conversed only with members of his own *mesnie*. Even Roland had neglected his normal position at the point, having handed his household banner to someone else, a lesser man, so that he could ride in the centre alone with his thoughts. This worried Cerdic more than anything, even more than Yvette, who also rode in the centre and kept her own counsel. In Yvette's case, he suspected, it was simple pique, an understandable sadness and frustration that the course of her life was changing daily even though she never had any say in it. But the full meaning of the drastic decisions taken the previous day were impacting on Roland in a different way. He'd confided in Turold that from the moment they'd embarked that morning, he'd felt torn about where his real duty lay. As Seneschal of House Tancarville, he should serve on in that capacity, no matter that the man who'd appointed him had died, so now, having sided against Joubert, who while he wasn't the new Count of Tancarville, was certainly his lawful representative, the knight was deeply conflicted.

'I thought it was a simple case of Roland taking longer to adjust to our new *wyrd* than you did,' Cerdic said to Turold, as they rode side by side. 'But that he'd come on board eventually, because he had a sense of what was right.'

'And now you fear he's having doubts?'

'Don't you?'

Turold pondered. 'Roland usually does what's right.' He noticed Cerdic's expression. 'Be sceptical of that if you wish. Yes, he commanded knights who invaded your country and made hay among your people. But in Roland's mind at least that would have been the prelude to a greater good. The imposition on a depraved, semi-pagan state of a pious king who would bring law, order and restore Godliness.'

Cerdic didn't bother arguing that this was pure nonsense, because Turold now knew that it was too. They all did. But the big knight hadn't finished.

'No doubt, Joubert would in time issue evil orders that no man, least of all Roland Casterborus, could ever delude himself into believing would lead to a greater good. Serving Lord Joubert would have tormented him to death. Eventually, he'd have sought a way back to Normandy, to reconcile himself with Dagobert.'

'I'm surprised others aren't doing the same already,' Cerdic said. 'Or at least heading south to join with the other great Norman households.'

Turold shrugged. 'They want what they've come for. A share in a wealthy earldom. Don't be fooled into thinking they're following *you*, Cerdic.'

'And if we recapture Wulfbury, and Joubert meets me in combat, and I defeat him, what will they do then?'

A grim smile broke on Turold's face. 'You ask too much. I'm the household champion. I also knighted you, which means I'm your mentor. But I've no gift for prophecy.'

—

The villages on this stretch of the journey weren't so much closed and unwelcoming as empty and abandoned. It was the dead of winter, not a time for travel, but most occupants would now have learned about the disaster in the south, and how the Normans treated those who fell into their hands. They'd also likely have heard about the new Norman-approved Earl of Northumbria, Copsi, a man known as a murderer even before he fell in with King William the Bastard, and now due to arrive at York. If additional word had then reached them that Norman soldiers were on the road, there'd only be one response.

It hurt Cerdic to sit astride his horse and watch while, under Turold's direction, the company looted the cottages, long-halls and storehouses, though he didn't blame Turold as much as he might once have. How could he? This force was heading northward at Cerdic's own request, its aim to liberate *his* personal holding, and having travelled so far already, it was in constant need of resupply. But he still couldn't help wondering at the price his fellow north-country folk were paying for that. Hiding in the encircling wastes, wearing only the clothes they'd run away in, seeking shelter amid frozen bracken, only to return on the morrow to find everything of value purloined. At least, under

Turold, nothing was needlessly burned, though pigs were taken from sties, geese from yards, chickens from coops.

At the end of the first day, they halted at a stockaded settlement called Langthorpe, which from Cerdic's memory was in the wapentake of Hallilkeld, not far from the monastery of Ripon itself, and about a third of the distance from York to Wulfbury. Again, it was open and empty, and they opted to stay there for the night. There was also a blacksmith's forge, which, at Cerdic's suggestion, they had Haco revive. They then cobbled together any bits of spare or broken weaponry, not to mention any iron lying around the smith's shop itself, and with some assistance from those who lacked skill but at least had eyes, had him fashion a number of crude but useable grappling hooks. This was a useful task of course, and should pay them dividends, but even so it was sobering for Cerdic to look out from the forge while the work was in progress and see the rest of the knights and men-at-arms rushing about as they sought the best berths for themselves and of course anything else of value.

Roland sat mounted nearby, aloof from it all.

'You feel like a real *seigneur* now?' he asked the lad, to which no honest answer was possible.

It was colder that night than it had been the previous week. A sharp frost turned the air brittle, so most of the company lodged themselves in the long-hall, where they banked the hearth up into a furious blaze, though Yvette was allocated an outbuilding of her own. This contained a small fireplace, which Turold had a couple of camp-boys light for her, and a bed with a straw-stuffed pillow and sheepskin coverlet.

'What are you doing?' she asked, about an hour after she'd settled under the fleece, only for Cerdic to let himself in and crouch in front of the fire.

He threw off his Leopard cloak and commenced unbuckling his hauberk, but he also looked puzzled. 'I'm coming to bed.'

'You mean to sleep here?'

He stood up. 'We're married. You're not saying you want us to sleep apart?'

'It wasn't a real marriage, Cerdic.'

'Of course it was a real marriage. Aethelbald's a real priest.'

'But we were coerced. Both of us.'

'I understand that, but...' He struggled to explain. 'How's it going to look to the rest of the troop if I allow my wife to throw me out of my own wedding bed?'

Her expression softened. She clearly understood his dilemma, but still looked uneasy.

'I'm sorry it happened the way it did,' he said, 'but is it really so bad? It's not as if we haven't shared billets before. We had a bath together, for God's sake. And I thought, I mean... well, we nearly...'

'Nearly coupled? Yes, we *nearly* did.' She regarded him with reproach. 'I even told you I thought you were someone I could love. And you threw that back at me.'

'I never said I couldn't love you. Just that at present we need to survive...'

She shook her head. 'This mission isn't about survival, Cerdic. It's about power, control. Which all men seem to seek... all the time. As much here as in Normandy.'

'You think I should just have accepted slavery?' He stood with his back to the flames. 'Or death? You saw what happened in that wood near Senlac Ridge.'

He referred to the fate of several other prisoners taken by Count Cynric after the battle there, all of whom were summarily executed in a woodland glade because they had no wealth or property to trade for their lives.

'I just...' She looked away. 'I just thought it would never happen. You finding yourself in a position to actually *fight* for your title again.'

'It didn't seem likely, I'll admit.'

'Cerdic!' she pleaded. 'Is revenge really so important?'

'It isn't revenge. It's justice. I'm having what's mine, and that's all there is to it.'

'No matter how many die in the process?'

'Yvette!' he protested. 'I'm not the aggressor here.'

'Are you so sure?' She stared at him, now with a hint of steel. 'You swore the oath of knighthood so willingly because you've been intrigued by the whole idea of it for weeks. But understand this, Cerdic... Turold holds rank because he kills on his master's command. Roland espouses the ideal, but that didn't stop him invading an innocent land.'

He heard this out before grabbing his cloak, swinging it over his shoulders and striding to the door. 'It must be wonderful to have a soul as spotless as yours.'

'Where are you going?'

'To find space in the back of a cart somewhere. It's not like I'm unused to it.'

'I just want us to have a better life.'

He looked back. 'All those love poems you mooned over in Lady Edith's boudoir have addled your brain.'

'If my dreams are a fantasy, then so are yours,' she said. 'Even if you win this war, you think there won't be another one after that, and another after that?'

'I don't *want* this, Yvette.' His voice almost broke, so earnestly did he try to express this. 'As a boy, I did. Or I thought I did. As an adult... *no*. I'd do anything to arrive at Wulfbury and find Ragnarsson gone, and that all we need do is rebuild. You never know, that may be the case. You could even pray for it, if you like.' He opened the door to leave. 'Though I'm sure you'd agree... thus far, prayers have availed us little.'

—

'Cerdic of Wulfbury!'

Cerdic glanced around. They were midway through their second day on the York road, probably just short of halfway to Swaledale, and well into territory where he'd expect to encounter Ragnarsson patrols. Earlier that day, they'd managed to capture a ceorl, and he'd told them that, as far as he knew, the Norse power was still ensconced at Wulfbury Hall, but that they'd only come out now and then, to raid the surrounding villages for extra food and animals, and to advise all headmen that new, stiffer taxes would shortly be imposed. Some Viking carls had installed themselves in halls vacated by local thegns slain in the recent wars, though that was mainly to the north and west, in Swaledale itself.

'Cerdic of Wulfbury!' the voice came again.

Cerdic turned properly and saw two horsemen cantering up to join him at the front of the troop. The speaker was Arne of Brabant, the other the giant Viking.

'May I present Tyrkil Hellasson of Fjelldal,' Arne said. 'Also called Widow-Maker.'

Cerdic assessed the Northman. He was truly a colossus. He had several inches on Turold, but was immense of chest and shoulder, an impression no doubt enhanced by his thick fur and gleaming ring-mail, though his neck itself had the girth of an oak trunk. His head was large and square, his thick, tawny hair hanging past his shoulders in multiple braids, his beard full and lush. Cerdic noted that, now he was back among allies, the Viking had adorned his knuckles with gold and silver rings, all elaborately wrought, and his heavy-thewed arms with an equal number of handsome torques. Presumably these treasures had been hidden on his person somewhere when he was first captured, which the lad didn't blame him for. Viking jewellery was awarded by chieftains for courage in battle. That made it far more to them than mere decoration. Tyrkil's exploits must have been valorous indeed.

Cerdic nodded at the huge Northman, who nodded back.

'Before I speak with Lord Widow-Maker,' the lad said, 'I thank you, Arne, for your support on the day Count Cynric died.'

'Ah.' Arne nodded. 'You think you needed it?'

'It's hard to say. Joubert is good with a sword, or so I'm told. And Yvo de Taillebois is *very* good with a sword. As for the rest of his *mesnie*, they're certainly killers, otherwise they wouldn't be following him. I'm interested to know why you did it? An ordinary sellsword would have fallen in with the new commander.'

Arne shrugged as if the decision hadn't been difficult. 'Now, we know you are not a fraud. You indeed have wealth, which you will share with us.'

'Joubert would have shared it with you.'

'Hah! You think? The morning after our attack on your camp, Lord Joubert wanted us dead. You were one of only a few voices to speak for us.'

'So, you spared me out of gratitude?'

'If you wish. But you still must pay us.'

Cerdic smiled. 'If you and your men help me recapture Wulfbury, you'll be paid twice over. I have a crucial role in mind for you.'

Cerdic hoped this wasn't an unwise promise, but the latter at least was true. The strategy unfolding in his mind increasingly relied on the Flemish crossbowmen.

'I am fascinated,' Arne said.

'I'll tell you about it when we get there,' Cerdic replied. 'When you can see the lay of the land for yourself.'

'As you wish. Now you'll speak with Tyrkil, yes?'

'Does he understand English?'

'He has mingled with Flemings a long time, so his French is better.'

'Tyrkil... how may I help?'

The Viking grunted and groped for the right words. 'Lord Cerdic...'

The lad was about to correct him straight away, only to remember that now he *was* a lord. He'd been lawfully knighted, which awarded him a status the Northmen had learned to respect in their clashes with the Franks. It was something he was going to have to get used to, himself, but it wasn't displeasing.

'I hear you say,' the Viking stumbled on, 'this Wulfgar... he betray Hardraada?'

'You were part of Harald the Hardraada's *drengr*?' Cerdic asked. He'd heard this mentioned, but now that he thought about it properly, it was more than impressive. No wonder the giant called Widow-Maker wore so many arm-rings.

Tyrkil nodded. 'I am... all who remain.'

'Wulfgar Ragnarsson did exactly that, my friend,' Cerdic said. 'He created a secret army of his own and hid it inside the Hardraada's greater army. He then sailed it to England in the Hardraada's ships. Supposedly he came here to help your prince conquer his new kingdom, but they left his ranks after my people and yours crossed swords at Fulford.'

'They fight on river?'

'At Stamford Bridge? No, they didn't. By then, they'd gone north to Wulfbury, where they attacked my father's unprotected homestead and slew many of his people.'

Tyrkil nodded as he absorbed this. 'So, when Hardraada die, this Wulfgar...?'

'He wasn't there, Tyrkil. While your prince and comrades fell around the Raven banner, he was far away, looking out for himself.'

Arne interjected. 'You think this Wulfgar Ragnarsson's action would have weakened the Hardraada much before that fatal fight?'

'I don't know,' Cerdic said with full honesty. 'It can't have helped him.' He turned to Tyrkil again. 'This pretender called Wulfgar... you know he claims descent from Ragnar Lodbrok?'

Tyrkil nodded. 'I hear this.'

'You should also know that it's a lie. Is that not a crime in itself? To falsely wear the names of Ragnar and his sons?'

The Widow-Maker's heavy-set features tightened like sun-burnished wood. He reddened, his eyes burning. 'He... what is this word... *dishonour*, yes. He dishonours us.'

'Harald Sigurdsson's men fought bravely at Stamford Bridge, for many hours,' Cerdic said. 'The battle went against you. It can happen. There is no loss of pride. But while this was going on, this other fellow was raping and stealing in far-off places.'

The Viking said nothing for several moments.

'Tyrkil,' Cerdic said, 'to have served the Hardraada closely, to have been among his favoured hearth-men... you must be a great warrior.'

The Viking grunted and nodded, as if this went without saying.

'Will you serve me?' Cerdic asked. 'I don't mean just for pay, I mean as a matter of honour… to right this wrong, and avenge your king?'

Rather to Cerdic's surprise, the Viking didn't reply straight away. Something still troubled him. But then he said: 'I ask you first… this cloak?'

'Cloak?' Cerdic was confused.

'He means the cloak and surcoat brought back from York by Lord Joubert,' Arne said. 'The one bearing the Boar's Head crest.'

Cerdic nodded. 'Yes.'

'Is yours?' Tyrkil asked.

'The blue boar on white is my family's emblem,' Cerdic confirmed. 'That particular cloak likely belonged to one of our housecarls. It was probably taken from his corpse.' He now posed a question of his own. 'Have you seen it before?'

Tyrkil nodded slowly.

'Where?'

'Fulford… I fight your house.'

Cerdic looking frontward again. 'I see.'

'Your men die bravely.'

'I heard that, yes.'

'Great loss to you?' Tyrkil enquired.

'I…' Initially, Cerdic wasn't sure how to respond, then decided that sincerity was the best course. Tyrkil had suffered his own losses under English blades, worst of all his king, but he was adopting the brothers-in-arms approach, the one that blamed war itself for the deaths of friends rather than those who waged it.

'My father,' the lad said.

Tyrkil nodded as if he knew this pain. 'He die on field?'

'Yes.'

'Then place in Valhalla for him… mead and song. Allfather will welcome.'

'We Christians don't go to Valhalla,' Cerdic replied. 'But I'm hopeful he'll find his own Heaven.'

'*Jaja.*' The Viking nodded vigorously. 'Brave will. Always. Me and my five, we serve.'

Cerdic glanced at him. 'Your five?'

'We have six Northmen left in our company,' Arne explained. 'Tyrkil, for reasons maybe obvious, has become their leader.'

'I'm glad to have you all,' Cerdic told the Viking.

Tyrkil nodded, before turning his horse around and heading back along the column.

'He'll seriously fight against other Vikings?' Cerdic asked.

'Wulfgar Ragnarsson is no Viking,' Arne replied.

'He has real Vikings in his retinue.'

Arne chuckled. 'You English should know Northmen better. They have no concept of national brotherhood. To them, sworn oaths and loyalty to leaders are all. These are bonds that cannot break without a price.'

Cerdic saw no reason to dispute this, even if he still harboured doubts.

'It's a mixed band you've put together, no?' Arne said. 'Flemings, Vikings, Normans... all under the captaincy of an Englishman.'

'I'm hardly their captain. But we *do* have a common interest.'

They rode on for a short time without speaking.

'It's good, I think,' Arne said. 'But watch your back... and watch this Joubert. He forswears his knighthood for personal gain. There is no honour there.'

Before Cerdic could respond, they both of them reined their horses up sharply. About sixty yards in front, just left of the road, stretches of marshland glimmered white, stands of frost-stiffened bullrushes dotting an extensive sheet of ice, which now that the sun was almost at its zenith, was slowly thawing. Close to the road, it had given way completely, and two horses stood there, drinking. Their riders were young men in ring-mail, carrying spears and circular shields painted with pagan symbols. They had helmets on, but these didn't conceal their long blond tresses and thin, hard faces.

They peered at the newly arrived force, at first with astonishment, and then unashamed fear, the pair of them spurring their beasts furiously. As soon as the animals regained the road, they galloped north at speed, cloaks billowing.

'Do we chase?' Arne asked. 'My mounted crossbows can...'

'No.'

'They will raise the alarm in this Wulfbury of yours.'

'Let them,' Cerdric said. 'Those rewarded with lands and lordships will be summoned to the central burh. They'll all be in one place... so we can destroy them together.'

CHAPTER 28

When they broke camp on the third morning, Cerdic felt especially wary. Though the countryside remained bleak and bare, the trees had thickened on either side of the road, the marshy ground diminishing, and to the west the land rose up into hillocks and densely wooded bluffs. He spied Cataractonium again, the old Roman fort. Apart from his journey south, when he'd blundered into it in the dark and in a state of panic, his natural inclination had always been to give it wide margin thanks to its ghostly reputation. On this occasion, as they spied its distant, lonesome outline from the road, he felt only concern that they were now less than a day's ride from Wulfbury.

He told Roland this as they fell into formation, but the knight-seneschal, still wrapped in a pall of his personal gloom, was unresponsive. When Cerdic mentioned this to Turold, the champion became thoughtful. 'How will we be received by your people?' he asked.

'We've been looting. The reception won't be overly warm.'

'They won't recognise you? They won't think their saviour has returned?'

'People adapt, Turold… because they have to. I don't like that we have a Norman on the throne of England. But what's the alternative? The Godwinsons are vanquished. Likewise, to the people of Swaledale, our house is gone. They may not be happy with their new earl, but they might now have accepted him.'

'Will they fight for him?'

'None of the last few villages we've passed have been torched. So, he hasn't spread his terror this far south. That must mean he thinks he can win them over. But we haven't been ambushed as yet, and he's known we've been here for the last half-day at least. If they've decided they love him, they don't love him enough to put their lives on the line.'

Turold sniffed. 'We still need to be cautious. I'll advise Arne to pass word to his outriders. From this point on, anyone who approaches us should be considered hostile unless they prove otherwise.'

'It would help if his men don't shoot barbs into the innocent,' Cerdic said.

'I'll tell him that, too.'

Turold headed back along the column. Almost immediately, he was replaced at the point, rather to Cerdic's surprise, by Roland, who had slowly been making his way forward. Without speaking, Roland took the banner from the man-at-arms who had replaced him and slid it into his own pannier. His features, though, were waxen.

'We were sighted yesterday,' Cerdic said. 'That means Ragnarsson will be ready.'

'I heard,' Roland replied. 'Turold is putting everyone on guard.'

'I don't think they'll attack. Rather than fight us in a pitched battle, they'll prefer to see us smash ourselves against Wulfbury's bulwarks.'

'If you say so.'

Cerdic had been amused how, almost overnight since he'd been knighted, the entire attitude of House Tancarville appeared to have changed to him. It wasn't so much that his fellow knights deferred to him, but there was a difference, a civility he'd never known before. The order of merit was a genuine thing in knightly eyes. But that was no explanation for Roland's ongoing lack of enthusiasm.

'Roland, what ails you?' the lad asked.

'That's a strange question. Only three days after our entire world drowned under the ice. You *do* understand how serious our problem is, Cerdic? It won't be resolved by simply persevering with the quest.'

'It was Joubert's decision to have the count temporarily interred...'

'I don't mean that.' Roland's voice tautened. 'That's as it should be. Count Cynric of Tancarville can't be laid to rest permanently anywhere save in his family vaults. I mean that I think we acted rashly back there.'

'You regret my knighting?'

'No. As Turold said, had Cynric lived and seen his plans to fruition, you'd have been knighted anyway. You couldn't take his daughter's hand otherwise. Of course... now you *can't* do that. And never will. His plan has been thwarted already, and with *my* connivance.'

'But Joubert...'

'Joubert be damned!' Roland snapped. 'When we put it to the test, we saw how few were prepared to die for him.' He shook his head. 'And by then it was too late.'

'I only married Yvette to...'

'It's more than a marriage, Cerdic. If you go on to inherit the earldom of Ripon, as is your right, we'll have empowered House Hiemois.'

Cerdic thought on this. 'Is House Hiemois an enemy of House Tancarville?'

'Not by blood. But allegiances change. And until I am officially discharged from office, I serve the Tancarville banner.'

'Is House Tancarville really what it was?'

'It still exists. Dagobert heads it now.'

'And is Dagobert a better man than Joubert?'

'The shaggy folk we call woodwose would be better men than Joubert. The average dog snuffling in the refuse piles of Rouen would be better than Joubert.'

Cerdic mulled it over. It was hardly a glowing recommendation. But like it or not, Dagobert FitzOslac was now Count of Tancarville.

'If Dagobert is a worthy lord, he'll understand that the circumstances were unusual,' Cerdic said. 'He'll also need to be told that Joubert killed their father.'

'There's no proof he did.'

'But what do you believe?'

Roland shrugged. 'Without proof, it doesn't matter. But yes… it was a dangerous moment. The company set to turn on itself. We took action to secure unity. But that won't mean House Hiemois won't now be a greater force to be reckoned with. The king himself will be angered.'

'If the king's looking for a way to make peace with Rodric of Hiemois, won't this encourage him all the more?'

'Of course, but not necessarily on the terms he'd have wanted. But none of that is a concern at present. I have an obligation to this company. I am now its senior officer, if not its commander. How far is Wulfbury?'

'Less than a day.'

Roland nodded. 'Then I'm almost finished here. I can't partake in a battle where victory would only strengthen a potential enemy of my overlord.'

'Turold sees thing differently…'

'Turold is a fighting man through and through. He has no overview. He makes decisions based on the needs of the moment. The long-term consequences may be bad for him, but he'll cope with that by going somewhere else. Any lord in Normandy and beyond, in Anjou, Maine, Touraine, even the Aquitaine, would be glad to have him.'

'It wouldn't trouble him?' Cerdic asked.

'The man he championed is dead, so no, it wouldn't. Not now.'

Cerdic was thoughtful, the potential wider context of his marriage to Yvette unfolding before him. 'It has occurred to you, Roland, that, if we capture the earldom of Ripon, I still must share it?'

Roland gave a humourless smile. 'Sharing it will be easier said than done.'

'But all these men need rewarding. So, even in victory, I'll be greatly weakened and no huge addition to House Hiemois.'

'That too remains to be seen,' Roland said. 'But you won't change my mind, Cerdic. In marrying you to Yvette, we made a mistake. It was a mistake born of necessity, but a mistake all the same. So, it's now my duty as knight-seneschal to correct it.'

'So... you won't fight?'

'I can't. And I must announce that decision to the company, then turn around and return to Normandy. En route, I'll collect Count Cynric's...'

'You're leaving us *now*?' Cerdic blurted. 'This very minute?'

'I'm one man, Cerdic. You won't miss me.'

'You're not one man, Roland. If you leave us now, the last vestige of Tancarville authority will have departed. There'll be nothing to keep the rest of the men here.'

Roland smiled. 'On the contrary. You're in sight of the prize. There's everything to keep them here. I'm sorry, but this is the other side of the chivalrous ideal. Vows mean something. Oaths cannot be forsworn.'

Cerdic shook his head. 'And for that reason, I still think a portion of our best men will go with you. And I'll be left with the sellswords, most of whom are more likely to join with Ragnarsson once they see his power.'

'The decision's made, Cerdic. And I can't delay. Count Cynric lies in a crude box, in the vault of an abbey church he's never even visited...'

'And my father lies under a few inches of soil, while my brother isn't buried at all. They're corpses, Roland. Lumps of clay. In the meantime, your living comrades have greater need of you.'

Roland brooded on this for several long moments. 'I've told you, I won't draw my sword if it means disadvantage to House Tancarville.'

'But you'll captain us for the remainder of this journey? At least until we get there?'

'After that, I take my overlord home.'

'Alone… that whole distance?'

'If I don't make it, that will be God's justice, which in due course we must all accept.'

'And Dagobert's justice if you do. I wonder which you fear the most? Do you have lands of your own, Roland? Do you now feel you must repossess them before your new master does?'

Roland eyed him closely. But whether or not he realised the lad was playing Devil's advocate, he chose to treat the question seriously.

'I won't deny it,' he said. 'My wife, Charmaine, and my daughter, Isabel, died several years ago. But I have a small estate on the greater demesnes of Tancarville. It isn't much, but it's home. Whether it's still mine of course… who knows, but Dagobert has no reason to disinherit me.'

'Then why…?'

'I've told you!' Roland became vexed, red-faced. '*This* is my duty as seneschal. Cerdic, it isn't just my oath to House Tancarville… the fact is I can't keep pretending. Look at this country of yours. No doubt it's the fairest of all come springtime and summer. But at present it's a hellscape. In soul if not appearance. It's difficult enough steering a chivalrous path through the treacheries and betrayals of everyday life in Normandy. But at least there is a semblance of law there. Here…?'

'It's William the Bastard's doing.'

'Whoever's fault it is, this is no place for a man seeking a righteous path. *You* seek one too, or so you say, but again there'll be slaughter. And most of those others here make no pretence that righteousness has any part in their ambition.' He shook his head, deeply regretful. Of many things, it now seemed. 'I think it will be decades, if not generations, before the dream that was England is restored. And I want no part in it anymore…'

Before they could speak further, Turold spurred his horse up from behind. 'We're being followed,' he said.

'How many?' Roland asked.

Turold looked grim. 'Enough.'

They formed a temporary bivouac to discuss the matter, the company circled around a small fire. It was perhaps inevitable that Joubert, cold and sullen though he remained, would occupy Count Cynric's seat of judgement. All the more so because it was a member of his *mesnie* who, riding some distance behind the rest as a rear-guard, had brought the alert that there were soldiers about two miles back.

'We believe it to be Earl Copsi himself,' Joubert said. 'He's evidently arrived in York and been advised that we are here.'

'Interesting,' Roland said. 'The same fellow you assured us was not supported by useful men?' Joubert curled his lip with irritation. 'How many?' Roland asked.

'Forty or so,' Yvo de Taillebois answered, 'but they had the air of an advance guard.'

'So more may be coming behind?' Turold said.

Taillebois nodded. 'Obviously, our man could not check.'

Joubert stood up. 'Allow *me* to discover the truth.'

'My lord?' Roland protested, clearly thinking this some ruse to break the company further.

Joubert snarled. 'Don't "my lord" me, Roland Traitorous. You think this error is mine. You *all* do. You think I failed in my task to reconnoitre York and establish whether there was danger there...'

No one responded, though all remembered his casual confidence that only a smattering of unwashed sellswords were in the city, despite Turold's doubts on the matter.

'Very well!' Joubert pivoted around. 'My *mesnie* and I will return along the road until we find a suitable place, and then we'll lie up and wait for these curs. We'll find out if others are following, or die in the attempt. Either way, you'll all be happy. Is that not so?'

'No one will be happy to see our numbers depleted further,' Roland said.

'Don't fret, Casterborus! We'll deal with these mercenary scum in very short order. And then we'll catch up with the rest of you.'

'I'll say something for that one,' Roland muttered, as Joubert and his thirty companions rode south, 'he never lacks for swagger.'

Turold gazed after them with a frown.

'What's troubling *you*?' Cerdic asked.

The big knight shrugged.

'You think he'll fall foul of these sellswords himself?' Roland wondered.

'No.' Turold smiled grimly. 'Definitely not that.'

CHAPTER 29

As they made their way up the south side of the valley, Turold continually checked that none of his sixteen-strong party of horsemen had disobeyed his orders and were wearing visible livery. He wasn't even happy about their chain-mail hauberks, though to have gone completely unarmoured would have been sheer folly, so he'd had as many as possible wear leather or russet homespun over the top.

Cerdic himself was less concerned.

'They know we're here,' he said. 'And I expect they'll be preparing to receive us on the Keld Brae. That will give them best vantage over us. Chancing these woods, which they don't really know, just to massacre a scouting party, would gain them little.'

Turold smiled to himself. 'Listen to *you*, the great tactician. A couple of months ago you were being lugged at the cart-arse. Now you're a true battle lord.'

Cerdic didn't reply. He knew that Turold spoke partly in jest. He was lord of nothing yet, though his knowledge of this district, its rocks, rivers and secret ways, had enabled him to lay plans that would yield them benefits in the coming fight. He focused instead on the hillside path winding ahead.

Turold glanced at Roland, who was riding close behind. 'What do *you* think?'

'I think there's too much talk,' the knight-seneschal replied. 'Even if they already know you're here, there's no reason to let them pinpoint you.'

'Well, I don't suppose it would do for *you* to die,' Turold said. 'Not when you're planning to desert us before the battle even starts.'

Roland said nothing to that, and they proceeded in silence, snaking two by two along the heavily wooded hillside. Cerdic had picked their pathway carefully. There were many evergreens here, which created effective cover, but there were deciduous trees too, all now bare of leaf, while the whole of the vast valley was blotchy with patches of glistening white snow, which could also betray a party of moving horsemen.

He'd grown up romping over these hills, but it was painful to be here now. The echoing silence was all wrong. Had Wulfgar Ragnarsson depopulated Wulfbury and its adjacent villages *so* thoroughly? When they came within sight of Brackley-on-the-Water, they reined up. From this height, the village was no more than a black stain straddling the river far below. There was no sign of movement down there, though when they looked to the top of the Keld Brae, the high plateau on the north side of the dale, where Wulfbury burh nestled behind its great palisade, things were different. Over the front gates, a heathen flag fluttered in the breeze, the fearsome *hrafnsmerki*, the great banner depicting Land Waster, Odin's battle-bird, a huge black raven with wings spread. The palisade's parapet meanwhile was hung all along with circular limewood shields, each one painted with its own demonic device, while the helmets and spear-tips of numerous sentries glinted on the gantry. Many pillars of slow-rising smoke indicated the presence of cooking-fires within, far more than would normally be needed on an ordinary day, which indicated there were many more present in the burh than usual.

'The whole horde is here,' Cerdic said, half to himself. 'As I hoped.'

He could even see smoke ascending from the chimney apertures in the apex of the dragon hall roof. Had he not been so conscious of his company, he'd have whooped with relief. The home in which he'd been raised wasn't just here, it was still in use. Who knew what vile desecrations had occurred inside it, but at least it hadn't been torched. That was no small mercy. Despite it being a self-defeating act, it had long been a tradition of triumphant Northmen to burn the halls of their broken enemies, preferably with those enemies and their families still inside. But Wulfgar Ragnarsson, somewhat true to form, had put his own personal comfort ahead of vainglorious gesturing.

Aside from that though, much else had gone to rack and ruin. The business of the estate had not yet recommenced. There'd been no new ploughing or planting along the valley bottom, no repairs made to walls or pens damaged by the winter weather. The one or two animals they hadn't butchered and consumed wandered freely and unmanaged.

One by one, the troop dismounted, surveying the fortress on the far side of the valley.

'A hard nut to crack,' Arne commented, crossbow resting at his shoulder.

'You say your father's host was absent when the Northmen took this place?' Turold said.

Cerdic nodded. For the first time now, he saw how filthy with rubbish the slopes of the Keld Brae had become, as if the occupants had simply tossed their leavings over the palisade. Even from this distance, he recognised some of those leavings as human bones.

'*I* was here,' he replied. 'There was a handful of others too. Old men, girls… but I should have done better.'

No one answered that. Likely, it was true. But how would any of them have coped in such a predicament, at seventeen, having never seen a day of combat before?

'How did they get inside?' Roland asked.

Briefly, he seemed interested in the mission, though he'd only accompanied them on this reconnaissance at Turold's insistence that, even if he had no intention of drawing steel against House Tancarville's interests, appraising the enemy's stronghold and advising on its capture surely fell within those final duties he'd promised to carry out.

'Through sheer weight of numbers,' Cerdic replied. 'There just weren't enough of us to hold them at bay.'

'You mentioned you had a plan?' Turold said.

Cerdic nodded. 'It will involve a cavalry charge on the palisade gates.'

One by one, they turned to look at him.

Turold chuckled to himself. 'Would you care to explain that further?'

'We have ropes and grapples, do we not? If we can assail the main gates with heavy horse, and hook them... we can pull them open.'

Even Roland, who'd been determined to involve himself in the conversation as little as possible, looked aghast. 'Are you mad? Charge up that steep track? Against that huge gate? They'll hide behind their rampart and pound you with everything they have.'

Cerdic shrugged. 'That's what I'm hoping for.'

Arne snorted. 'And you're looking for volunteers? Last time you fought this battle with only a handful. This time you'll have even less.'

'Not if there's someone fearless and respected to lead the charge.'

More bewildered glances were exchanged.

Turold sighed. 'What a pity Lord Joubert didn't catch up with us in time, as he'd said he would. He'd have been perfect for such a task. Meantime, I'm assuming this is only part of the plan? You haven't led us the whole length of the country to send us to certain death?'

Cerdic nodded. 'This is only part of the plan.'

'You and this Blood-Hair clearly know each other?' Turold said in a voice of disapproval. He was never pleased to learn that crucial information had been kept from him.

'Now you know what happened,' Cerdic replied. 'You saw for yourself what he and those others have done. You surely understand why I had to come back here?'

He'd taken them much further westward along the valley, until they were well past Wulfbury and far out of sight of its sentries, before descending to the bottom and there presenting to his comrades the second half of his scheme. They discussed it for a brief time only. It was mid-afternoon by then, and they didn't wish to make their way back along the fellside in the dark. However, on returning the way they had come, they'd looked down through the trees again and seen that a clutch of Viking warriors, maybe twelve in total, had emerged from the gates to the burh, and were waiting at the top of the brae track under a banner bearing the crossed staffs of the *Vaergenga*, which Arne recognised as a peace sign. Turold had thus instructed them to shuck off their leather and homespun, raise their pennons and descend to the ford in the village called Brackley, and receive any parley that was offered as knights of Normandy.

As Cerdic had expected, it was unproductive.

The party of Vikings they spoke with, thinking this the advance guard for an invasion of the north, had initially sought to curry favour, offering to hold the earldom in fealty to the new Norman king, but on seeing that Cerdic was with them, all that had changed. They clearly didn't understand how he'd come to be a Norman, but they wouldn't need to. They were Norse, and oath-sworn to Jarl Wulfgar, whom Cerdic had promised to kill. All that could pass between them after that was steel.

'Yes, I *do* understand why you sought to come back,' Turold said later, as he and Cerdic waited on horseback beside the York road. 'Most times, war is not personal. But this one undoubtedly *will* be.'

Cerdic shrugged. 'These dogs slew many who mattered to me.'

'Then you shouldn't fight,' Roland interjected, emerging through a thicket of wintry trees fast turning spectral in the purple dusk.

They waited in wafts of smoky breath as he approached, riding his own horse but with a pack-animal laden with gear and supplies trundling behind. They were a mile south of Wulfbury. Beyond the nearby wood, hidden by the encroaching night, they'd built their main camp in a low valley. It was convenient and well-concealed from the road. The rest of the troop had now returned to it.

Roland reined up, his Leopard cloak belted tight over his chain-mail. 'When one man seeks another on the field, often-times he neglects other responsibilities.'

'I won't,' Cerdic said simply.

'You say that now, but when the blood is up... when your foe stands before you, your vision tunnels. You see nothing else, and men may die because of that.'

'I'm not the commander here, Roland.'

'You're leading nevertheless. Somehow, the success of this battle has come to rely on *your* plan, on *your* ability to make *your* vision real.'

They regarded each other in the dimness, the older Norman with his air of caution and experience, the younger Englishman with his energy and fire, though inwardly Cerdic hated the fact they were losing their most seasoned officer.

'If you were staying, *you'd* be commanding,' Turold said. 'You could take care of all these matters. As you have so many times before.'

Roland said nothing. They'd already had this conversation, and now the road south awaited him. In normal times, it would make no sense for any knight, not even a knight like Roland Casterborus, to embark on his solo quest at such an hour. But the battle of Wulfbury would commence before dawn, when the burh's defenders were likely to be at their dullest-witted, and the knight-seneschal, by his own admission, could not remain in the camp alone, listening to the sound of combat and taking no part. He needed to be far away by then.

'Nothing will keep me off that field today, Roland,' Cerdic said. 'Maybe it's a bad thing in God's eyes, but it was God who allowed this disaster to fall on us.'

'In war, vengeance can be useful,' Turold opined. 'It can focus a man's hatred in the correct place. Is it not better if only the guilty die?'

Roland smiled wryly. 'Vengeance is mine, said the Lord.'

'Overcome evil with good,' Turold replied, surprising them both with his own quote from scripture.

Roland smiled all the more. 'Good, it seems, is a moveable feast these days.'

'We're here, and the fight is going to happen,' Cerdic stated flatly. 'If I stay out of it, what will it tell the rest of our men? Men who may die in my cause.'

Roland nodded. He had no dispute with that.

'You should go,' Cerdic said decidedly.

The knight-seneschal nodded again. 'Your plan is a good one, for what it's worth.'

'Just go.' Cerdic was as clipped and curt as he could manage.

Roland seemed surprised, even a little hurt, to have been so abruptly dismissed. He glanced at Turold, who returned his stare impassively, and then at Cerdic, who'd now turned his head away. Silently, he wheeled his animals and headed south, where he was quickly swallowed by the encroaching darkness.

'A good thing the rest of us have no time for such things,' Turold said.

'Such things?'

'Such things as conscience.' The knight guided his horse back towards the trees.

Cerdic hastened to follow. 'Turold… when this is over, we'll have a peace in which everyone can share, which will improve life for the ordinary people.'

'Spoken like a true nobleman. Like the Duke of Normandy himself.'

CHAPTER 30

Yvette found no sleep that night. There was too much bustle in the camp, too much hurried conversation, too much clinking of mail and weaponry. The men were clearly under orders to be quiet, but it wasn't possible with so many of them, while the atmosphere was one of urgency and tension. That alone would have kept her awake.

Cerdic then stooped in through the tent's entrance. 'Hello, my wife.'

She had no idea what hour it was. Even with the whale-oil lamp by her bedside, it was pitch-black outside. Despite that though, she could see that he hadn't slept either. He was bright-eyed and ruddy-cheeked, eager to be off, so determined to right the wrongs done to him that scarcely a hint of nerves was visible. As she sat up, she saw that he wore a plain dark tunic and breeches rather than mail.

'I just thought I'd tell you that we're going,' he said.

'Battle plans drawn?' she asked.

'As much as they can be.' He gazed at her earnestly. 'You should know that I met them on the river this afternoon. Representatives of the Northmen. We tried to get them to surrender, but there's no possibility of it.'

'Did you think there would be?'

'If I'm honest, no.'

'I hear that Roland has left us?'

He shrugged, feigning disinterest. 'He's gone to retrieve Count Cynric's body. And then he's heading back to Normandy.'

She fought visibly to suppress emotion.

Cerdic didn't point out the contradiction that only a couple of nights ago she'd described Roland as epitomising the Norman knights' failure to demonstrate chivalry in England, because both he and she knew that, even then, some were still better than others.

'You know,' he said, 'Wulfgar Ragnarsson's Vikings created a nickname for me. *Vargrkind*... it means a young wolf, but a bad one too. Someone or something who should be despised and hunted for sport because he exists outside the law. But that's *their* law, Yvette. The law that says Wulfgar takes everything. Much the way, in Joubert's mind, the law he will impose once he comes to power will state that *he* takes everything.'

'It's the law of all powerful men,' she replied.

'Not quite. You never knew my father. You say you think you'd have liked him. I *know* you would.'

Yvette didn't respond, but, though she'd never met him personally, she actually *did* know about Earl Rothgar. From Lady Edith, because he'd been a friend and ally of Earl Harold's. She'd often heard about his wisdom and probity, but also about his unusual marriage to Lady Eallana of Worcester.

It had happened over thirty years ago now, when the hated Harthacanute was King of England. Two of his tax-gatherers were slain in the city of Worcester. In response, he'd ordered its destruction. To protect the citizens, Lady Eallana, the young noblewoman in whose jurisdiction the city fell, arrested and handed over the real murderers. But this wasn't enough for Harthacanute. Eallana, unmarried but betrothed to Rothgar Aelfricsson, who was in line to inherit the earldom of Ripon, was renowned for her virginal beauty. Harthacanute, covetous as ever, demanded conjugal rights with her – and to save her people, she acquiesced, even though it stained her reputation. Ever afterwards she was referred to as 'the Viking's whore', though secretly her people loved her all the more for her huge sacrifice, and it didn't stop Earl Rothgar making her his wife.

Such stories of selfless duty, particularly when tinged with romance, had been regular favourites with Edith Swan-Neck, though Yvette would not reveal that she possessed this knowledge for fear that it might embarrass her husband.

'So, it's the memory of my father,' he said, 'whose firm but fair rule made Swaledale a good place to live, which makes me determined to restore it.'

'In itself, that's not ignoble,' she replied.

'They can call me names all they want, dismiss me as a bad and worthless wolf... but I think my quest is good. That's why I'll wear that insult as a badge of honour.'

'Earl Harold sought to be a good ruler too,' she said. 'He wanted to rule fairly. And look what they did to him.'

'One thing I can assure you, Yvette, they're not doing that to me.'

'Oh, Cerdic!' she pleaded. 'Why didn't you just escape when I told you to? You had so many chances.'

He frowned. 'And be hunted like a real outlaw?'

'They'd never have found you.'

'But they wouldn't have stopped trying. And now you know why. Because of who I am... *what* I am. Even Joubert. Something about me has terrified him from the start. Can't you tell? He knows intuitively when someone threatens his ambition.'

'Oh, God,' she moaned aloud. 'Ambition, badges of honour. All *I* see are hillsides covered with dead men.'

'Yvette...' He crouched, taking her hands. 'You hate being a pawn in these brutal games. I understand that, and I have to respect it. But we *are* husband and wife.'

'We are indeed.' She averted her gaze downward.

'Whatever happens tonight, I hope this union of ours may come to mean more to you at some point than it does now.'

She peered up at him. 'How much does it mean to *you*, Cerdic? Truthfully?'

Even in the wavering lamplight, wet-eyed suddenly, she was so beautiful that his heart ached.

'Look,' he said. 'I'm a stripling. If I told anyone I was in love, they'd laugh and say I don't know what love is. And they'd be right. I have no idea. But I know I feel a *closeness* to you. Calling you my wife… thinking I'm your husband. These aren't just words. It feels special. I know it's all happened in the strangest circumstance, and it's not the way either of us would have wanted. But you should know, before I go, that I'm *glad* we're joined together. My life's been shattered, Yvette… ruined. But you are without doubt the one good thing that's emerged from it. Maybe the only good thing. I can't explain it, but I feel so much better with you close by. But if you truly don't share that, well… there might be something we can do in due course.'

She'd been a little taken aback by the emotion in his voice. It was possibly the most she'd ever heard him say about anything that didn't involve hatred for the Normans or a yearning to kill the Vikings. But now she was even more surprised. 'You'd seek an annulment?'

'It's not a choice I'd make happily,' he said. 'I'd like us to at least try. But if you can't do that, I'll understand. Either way, tonight we should part friends at least.'

Her lip quivered. Then she offered her cheek so that he could kiss her. Briefly, she felt guilt at the chasteness of it. He was her husband, after all, and his unwillingness to ask for anything else, to make any physical requirement of her, despite the fact they'd once come very close to being lovers, was a kindness on his part that seemed to merit greater reward.

'Cerdic, wait,' she said, as he made to leave.

He glanced back.

She rummaged through the bedclothes and her few belongings, locating a white linen sack and opening it. From inside this came a neat roll of material, which when she shook it out, he was startled to see was the surcoat and cloak with the Boar's Head crest that Joubert had brought back from York, though now it sparkled as though it had been washed. There were no longer tears and slashes in it.

She handed it to him. 'I cleaned and darned it as best I could. It's so your people will know who you are when you return to them.'

At first he couldn't speak. He turned it reverentially in his hands, his eyes glistening. 'It's magnificent.'

'It's far from that, I'm afraid.'

He looked up at her. The tears had seeped onto his cheeks. 'It's…'

'Don't thank me too much.' She forced herself to be terse again. 'I hate war. But the world is the way it is. So, I know I must play my part too.'

He nodded, pulling himself together, carefully re-rolling the surcoat.

'The fact you feel that way makes this a genuine sacrifice,' he said. He placed a kiss on the cloth. 'I'll honour you when I wear this.'

'Heavens,' she said. 'You sound like a chivalrous knight already.'

He half-smiled at that. Then left the tent.

—

Cerdic took one hundred men with him, once again cutting west along the valley's southern side, though this time they followed a different route, which led up to much higher ground. Partly, this was because the Viking lookouts at Wulfbury had seen them when they'd traversed the valley wall earlier, and if so, it wasn't impossible that they'd have men posted on that particular path, waiting to ambush any second party who chanced it, but also it was because this time they couldn't afford to be seen at all. Not that it was likely. The men had brought their mail and weapons, but all of this was wrapped in bolsters or haversacks, which they carried on their backs. In addition, every man present wore dark clothing and carried his own coil of knotted rope.

Cerdic had Arne with him and all seventy-five Flemish cross-bowmen. He also had Tyrkil and the five other Northmen who had sworn to serve. In addition, he had ten Norman knights and ten men-at-arms, all under the command of Ivan d'Avranches.

They ascended the fellside slowly, again on a path familiar to Cerdic. Even though it was partly lit by shafts of winter moonlight poking through the firs, he constantly had to issue warnings about low-hanging boughs or roots or rocks jutting through the snowy soil. It was an hour before they reached the highest point of the valley without actually emerging onto the windswept tops. From here, they followed a more level path, bypassing Brackley-on-the-Water and Wulfbury burh, both so deep in the valley now that they couldn't see either. They only descended again about two miles west of there, on the opposite side of the river from the grove that Cerdic knew as Gonwyn's Orchard. Once they'd arrived in the riverside meadows, they dismounted and tethered their beasts along the treeline.

'This will be the difficult part,' Cerdic said as they huddled in a tight circle. 'That river will be very cold.'

'It's running deep too.' Ivan d'Avranches' voice sounded a warning note. 'Are there no other crossing-points?'

'None within several miles. We can go back to the ford at Brackley, but that would defeat the whole purpose.'

There were muted grumbles, in response to which Tyrkil the Widow-Maker snickered. 'My people learn to fight at sea. Snow, ice, saltwater... these are nothing. When man fight, his blood should pump. Warm him from inside.'

No one made any complaints after that. It was unlikely they agreed with the giant warrior; getting wet on a bitter winter's night could easily see a man dead by morning, but all of them prided themselves on their martial prowess. They'd never have made it this far north if they didn't, and this oafish barbarian, colossal though he was, would not make them feel bad about themselves before a blow had been struck.

They fanned out as they crossed the meadow towards the river. There was much snow here, all of it deep-frozen, its crust crunching underfoot. But there was nothing they could do about that. The nearest habitation was Oswalda and Guthlac's homestead, one mile to the west. Cerdic tried not to dwell on what state it might be in now, but his blood simmered at the memory of how his old wet-nurse and her husband had been treated by the insurgent Northmen. There were some wrongs that could never be righted, though he'd damn well do his best about that one before winter sunlight flooded Swaledale again.

He halted by the river's edge, unnerved by how broad it was, and yes, how deep. It was so swollen with meltwater that instead of flowing past and among scores of toothlike rocks, it ran smoothly, an unbroken sheet of black glass. Fleetingly, Cerdic wondered if they'd be able to manage it. There'd be nothing more likely to alert the Northmen to a surprise attack than the sight of drowned men trailing past along the river below their strongpoint. But again, there was no option. Looking at the sky, the moon was almost down. They had another forty minutes before the first hints of dawn glimmered on the tops to the east. Turold and his men ought to be in position by then, which meant that Cerdic and his men must be too.

'Every man stay close to another.' He waded cautiously down, bolts of frozen lightning shooting up his legs as the chill gripped them. 'If anyone loses his footing, it's down to the man next to him to catch hold.'

They followed him stoically, though again there were hisses and curses. The current was indeed strong, and the depth came almost to Cerdic's chin as he struggled against it, ensuring to hold high the single whale-oil lamp that he'd need to light the way up the Elf Stair. Tyrkil was nearby, and even he was advancing with careful, ponderous steps. Close behind him came Arne and his crossbowmen, all ensuring to hold their bows and missile-bags above their heads; a wet drawstring could render a crossbow completely ineffective.

'Christ help us, I can't feel my feet,' someone grunted.

'Colder than Lillith's tit,' another replied.

As they approached the other side, none had been swept under, though they'd been driven apart over many yards. Climbing out onto the snowy north bank afforded them next to no relief, but briefly there was that curious sensation one gets in the depths of a truly biting winter, when plunging frozen hands into the snow almost seems to warm them.

It was Tyrkil who egged them on as they slumped on their knees, lungs heaving, some even lying flat. 'You lie down, you die.' He stalked among them. 'Your only warm is *here*...' He thumped his chest. 'Move your raggedy arse, Frankish men. Heart will pump hot blood. Warm limbs before fingers drop off.'

They grumbled but got to their feet. Cerdic took point again, leading them across the valley road, through the orchard and along the course of Brackley Beck into the thicker woods under the cliff. There were fewer problems here than he'd expected. Normally this sloped section of woodland was swampy, but now it was deep-frozen, so they were able to pass through with minimum difficulty. Up ahead, beyond the twisting mesh of frosted branches, they heard the rumbling churn of a waterfall's plunge-pool. By the sounds of it, it was still in full flood. That was a good thing, for once they were behind the cataract itself, they could climb the Elf Stair with no danger of being seen.

The Elf Stair was a tilted limestone rockface, riddled with man-size grikes and fissures, which stood concealed behind a powerful curtain of water discharged down into the valley from under a place called the Upper Meadow, which was located just west of Wulfbury burh. As children, Cerdic and his friends had scaled it many times, both top to bottom and bottom to top, always hidden from view by the vertical sheet of thundering foam.

Children were agile as cats, of course. And often recklessly brave.

Whether, as adults, it would be quite so easy, especially with fingers now numbed and stiffening into icy claws, remained to be seen.

CHAPTER 31

'You've staked a lot on that lad's trustworthiness, Turold,' Will Malet said. 'A lad who has every reason to despise us.'

'Did Joubert have reason to despise us?' Turold replied, as they rode quietly along the valley road at the head of the troop.

'What are you talking about?'

'Because unless I've gone as blind as that madman who latched on to us in York, he isn't here. Even though he said he would be. And that means his *mesnie* isn't here either. Which weakens us in the face of the enemy.'

Malet looked puzzled. 'What has that got to do with anything I said?'

'You're questioning my judgement, aren't you? My decision to trust Cerdic more than Joubert... but where is Joubert? When we need him most?'

Malet pondered. 'Speaking of the blind man, I didn't see him around the camp today either.'

'Because Joubert took him with him.'

'Why?'

'I imagine he felt he might need a guide of his own.'

Malet sighed. 'I wish I understood why we are doing this.'

'You've seen Wulfbury for yourself, haven't you? It's real. Why wouldn't everything else the lad told us about also be real? The silver, for instance.'

Malet had no answer for that.

'You came to this land seeking to improve your standing, did you not?' Turold told his former squire. 'Well, this is your chance.

Fight like the devil and prove your mettle. Win renown, and it will earn you position. And you might even get rich in the process.'

Malet glanced backward, presumably wishing there were ten thousand men behind them rather than a measly four hundred. 'I didn't know it would be like this.'

'You didn't know that taking other men's possessions would be difficult? Things could be worse, Will. You could be sitting in a Godforsaken village in the south now, billeted in some damp, flea-infested hovel, awaiting the duke's return, whenever that might be, not even knowing if he plans to reward you. At least this way, it's in our own power.'

The road ahead of them bent, and the burnt ruins of Brackley-on-the-Water came in view.

'Torches!' Turold shouted, no longer concerned about stealth. 'You want to get something out of this wretched war, Will, this is your best hope.'

The two of them reined up, Turold opening the window to his whale-oil lamp. The other horsemen passed him in single file, each one carrying a staff, the end of which was tied with rope and smeared with pitch and resin, so that when it was poked into the oil-flame, it ignited. In a short time, every member of the company had his own firebrand. They proceeded through the village on the south side of the river, halting at the crossing point. Again, the shops and houses here were blackened shells, but where possible, they lit them up again. The majority of the host then arrayed itself along the south riverbank, conversing loudly, their animals neighing and whickering.

The purpose was to ensure that the defenders of the burh would realise they were here, and it didn't take long. High on the Keld Brae, more and more torches sprang to life atop the palisade. There was a harsh shouting, a clattering of mail and timber as additional men were called from their barracks. Soon, there was so much flickering light up there that almost the entirety of the brae track was visible, not to mention the burh's entry gates, which, by the looks of them, had not just been repaired since the Vikings broke them open the previous September, but strengthened. An outer layer of overlapping, hide-covered shields had been nailed over them, and even as Turold watched, figures on the gantry spanning the top of the gates were emptying pails of water down through them, to reduce the fire risk.

'We haven't been anywhere else in England as defensible as this,' Malet said.

Turold had to admit that. In truth, he marvelled that it had fallen the first time, though Cerdic and his people had not been expecting an assault. In sharp contrast now, the burh's palisade bristled with weapons. However, only a small portion of these men would be useful should someone attack the gates. With no room for more than a few on the gate-top gantry, the majority were ranged along the south-facing palisade, which was a waste as the chances of anyone assailing Wulfbury on that side were negligible given that the slope was steep and implanted with sharpened stakes. Archers on that side might angle their shots to try to hit men ascending the track, but it wouldn't be easy. Thickets of defenders manned the parapets to the immediate left and right of the gates of course, and they'd pose a problem, but there weren't great numbers of them either as there wasn't enough room.

In Turold's lengthy experience, the biggest threat waited inside. They'd take losses attacking the gates, heavy losses possibly, but that would be nothing compared to the reception they'd receive if they got the damn gates open. Most likely, the entire bulk of the Viking horde would be waiting behind them.

'You'd better hope and pray this boy comes through for us, Turold,' Malet said. 'If he doesn't, we face disaster.'

Turold didn't bother arguing, because this time it was true.

—

Cerdic's company edged over the jagged, ice-sheathed rocks circling the frothing pool into which the cataract descended, finally sliding behind the curtain of water into the recess containing the Elf Stair. Several fell, bruising and winding themselves, but then they peered up the cracked, unevenly stacked boulders they intended to climb, a near-vertical pathway towering to a height of sixty feet at least, and the sight took the breath out of them.

Once again, Cerdic assured them that it wasn't as terrifying as it looked.

'There are many nooks and crevices in that rock face, all of them wide enough for a man to insert himself,' he said. 'Many lead upward at easy angles, and interconnect. In addition, you can't quite tell in the dark, but the Stair itself tilts slowly backward. So, it's not a sheer climb. At no point will anyone find himself hanging over an abyss.'

It was true, he admitted, that many of the foot and handholds would be slick with frost, the spray from the cataract having frozen on contact with the rock, but the lead climbers would just have to be careful and scrape it away as they progressed. To prove to them though, that this could be done, he went first himself, the oil lamp, now lit, clipped to his belt.

As he effortlessly took the upward route he'd taken so many times in his youth, Cerdic recalled his conversation with Turold and Arne on first telling them this plan.

'Even the majority of my own people know nothing of the Elf Stair. We discovered it as children, and we kept it secret. It's the easiest way to approach the burh unseen. If there are any sentries on the west wall, all they'll see is the Upper Meadow, a stretch of moorland sloping downhill to a cliff-edge. The cataract plunges from just below there, so it can't be seen even from the highest point in the burh. I can carry a light up the Stair in complete safety. No one will know we are coming.'

'It can't be any worse than the outer wall of Chateau Namur,' Arne had replied. 'Which I scaled in the service of Baldwin of Hainaut.'

'Did you win that day?' Cerdic had asked.

'I took a full complement in and brought a full complement out.'

'I take that as a good omen.'

There was much grunting and puffing as the troop climbed, but the Elf Stair proved every inch the unexpectedly easy access to higher ground that Cerdic had promised. Near the top there was an eerie effect, blurred striated moonlight spilling over them as it shimmered through the cascading water, though this made it even easier to find niches and crannies to grip onto. After half an hour, they'd all of them emerged from under the limestone overhang and filed out along a ledge, where for a very short distance, no more than three yards, they truly did teeter on the edge of a gulf, though there was still space enough for them to draw up their bundles by rope. From here, they ascended a slope conveniently studded with juts of half-buried rock, moving then onto the Upper Meadow itself. Above the snow-clad crest of it, they could just about discern the topmost parapet of Wulfbury's west-facing palisade.

They crouched or knelt, regaining their breath, watching.

The pristine blanket of snow covering the meadow would not help them on the final approach, but not a single torch glimmered on the west-side parapet, and it soon became apparent why. Cries rent the frigid air. Impacts sounded: missiles striking woodwork, the clatter of throwing spears rebounding from shields or helmets. The sky to the east had turned orange with fire.

'The perfect cover,' Cerdic said.

He unravelled his pack, taking out his gauntlets, his helmet and coif, and then his mail hauberk. Armoured, he donned the cloak and surcoat bearing the Boar's Head emblem of Earl Rothgar and Wulfbury, which Yvette had repaired for him, buckling the surcoat at the waist. He hung his sheathed longsword over his back, along with his shield, and stuck a seax in his belt.

Fully girt, they ran forward silently, only to falter on twenty yards, Cerdic hissing a warning. They slid to a standstill, every man's eyes having now attuned to the firelit snowscape and thus spying the lone figure on top of the palisade. A single guard, it seemed, who'd been parading back and forth, had now stopped and peered down at them, his shoulders square and rigid as if he couldn't believe what he was seeing. Arne dropped to one knee, took aim with his crossbow and loosed. The bolt flew silently, hitting its target in the side of the neck. The guard staggered and gargled with pain, clamping the wound with his hand, only for a second bolt to streak through the darkness, courtesy of Henrik, Arne's deputy, hitting him in the throat.

The guard slumped forward, hanging limp over the parapet.

Arne looked at Cerdic, his face gleaming with sweat.

Cerdic nodded his acknowledgement of the close call, then turned to the others. His heart thudded in his chest. This was it. After all the torture, hardship and hopelessness he'd suffered since Wulfgar Ragnarsson had first driven him away from here, this was finally it.

'Ready yourselves. It's time.'

CHAPTER 32

Turold's first assault on the gates of Wulfbury was made by infantry, a hundred men-at-arms advancing behind a wall of shields, and behind them, moving at a near-crouch, the forty archers they had left. Once within striking range, the shield men would squat in unison, and the archers rise up and launch a volley. They'd then advance another few yards and do the same again, and then again.

It was an attempt to thin out the defenders on the gantry above the gates and those sections of palisade on either side. Certain shafts found their targets, but more by luck than design. The Northmen meanwhile bombarded them with rocks, of which they'd clearly amassed a great many, javelins, arrows and darts.

In no time the attackers' shields were dented, gashed and riddled with feathered shafts. Several of the shield men were wounded, a couple killed. They persevered, sending up flight after flight of their own. It was difficult to tell whether they were making any impact, because even those they hit cleanly were replaced by others from behind, and very quickly their quivers were empty.

At this point, they shuffled aside, allowing the first squadron of Norman horsemen, Turold at their head, to gallop through.

The cavalry had ascended the brae track behind the line of infantry at a walking pace so as not to exhaust their animals, but now there was no option but to charge. The first squadron barrelled uphill the last fifty yards, spreading out as they closed on the gates. Many threw bundles of tied sticks and branches at the base of the portal, while others were armed with fire-pots, small clay jars filled with whale-oil, and with burning rags stuffed into the neck, so they could be thrown as incendiary grenades. Others meanwhile carried ropes and grappling hooks. Again, they received stones, spears and arrows in response. Turold bore through it behind his shield, though the impacts rang in his ears, especially when a slingstone clattered from the side of his helmet. Twenty yards in front of the gates, he wheeled his horse sideways and hurled his grappling hook. It lodged in the shield cladding rather than catching on the top of the gate, and when he rode away again, the rope tied to the pommel of his saddle and pulled taut behind him, layers of defensive linden wood were torn loose, but the gate itself remained undamaged.

Those with him were equally unsuccessful. Milo de Hauteville's grapple caught the top of the gate, but a Viking on the gantry above chopped down with his broadsword, and the rope was severed.

'This is futile!' Hauteville bellowed, riding back.

Most of those others throwing grapples had missed the mark, while many of the incendiaries had struck the bundles of sticks and even the gates, and flame had blossomed, only for the defenders to pour further pails of water down and quench it.

Once the first squadron was back out of range, another squadron charged, similarly equipped. Will Malet rode at their head.

'This is sheer madness!' he called to Turold as they passed.

'Damn it, Cerdic!' Turold said through gritted teeth.

If the lad didn't come through for them soon, they'd all die here.

—

Using their ropes and several hooks, Cerdic's party was over the west-facing palisade in a relatively short time. Once on its gantry, they divided into two groups, Arne taking his crossbows up onto the thatched roofs of Wulfbury's many outbuildings, leaping quietly from one to the next, while Cerdic stayed at ground level, leading Tyrkil and his five Norse, and the twenty Norman footmen, through the maze of cramped passageways, the roars and screams of battle drawing them steadily.

Only once did they encounter anyone, two Vikings emerging from the doorway to a billet, hurriedly pulling on their mail shirts and buckling their weapons in place. Cerdic, with longsword already drawn, ran the first one through silently, but the second, just ahead of his comrade, spun to face them, battle-axe in hand, teeth bared in his mead-sodden beard. Tyrkil pushed forward to engage, but that would have meant noise. Instead, Arne shot him from overhead, punching a crossbow bolt between his jugular and collarbone.

Fleetingly, the air was tense, Cerdic watching as Tyrkil turned the corpses over with his foot, his own Vikings ranked behind him, looking on sullenly. Could these violent sea-roving warriors really be trusted in a situation like this? Could he seriously expect them to make sword-brothers of English and Normans when fellow Norse lay slain at their feet?

He waited as Tyrkil squatted beside the bodies but was relieved when instead of performing some kind of respectful ritual, the Widow-Maker simply loosened the first one's belt, the clasp to which had been worked with silver, then stripped off both their arm-rings and weapons, handing them out, item by item, to his own *drengr*.

From here on they proceeded unhindered, passing the drill yard and allotments, and coming finally to the end of an alley that opened into the dragon hall square. Here, they could see clear across it and down Wulfbury's central thoroughfare to the main gates. Wulfgar Ragnarsson's entire host was crammed all the way along it, rank after rank of mailed and helmeted fighters standing shoulder-to-shoulder, weapons brandished, impatiently awaiting the great gates' collapse so they could launch themselves on the enemy.

Not that this was likely to happen soon. From what Cerdic could see, significant numbers of Norse were also on the gantries both above the gates and to either side. Many also crowded the gantry running atop the palisade on the burh's south-facing side, though not anticipating attack from that direction – they were turned to the east, watching the brae track. Some of those posted towards the east end of the south parapet flung stones and even spears, but with little hope of hitting anything.

For all the mental preparations he'd made for this night, Cerdic was still stricken by the huge number of Northmen they had to overcome.

By his own reckoning, Wulfgar Ragnarsson had first attacked with several hundred warriors. Now, there appeared to be more than that. An accurate headcount was impossible but even from a single glance, the lad estimated they faced five hundred at least. A doubtful voice in his head wondered if he'd made a terrible mistake, but then, even from this distance, he heard the renewed shouting and bellowing from beyond those great gates, and a Viking fell backward from the gantry, a fire-pot having enveloped him in flame. At the same time, a grappling hook on a rope latched itself to the top of the gates, and even though a defender struck with an axe, and sheared it loose, Cerdic was reminded of the force of Norman arms just outside. Altogether, they weren't far off matching this number.

They could still win this battle if they stuck to his plan.

He glanced overhead. Arne, like a guardian angel, was bent to one knee on the overhanging thatch of an outhouse. They locked gazes. Cerdic nodded, and Arne nodded back. He was proving an able subcommander. He knew exactly what to do.

—

Turold's third assault on the gates was beaten back with no loss of men or horses, but though many more fire-pots struck home, most of the resulting blazes were extinguished, while the two hooks and lines connected at the top of the gate were severed. The grappling hooks were now much reduced in number. Most lay at the foot of the gate, while others were stuck in the timber itself, and it would have been suicide to dash up and try to retrieve them.

'This plan is not going to work,' Turold told himself, as he and his battered party descended the brae until they were out of range again. He scanned the various groups of horsemen waiting on the lower slope for orders to advance, but then fixed on the company of archers who'd strafed the palisade with arrows before.

'Get back up there!' he ordered. 'Thin out that herd of pigshit!'

'With what, my lord?' their captain replied, holding out his bow and his empty quiver. 'All our shafts are spent.'

'Damn it!' Turold swung round in the saddle. 'Will Malet, your turn again! Get back up there. Lug those damn gates open.'

'Turold, are you mad?' Malet dabbed at his face with a blood-soaked rag, his shield thick with the husks of arrows. The rest of his squadron were in a similar state.

Turold looked to others of his subcommanders. All looked beaten and bedraggled. Each had forty or so horsemen under his control, both knights and mounted men-at-arms, but several were visibly wounded in each cohort. The captain of the men-at-arms had been shot through his left shoulder with an arrow, and once again, others of his troop adorned the higher slopes and wouldn't be coming down again.

Exhausted but angry, Turold stood in his stirrups. 'I'm going back up there one more time!' he proclaimed. 'No one has to follow me, but anyone who wishes to, you're welcome... and the more of you the merrier.'

He grabbed a couple more ropes and hooks from the camp-boys charged with running round and distributing them, and backheeled his horse up the slope, the animal now heavy and sluggish, lathered with sweat, its breath pumping in dense clouds. Loyal to the last, a number of others rode too. They couldn't all carry hooks, as there simply weren't enough, while their fire-pots were also used up, the whale-oil exhausted, but all along, the strategy had been that some of the men would ride up to the gates as decoys, so the defenders weren't entirely focused on the handful who could do them harm.

Another deluge of missiles greeted them, though mainly these were now stones. The Vikings weren't known for their archery, so they hadn't had many skilled men with bows to start with, and they'd likely used most of their javelins and throwing spears, but they were still hurling lumps of rock, many of which were large enough to split the skulls of oxes. Their impacts on helmets and hauberks were enormous.

The shield-cladding had now been torn off the gate in its entirety, but the heavy wooden timber behind it remained formidable, even if parts of it were on fire.

Turold swung and hurled his first hook. It missed entirely, but he drew it back and swung it again, and this time it caught at the top of the gate. He yanked on the rope to pull it tight. A defender on the gantry swiped down with his axe. The first blow missed. He straightened up to aim a second, but then jerked and twisted, and toppled forward, spiralling down and landing heavily in the wreckage of shields and smouldering wood. A few yards to the left of him, also on the gate-top gantry, another one twisted, screeched and slumped over the palisade, landing a few feet from Turold's horse.

The knight's attention closed on the feathered stub of a crossbow bolt protruding from the base of the defender's unhelmeted skull.

They're in, he thought. *They're into the compound.*

He pulled harder on the rope, looping it round the pommel of his saddle. Another Northman slashed with his sword, and the rope came free. Cursing, Turold threw his second hook and missed, but he no longer cared. He spurred his horse downslope, the rest of the squadron following. Before he was out of range, he reined his animal around to look back.

Another Viking fell from the parapet. And another.

The rest of them, that great mob of mop-haired, beard-faced barbarians, were so convinced they were winning the battle now, and so much more easily than they'd anticipated, that they were too busy jeering and shouting insults to notice that one by one, they were being struck from behind.

CHAPTER 33

Many minutes passed before the Northmen inside the burh realised where the real danger lay.

During that time, Arne's crossbowmen, ranging widely across the Wulfbury rooftops, were able to pick their targets, the bolts flying silent and efficient. Mostly, they concentrated on those defenders manning the gate-top gantry and to either side of it. One by one, at an increasingly rapid rate, they hit their marks cleanly. Ring-mail did not afford the protection that chain-mail did, but some of them sported only fur, leather or woollen jerkins, and they were the easiest meat of all. Several gasped and choked, and were not immediately slain, but for a time, their comrades, not having seen the fatal missiles, assumed such injuries were coming from the front, where the Normans were still staging reckless, headlong charges.

Five particular crossbows had been detailed to focus on the gantry on the south palisade, as this was the route that Cerdic and his fellow footmen needed to take if they were to seize the gates. The Northmen posted along this section were lesser in number and one by one they too fell, either backward or forward. The result was confusion; they couldn't understand from whence the blows fell, and as they cast around in panic, they spied Cerdic and his four henchmen, who'd ascended to that gantry at its undefended western end, and now stole along it towards them. Battle was joined immediately, shouts raised as swords rang, but the gantry wasn't wide enough for more than two men to fight two at a time, and the five crossbows on the nearest roof continued their work, hitting Northman after Northman, so that even as

Cerdic's longsword clove one fellow's shoulder, a flying bolt hit his temple, piercing him to its feathers. They thus advanced quickly, meeting fewer and fewer opponents, and every time they came to a ladder, they heaved it up and threw it out of the compound, to make it harder for anyone else to assail their position.

Down in the thoroughfare, meanwhile, the phalanx broke apart slowly and messily as the Norse wolves began to realise the enemy was within. Arne's orders echoed across the rooftops, additional squads of his men shifting their aim to the chaotic whirl of bodies below. Vikings shouted and jostled each other as bolts slanted down, burying themselves in necks, chests, skulls. Shrieking in rage, the ship-brothers toppled like skittles, and still they couldn't see who was responsible. Eventually, one of them glanced upward by accident, and spied the shadowy shapes on the eaves overhead, but though he tried to raise the alarm, his cry was lost in the furore, and then a bolt hit his open mouth, and he dropped to his knees, gagging on blood.

—

With fewer and fewer Northmen defending the gate-top gantry or the palisades on either side, it was easier for Turold to marshal his men and launch another attack. He personally had only one grappling hook left, though two or three of the others had one each too. They twirled them around their heads as they rampaged up the hill. A thinner cloud of missiles descended to greet them, and they bore through it, unleashing their payloads from twenty yards short.

With insufficient defenders up there now to throw water, the right-hand gate was still burning, the flames eating into the timber. Turold's hook caught there, midway down in a section now blackened and splintered. He leapt from his horse so as to yank it downward further, lodging it fast rather than simply tearing it loose in a cloud of cinders. It worked; the hook became wedged. He scrambled back into the saddle, wound his tow-line around its pommel, and galloped back downhill. The line went taut, the gate creaking outward, a fracture running down it to the bottom. At the same time, one of the other grapples had also caught, this time on top of the right-hand gate. One of the few Vikings still up there struck at it with his sword, but by now the Norman archers had recovered some of the arrows shot down at them by the defenders, and one had come close enough to take a pot-shot in return. It hit the Viking in the side of the chest, and he fell silently into the flotsam below, that second grapple still attached, this rope also pulling taut as Will Malet, who'd thrown it, retreated downhill. Once the horsemen were out of range, other men, both mounted and on foot, came forward to grab the ropes and haul on them. The gates whined and creaked as they bowed outward. The one on the right, now clad in flames, was threatening to come apart on its own.

'Give it everything!' Turold spurred his horse downhill as hard as he could, before looking to the rest of the company, still sheltering from missiles on the lower slope, signalling for them to mount up and draw swords.

—

It was Tyrkil who led the foot-charge across the dragon hall square.

Countless members of the horde cramming the thoroughfare now lay dead or wounded, while others were distracted by their attempts to get to the bowmen on the roofs. Some had thrown torches, which at any other time of year might have lit the thatchwork, but much of it was still encrusted with ice and snow. Others had managed to clamber up, only to be shot from close range, or stabbed and clubbed. The last thing any of them expected was twenty warriors to range into them from the direction of the dragon hall, in Tyrkil's case both arms windmilling, his axe and sword wreaking red devastation all on their own. The Ragnarsson host outnumbered them by far, but the shock of the overhead assault was still reverberating through them, and then they found they were under attack at ground level, too.

Mayhem resulted.

'Traitors all!' the Widow-Maker roared in his own tongue, as he tore his way through, hammering helms and chopping limbs.

The others formed a shieldwall behind him, Viking standing shoulder-to-shoulder with Norman, all their momentum forward, their steel biting mail and flesh as they advanced.

It was an impossible task overall, of course, so few challenging so many. Their initial impetus was a huge advantage, carrying them over one scattered group after another, and even when it inevitably slowed as they met ever more opposition, the intent was to divert Ragnarsson's men both from Arne's Flemings and Cerdic's small band on the gantry, and in that it was successful. But as awareness spread that Tyrkil's numbers were limited, more and more Northmen rounded on them. Tyrkil himself slew on with ferocity, but soon was pushed back among his shields, and now his entire line of warriors was retreating, shuffling backward across the square, each man of them fighting two or three adversaries at the same time. One by one, they fell, and even if only wounded, were brutally hewn where they lay.

Tyrkil proved harder to take down than any of his comrades. Blades struck him repeatedly, but his own blows were lethal. He killed all those who came directly against him, but as each wave of opponents fell back to get their breath, a fresh one always surged in. The Hardraada loyalist knew that it was too much. Sideways glances showed him that his numbers had already thinned from twenty to ten. A fighting-retreat wasn't enough. He personally strove on, delivering mighty strokes, splitting heads down the middle, cleaving shoulders from trunks, but had now realised that the only hope for his men's survival was to get them under cover. Praying to his gods that he'd bought Cerdic enough time, he ordered his band to take refuge in the nearest outbuilding, a simple storage shed on the north side of the square. When he gave the actual command, they broke and ran.

The Widow-Maker covered their backs himself, hacking and slashing like a thing possessed, only to receive a stunning blow in the face. Whether from axe, mattock or broadsword, he couldn't tell, but it sent him reeling, and his opponent would almost certainly have followed through and finished him, had a crossbow barb not struck him in the throat and dropped him to his knees. With help from his eight remaining warriors, Tyrkil was steered into the refuge of the shed, its doors and windows then closed and battened. A huge bombardment immediately set the structure rocking.

Inside, they could only lean on each other, panting, aching, smeared head to foot with glutinous gore. With luck they'd have a few minutes in which to regain their strength, and so assail anyone who hacked his way in. The greatest threat of course was that their foes might bring torches to this timber sanctuary. The snow cladding the thatch on top might dissuade any such action, but at present all they could do was breathe hard and heavy, and hope.

High on the south gantry, Cerdic had made swift progress, aided both by Tyrkil's distraction attack below and the marksmen on the nearby roofs, though the rate of flying bolts was dwindling now as the Flemings' ammunition ran out. However, they'd made it all the way to the burh's southeast corner. Again, they heaved up every ladder and threw it out of the compound, which ensured that no one could come up from behind. Those in front they traded steel with ferociously, Cerdic cutting and stabbing with every inch of his new-found skill. But it might still be for nothing. The majority of those below were not just congregated in the thoroughfare now but spilling through the narrow passages between the outbuildings. They still had superior numbers, which would shortly tell unless Cerdic took charge of the gates. He and his band rounded the corner onto the east palisade, where some twenty yards ahead, a flight of narrow wooden stairs connected with the gate-top gantry itself. Only dead Vikings occupied that crucial twenty yards, though a ladder on the left, the gatekeeper's ladder, was fixed in place, and reinforcements were clambering up it. Cerdic kicked the first two down with hefty blows of his boot, but more and more were ascending.

Ivan d'Avranches was close behind. 'Hold these men off, if you can!' Cerdic shouted, moving on towards the staircase. Behind him, a Viking squawked as he reached the gantry and D'Avranches' blade punctured his throat.

Thus far it had been difficult for Cerdic to establish how much progress Turold had been making outside, if any. The din of battle had drowned out all individual sounds, and even now, at the front of the burh, and with a silver-grey dawn breaking over the eastern ridges of Swaledale, smoke hung thick, obscuring his view. But as he reached the foot of the staircase, the smoke wafted clear, and he looked down onto the brae and saw teams of men and horses lugging for all they were worth on two ropes snagged firmly to one of the gates, which wasn't just burning but bulging outward.

Hurriedly, he clambered the narrow stair. At first, he'd assumed there were no Northmen left alive on the gate-top gantry to hack at the lines, but when he got up, he realised that another one had taken position there, in fact had posted himself directly beneath the great raven banner, which Cerdic could now see flew from the top of a nine-foot fighting spear lashed with ropes to the upright posts of the parapet. That sole defender had a hunting bow and an open sack of arrows at his thigh. One after another, he took carefully aimed shots at the men below, each time striking clean, an individual always staggering and dropping to his knees or face.

More important than any of this, to Cerdic at least, was the name of this defender.

The lad took a long breath, before wiping the sweat from his face with his chain-mail sleeve, and shouting. He shouted with such gusto that even over the clamour of battle, his opponent heard him.

'*Blood-Hair!*'

CHAPTER 34

'*Vargrkind!*' Blood-Hair grinned, that hole in the middle of his teeth visibly rotting.

He wore a ring-coat with steel shoulder plates, a fleece doublet belted over the top. For some reason he'd discarded his helmet, so his full mop of crimson hair hung to his shoulders. It would have seemed absurd to the Cerdic of several months ago, but to even things up, the lad now unfastened the strap under his chin and pulled off his own helm, pushing back his chain-mail coif.

But this wasn't just the chivalrous influence of Roland Casterborus.

'This fight has to be perfectly fair,' Cerdic said. 'When the skalds sing of this, I want their listeners to know that I had no advantage on the night I slew you.'

Blood-Hair grinned again and nodded. And then he threw away his bow and its empty quiver, took a war-axe from his belt and picked up his circular shield. The hide on the latter was painted purple, the single crimson eye of Odin at its centre, the iron boss serving as its pupil. Before they joined, Cerdic twirled his sword as Turold had taught him. Forward, then back, a perfect flourish each way. Blood-Hair noted this, a tiny hint of uncertainty creasing his face before, with a roar that verged on a scream, he came forward at pace.

Cerdic met him silently, with a solid, foot-forward stance. Blood-Hair's blows were earth-shattering. The axe struck Cerdic's shield again and again, and he felt it in his marrow. The clangour tortured his ears, he was rocked on his heels, but he struck back firmly, thrusting and stabbing as well as slashing, hewing the circular shield repeatedly, but often reaching past it with his extra half-foot of steel.

They travelled back and forth along the gate-top, eyes wild, sweat flying. Twice Cerdic almost gained the upper hand, his longsword sideswiping the Northman's shoulder guard, sending him tottering, then a furious backhand only missing because his opponent ducked, striking the upright haft of the spear on which Land Waster was mounted, severing it clean, the dreaded raven totem fluttering down from its perch, which could only, surely, be a good sign.

Of course, Blood-Hair read it differently.

'You came here ready for this,' he said, spittle seething through the black gap in his tight-locked teeth. 'That pleases me. Only a true warrior is worthy of my axe.'

'I know at least one young woman who'd disagree with that,' Cerdic panted. 'And it's in her name, now, and many others, that you're going to pay with your guts…'

With a wild yell, he hurled himself forward.

—

Outside, revived flames licked their way up the right-hand gate, the entire structure creaking and shuddering as the two teams of men and horses expended immense strength heaving on it, their tow-lines taut as bowstrings, though Turold had now detached to watch the two-man combat on the gate-top gantry. Alongside him, an archer nocked an arrow.

'If they break apart again,' the archer said, 'I've got that pagan bastard dead.'

Turold tapped his shoulder with his sword-tip. Surprised, the archer lowered his bow.

'He didn't come all this way to be denied now,' the knight said.

—

The combatants broke apart, gasping. Cerdic twirled his longsword again.

'You've learned a trick or two,' the Viking sneered. 'But this is a war between gods. And fancy work means nothing when thunderheads collide.'

He swept back in, his axe looping over and down. This blow bit deep into Cerdic's shield, the blade briefly wedging before Blood-Hair yanked it free. The damaged shield now felt flimsy in Cerdic's hand. A second such blow hit the same cleft crosswise, and Cerdic drove in with a flurry of his own. Briefly, his blade too was embedded in his opponent's shield, but he worked it free in time to leap back and evade a reverse slash.

Though considerably older, Blood-Hair kept going, sobbing for breath, his locks hanging in sodden rat-tails. A third colossal blow landed, and Cerdic's shield broke in half. Cursing, he tossed it and replied with a succession of arcing two-handed swipes from left and right. Blood-Hair backed up, forced to parry with the haft of his axe and then his shield. This time, the sword's edge smote the limewood deep; a huge rent appeared, and the Viking flung it aside. Cerdic's hope surged. A hand axe was no use in swordplay. He only needed to catch the haft again, and it would give. But as they closed, weapons braced against each other, Blood-Hair headbutted him in the face. Skull spinning, Cerdic tottered. He sensed the axe scything down and raised his sword. The blades met, but it was the sword that gave, or rather Cerdic's grip, which had slackened in his grogginess.

The hilt left his shaking hand, and his steel spun away.

Howling triumphantly, Blood-Hair aimed a backhand. Cerdic dropped to a squat, the blade swishing over his head, then lunged forward, bearhugging Blood-Hair's hips. Blood-Hair struck down again and again, striking the middle of Cerdic's back with the heel of the axe-haft, then trying to knee him loose, first with the left and then with the right, putting himself off balance, enabling Cerdic to grip him harder, rock back onto the flats of his boots and lever himself upward, using every inch of strength in his thighs and calves.

The Viking was lifted clean off his feet, then off the timber platform itself, falling bodily forward over Cerdic's shoulder, the lad pushing him upward and back.

But before he could plummet the full sixteen feet to the hard-packed floor inside the gates, Blood-Hair clawed out, catching Cerdic's belt. And the lad went too.

They fell together, but the Viking was underneath and travelling head-first.

He landed with a sickening crunch of bone and flesh, Cerdic landing on top of him, the hefty but broken body, part covered in thick fleece, providing an essential cushion. Cerdic rolled away, gasping and stunned, but got quickly to his feet, backing up a couple of steps, mopping sweat from his brow as he peered at Blood-Hair's lifeless face, which was clearly visible as his head had turned at a grotesque angle. The mangled mouth hung agape, the eyes staring glassily in different directions.

Fleetingly, all energy drained from Cerdic's bruised, tired body. His sweat cooled; his shoulders sagged. And then, more by instinct than design, he glanced up.

And saw all the other faces enclosing him.

From three different sides.

The scowls etched onto them like devil images cut in wood.

One by one, swords and axes were unharnessed.

Swiftly, he cast around for any weapon he could find, but saw nothing. Even Blood-Hair's hand axe was lost to view.

'You are looking for this?' someone enquired.

On the other side of Blood-Hair's corpse, one particular Viking had pushed his way through the angry huddle. A figure in shimmering, high-quality armour and a full-head helmet, its faceplates fashioned demonically.

It was Ragnarsson himself, Jarl Wulfgar, and the weapon he offered was a magnificent broadsword, its cross-hilt bound with wolf fur, its pommel set with an immense emerald. The brigand chief had clearly had one of his smiths polish the fine blade, for the heathen lettering engraved down the length of it glinted in the firelight.

Cerdic glared at him with hatred. 'That's my sword! My family won it at Tettenhall. It came down through generations of our warriors.'

'You are wrong,' Ragnarsson said simply. '*This* is your sword.'

One of those close by handed the jarl a secondary broadsword, this one minus ornamentation, its blade dull, chipped along its edges. It might have seen many battles, but it was past its best. A pauper's sword. Which was clearly Wulfgar's point as he tossed it to Cerdic hilt-first. Cerdic caught it, glancing again at the encircling faces, many now grimly amused. No doubt they'd been told the son of the earl who'd once claimed this place had come to steal it back, and the Boar's Head crest on his surcoat indicated that this was he, though in a dirtied and dishevelled state, not to mention alone.

One glance at the gantry atop the gatekeeper's ladder showed Ivan d'Avranches and the rest of the small band who'd gone up there with him dead, the Norse who'd finally fought their way up standing over them. It would have been nice if crossbow bolts still sleeted down, but clearly all the Flemings' missiles were spent. Maybe the Flemings were spent too. Behind him, the gates creaked and groaned, flames licking over the top, but they remained standing. He looked again at Wulfgar. The jarl's wealth was written all over him. It wasn't just his exquisitely worked helmet. He wore a shirt of iron scales rather than rings, a polished *byrnie*, which extended all the way from his shoulders to his knees. A thick sword-belt, the buckle of which was inlaid with gold and silver, and which had once belonged to Cerdic's father, clasped it at the waist. Though Usurper's scabbard hung empty, a dragon-headed war hammer was fastened at his other hip.

Unlike many Northmen, he wore his valuables into battle: the snake-headed torque at his throat, the gold and silver rings around his muscle-heavy arms, which he clearly displayed as a direct challenge to anyone he encountered on the field of honour.

These are your trophies. All you need do is take them.

The twosome circled each other. Cerdic was still winded after his fall from the parapet, his right hip and shoulder hurt abominably, and his lungs ached. He ran with cold sweat; his arms heavy as lead. Laughter and scorn sounded amid the Norse ranks. If he strayed too near, they pushed and slapped him. Wulfgar merely grinned, his teeth white in his thick, braided beard.

'Good of you to come to find me,' he said. 'You saved me the trouble of finding you. You see, friends, the gods favour those who serve them. When the jarl calls, they know their own.'

'The gods know *you* for an oath-breaker!'

The accusation was made in Norse, so Cerdic only partially understood it, but he gazed around in fascination. Wulfgar looked too, angered, bewildered. And then a third party pushed his way through the surrounding men and stepped into the firelight.

Tyrkil was a bestial sight, slashed and bloody all over, one blow having bisected the upper part of his nose, but he still towered to his near seven feet of height, while his battle-axe and broadsword, one in either hand, glimmered with gore.

'Is there any man here who doesn't know me?' he enquired.

A numb silence followed, for if they didn't know him, they certainly knew *of* him.

CHAPTER 35

'I am Tyrkil Hellasson, Widow-Maker of Fjelldal.'

Silence lingered as the hulking, blood-soaked phantom slowly pivoted in their midst.

While they were familiar with his reputation, the majority of them hadn't known that he was present. Those among them who'd fought him into the storage shed on the dragon hall square either hadn't recognised him or had assumed his part in the battle was finished owing to his severe facial wound, and thus, when the army's attention switched back to the front of the burh, had left him there to die. Clearly though, he was still very much alive.

'I fought with Harald the Hardraada. On fields as far apart as Olivento and Ostrovo, Jerusalem and Kiev,' Tyrkil said. 'I fought ship-to-ship with him at Niså, stood with him in the shieldwall at Fulford, when we drove the English earls from the field, and then at Stamford Bridge, where our mighty lord fell and our cause in England was dashed. And where were *you* that fatal day?' He eyed them one by one. 'And *you* in particular, Wulfgar Ragnarsson? Here. Seeking your private fortune. Sacking homesteads manned by boys and women. I piss on your name the way I piss on your title, *Jarl* Wulfgar.'

Again he turned, staring the gathered warriors in the eye.

'You hear that, spear-brothers? I piss on it. Because it is fake. This is no jarl you follow. He claims descent from Ragnar Lodbrok. But he lies...'

'You dare...' Wulfgar snarled.

'I dare because it's the truth,' Tyrkil retorted. 'He lied to you that he is noble-born, and honour-bound to restore the lost lands of his fathers. In truth he murdered his father, and fled to Flanders to escape justice, where he lived as a common sellsword. He lied about his ancestors. His father was Danish, but his mother English.'

Disbelieving murmurs greeted this.

'Yes, my friends, you hear that rightly. It is English blood that runs in his veins. He was raised a Christian, and yet here he dares stand under his own false image of Land Waster, a bogus idol, blessed neither by *goði* nor *gyðja*... when the real one, the Hardraada's own, had to be pried from the cold, dead hands of Jarl Frirek, who died by his side...'

The Northmen glanced at each other askance, for all of them shared their master's guilt at having abandoned Harald the Hardraada at his hour of need.

'He named himself Ragnarsson to bring warriors to the house of Tostig Godwinson,' Tyrkil said. 'It was Earl Tostig who told him about this hall, this earldom. This, then, is your jarl, my friends. A liar, a murderer, an imposter.'

More fearful murmurs sounded. There were many among them who'd already been jittery about their betrayal of the Hardraada, and still were. But to learn that it had all been for nothing... to follow a scoundrel, a pretender, who'd even had the gall to claim kinship with the Ragnarssons of legend when he was no such thing.

'Liar and whoreson!' Wulfgar bellowed. 'You think your past glory excuses you such deceit, such treason as to ally yourself with these English... these Normans.'

'Enough talk!' the Widow-Maker retorted, red spume flying from his lips. 'If the blood of Ragnar flows in your body, you will cut me down now as a betrayer of all our fathers.' He raised his own sword. 'If not, lower your head for the stroke of justice.'

With a strangled cry, Wulfgar leapt across Blood-Hair's corpse. Their blades met in flashes of sparks, their blows furious, unrelenting.

Cerdic backed away to give them room but watched intently.

Steamy breath leaked as much from Tyrkil's wounded upper nose as from his blood-glutted mouth. He was a *berzerker* in all but name, a giant, a genuine battle lord, but he was injured and weary for he'd been fighting huge odds for an hour at least, whereas Wulfgar, though a pretender, was no mean warrior himself, and was fresh. Very rapidly, this told, for though Tyrkil fought like a devil, his sword and axe swinging down in mighty overhead slashes, Wulfgar parried all and dealt him a smashing impact on his half-severed nose with Usurper's emerald pommel. There was a crack of cartilage, fresh blood spurting. Tyrkil yowled like a wounded animal, tottering backward. Wulfgar struck at Tyrkil's heart. Tyrkil parried it with his sword, but the axe in his other hand wobbled, and Wulfgar caught it with a lightning reverse-slash, the weapon flying wide and free.

Gasping, the twosome fell apart, but still Wulfgar was the fresher.

He leapt again over his henchman's corpse, Tyrkil fending him off, though the larger warrior now seemed exhausted by pain. He stumbled, lost in the haze of blood that masked his face, only to throw himself bodily forward, grappling with his foe chest-to-chest. And then it was Wulfgar who choked as the giant hugged him and hugged him, bones cracking inside the coat of scales. Desperate, Wulfgar clawed at Tyrkil's eyes and then at the gory mess of his nose, his finger hooking into the exposed nasal cavity.

Tyrkil's growls became piercing shrieks. He released his opponent and lumbered backward, blinded by agony, and as he did, Wulfgar caught his sword with a mighty backslash and sent that spinning away too. Completely disarmed, Tyrkil now fell over Blood-Hair's corpse. Wulfgar wheezed with pain himself, but barked with laughter.

'Odin speaks! You're witness to this, you wargs, you hell-hounds… Odin speaks!'

Tyrkil tried to get up to meet him, but Wulfgar lurched forward, kicking at him, knocking him back onto his rump and raising Usurper for the final killing blow.

'*Bróðir!*' Cerdic cried, throwing something from the side.

It was the severed spear-shaft from the palisade atop the gates, the bogus *hrafnsmerki*, depicting the raven Land-Waster, ragged now and blackened by smoke, but still attached, the spear-tip at the top of it gleaming with sharpness. With a roar, Tyrkil caught it and thrust it upward as he rose to his feet, driving it with all his strength into Wulfgar's barrel chest, piercing the scales of his *byrnie*, and going deep through the ribs into the soft organs beneath.

Wulfgar toppled into retreat, agog, gagging on the crimson cataract that pulsed from his mouth, finally slumping backward over his friend. Tyrkil leaned on him ever harder, forcing the shaft of the raven banner ever downward, lodging its steel point in the very heart of his sworn enemy, whose eyes glazed over with undeservedly merciful speed.

'Yes,' Tyrkil said, eventually stepping back, a hideous sight himself, so gashed and mutilated was he. 'Odin speaks.'

The stupefied silence lasted several seconds. And then the encircling ranks exploded with rage. More swords were drawn, more axes hefted.

'Arnulf... Olaf!' Tyrkil shouted, stumbling towards Cerdic. 'To me!'

Two more Northmen pushed into the open space and hurried to join him, one wielding a spear, the other a seax. Cerdic recognised them as two of the five Vikings who'd accompanied them up the Elf Stair. Clearly the others were dead, though like their leader, these two were slashed and bloodied.

The foursome stood with backs to the burh gate as the rest of the horde pressed towards them, eyes livid in mottled faces, beards filled with spittle. The plan hadn't worked, Cerdic realised with disbelief. The Flemish bowmen had killed innumerable of them, but there were still hundreds left, and even without their leader, they were ready to lay waste their enemies.

But then, in most timely fashion, and with a cacophony of ripping and rending timber, the great solid uprights behind them fell away, the huge gate on the right collapsing outward, engulfed by flames. Working on pure instinct rather than knowledge, they all four of them scampered aside as the Norman cavalry, Turold at its head, surged in.

Even amid roiling smoke, the dawn light glinted on the tips of lowered lances, the edges of swords. The mass of the Vikings, neither with shields to the fore, nor spears braced, were in no position to face a charge and attempted to turn backward en masse, but they were too bottled up in the thoroughfare.

The Norman heavy horse crashed into and over them, lances ramming home, longswords rising and falling in a blur of blood-spray. Even Cerdic, who'd expected to be sword-meat himself, watched aghast as the war-steeds ploughed steadily onward, a carpet of torn and shattered men under their hooves. He glanced left. He and his companions were pressed against the palisade on the right side of the entrance. Tyrkil, next to him, slid slowly down the woodwork, smearing it with blood. Cerdic grabbed him, trying to hold him up.

Tyrkil shook his disfigured head. 'This… *yours?*'

Cerdic's eyes fell on the emerald in Usurper's hilt. He grabbed the weapon gratefully, slotting it into the scabbard on his back, but still trying to assist the fallen giant. The Widow-Maker shook his head again, more breath steaming from the bridge of his nose as he landed on his backside, his entire upper body slumped forward.

Olaf, a brawny middle-sized man, his fair hair tied in lengthy, flaxen ropes, crouched at the other side of him, probing at his neck. 'He live,' he muttered in broken Frisian French.

Cerdic swayed back to his feet. He glanced along the central thoroughfare, a worse scene of crushed and broken forms than he'd seen even in the precincts of the West Minster.

Sickly dawn light spilled over it in full, not a single grisly detail hidden.

The bulk of the Norman horse had passed through and were now engaging their foe in the dragon hall square. Cerdic stumbled after them, struggling to find footholds in the meshed, gory wreckage. When he reached the end, he couldn't get into the square; it was too crowded, the entrance jam-packed with horsemen.

'Cerdic!' a voice called from overhead.

Directly above, Arne leaned down from a thatched overhang, extending his arm. Cerdic snatched hold and the Fleming pulled him up. Several other crossbowmen were up there with him, though all, as Cerdic had suspected, had now discarded their bows and were simply sheltering from the storm below. He stood upright and in the spreading dawn was able to see clear across the interior of the burh. More Flemings were scattered over the other rooftops, but fewer than he'd expected.

'Once we were out of shafts, they pulled us down,' Arne said, wiping sweat and dirt from his face. 'Until your fight with the redhead drew their attention.'

Cerdic had no answer for that, though he'd need to find one soon, because yet more men had now sacrificed their lives in the quest to recover *his* earldom.

He turned to the square, over which he had an unrestricted view.

What remained of Ragnarsson's horde, no more than a hundred strong, was packed into the centre, the Norman horsemen encircling them, thrusting with lances, laying down hard with blades and maces.

'Enough!' Cerdic shouted, raising both arms. '*Enough!*'

It was Turold who did the honours, reining his animal back when he spotted the lad, shouting an order that passed through the rest of them. One by one, spears were raised, swords hefted back to mail-clad shoulders.

The Viking remnants clung together, gasping, exhausted, hemmed in not just by spears but by the corpses of their friends, but defiant too, threatening all comers with what few weapons they had left. Before he could say more, Cerdic heard a scrambling and scuffing of thatchwork to his rear. He turned. Arne was pulling another fellow up. It was Olaf.

Relieved, Cerdic beckoned him forward.

'Tyrkil sleep,' Olaf said.

Cerdic nodded. 'You will translate for me, yes?'

Olaf nodded too. Cerdic turned back to the expectant crowd. 'Northmen!' he shouted.

Olaf repeated it in Norse.

'You have been told this once and should not need to be told it twice. Be under no illusions, you will not be told a third time.' He paused to let that sink in. 'You were brought here under a false promise. The warrior Wulfgar, who called himself Ragnarsson, never held any rights, by descent or otherwise, to these lands. He was not of noble blood, neither English nor Norse. He shared no kinship with Ragnar Lodbrok. He was a liar and a cheat, who set himself against everything that is great in your culture. He rode on the glory of others to obtain wealth and power for himself. In doing this, he betrayed your great king, Harald "the Hardraada" Sigurdsson... and because of this, the Hardraada's kingdom is no more now than six feet of English earth.'

He paused again, watching them. They listened, rapt.

'All of you share in this guilt... though you are lesser offenders than your master, for you thought you were following an honourable man, a jarl. But even then, he brought you to make war on a part of this land where English and Norse have lived in peace for many years. Think on that crime, think on all the crimes Wulfgar, the man who claimed descent from greatness but was merely a thief, induced you to commit.'

Olaf translated word for word.

'Because you were led here on a lie, I... Cerdic of Wulfbury, knight of this realm, and Earl of Ripon, will spare your lives.' He paused for effect. 'If you throw down your weapons now.'

As one, they refused.

He shook his head. 'Listen to me, Northmen. When you first attacked this place, which had done you no wrong, many died at your hands. My blood boiled at my helplessness that day. I heard the screams of the women you defiled, the babes you orphaned. It would be very easy, and it is very tempting, trust me, to bid my Norman comrades continue their Godly work... to take you man by man, make you first embrace our God, and then kill you afterward, so the Hall of Heroes will never be yours. And yet still I offer mercy if you disarm now. Think hard on this, Northmen. You have committed grave offences here. This day could still go against you. You have one minute to decide.'

He turned away, looking first at Arne and then at Olaf.

They regarded him blankly.

And then a clattering sounded from the square.

It was the echo of swords, axes and spears being cast to the paving stones.

—

'Taking so many alive is a laudable Christian act,' Turold said, leading his horse up to Cerdic, who stood to one side of the Viking prisoners, mostly now seated in the centre of the square, many looking disgruntled as their weapons were gathered by their captors. 'The question now is what do you do with them all?'

Cerdic was tempted to reply that he'd treat them better than Duke William did his. But that would be a glib response given that this was a real problem and required a real solution. Before he could say more, a horseman cantered into view from the main gate. It was Will Malet, looking grimy and bloodied.

'Turold!' he said. 'Cerdic! Something you need to see.'

'As soon as we can,' Turold replied. 'First...'

'It won't wait.' Malet saw their puzzled expressions and added: 'Joubert has arrived.'

'Better late than never,' Cerdic said.

Malet remained grim. 'Not quite.'

CHAPTER 36

The army was arrayed broadly along the southern side of the river. Even from the top of the Keld Brae, it was obvious that most of them were sellswords, such were the disparate types of armour and weaponry on view. But all were mounted, there was somewhere between six and seven hundred of them, and in their centre, facing the crossing-point, sat Joubert and his *mesnie*, alongside a heavy-set fellow with long copper hair hanging from under his Norman helm. Over his hauberk, this new fellow wore an orange tabard bearing the image of a black ram's head, and a heavy cloak patched together from many fleeces. He held a hefty kite-shaped shield and a broadsword already drawn, while a two-headed war-axe hung sheathed on his back.

'Copsi,' Cerdic said. 'I should have known that Joubert would try something like this.'

He eyed the infamous figure warily. Copsi might be English to his toenails, and a Northumbrian to boot, but his avowed opposition to Harold Godwinson, and his murderous reputation generally, had clearly won him support in high places, for by the looks of the twenty or so knights ranked behind him, doubtless all handpicked for their efficiency in battle, he now had a *mesnie* of his own.

'We should both have known,' Turold said. 'I never believed Joubert had gone off to ambush Copsi's men. Not when he could have made use of them in his war against you.'

'That's a significant force,' Will Malet observed. 'And we have three hundred or so left who are fit to fight.'

'We also need to allocate men to guard the prisoners,' Alain le Roux commented, coming to join them outside the burnt-down gateway.

Tyrkil and Arne now arrived as well. The former was grey of complexion, his face so wound with dirty bandages that he was only just able to see. Even so, what little colour remained in his mangled features drained slowly away as he gazed downhill.

'Even if we'd killed them instead,' Turold said, 'we'd not have enough men to hold this palisade for more than a day. And that's assuming we'd be able to repair the gate in time, which we wouldn't. And all the while, of course, Copsi could be sending south for reinforcements. He has the power of the king, remember.'

'Isn't it a fact that these men are nothing more than *routier* scum?' Cerdic said.

'The ones I saw in York were,' Turold confirmed. 'But if the riches of Wulfbury are theirs for the taking, they'll be highly motivated.'

The lad sighed. 'As I see it, we have two options. We fight as one. As the same war-band that captured this place, now defending it. Or... you all surrender to Joubert and hand me over as a prisoner.'

They responded to this with silence.

'The latter choice is worthy of long consideration,' Cerdic said. 'But remember, Joubert is not the one commanding down there, and even if he was, he murdered his father... and *you* were witnesses to that.'

Le Roux snorted. 'None of us actually saw...'

'But what do you *think*, Alain?' Cerdic asked him. 'What do you *believe*?'

Le Roux relapsed into silence.

Turold spoke next. 'The probability is that in return for his revealing our presence here, Earl Copsi has offered Joubert the Hold of Ripon. And all the wealth associated. Whether Joubert will share with those he thinks betrayed him, even if we hand you over, is a different matter.'

'If you join with him, he'll definitely share,' Arne said. 'He'll share the responsibility for his father's murder.'

'He'd prefer us dead?' Malet replied. 'Is that what you're all saying?'

Cerdic nodded. 'It would be easier for him. He has new friends now, after all.' He nodded at the wide deployment on the river below.

'Let's be blunt,' Turold cut in. 'Joubert can't risk even one of us returning alive to Normandy. Dagobert may not be sorry to hear that his father is dead, but when the story gets around that Cynric was murdered, he can't afford not to act. At the very least, he'll appeal for justice to the king. And if that happens, even sitting pretty here in Wulfbury will be no protection for Joubert.'

'Especially not if his new mentor, Earl Copsi, has been killed by Oswulf of Bamburgh,' Cerdic said, reminding them that even Copsi was under threat in this hard northern realm. 'He *needs* us dead, all of us. And this is his chance.'

Will Malet had heard enough. He wheeled his horse back through the blackened entranceway. 'I'll explain the situation to the men.'

'Apologise that we're asking them to do it all again,' Turold said, 'but point out that all our lives and fortunes depend on it.'

'Tyrkil… Arne,' Cerdic said. 'You are soldiers of fortune, and you've done exactly what you were contracted to. I can't order you into this additional battle. I'd just say this. There's no time at present for me to locate my father's silver and pay you what you're owed. I can do it later, of course. If I'm victorious.'

Arne gave a crooked smile. 'And if you're not?'

Cerdic arched an eyebrow.

They grunted with frustration, but also acceptance. Neither expected that Joubert would show mercy to them, but they had nothing to offer Cerdic anyway. Tyrkil had only two men left, and while Arne's survivors numbered around thirty and were busy inside the burh, retrieving what crossbow bolts they could find, they looked tired and listless, the paltry survivors of a once-mighty force now decimated.

'Very well,' Cerdic said. 'Wait on us here.'

He crossed the corpse-strewn hilltop to where Turold had commandeered two riderless horses. They climbed up, side by side.

'We're very outnumbered,' Turold said, fitting his helmet into place.

Cerdic hefted the battered shield hanging on his animal's flank. 'The downhill charge will give us momentum.'

'I think I've fought too many battles.'

'I can't even promise this will be the last.'

—

When the three hundred or so Norman knights and men-at-arms staged a mass charge down the brae track, the earth shaking, snow and dirt flying from their hooves, Arne and Tyrkil could only watch from the top in disbelief.

'I cannot believe what I'm seeing,' Arne said.

Tyrkil yanked off his bandages to get a better view, even though it exposed his gruesome nose-wound. He laughed aloud. 'Balls of Thor! That boy is wasted on the White Christ.'

—

At first, the enemy seemed stunned by the reckless downhill charge. Even when the Norman force reached the bottom of the brae track, weaving between the charred shells of Brackley-on-the-Water, and hit the river at chaotic speed, plunging through it in fountains of foam, the opposition were slow to launch themselves forward. When the collision came, it was on the river's edge on its south side, many of the Norman knights striking clean through onto dry ground, which threw Copsi's army into immediate wild confusion.

The battle spread quickly between the few ruined cottages on that side, and then all along the riverbank. There were open spaces among the trees here, sufficient for horsemen to zigzag in and out as they dashed at each other. Again, the clatter of blade on shield, mace on helm was ear-numbing. However, such cramped confines prevented Copsi's mercenaries from using their weight of numbers effectively. Cerdic felled a couple straight away. They bristled with weapons, mauls, axes, cleavers, but compared to the Norman chain-mail, their inferior ring-mail and patchwork leather was easily penetrated by longsword and lance, while Usurper was harvesting men like wheat. One sellsword wasn't even helmeted, Cerdic splitting his skull like a melon. A second wore only homespun under a leather vest, and Cerdic clove his chest. It was another clean, straight blow, and it sliced him to the heart.

Alongside him of course, Turold wrought his customary havoc. His shield was speared through on the first charge, making it an impossible encumbrance, so he'd dropped it and drawn his chain-mace, and now he fought with that in his left hand and his sword in his right. None he met were a match for him, all falling from the saddle in welters of blood and brains.

Cerdic spied Earl Copsi only a couple of times, despite more than once standing in his stirrups to pinpoint him. For all his hefty frame, and the strength and vigour with which he wielded his battle-axe, the new Earl of Northumbria was closely attended by his cohort of heavily mailed horsemen, who shielded him from the worst of the exchanges. More involved was Joubert, and this surprised Cerdic greatly. Not because he thought Joubert a coward – he didn't – but because these men the count's son was at war with had until recently been his own comrades, and yet he and Yvo de Taillebois, who was never far from his shoulder, slashed and thrust, hacking men down in what seemed a frenzy of rage and hatred.

'To Joubert we're nothing but traitors,' Turold said, halting briefly, sweat streaming from under his gashed helm. 'With Joubert, you're with him or against him. There's no in between. And no mercy if it's the latter.'

'We need to end this.' Cerdic yanked at the shaft of a lance driven so forcefully into a mercenary that it had impaled both him and his horse to the ground, and once he'd freed it, levelled it and charged along the riverbank. 'Joubert!' he shouted. *'Joubert!'*

Joubert spotted him. Grinning with typical malevolence, he was handed a lance by Taillebois, and lowered it, kicking his own horse into furious forward motion. The twosome hurtled at each other, only for an entire pack of riders, whirling back and forth as they hewed and struck, to barge into the space between them, forcing them far apart again.

—

'Oath-breaking pigs!' an angry voice pealed.

The Vikings sitting miserable and bedraggled in the dragon hall square glanced around. They weren't chained, but they were disarmed, a body of Flemish crossbowmen standing guard over their heaped war-gear, a bolt on every string.

'You betrayed your ring-giver, Harald the Hardraada!' the angry voice said.

It was Tyrkil Widow-Maker again, the former captain of King Harald's own *drengr*, a warrior of such prodigious strength that legend held he'd single-handedly dragged a longship across a frozen river in the land of the Rus, a warrior whose ferocity they'd seen for themselves that very day, when he'd fed a number of their men to the crows, and cut down the false but still-mighty fighter, Wulfgar Ragnarsson. He'd suffered grievously, as they were now reminded – for he stood above them on a straw-thatched roof, his nose streaming fresh blood – but he was far from feeble yet.

'Now your other false lord, the imposter, Ragnarsson, also feeds the worms, and yet still *you* live.' His eyes filled with murder as they roved the beaten, craven band. 'For this abomination, Niflheim awaits you! That you have the nerve to sit unmarked by axe or spear dooms you to eternal mist!'

None could dispute this, for it was true. They hung their heads.

'Despite this,' he said, voice still ringing but his tone more even, 'the goddess Freyja, ever a mother to the brave, has interceded on your behalf, and though it pains me to say it, your names may yet be carved on the Allfather's mead-benches.'

One by one, they glanced up.

Tyrkil nodded. 'The One-Eyed Lord offers you a chance to redeem yourselves, and maybe... if you are lucky, a chance to die such deaths that the Valkyrie will be proud to swoop for your souls.'

—

Cerdic found himself forced out into the river, the water sloshing as deep as his horse's thighs. The animal panicked and he had to battle to keep control of it. At the same time, he was fending off foes.

Fighting from horseback was relatively new to him. He'd practised with Turold, and the big knight had told him that if he could learn to wield the longsword on foot, which he had done, engaging from the saddle would be easier as mounted knights rarely came nose-to-nose for protracted periods. However, there were added difficulties here: more opponents; a river level that rose the more his horse wheeled and bucked its way out into midstream. In consolation, he was fighting brute mercenaries rather than professionally trained knights, but somehow, he seemed to be far from his comrades, more and more sellswords, odd-eyed and pig-faced, surging through the foam towards him.

Usurper took its toll. One fellow, wearing a leather cap rather than a helmet, spun a chain-mace at him, the spiked ball landing with smashing impacts on his shield, the woodwork splintering inward, before catching him on the shoulder. It was a stinging blow, but the spikes lodged in Cerdic's chain-mail. The mercenary couldn't pull it free, and Cerdic rammed his blade into the fellow's gullet. A second one, wearing a flat-topped helm but with its faceplate missing, loomed in, swinging a broadsword. Cerdic parried, and pierced him through the open mouth.

The river boiled around their thrashing beasts, swirling crimson. But still they came, and Cerdic, though pumped with hot blood, was dizzied from the constant ducking, weaving and dodging. His left arm throbbed as blades and mattocks pounded his shield, his right arm weary from wielding his sword. When it lodged in the midriff of a big-bellied oaf on his left, and he couldn't retrieve it, he had sufficient speed of thought to draw his seax, hack off a row of fingers and plunge it to the hilt into another sellsword's eye (*a second score for King Harold*, he thought), before releasing the seax, grabbing Usurper's hilt and wrenching it free from the oaf, who fell twisting from his saddle, guts loosened like a brood of vipers.

But still he was out in the river, and the nearest of his sword-brothers were snarled amid superior numbers on the southern shore. Till now, it hadn't entered his head to shout for help. Firstly, it was unthinkable; he was a knight, an example to others; a leader. Secondly, because he couldn't draw sufficient air into his hard-pressed lungs.

But whether he summoned it or not, help came.

With thunderous belly-roars, an avalanche of men cascaded down the Keld Brae. Cerdic stared at them, baffled and terrified. It was the hundred or so Viking prisoners, now rearmed with their hammers and axes. But on whose side did they intend to fight? Then he saw Tyrkil Widow-Maker at the front, leaping down the rugged slope, a cleaver in one hand, a broadsword in the other, and he had his answer.

CHAPTER 37

Yvette didn't know if praying served any purpose.

As a young girl she'd been taught there was a different prayer, and indeed a different saint, for every crisis. And she'd believed it. Of course she had. Why not? Who didn't like the thought that a ceiling of kindly faces looked down on you wherever you went? Of course, it was relatively easy when so few of the crises she'd faced in those long-ago halcyon days of innocence and joy had qualified as *real* crises. Now, it was tempting to believe that any wrong thing in her life back then had, in truth, been resolved by her father's wealth and power... though he hadn't been able to breathe life back into her mother, who'd died when Yvette was four years old. Of course, God hadn't done that either, though Yvette had always explained this away by reminding herself that she'd never asked for any such miracle, even in her most desperate, tear-sodden prayers, because as the priests in Hiemois repeatedly told her, God had taken her mother for a reason, which she would only understand when she joined Countess Constantia in Heaven at the end of her own days.

After the last few months, she wondered if Countess Constantia had died while her only child was still a babe because God was simply content to let bad things happen. It was inconceivable to think that – and a grave sin, she was sure – but how else could one explain the appalling events since the October of last year? Some of the things she'd seen in this land would stay printed on her mind forever, the evil she'd witnessed had terrified her out of her wits, the injustice sickened her to the point of being physically ill. She'd been spared the worst of it in Normandy, when her father sent her overseas to the idyllic sanctuary of Walsingham, only, in due course, for the tide of hatred to arrive there too.

Maybe subconsciously it had undermined her faith in the effectiveness of prayer.

Not to the saints this time, but to God himself and even the Virgin Mother, whose unwillingness to hold back the darkness had ensured that never again would Yvette spend time in the care, kindness and tutelage of Edith Swan-Neck, a damsel the beauty of whose soul matched only the beauty of her body, driven finally to madness and death.

And yet she prayed again now, feverishly, intently, kneeling inside her tent, clasping a crucifix that she'd lashed together from two sticks. Even if God was genuinely unconcerned about mankind, if He was happy to let the darkness rampage, she had to try. If there was only the most infinitesimal chance that He might hear her, it had to be worth it. So, she poured out all the verses and psalms she knew for hours, even though all the time that terrible cacophony rang across the valley: the clangour of blades, the screams of dying men and horses.

How could human voices be filled with so much hate and rage?

What needed men of trolls and ogres when they themselves were so much worse?

And then, with a deafening rending of material, the entrance to her tent, which she'd laced closed, was torn wide open, and two filthy brutes stooped in.

Yvette would have laughed at the irony of it – it was the precise opposite of what she'd prayed for – had their faces alone not been enough to provoke terror: scarred, pock-marked, low-browed, their noses flattened, their mouths filled with brown and broken teeth.

One of them, the leaner of the two, crowed like a cockerel as they hauled her out into the otherwise deserted camp. Even outside, the stink of their sweat and dirt was overwhelming, their hair whipping in greasy, unwashed hanks. They wore patchwork armour of ring-mail and leather, and harnesses filled with every kind of edged weapon.

'He said she'd be here,' the heavier of the two said in Breton French, his voice guttural and croaky thanks to the ancient gash now hardened into a jagged white scar on his throat. 'What a goddess. I'm not surprised they want this one kept safe.'

'Just a shame we weren't able to,' the leaner one replied in a snivelly, weaselly voice, before giggling. Yvette wailed as they flung her between them, pawing at her with callused, grime-encrusted hands, tearing at her clothes.

'We have to give her back for what they're paying,' Scar-Throat replied, in a voice that suggested he could be persuaded otherwise.

'Please…' she wept.

'They'll get her back,' Weasel squawked. 'We want our money. Whether she'll be worth having by then, that's another matter.'

They brayed with laughter. Up close, their breaths reeked of excrement.

'No,' she begged.

'No?' Weasel said. 'You need to be nicer than that, you snot-nosed baronial whore.'

'Don't matter what she says,' Scar-Throat replied. 'When a filly needs riding, that's all there is to it.'

They brayed with laughter again.

'Oh my God,' she pleaded aloud.

This was surely the time. Where was He? Where in Heaven's name…

And with a whistle of unclad steel, a longsword hit Weasel in the neck, biting through the leather coif and the stringy muscle beneath, slicing into the neck-bones.

The sellsword capered sideways like a chicken, head lolling to the left, a cavernous wound spraying blood like a fountain. So shocked was Scar-Throat that he released Yvette, and she staggered away a few yards before turning. *'Roland!'*

The knight leapt forward, his bloodied battle-blade levelled. Scar-Throat ripped out a scramasax, but Roland parried the blow, and with an invisibly fast backhand, opened his larynx again. Scar-Throat staggered, eyes bulging, choking on the tide of blood that surged down his chest. For good measure, Yvette grabbed an iron cooking pot from the embers of a nearby fire, and smashed him across the skull with it. He dropped heavily to his knees, still clawing at his slashed-open throat. For half a second, she thought he would force himself up to his feet again, but then, instead, he tottered and fell full length, landing face-first in the embers, his brutish features immediately sizzling.

Yvette thought she'd hate herself for that, but somehow, she just didn't.

When she turned, Roland was cleaning his sword on a handful of cloth.

'Has the tide of battle changed?' he asked. 'Who are these goblins?'

She shook her head. 'I don't know... I couldn't watch it.'

He sheathed his weapon. 'Probably for the best.'

—

Tyrkil and his Nordic wave crashed across the river and struck Copsi's mercenaries hard. They had support from Arne and his crossbowmen, though the Flemings hung back on the other bank, instructed by their captain to pick off targets from a distance.

It told immediately.

Those surrounding Cerdic were pulled from their saddles and plunged headfirst under the blood-red surface. Others, even those mounted, were split apart by sweeping strokes of the Dane-axe or saw limbs sundered by flashing broadswords. But even with the ferocious downhill charge and the fearless abandon with which these redemption-seeking Northmen entered the fray, the energy of the attack didn't last long enough to tip the balance. The river slowed and exhausted them. In addition, there were only a hundred of them, which still didn't bring Cerdic's overall force to an equal number with Copsi's. Plus, they were on foot, and once on dry ground on the river's southern bank, that gave them disadvantage.

Cerdic, for his part, worked his horse hard to mount the bank again.

There, he halted, sweat-drenched, reins tight in his gauntleted fist. The melee raged on and on between the trees and the burnt cottages, and all along the waterside. But though Tyrkil in particular was hauling men from the saddle and chopping them like meat, many of his new-found colleagues were lanced or speared, or went down with shattered crania. Turold still ranged back and forth, laying waste to each opponent either with longsword or chain-mace, he and his mighty black steed both shining with sweat, patterned all over with gore. But he wasn't so distracted that he couldn't suddenly direct a warning shout at Cerdic.

The lad glanced left and saw two mercenaries driving at him, spears levelled.

He wheeled to meet them. The first spear transfixed what remained of his shield, the hacked, hide-clad woodwork splintering apart. He responded with steel, severing the shaft and ripping it through his assailant's guts. The other fellow turned his beast deftly to strike from behind. Cerdic turned too but wasn't quick enough. The blow from a flail caught him between the shoulders. His body spasmed, but his mail absorbed the worst of it. He completed his turn, parried another blow, and thrust with Usurper, punching through his opponent's leather corselet, driving the blade under his ribs.

As Cerdic swung his animal around a third time, he was confronted by Milo de Hauteville, coming towards him minus helmet, lolling in the saddle, blood gushing from two ghastly wounds, one in his chest, one in his throat. A passing sellsword added a third, striking with a backhand, removing the top of Hauteville's skull.

Cerdic shouted and was about to spur his steed in pursuit, when he saw Joubert again, distanced about a hundred yards back from the river, among trees. He still hung close to his *mesnie*, or the ten or so that remained, Yvo the Slayer always at hand. Both Cynric's son and his guard-dog were fully engaged, swapping savage blows with men who had formerly been friends, but mostly now with Tyrkil's Vikings, several of whom had managed to mount horses, though they'd never been trained as cavalry, and thus fell easily to Joubert and his henchman's blades. Even the Normans who tackled them, and again it was full-blooded, Cerdic's reminder that this young dog had slain their count still ringing in their ears, appeared to be outmatched. Joubert smote one in the neck. Another he impaled through the heart. Though the Slayer was all that and more. Three knights and a mounted man-at-arms tackled him at the same time. He despatched them one by one, with clean but furious strokes.

But it didn't matter how good Joubert and his sidekick were. Cerdic knew that this had always been their fate. To meet on the field. Joubert represented all that was worst in the Norman conquerors. He'd massacred, raped, burned, treated all before him as subhuman, animals to be yoked, or lice to be trodden. He'd be the worst tyrant imaginable should he gain this earldom.

'*Joubert FitzOslac!*' Cerdic shouted.

Joubert turned again, wiped the red froth from his eyes, and for the second time that day, sighted Cerdic and his face split in a maniacal grin.

This time there was no one between them.

They struck each other once only on the first pass, their blades singing, before bringing their animals around and charging again. This time, they reined up, exchanging blows so forcefully that sparks flickered. Joubert's eyes glared like soulless baubles from either side of his nosepiece. Sweat seethed down a face not just flecked with other men's blood but flushed and bulging with effort. Cerdic also sweated and ached, but every stroke from the Norman he countered. Until he parried Joubert's blade downward, and it cut through his saddle, scoring the horseflesh beneath. His mount reared, and Cerdic battled the reins to avoid being thrown. Joubert, wheeling his steed around him, aimed a thrust from the side that would have skewered his ribs had Cerdic not turned the point with his elbow and landed a counterstroke on Joubert's neck. It failed to slice his steel-studded aventail, but the count's son was stunned by the blow. His head drooped and he tilted sideways.

Cerdic was about to slam his blade home, when he sensed another opponent closing. He ducked, just in time to evade a throwing spear.

And then Yvo the Slayer, sword drawn, was on him.

Cerdic swayed exhaustedly, the rank air dragging in his lungs as he fended off a succession of cuts and thrusts. At the same time, he sensed others coming. More of Joubert's personal guard. He took a mace to his helm, its impact shuddersome, and then a blow in the back, which again failed to penetrate. Terrified, his mount thrashed, turning and rearing. He lashed out, by pure luck cleaving an exposed throat. But now he was being hit from everywhere. A seax drove point-on into his ribs. The chain-mail held, but the force of the blow was horrendous, crushing pain filling the side of his chest. An axe-blade glanced from his helmet, and he saw dazzling lights.

He was barely aware of Joubert materialising in front of him, drawing back his longsword. It would be a clear, unobstructed thrust to the chest. Cerdic had nothing left. And then, with colossal impact, another knight crashed full-on, horse and all, into the count's son. The two animals squealed with terror as they stumbled apart, the mail-clad riders only just clinging on.

'*Murderer!*' the newcomer shouted. '*Patricide.*'

It was Roland Casterborus.

The knight-seneschal closed eagerly with his former master's son, the duo swapping steel in a frenzy. Cerdic could do no more than lean over his horse's head. He was numbed down half his body as he watched them circle each other in a lethal dance. The clangour of impacts was torturous. Their sweat flew, faces wild.

But Joubert was waning the fastest, his defence faltering.

'*Traitor!*' the knight-seneschal shouted. '*Assassin! Betrayer!*'

Joubert gaped in horror. He couldn't breathe, foam and sputum slathering his jaw. He blinked to clear the sweat from his eyes. And then, from nowhere again, Yvo the Slayer galloped past with seax in fist, stopping only to deal a downward blow to the space between Roland's shoulders.

'*Bastard!*' Cerdic screamed, riding in from behind.

The Slayer glanced back, then spurred his horse away, seeking to put ground between them so that he could wheel. But Cerdic was too distracted to follow. More attackers struck at him, and he fought back furiously.

Roland meanwhile had arced with agony, limbs twisting out of shape, the seax buried to its hilt just left of his spine. Joubert kicked his horse's foaming sides, urging it the last two yards, and slammed his sword home, driving it clean through Roland's mail. Withdrawing it quickly, he slumped back in the saddle, stuttering with harsh, broken laughter.

Roland gazed at him white-faced... and yet somehow found sufficient strength to lunge forward with his own blade. Unexpectant of this, Joubert failed to respond, the sword tip piercing the mail over his solar plexus, ripping through muscle, flesh and organ.

Gargling bile from a mouth gaped impossibly wide, his eyes literally popping, the count's son fell back lengthways along his horse, which reared and galloped from the fray.

Roland now tipped sideways and fell to the ground.

Cerdic would have jumped down to assist him, but there was still danger all around. In those two terrible seconds, he'd made sufficient space for himself to wheel part-way about, so as to keep one eye on Taillebois, and the other on the rest of Joubert's *mesnie*, though now the whole pack of them seemed hesitant. They exchanged nervous glances, some standing in their stirrups to stare after their master's departing horse. A swift thunder of hooves drew him around to face Taillebois, but Joubert's champion, though riding pell-mell, was now veering away from him towards the edge of what little of the battle remained. He didn't look back as he vanished through the trees.

Glancing further, Cerdic tried to understand what was happening.

The riverside woods were filled with corpses for hundreds of yards, though here and there twosomes still fought it out, blades clanging. His eyes fell upon Copsi, now on higher ground, a posse of bodyguards close around him. Many slain lay to his fore, but he too it seemed was on the verge of retreat. There were ten of them left in total. They could wreak some damage on the remnants of Cerdic's command, but instead, after heated, hurried discussion, they turned around as one, and rode eastward through the woods, not at breakneck speed but quickly enough to soon be clear of the fray.

Cerdic glanced back towards the river. It ran crimson, its shoreline choked with dead and wounded men. Of those groups still standing, more looked like Copsi's mercenaries than Norman knights, but without their master they had no reason to stay. They too commenced quitting the field, in rags and tags at first, but then in larger numbers, most walking, many limping or leaning on each other. They were bloodied and bedraggled, but all brandished weapons in case anyone sought to challenge them again.

No one did. Even Tyrkil Widow-Maker leaned against a tree trunk, watching tiredly as they departed. Arne stood by the waterside, a handful of surviving bowmen with him, all with weapons dressed down. Other knights Cerdic had become respectful of, Will Malet and Alain le Roux, were still on their feet, but both of them filthy, pale-faced and nursing gory wounds.

Roland of course was in a worse state than anyone.

Cerdic dismounted and dropped to one knee alongside him.

The fallen knight tried to smile. 'I paid him back,' he said through crimson bubbles.

'And you saved my life,' Cerdic said.

'You're a good lad, Cerdic...'

A hand touched Cerdic's shoulder. He glanced up and was startled to see Yvette standing there, hugging herself, her own features ashen as she gazed tearfully down.

'You're now Earl of Ripon,' Roland whispered. 'And Comte of Hiemois-in-waiting. A glorious future beckons you.'

'And you, Roland,' Cerdic said. 'You can be my seneschal. What do you think?'

'I'm sorry for what we did to your country... for my part.'

'Just accept my offer...'

Roland clawed at him in agony.

'*Roland!*'

Roland's grimace forcibly twisted itself into a smile. 'Charmaine...'

The smile froze.

Seconds passed before Cerdic was able to stand and put his arms around Yvette, who wept quietly into his shoulder.

'Did he die well?' someone asked.

It was Turold. He'd approached on foot through the carnage, leading his horse by the reins, both man and beast covered in livid slashes. His own sword was still drawn, crimson to its hilt. He regarded Roland with stoic manliness.

'His final blow was his greatest,' Cerdic said, pointing.

Forty yards away, its flanks quivering and steaming, Joubert's horse stood by the water's edge. A limp shape hung upside down from its saddle, the cross-hilt of Roland's longsword still jutting out from it.

Turold nodded, satisfied by that if not exactly pleased.

'He mentioned someone called Charmaine,' Yvette said.

'His wife,' the big knight said. 'He's with her again at last.'

The girl nodded, swallowing back more tears.

Turold looked further afield. 'What of Earl Copsi?'

'He left,' Cerdic said, still kneeling. 'At speed.'

Turold gave a grim smile. 'It's no surprise. He landed on his feet here. Became an earl without ever having to fight a real opponent. Today that ended, and he was found wanting. I doubt you'll see him again... until he has the king with him.'

'The Slayer fled too,' Cerdic said.

'A deadly foe to be sure, but he served only Joubert... with Joubert dead, there was nothing else for him here.'

'We owe him nevertheless. That's his blade in Roland's back.'

Turold scrunched a handful of rag with which to strop his steel. 'Fate can play strange tricks. We may meet him again. In the meantime, you have important matters to attend.'

Cerdic nodded, rising to his feet and glancing round. At the innumerable bodies in need of burial, at the wounded in need of care, and at the survivors, not just Normans, but Vikings too, and Flemings, who watched him, waxen faced and weary.

'Where do I start?' he wondered aloud.

'Don't ask me,' Turold said. 'I'm only a knight. *You're* the earl.'

CHAPTER 38

At first, things seemed so normal that Cerdic was forced to take a breath.

The homestead stood as it always had on so many winter mornings past, the steep sod-covered roof partially clad with snow, the gable window shuttered against the cold. In normal times, Guthlac or Oswalda would have lined it inside with flax or wool, but most likely only rats and beetles dwelled there now. The encircling sward was mostly carpeted white, and where the ordinary ground was exposed, frozen and barren. The outbuildings looked dilapidated, untended. Where the vegetable allotments lay, only brown stalks protruded. The pigpen was empty, its fences broken. There was no sound of animals from the rickety, ramshackle stable that Guthlac had built himself, neither horses nor cattle. Likewise, the long rope on which Hyrrokkin, the nanny-goat, was normally tethered, lay cut, Hyrrokkin herself missing. Probably eaten.

Cerdic sat rigid astride his horse.

'There'd always be a pillar of smoke rising at this time of year,' he said. 'In winter, Oswalda used to burn holly logs, so the fire would crackle and the smoke would be white and pungent... almost sweet.'

Needless to say, no smoke hung over the cottage now.

'I'm so sorry, Cerdic,' Yvette said, mounted next to him.

He didn't reply, because his gaze had fallen elsewhere.

Fifty yards from the farmhouse, down by the river's edge, two low, oblong hummocks lay side by side. Again, they were partially covered by snow, though that didn't obscure the homemade wooden crosses that stood at the head of each one.

He slid from his horse and walked slowly over there.

Yvette watched, saddened by his air of weariness and defeat, even though he'd anticipated something like this all the way from Wulfbury.

There were so few *real* victors in war.

She'd only been young when sent for her own safety to England. But she'd already garnered enough life experience, mainly by witnessing the feuds and battles waged by her father, to know that it never brought solace for long. Reprisal was a drive that seemed to motivate every man she knew, yet they never learned from it. Cutting off hands or heads, nailing bodies to castle doors, even slaying your foe more honourably on the field of combat – none of it reversed loss, nor salved the pain of a loved one killed.

And yet, maybe peace was not worth *any* price.

Queen Ealdgyth had handed over her kingdom's treasure to buy a cessation of slaughter. Lady Eallana had allowed a cruel and despotic king to have his way with her if it would spare her subjects. But Edith Swan-Neck, the woman she'd revered more than any other, had died rather than surrender to brutes. Yvette herself had struck the killing blow to the man who would have raped her. And she'd done it without a thought, without a qualm.

This troubled world of theirs was not nearly so simple as she'd have liked.

She dismounted, leading the two animals forward, stopping again as they nosed at a tussock of exposed grass. She advanced a few more yards alone, halting beside the stable. At least the sun was up, not exactly warm, but sparkling from the river's crystal waters, casting blue shadows through the pines on the opposite slope.

Cerdic stood stiff beside the graves. Either in prayer or simple contemplation, Yvette wasn't sure which. It cut her again to see him knuckling tears from his eyes.

There was much in him to like. Ever since she'd known him, he'd shown courage and daring, somewhat naïve daring at times, though in its own way that was endearing. He'd also shown determination to survive, defying many odds. These were all qualities to admire. They outweighed the entitlement he felt to the right of command, the vanity that drove him to involve other men in his personal war. All these faults were Cerdic's, for that was his culture. But there'd been times when she'd genuinely needed tenderness, and he'd shown it to her, or when wisdom had been called for instead of bravery, and in due course he'd come to show that too. All these things could make women fond of him, love him even.

Except for her? she wondered.

His wife, whose hand he hadn't asked for, yet whose companionship he seemed to cherish rather than whose body he simply lusted after. It wasn't something she'd felt or shown in return, not abundantly. And yet now, ironically, as he stood by the two graves, a figure of dejection, a broken soul, her heart went out to him. The young captain, the fearless fighter, the winner of battles? No, just a man. A boy in fact, who'd been very sweet to her and had a sensitive side that he tried in vain to conceal but was never quite able to.

This, she *could* love. She knew that now.

She'd wait a little longer. Let him alone with his thoughts.

So engrossed was she in this idea that she never saw the figure shuffle out from the stable behind her. The ragged, scarecrow-thin horror that had once been a man, but now was cruelly blinded, his turnip head a mass of lice-ridden hair and beard, a filthy strip of cloth concealing his empty sockets, his clothes in black tatters.

She saw neither him nor the broad-bladed hunting knife in his claw-like left hand.

In fact, Cerdic saw Haco before Yvette did. By pure chance he glanced back, and a bolt of ice went through him as the spindly but monstrous shape hooked its wiry arm around her throat, cutting off any hope of a cry.

Cerdic broke into a run, shouting, slipping and stumbling in the snow, none of which stopped or even slowed the unseeing creature that now existed purely on hate, as it raised its blade for a downward blow into Yvette's soft, heaving body.

Cerdic screamed.

Yvette got one last breath out, and she too screamed.

And then another figure, which had come around the side of the main house and been startled to a standstill, lunged forward, speedy for all its ungainly outline, raised the spade it had been carrying, and crashed it down on the blinded murderer's head.

Yvette staggered forward, gasping but unhurt.

Cerdic slowed to a disbelieving halt, unable to believe it... firstly because Yvette was still alive. For half a second then, for the worst half-second in his entire life, he'd felt certain...

He grabbed her, hugged her to him. She hugged him back, still heaving for breath. But then, almost as quickly, Cerdic turned to her saviour, thoughts still reeling, eyes goggling.

This was the thing he *really* couldn't believe.

'Oswalda?' he whispered, unsure if it was a dream. And then, with an elated and joyous shout: '*OSWALDA!*'

—

'I thought you dead,' Cerdic wept, his arms tight around his old nurse's hefty form.

She wept too, her hands all over his face and hair, then roving down his shoulders and chest. 'I... I thought *you* were dead,' she stammered. 'How can you be here?'

'It's a long story, trust me. But I... I...' He could barely get the words out. 'But... Yvette... this is Oswalda, she was... a mother to me.'

'I... I, erm, I know...' Yvette, still badly shaken, only managed half a smile.

'Oswalda,' he stuttered. 'I saw the graves and...'

'Guthlac and Eadora.'

'Ahhh...' He hung his head, abashed. 'Of course.'

'Once the Danes left here, I buried them myself,' the woman said.

'Alone?'

'How else?'

'I'm staggered you were able to.'

'It wasn't easy. Those devils left me in great pain, but I've been through worse.'

Cerdic nodded, remembering that Oswalda had only become his wet-nurse after giving birth to two children of her own, both of which, having torn her open in the process, promptly died.

'They left me alone after that,' she said. 'But the main thing is you're here. Cerdic… *you're here*.' And then she looked frightened and clutched his shoulders. 'And the Danes are only down the road. In the burh…'

'The Danes are destroyed,' he said. 'Totally. Less than a handful remain.'

She regarded him incredulously. And only now seemed to realise that his hair was clipped short, and that he wore hefty chain-mail under a bloodstained surcoat.

'You brought soldiers?' she said.

'I did.'

Oswalda still looked flummoxed. 'And this young lady?'

'Yvette of Hiemois.'

'Hiemois?' Oswalda's eyebrows arched. 'You're a Frank?'

'By birth.' Yvette offered a cautious hand. 'Thank you for the gift of my life.'

Despite everything, Oswalda seemed hesitant, but then she took it.

Cerdic crouched and felt briefly at Haco's neck. 'This one will never torment anyone again.' He saw Oswalda's shocked response and put a hand on her shoulder. 'Don't be upset. Anything that was ever worthwhile in him was burned up in his desire to hurt. He came to the end he chose for himself. Infinitely more terrible things have happened in the kingdom.'

Oswalda nodded. 'I've heard as much.'

'They may yet happen here.' He shook his head. 'I don't know. But at least Wulfgar Ragnarsson and his horde are defeated.'

'So...?' His old nurse sounded as if she hardly dared ask. 'Does this mean you have returned to us... as Lord of Wulfbury?'

'Maybe... I hope so.'

'And you...?' Oswalda looked at Yvette. 'You are the Lady of Wulfbury?'

Yvette took Cerdic's hand. 'I'm Cerdic's wife. And I will be a mother to his people. If you'll have me.'

Cerdic stiffened and swallowed, but Oswalda threw all her reticence aside and her arms out as she embraced them both. 'Oh, my dears... my dears!'

The communal hug lasted for almost a minute, before Cerdic was able to extricate himself. 'There's too much to do for us to celebrate, I'm afraid. The estate is in ruins, and the people... where are they?'

'Mostly in hiding,' Oswalda sighed. 'But they'll come back now, Cerdic. Now there's an Aelfricsson at Wulfbury Hall again.'

'I'll send riders to find them,' he said.

'God be praised.' Oswalda shed more tears. 'I never thought my prayers would be answered like this.'

'I don't know if they've been answered yet,' Cerdic replied. 'I have a company of tired, hungry warriors at Wulfbury, many nursing wounds. Yesterday was hard. Last night even harder. I'm hoping to build my household out of the survivors. There's one sturdy fellow who's already seen us through difficult times. He's agreed to be my marshal and household champion.'

'If you have thegns among them, there are many vacant halls in Swaledale,' Oswalda said. 'Their original masters never returned.'

Cerdic considered that. 'We have knights certainly.'

'Knights?' The word clearly meant nothing to her.

'Thegns in all but name. The elite class of Normandy's fighting men.'

'Normans?' She appraised his short hair again, and the coat of mail he wore, so noticeably different from those sported by Earl Rothgar and his housecarls.

Cerdic gave her as frank a stare as he could. 'Much has changed, Oswalda. I detest saying this, but... the England we knew has gone.' He shrugged. 'A new one will emerge. Whether better, I cannot say. Either way, it won't be an easy transition. But we have to make do, and without these Norman warriors I mention… I would not have regained the earldom.'

'And they are staying with you?' she asked. 'As your hearthmen?'

'Some may.' He couldn't help but looked troubled by this, because he didn't really know. Aside from Turold, none had accepted his invitation as yet.

'Cerdic found a hiding place in the burh chapel,' Yvette said. 'It contained vital documents. Deeds and ownership details for the estate. It names him as direct heir.'

'But now we have a new king, do we not?' Oswalda said. 'A *Norman*.' Clearly, the very word was difficult for her, and both Cerdic and Yvette understood why. 'Won't he differ?'

'He may,' Cerdic admitted. 'Or he may not. If I can pay adequate homage to him, who knows. But if the worse comes to the worst, we are all of us well provided for. There were other papers hidden too. One directed us to the northwest side of the burh, and the location of twenty chests of silver.'

Even Oswalda gasped at that.

'Buried in a disused midden,' he said. 'And these in addition to the eight chests in the hall, which most people knew about. That first eight persuaded the Norse that Father's hoard had been found. So, the others lay undiscovered. Much of what they contain is hacksilver, but it's still wealth, is it not? There's more than enough there to pay those knights of mine who wish to leave.'

'Maybe half will remain with us,' Yvette said. 'For there is much disruption in the house they came from.'

Oswalda thought on this, and on the earnestness in their young faces.

'At least it will be settled by talking rather than fighting,' she said.

'Let's hope so,' Cerdic replied. 'I've sent word to Aethelbald, a priest in York. I've asked him to be my chaplain here. Even if he refuses, I've requested he attend us as soon as possible. There are many funerals to be said.'

Oswalda glanced east along the valley road. 'If there are wounded men at the burh, I might be able to help.'

Cerdic nodded. She'd been his nurse as a child, but he also remembered her skill as healer and midwife. 'It can't hurt if you go along there, I think.'

Without another word, she bustled into her cottage.

Cerdic drifted back towards the graves. This time, Yvette accompanied him.

'Are you sure you want to be part of this?' he asked her.

'I'm part of it regardless,' she replied. 'The real question is, do *you* want me to be part of it?'

He pondered that as he stood by the narrower of the two mounds, the one he assumed was Eadora's. In truth, like so many people in his life, he'd never really known Eadora until it was too late. Only then had he come to understand how much more she was than the village beauty, than the May Queen. How precious a person she'd been all-round. How grievous a loss she'd have been to this place, even if she'd been the only one who'd died.

He gazed up the tree-clad slopes to a sky now pearlescent blue, only shreds of cloud hanging there motionless. One or two birds twittered. Spring wasn't too far away.

He wondered where they all were. Really. Eadora, Guthlac, Letwold, Aethelric, Unferth, his father. In most cases, he didn't even know the fate of their mortal remains, much less those parts that had genuinely lived, those happy souls dismissed from this world so abruptly. In many cases with God, he was sure, though during the course of these horrors he himself had called slurs upon God, had come to doubt His beneficence.

He told himself that he didn't doubt it now. At least, he hoped he didn't.

That was one more thing that would never be the same, he realised. Whatever happened here in the weeks and months to come, his old *wyrd* had expired. His new *wyrd*... well, he'd yet to establish exactly what that meant for him. There were so many questions unanswered, but some worrying certainties remained.

'I have a disconcerting habit, Yvette,' he said, 'of being the sole survivor. I once said you were the only good thing to emerge from all this. And I meant it. That means I want you with me here. Now and forever. But my original question to you stands. Because I fear this thing hasn't ended yet.'

'I know that,' she said as they walked back together. 'But these things never really end.'

'I wouldn't say never. But there's no way out of them that doesn't cost.'

He buried Haco under a mound of snow, making a mental note to inter him properly when the ground thawed. As the last shovelful was patted in place, Oswalda emerged from the house. She carried a battered old leather bag with a shoulder-strap. Cerdic recognised it as her bag of medications. There'd been all kinds of weird and wonderful phials and salves in there in the past, which she'd used on a range of his childhood cuts and abrasions.

'Are you ready, my dears?'

'You still have a horse?' he asked her.

She ambled to the stable. 'It's an old nag. That's why the Danes didn't steal it.'

They headed east along the valley road, Oswalda ahead of the others, her maternal instinct drawing her along swiftly. Cerdic reined up to look back, wondering, as so many did once bereaved, what he'd do if he saw those they'd lost now standing in a group, watching, maybe smiling as the morning sun lit their faces. But the valley remained winter-bare, with no sign of those who'd once dwelled here.

'I've realised you can't just walk away from troubles like these,' Yvette said, as they rode on. 'But, Cerdic... you can't provoke them either. You can't go looking for discord, and then claim that you're a victim.'

He nodded. 'I realise that. Though I doubt there's ever been a harder lesson taught.'

'If it's any consolation, I've now seen Swaledale for myself. Or part of it. And I think it probably was worth fighting for. The world is full of savage beasts, Cerdic. When one finds good people, and good places, one should do everything one can to cling to them.'

'That's why I said I wanted you here with me.'

'Is that the only reason?'

'In… in times of tumult, it isn't easy to profess love in the normal way.'

'There are distractions, that's true.'

'But I know my feelings. And for a moment then…' he shook his head, shuddering, 'when that blind madman…'

'Heaven stepped in,' she replied. 'Which surely means that neither your feelings, nor mine, are misplaced.'

He smiled at that, only now daring to reach a hand to her. When she took it, it was a deeper joy than he'd thought he'd ever feel again.

'I hear you spared many enemies yesterday?' she said.

'Once they were beaten, a number fled. I could have pursued and killed them.'

'I'm proud of you for not doing that.'

'Don't be too proud. Like as not, they'll be among the first to come back.'

'And if they do, this time you'll be ready.'

He stole a glance at her. '*We'll* be ready.'

'Yes.' Her grip on his hand tightened. '*We'll* be ready.'